Mr. Pilbeam Built a Boat

Bill Jones

isbn 978-1-912728-27-5

Set in twelve point Baskerville, justified with occasional text italicising, headings centred in Baskerville bold. Page size 152x229mm printed litho on a one hundred gsm chosen for its sustainability.

Published and printed by
Quacks Books
7 Grape Lane
Petergate
York Yo1 7hu
info@quacks.info
www.radiusonline.info
01904 635967

About the author

Bill Jones started his career in newspapers before joining Granada Television in the early 80's. Over the next three decades, he turned his hand to documentary filmmaking, making many award-programmes films for the BBC, Channel 4, Discovery, ITV, PBS, Sky, National Geographic, and others. Along the way, he worked with Billy Connolly, Michael Apted, Sir Trevor McDonald, Joanna Lumley, and Sir Peter Ustinov.

In 2011, Bill wrote his acclaimed first book THE GHOST RUNNER (Mainstream), winner of the British Sports Book Awards 'Best New Writer' category. In 2014, he followed this up with ALONE : THE TRIUMPH & TRAGEDY OF JOHN CURRY (Bloomsbury), winner of the British Sports Book Awards 'Outstanding Writing' category. Both books were shortlisted for the William Hill Award. Both are in advanced development as feature films.

In 2018, his first novel, BLACK CAMP 21 (Birlinn) came 'highly recommended' by Lee Child. The novel was shortlisted for the 2019 McIlvanney Prize for Debut Crime Fiction.

Bill says his taste for writing was stirred after winning a short story competition about trees when he was 11 years old. The event was organised by Hull City Council and earned him a £1 prize. "Word for word (if you allow for inflation)," he says. "That was possibly my biggest royalty."

He now lives in Ampleforth, North Yorkshire, although he was born in the town where the following story unfolds......

"A smooth sea never made skilled mariner"

Old English proverb

Mr. Pilbeam Built a Boat

Part One

'Goodrun'

1925-1967

Chapter One

There were lots of boats in Seymour Pilbeam's story.

Most of them were the toys in his box or the photographs of giant three-masters he scissored lovingly from old yachting magazines. Only three were ever big enough for a person to step into and sail away and yet these were the boats which changed his life – and the lives of one or two other people – forever.

Their names were 'Goodrun', 'Phoenix' and 'Gratitude' and – for very different reasons – Seymour's heart was swamped in turn by each of them. Ever since his childhood, he'd dreamed about owning and maybe building a boat of his own. But as he grew older, the dream slowly mutated into an obsession, bringing times when nothing (and nobody) else mattered. But that was before he knew the trouble they'd cause. Or the wounds they would inflict.

In the beginning, Seymour hadn't bargained with any of this. In fact, if he'd known what he later knew, he might – just might – not have bothered. But right from the start, events drifted so rapidly out of control that by the time he could see what was happening, it was all a bit late; which isn't to say, it wasn't also extremely funny at times (or even joyful), because the story of his three boats was frequently both.

It's just that Seymour liked life best when it was simple. And that preference – as much as his boats – was where the trouble really lay…..

A long time later, when these events were all over (and he was more inclined towards introspection) he could pinpoint exactly when things had started to unravel. It would creep uninvited into his head; a single, horrible moment blasted into his memory like the photograph of a crime scene.

In the picture he sees a Yorkshire harbour in dazzling summer light. Around the edges of the frame, hordes of holidaymakers are looking intently towards the same point. Draw the image closer and the object of their curiosity is revealed as a wooden dinghy which appears to be sinking. On its fast-disappearing transom, a name is visible.

'GOODRUN'.

In the future, Seymour shudders. His brain zooms in. There's something else in the crime scene; something which he can only see when he squeezes his eyes tight and blots out all the extraordinary times that followed. There. There. In his head, it's always there. Tumbling down through the tangled ruins of the yacht is a pair of false teeth being sucked by gravity to their new home at the bottom of the sea.

And it's at this precise moment that the tableau unlocks allowing Seymour to step back into his own story; hoping that this time it makes sense and that – this time – there's a happy ending......

"Big day, Seymour? Ready for another pint?"

Maybe that had been his biggest mistake. Just one hour before the launch – the much-vaunted inaugural sail of his first-ever boat – he'd popped into The Ship for some lunchtime liquid courage.

"I'd better not. Everyone'll be here soon. Best if I keep a clear head."

"A half then? Or a rum?"

There were only two of them at the bar. Captain Rehab, Seymour's drinking companion, was rarely anywhere else. According to the harbour wags, there was only one thing Rehab sank more often than pints. And that was ships.

"Go on, then. Just a single. No. A large one, thanks."

Everyone drank in The Ship during the summer. No other pub could match its view of the bay or its potent smell of fish. From the rusty balcony, Seymour could see 'Goodrun', bobbing gently alongside a flotilla of black-hulled trawlers. She looked fragile and old, and – if he wasn't mistaken – her mast didn't look terribly straight.

"That's it then is it?" Rehab was holding a full pint glass in each hand. "How much did you pay?"

"Ten quid."

"Jesus. It's a tub. You were done."

Seymour had always liked Rehab (although perhaps not at this moment). He liked his broken nose, his leathered skin, his thinning shoulder-length hair. Better still, he loved the Captain's unfabricated air of mystery. No-one really knew where he lived or where he was from. Only one thing seemed beyond dispute. Despite all the jokes, Rehab was an authentic man of the sea.

"Please don't say that. I'll be in so much trouble if I was."

It hurt, but Rehab had a point. Seymour's life-long wait for a first boat had ended with an impulse buy barely one week before. Within a few minutes, his wife Lucy would be arriving with her family and (if he was honest) he wasn't even entirely sure how to get the sails up. Apart from the name – which he'd chosen himself – the boat's rigging was as mysterious as Rehab's antecedents. And the last time he'd held a tiller, he'd been an evacuee.

Seymour drained the rum down in one slurp. A stiff breeze was rolling across the waters of the harbour. Along the edge of a narrow wooden jetty, he could make out his wife at the front of a small knot of familiar-looking people; each one seemingly hypnotised by the tiny vessel lurching violently against an ancient, seaweed stanchion.

"Shit," said Seymour. "Shit. Shit. Shit."

"One for the road?" said Rehab.

But it was too late. By the time, he'd tottered down the worn stone steps to the quay, it was already far too late. Blown across the peeling varnish of the hull, he could hear the ripping of rotten wood, followed smartly by the metallic lashing of dislocated stays. Finally, with one feeble quiver, the mast fell sideways against the jetty.

It was at this precise moment that Seymour had seen his father-in-law's false teeth. Not in Bill's mouth (which is where they usually were unless their owner had jumped to avoid a broken mast) but spinning down from the quay; forever in slow motion; a macabre plastic grin swallowed up by the sea somewhere between a seagull and a discarded condom.

In that dreadful moment, Seymour stared at the widening circles as if the teeth might somehow return for an encore. Or better still, surface with a sensible explanation for what was surely just a terrible, terrible dream.

"Seymour. What the hell has just happened here?" Lucy was surging towards him, magnificently furious in a yellow gingham dress. "Speak. Say something."

"I can't understand it," he stammered. It really wasn't a dream.

"Imbecile. How could you? With the whole family here? The whole bloody town, in fact."

"If you can give me half an hour?"

Everyone left on the quay was shuffling closer to listen. Behind them, in the stiffening wind, Seymour could hear wood splintering against stone.

"Is your dad alright?"

"He's lost his teeth," she hissed. "What do you think?"

Over Lucy's quivering shoulder, Seymour could see his father-in-law happily gumming an ice cream. Alongside him, all the rest of his wife's incomprehensible family were gurning joyfully in his direction.

"Lovely day for a picture?"

Seymour span round. A small middle-aged man in an orange cap and blazer with the word 'Snaps' embroidered on its chest pocket was pointing hopefully at a battered camera. Up on the balcony of The Ship, Seymour could see the tall outline of Captain Rehab wafting another full pint (with whisky chaser) in the general direction of the sea.

"Maybe just you and the wife, Seymour? Ready to collect in the morning? 9am sharp. Black and white or colour. And free for a mate."

"Go away, Frank."

"A family shot, then? With what's left of that boat in the background?"

"Go away, Frank."

There was a loud crack and a jingle of rigging from Seymour's stricken dinghy. As the tide climbed, the mast had been pushed up under the quay's wooden sub-structure and water was swamping the remnants of its decks. Amidst a gurgle of sodden chip forks, he could still make out the red letters of 'GOODRUN' and then just 'RUN', followed by a wet, grey nothing.

"Just a snap of you on your own then, perhaps?"

"Go away, Frank," said Seymour, scanning the ebbing pack of rubber-neckers for a glimpse of his wife.

She was never difficult to spot. They'd called her 'Stifflegs' at school and no-one he knew walked with a straighter back than his wife's.

7

Alongside her trailed Bill, his toothless father-in-law, nose deep in the soft foundations of a cornet. In a few moments, they'd be lost in the weekend crowd; her face set hard and turned towards home.

"If I can sort it we can try again next weekend," bellowed Seymour, hopelessly. "I promise."

If Lucy had heard, she didn't respond. Only her father had halted briefly in his tracks.

"You're totally fucked," mouthed Bill silently, drawing an imaginary knife across his throat before slipping out of view.

Seymour turned wearily to assess the damage. Where his dinghy had once been, there was now just a jungle of wires. In every other respect, the harbour had already lost interest in him. Even Frank the photographer had sensibly vanished.

Under full sail, yachts of every age and size were sliding out into the open sea, their crews wrapped up in thick sweaters and braced for the wind. Unable to watch them, he closed his eyes against the tears and slumped on a bench.

"Can I have some money for a donut, dad?"

Seymour lifted his head. The remnants of his launch party had gathered around in a circle to gloat. Standing slightly to one side of them was his son, sporting a tie-dyed t-shirt and scout shorts. His top gave him the air of a 20-year-old. His bottoms were more suited to a child. In actual fact, he was aged somewhere in between.

"Isaac. I didn't know you'd come."

"I wish I hadn't. Money. Donut. Now."

"I'll join you," said Seymour. "If I don't eat something soon, I'll be sick."

A nearby kiosk had opened for business, discharging the sweet smell of deep-fried dough. Everywhere he looked, people had their faces buried in food.

"Don't be shovelling rubbish into the boy. He'll only get fat."

Seymour felt his son shrivel. The tweed-suited figure of his wife's mother, Olive, had hoved into view, clutching a bulky and expressionless black dog.

"Just like that thing then," said Isaac, brushing a sugared donut across the dog's nose.

"Seymour. Stop him. Restrain him. He's rude, he's disrespectful and he's dressed like a…a….hippy."

"He's a teenager," said Seymour.

"Who doesn't look like a sprout," added Isaac.

Which was true, or partly so. From childhood (or somewhere near it) Lucy's mother had only ever been known to wear green. Green hat, scarf, suit, stockings and shoes. Green everything. Even it was said – although only her husband had dared to investigate – green underwear. On a summer's day in a forest, she could reportedly vanish without trace. Only the dress size had changed over the years. Green was a constant without challenge.

As, indeed, was the second constant in her life; a substantial and seemingly immortal bulldog called Arthur whose aversion to exercise was matched only by his passion for cakes (and donuts); two weaknesses which ensured that he was pushed almost everywhere in an ancient metal pram. Very few people had ever seen Arthur standing up unaided. An even smaller number had witnessed him in independent motion.

"Apologise. Apologise at once." Isaac's grandmother was spinning round looking for her grandson.

"He's gone," said Seymour, in a tone of quiet desperation.

"Like Bill's teeth," said Olive.

A horn was blowing behind the north pier. The town's last-surviving (and horribly rusty) pleasure cruiser, The Burlingtonian, was returning from a bird-spotting excursion to the cliffs. As it entered the harbour, the skipper began waving wildly from the wheelhouse.

Seymour raised his arm in recognition. It hadn't been easy, but he loved this town, and its people, but he suddenly felt horribly adrift. A column of rain was marching off the North Sea and Rehab had scuttled inside the pub before it struck. Today was supposed to have been a celebration; a childhood dream finding its time. Now he just wanted the witnesses all gone.

"Please go. Bugger off. All of you. It's over."

None of the stragglers needed telling. Olive led the way silently pushing Arthur in his perambulator, followed by his wife's feckless brother Ralph (a garage owner from the West Riding) and Vietta, his wife's feckless brother's wife.

"Great day out, mate," shouted Ralph. "Wouldn't have missed it for the world. We should do it again some time."

"Fuck off, Ralph" returned Seymour.

Soon there was only one person left: the best-dressed person on the quay. Blue linen suit. Bespoke leather-soled shoes. Panama hat. A man who looked like he owned the place for one simple reason; he did own the place. Stan Clough: businessman, amusement arcade boss, barber, scholar, lothario, lifeboat skipper and previous owner of the boat which was now resting on the seabed.

"Before you even ask, Seymour. I never once had a problem with it."

"That's because it was sat rotting in your garden for fifteen years."

"I didn't say it hadn't."

"You didn't say it had, either."

"Which is why I only asked ten quid for it."

"You knew. You must have."

"Ten quid, Seymour. Think about it. Bought as seen."

"You saw me coming. You knew what it meant to me."

"Listen. It was a good little boat. I'm sorry about what happened here today. But Seymour, it wasn't my fault."

"Fuck off, Stan."

With a final look at the place where his first-ever boat should have been bobbing – Seymour turned away from the sea and set off after his wife. It wouldn't be easy, but he'd bring her round. The money wasn't the end of the world. And maybe – just maybe – he'd be able to salvage GOODRUN when the tide went out.......

It had taken Lucy ten furious minutes to get home. Normally, it took twice that long. Rushing past three sets of amusements, and a shop selling Guinness-flavoured rock; past the steamed-up Coin-Op and Johnny's Junk Shop; past Corky Brown's crab stall and over the level crossing, she had paused just once; sickened, as she always was, by the Victorian gasworks which loomed over the end of their street.

Somewhere along the way, she'd misplaced her father, either to the temptations of a slot machine or the warm embrace of a lunchtime pub. No doubt he'd turn up around teatime with a daft smile and a pocketful of filthy coppers. He needn't hurry. Watching his teeth disappearing into the harbour had been the final indignity on a day she'd been dreading in a town which she despised.

And now – in a way she hadn't thought possible – everything looked worse.

Puddles of filthy water pockmarked the narrow corridor of redbrick terraced houses which led to the large, detached Victorian villa they called home. On any other street – in any other town – it would have been a valuable dwelling. Except it wasn't another town, it was this one. And they didn't even own it, they paid rent.

The whole thing was a tragedy. At street level, behind a scruffy hedge of box, two paint-flaking bays guarded a panelled front door missing its letterbox. Above the entrance, two floors rose to a leaking slate roof interrupted by three dormer windows.

It looked exactly like the house a child would draw; solid, symmetrical, and seemingly prosperous. In its heyday it might even have had staff. But there were things a child would have ignored which Lucy couldn't. Like the perpetual whiff of gas and the noise from the working men's club across the road; like the clutter of dying cars along the street and the crusty piles of white dog dirt on the pavements.

"Alright darling? You look upset."

A neighbour (who Lucy didn't know) was tipping potato peelings into a dustbin. With a shudder, she unlocked the back door and stepped into the kitchen. There was a hacksaw on the dining table, and a stack of timber leaning against the back wall. On the sideboard, a dog-eared pile of manuals was being held in place by a large magnet. In a frying pan on the gas stove there were four filthy spark plugs.

Everyone loved Seymour, she knew that. She understood that. She loved him, too. But none of them saw this. None of them knew she lived in a grown man's glorified playroom.

Where the radio should have been, there was a rectangle in the dust and a clutter of glass valves. In the lounge, an electric train was winding its way endlessly around the edge of the skirting boards; and when she followed the lead to the wall, two bare wires had been pushed into the socket. Everything in the house was the same. It was a shambles; a death-trap; a living joke held together by solder and sticky tape.

12

Stifling a furious scream, she slumped back in an armchair and massaged her forehead. When she stood up a few minutes later, a tube of glue was stuck to her sleeve....

Walking the exact same route as his wife, Seymour was also inching his way home. There was no hurry. He was under no illusions about what was waiting for him and almost everyone he ran into wanted to chat. At the Coin-Op launderette, Mrs Cribbis needed to know when the kite for her grandson's birthday would be ready ("You'll be flying it by next weekend," he promised.) At the fish shop, Corky Brown took an order for three fillets of plaice, and at Johnny's Junk Shop, he found Isaac peering hungrily through the window at a battered electric guitar.

"You alright?" asked Seymour, putting an arm around his son.

"Delirious," said Isaac, detaching it.

Something brown and dingy was moving inside the shop towards the door. When the door opened, a bell rang somewhere, and a brown and dingy man wearing a mackintosh popped out.

"Seymour," mumbled the man's face. It too was of a beige colour.

"Clinkers," replied Seymour.

"Someone bought in an old sledge. Antique. Needs work. I thought maybe..."

"No problem at all," said Seymour. "I'll drop by next week."

"Nice one," said Clinkers, walking backwards into his shop and locking the door.

"Why has that man got curly hairs growing on the bridge of his nose?" asked Isaac after they'd moved a little further down the street.

"Not really sure, son," said Seymour.

But that had not been quite true. Johnny's nickname was 'Clinkers' for a reason. If the pub rumours were true, he'd once needed a skin graft on his nose which a pioneering surgeon in Doncaster had taken from the inside of Johnny's bottom (or from that general area) thereby making him the only man in town (or anywhere else) with pubic hair growing directly on his face.

"And why doesn't he sell new stuff?"

This was also a good question although, in fairness, nobody had ever actually seen Clinkers sell much of anything. For the most part, locals only ever crossed his portal to inspect a collection of 'Health & Efficiency' magazines, hidden between a stuffed badger and an old cork lifebelt. Like so many things in Seymour's town, the appeal of black and white pictures featuring rotund naturists wasn't an easy thing to explain. And so, he didn't.

"What will you say to mum?" asked Isaac.

"I'm not sure yet," said Seymour. "Any suggestions?"

They'd finally reached the open back gate of their house. In the small garden, a black cat was feverishly scraping soil over its mess, and the shrill whistle of a kettle was blowing from the kitchen door.

"Who's is the cat? Mum will go mental."

"I think you should go and play with your Meccano."

Isaac didn't need the hint. For as long as he could remember, weekends had been a mysterious confection of good times and dreadful ones. On Sunday afternoons (until very recently) he'd been packed off to church with a few pennies for the collection box and ordered to stay away until after three. When he returned – having doubled his money in the amusements – his parents were usually in bed sharing a cigarette. Sadly, not anymore. Now they often went days without speaking.

"You'll say you're sorry, won't you dad?"

"It'll be fine," he said, which is what he usually said.

Isaac ran upstairs, slammed his bedroom door, and turned his transistor radio as loud as it would go. In the room directly below, the relentless progress of Seymour's electric train had been halted by a book laid deliberately across the track.

"I've bought you a cup of tea."

She'd been asleep when he entered the lounge; or pretending to be. Now her lips were pursed, and she was stroking them between her thumb and forefinger. It was not a good sign.

"There are four spark plugs in the frying pan," she said, without opening her eyes.

Seymour kneeled to release his train. The engine was red hot and there was a bitter smell of burning flex. With a sharp tug he pulled the lead from the socket and picked up the book. D.H Lawrence. From what he could tell, his wife read no-one else.

"The car's not been starting. Rehab does it all the time on the boats. Warms them up."

"Rehab?"

"He's in the dominoes team? At the pub? He was there today, actually."

Lucy's eyes stayed shut. There was nothing new here. Not the glue on the sofa or the ancient pots of paint in the pantry. Not the sandpaper on the bookshelves or the screws which clogged up the Hoover. Not the perpetual wood shavings or the train spotter guides or her husband's endless quest to construct the ultimate kite.

"Have you any idea how I felt? Really?"

Her entire body tightened with anger. Of course, he'd no idea. Upstairs, Isaac pushed his radio up against his ear and climbed into bed. Through the raised voices, he heard something hard slam into a wall, followed by the scattering sound of broken metal pieces.

"That wasn't necessary." Seymour was collecting the fragments of his shattered train. "The boat only only cost ten quid."

"It's not about the money." As it always did, the rage had swiftly evaporated leaving her feeling puzzled and drained.

"I can fix it this week. I know what was wrong. It'll be perfect next weekend."

"I don't want you to fix it. You humiliated me. My dad's got no teeth. We're a laughing stock."

"I even chose the name for you. I thought you'd be pleased."

"Goodrun? G.O.O.D.R.U.N?"

"After the character in this book. 'Women In Love'. Yes."

"Open it. Read it. Look for that name."

Seymour flicked the pages quickly between the hard covers. He'd a very strong feeling that a disastrous day was about to get worse. He just wasn't sure why.

"You spelled it wrong. You oaf. You spelled it wrong."

Now he knew why.

"It's G.U.D.R.U.N. But then why would you know. You've never read a book since Janet and John. It's like everything else. You're still stuck in short trousers."

There was a noise from the kitchen; the yap of a dog, followed by the deeper growl of an elderly woman. In a blur of green, Lucy's mother blew into the living room, still holding Arthur tightly to her chest. With a single lacerating glance, her eyes moved from Seymour's face to the broken toy in his hand.

"My husband is drunk," she declared. "He has no teeth, and he is sucking a stick of black rock."

"Cup of tea?" chirruped Seymour, hopefully, tickling the dog under one of its chins.

"Where is he?" said Lucy.

"He is outside in the car. And no-one will be seeing him again until his teeth have been replaced. Goodbye."

In a swirl of camphor, Olive stormed from the building. Moments later, through the living room window, Seymour could see Bill's white Austin weaving dangerously towards the main road. In silhouette, Lucy's mother towered up out of the passenger seat. Somewhere to her right, slumped so low only his cap was visible, sat Bill and his rock.

Poor bugger, thought Seymour. He'd been through hell and back with those gnashers already.

According to family legend, Olive's first true love had died at the Somme. Later, when the war was over – although still in mourning – she'd accepted Bill's opportunistic proposal of marriage on one condition; that he have all his rotten, twisted teeth replaced with one of those nice modern sets of plastic ones.

No dentures. No wedding. No arguments.

It was a deal in which both parties were happy. Olive got a man she was happy to be seen in public with on special occasions. Bill got the girl he'd secretly always wanted. Except now his dentures were under six foot of seawater along with Seymour's ill-named dinghy.

"His life won't be worth living for weeks," said Lucy. "Poor sod. This is all your fault."

"Drop her a line, love. Tell her there's always a chance I'll find them when the tide's out."

There was no reply. As the tiny car joined the flow of headlights moving away from the town, Seymour drew the curtains on an empty room. Lucy had already gone to bed. Lately, whenever they argued, it was what she did; sometimes for days on end, sending notes to work with ever more desperate excuses. Like mother, like daughter, he thought. Maybe that's why he liked poor old Bill so much.

For the rest of the evening, Seymour pottered quietly about downstairs. After scooping up the ruined pieces of his train set, he fetched his toolbox from the pantry and lit the gas under his spark plugs. There was the kite to finish for Mrs.Cribbis; a new element to put on their dodgy heater and (now that he'd looked at it) he was pretty sure he could repair the smashed locomotive.

Three hours later, he looked at the clock (one of the few things that worked in the house). It was almost 10pm. He'd been tinkering for over four hours. From upstairs he could make out the muffled sound of Isaac's transistor radio. Poor kid, he thought. The two of them were just as confused as each other. The way Seymour saw it, their life should be perfect. Although they couldn't actually see it, they were living by the seaside. All that fresh air and boats. What could be better?

It's just a phase, he muttered to himself. That's all. It'll be fine.

Wrapping his spark plugs in an old shirt, Seymour stepped into the back yard for a few minutes with his pipe. The afternoon's wind had dropped leaving a warm, pink evening. With an oily thumb he tamped down the tobacco in its bowl and put a match to the strands.

There was no use trying to sugar it. His day had been a monumental disaster. Until he'd met Lucy, the only thing in life he'd ever wanted was a boat, his own boat. Not a picture cut from a magazine. A proper boat they could both sit in. It wasn't a secret. She'd always known that too. And now he'd finally got one, it had bloody well sunk.

Instead of surging out into the bay with his wife, he'd lost a tenner and a whole week's peace. There was only one thing for it. Moving quietly across the yard, he pushed open the swollen door of the outhouse. In the gloom, he could make out a sink, piles of ancient timber, and a child's swing knotted to the joists.

From a fusty mound of old blankets, Seymour wrestled a large shiny, black case. As he opened it, there was a gurgle of noise, a strange flash of pearl light and in the orange glow of his pipe, a broad smile could be seen returning to his face.

Chapter Two

Whilst it was true that 'Goodrun' had been the biggest (and shortest-lived) boat Seymour had ever owned in his forty-two years, it most certainly wasn't the first.

As a child he'd made dozens of them in his father's joinery workshop; toy boats, each one sanded smooth and painted in vivid colours; each one carefully named and stored on the shelves above the cheap pine coffins which underpinned the family's income.

From Mr.Pilbeam(Senior) he had inherited just two things; an aptitude for woodwork and a pair of short legs; proof, he was constantly being told, that somewhere beyond their undistinguished present lay a romantic Welsh past for which there was, as yet, no single shred of serious evidence.

"Look at me,' his father would say, citing his own dwarf-like physique as an incontrovertible genetic clue. "Long body, short legs. Therefore Welsh."

In fact, Mr.Pilbeam was a thoroughly habituated Northern bloke who, when he wasn't making cut-price coffins, pursued three principal obsessions; beer, rugby league, and sleep. And since home was a tight-knit, old-fashioned industrial town, almost every other adult male shared the same fixations. Sons (and wives) – if they were good for anything – were for weekends, which left Seymour free to do what he liked best.

By the age of ten, there was very little he couldn't do with wood. At Christmas he sold his own lathe-turned candlesticks for pocket money and when the snow came, he did the same with lethally contrived sledges, slabs of recycled oak panelling bolted to the iron pipes he'd pinched from a local scrap yard.

Almost every toy he owned, he'd made for himself; from soldiers to spinning tops; and since his dad's small business was run from a low brick building at the end of their long, scruffy back yard, Seymour never had far to go for his fix.

The simple act of drawing a saw blade across pine set him free. Nothing smelt sweeter than the sappy dust which he kicked gleefully around the floor, and nothing he made pleased him more than the kites and the boats he began to produce on an almost industrial scale.

At his school − where he was deemed sweet, creative and popular but irreversibly lazy − every playground child wanted a 'Pilbeam product'. In the spring, they clamoured for his kites, and on windy days, the skies above the town's heathery perimeter were thick with his creations, although none flew higher or steeper than his own. The wind, with its invisible moods and vacillations, had become Seymour's silent friend and its infinite possibilities presented a challenge he could neither resist nor grow tired of.

"How are you getting on at school?"

It was the question Mr. Pilbeam Senior posed just once a year, usually without waiting for an answer. This year was no different.

"Dad?"

"Hurry up lad. It's Saturday. You know what happens on Saturday."

He'd already been sitting in his best coat for an hour. When the clock on the mantelpiece reached two, there'd be a knock on the door.

"Dad. What's the thinnest dowel rod you can buy in the lightest wood?"

There was a sound of hobnails scuffling on the outside step, followed by an invasion of leery voices through the letterbox.

"Sorry son. Another time. Big match. Derby match. Kick off in an hour. See you tomorrow."

Seymour's question had already been troubling him for months. Behind it was his rising obsession to build the biggest box kite anyone had ever seen. To the boy, every kite was beautiful but none more so than the monstrous improbability that was a box kite.

Nothing seemed less capable of flight than these ramshackle cuboids of fabric and wood. And yet when Seymour unrolled his latest creations, everyone wound their own kites in to watch. In the beginning, even his mother had watched too, but when he was nine, Beryl had been struck by a tram while crossing a road in bad fog.

Although she survived – and although witnesses swore the vehicle had no lights on – Beryl's pelvis was so badly shattered, she was confined to bed in one of the family home's two grimy upstairs rooms.

For a while, his father had taken food on a tray for her to eat, followed by a nightly bowl of lukewarm water for a wash. After school (and on Sunday mornings) Seymour would slip in and silently hold her hand but as an adult, he could recall no memory of her dying. In a way, she'd just sort of disappeared. And soon after that, his father had stopped going upstairs.

From then on, Seymour flew his inventions alone, and if he thought of his mum, he didn't say. The only things in his head were his kites, and every summer evening he left his homework untouched and headed for the park; feeling the line of his kites ripping through bare hands until the skin burned red and his latest creation shrank to a quivering dot in the sky.

Somewhere, he felt sure, there was an equation – a perfect marriage of size and fabric weight and wind strength – which would ensure his kite kept on rising. And every week he added more line to the hank, sending it further and further away. But every week, long after they'd had passed from sight, the weight of the line would drag the kites back to earth and Seymour right back to the drawing board.

In a different way, his toy boats exerted a similar fascination, but from the beginning there was a void there he knew only a real boat could ever fill.

Making them was a joy, if anything more so. Each component required skills and tools unique to itself; from the smooth flanks of the hull and the taper of the boom to the delicate carving of the tiny cleats and the comical female figurehead he sculpted on every single bow. The act of sailing them, however, was always an immense disappointment.

With a kite, you could feel the earth's elemental power reaching down from the clouds into your arms. Once you slipped a model dinghy into a boating pool, you relinquished control. No matter how thoughtfully, you'd trimmed its tiny sails, there was no protection against the crashing insanity of clockwork power boats or the tidal waves generated by rampaging infants.

A falling kite had grace. Wading through stagnant water to retrieve a marooned wooden boat did not. And yet, on a warm spring Sunday afternoon, that's precisely what he'd been doing when he first met Lucy; and with different emotions, that's precisely why neither of them would ever forget it, although in just one symbolic way, their version of events always differed.

"You were wearing short trousers."

"No, I wasn't."

"They had a hole worn in the bottom. You'd got no pants on."

"Well alright. That bit's true. But they were longs. Not shorts."

Seymour's memory was correct, but it was an argument he was never keen to prolong for fear of reminding her of just how unsavoury his childhood had been. Back home, his mother's accident had led to a collapse of domestic order. Instead of toilet roll, they were now using pages from the pink Saturday sports paper; and when the kitchen dishcloths disappeared, Seymour's solitary pair of underpants had been drafted into action.

"I could see your backside. They were shorts."

In actual fact, Seymour's (long-ish) trousers had been rolled up to the knee, but what really mattered was that they'd met, and that – by some slightly sick twist of fate – he'd been holding a boat when they did so.

"Do you not think that meant something?" he asked her, some years later. More than once. And always with a vaguely hopeful tone in his voice. "An omen, perhaps?"

"No. Absolutely not," she would always reply. "And they were definitely shorts."

Whatever they were, he'd been standing in the middle of an artificial lake, where his model was becalmed under the still May sunshine. As he waded back to the edge, he'd slipped, instinctively reaching out for the girl's hand.

"Are you on your own?" she'd asked. "I've seen you here before."

"I caught the bus. I come every weekend," said the boy, carefully rolling the sails around the folded masts of his toy. "There's no boating pool where I live."

"Aren't you a little old for this? Do you like football?"

"Not really. Do you?"

"I hate it," she declared.

Beyond the hedge which circled the park, Seymour could hear the steady thwack of a hand slapping a bare leg. Seconds later, the howl of a child's cry rang out across the water.

"I'm thirteen. How old are you? What's your name?"

"Lucy. Fourteen. What's yours?"

"Seymour. Seymour Pilbeam." The girl was trying (and failing) to stifle a giggle. "It's alright. Everybody laughs. I'm used to it. My dad says it's Welsh."

"It doesn't sound Welsh. It sounds stupid."

"Thanks," said Seymour.

"Not an easy one to forget though." The girl pointed to a large woman dressed in green, picking herself up from a bench and moving in their direction. "I've got to go. That's my mother. We come here every Sunday."

"Every Sunday?"

"Yes, but boats are for kids. You're thirteen. And Seymour......"

"What?

"You need to get some underpants."

He'd watched her walk away, regally upright in a plaid skirt, straw hat and blazer, hoping for a final glance back that never came. Then on three more happy occasions that summer, they'd met in the park by the pool although by then Seymour had patched his own trousers and temporarily disposed of the little yachts.

"What does your dad do?" she'd asked. "Mine works in an office. He's called Bill. He's got false teeth."

"Mine makes coffins," he replied, desperately hoping that she'd let him hold her hand. "He's called Seymour Pilbeam, too."

Shortly after that, with German bombers threatening Northern cities, Seymour was readied for evacuation to a farm in North Wales.

"This is great news," said Mr. Pilbeam Senior, as he marched his son to the railway station. "Truly great news."

"Not for me it isn't," replied the boy.

"Of course it is. You're going back home. To Wales. The motherland. All those centuries of Pilbeam exile are over."

"We've got short legs, dad. That's all. We're not Welsh."

But there were two deeper reasons for Mr Pilbeam Snr's glee. Firstly, the price of coffins, he felt absolutely certain, was about to go through the roof. And secondly, he was struggling to raise a teenage son without help. A few weeks away from those kites and boats would be good for a lad who seemed trapped in a world of his own; and who showed not the slightest interest in Rugby League.

Surely, surrounded by the peaks of Snowdonia, he'd grow up eventually.

Because surely, eventually, everyone did.

Chapter Three

"So, you're not Welsh?"

"No. Absolutely not. It's an ancient family myth. I've just got short legs."

"I've got short legs too. Exactly how short do they have to be?"

There were many nights when Seymour wondered why he'd volunteered for the pub dominoes team. So far, this was one of them.

"Listen carefully, Frank. Everyone in the team has a nickname, so when I joined, people started calling me Taff."

"Because of that old story?"

"Yes."

"So, I'm not Welsh either?"

"No."

Frank's nickname was 'Dense'. Five minutes in his company was ample time to work out why. For twenty years he'd been taking holiday photographs of the town's trippers and every summer morning, they'd congregate outside the glass cabinet at 'Super Snaps' to scrutinise the results.

Usually they were delighted. Even when it was raining, Frank could charm a smile out of a moody lobster. For his satisfied customers, a solitary picture would be the only lasting evidence of their trip; a memory for which they paid dearly. During the off-season, most people in the town worried about money. After he'd packed his cameras away in October, Frank wasn't one of them.

"I took some cracking pictures of your boat going down," he chuckled. "I could drop them round at yours."

"No thanks," said Seymour. "I'd prefer it if you destroyed the negatives."

For one dismal moment, he could picture the scene back home. Lucy lying in bed in the darkness; an open book sliding from her pillow to the floor; Isaac watching Captain Scarlet (or The Avengers) alone with a bottle of pop and a packet of crisps.

Blinking the image away, he surveyed the fast-filling pub. Nothing beat the guilty thrill of The White Horse on a Friday night. As always, the place was rammed and a fug of spilled ale and rolling tobacco was seeping from the crush of men piling in off the street.

Everyone in town knew the drill. Hardly anyone was there for the sport. If you studied the fixtures, there was pub darts or dominoes somewhere every night of the week and no self-respecting landlady wanted her free half-time spread of pork pies and prawn sandwiches to be bested.

For the lonely hearts, drunks and transient trawler men, it meant no-cost grub. For the women who laid on the spreads, it ensured a never-ending arms race in which the outcome of the darts matches mattered far less to the punters than the quality of the puff pastry.

"You playing tonight?"

As the pub filled, Seymour had found himself pushed to the bar. A dark-haired woman in her mid-40's, with scarlet lips and a dizzying excess of cleavage, was leaning behind it.

"They need my brains, Nellie. I'm the only one who can count."

Seymour liked Nellie. She glowed, she kept a good pub, and as she was invariably the only woman in it, she never failed to give her male clientele something to gawp at.

"I heard about the boat. This one's on me."

With a nod, Seymour took the glass from her hand and raised it to his lips. It was funny. Almost everyone he could see really did have a nickname – everyone that is, except Nellie – and the five-man domino team was a perfect example.

The names were up there now on the noticeboard. "White Horse Doms A team. Taff. Clinkers. Rehab. Dense. Harry Spanners." Maybe it was a seaside town thing, but he hadn't got a clue what anyone was really called.

"Why is he called Harry Spanners?"

There was a brief lull in the scrum for drinks. Nellie turned back to Seymour and suspended a stained tea towel across the beer handles. It wasn't something she was likely to investigate, but she liked Seymour too. In a town full of oddballs, he was a rare touch of class.

"Harry? He had this metal caliper splint thing on his right leg when he was a kid…. polio, I think…the splint kept falling to pieces….so his parents put a tool kit in his school satchel. You know what kids are like. Tools. Spanners. Harry Spanners. Hey presto. I reckon he uses them now to keep The Burlingtonian afloat."

"I never knew. That's brilliant." Seymour put his empty glass down on the bar. "But what's his real name?"

"No idea", laughed Nellie. This close, he thought, she had a lovely smile. "We had a regular once called Steve, but everyone always referred to him as Vick."

"How come?"

"Because he got up everyone's nose." She waited a moment for the joke to settle. "Same again, chuck?"

It seemed odd to him how little people really knew about each other. Everyone was a headline. Captain Rehab was a drunken ex-trawler skipper. Clinkers ran a junk shop full of stolen goods. Beyond that, they were total strangers. And yet their company – because it demanded nothing of him – filled Seymour with joy, as if knowledge and intimacy were sometimes obstacles to true friendship, not a route to it.

Maybe it was the same with marriage, or with his marriage, at least. Almost a week had passed since Lucy had spoken to him and whilst they'd shared a bed, their bodies had not touched, and the day's one family meal had been conducted in chapel-like silence. After that, at around seven each night, she'd slipped quietly back upstairs with a book.

"You need to do something," Isaac had pleaded.

"Just give her time," said Seymour. "You know what she's like."

"She's stopped going to work. She'll get sacked."

"She might. I don't know. Her boss is a friend."

It didn't help that Seymour loved his job every bit as much as his wife hated her own. At one end of the long main street, Seymour prepared the pages for the town's (proud but dull) weekly newspaper. At the other end, Lucy helped elderly ladies select footwear at an airless shoe shop which smelled (not surprisingly) of other people's socks

"I'm better than this, Seymour. I'm wasting my time."

"I know. I know. You are. We need a plan. We need you strong again."

But in fifteen years, nothing had changed. Seymour still loved his pots of paste, and the click-clack of his scissors. He still loved the smell of the newsprint, and the whoosh of the compressed air tubes carrying the corrected copy into the thumping cauldron of the print room.

Lucy, on the other hand, still counted every minute until her shifts were over, and back home, she would endlessly scrub her hands, certain that the stink of geriatric feet was sinking deeper and deeper into her flesh.

It had been building up for a long time. Ever since they'd moved to the coast, something had been wrong. But just lately, Lucy's moods had been coming on more often. And after this last week of gloom, Seymour had needed to get out.

Although he never drank heavily, there was a soothing quality to public houses which he cherished. He loved the horse brasses and the framed hunting scenes. He loved the undemanding chat, and the glorious rootedness of being a part of somewhere.

Like his father, the pub somehow felt to Seymour like an entitlement. And like his father, he'd ended up with a wife living in the dark. It wasn't much to ask, he reasoned. Just a couple of pints on a Sunday lunchtime, and – providing he was in the team – one night a week of darts, dominoes and gelatinous pork pies.

"You shouldn't go, dad. You'll make it worse."

"I'll only be a couple of hours. And she's in bed anyway. It'll be fine."

He hadn't told Isaac, that with just two fixtures to go, the White Horse were in with a chance of silverware; or that victory over the Flying Horseshoes would bring the East Riding (East) Higginson's Bakery Domino League title within tantalisingly easy reach.

To Seymour, it was no less a sporting miracle than England winning the World Cup. Even after a lifetime spent in pubs, his team-mates seemed incapable of grasping the rules, and every match was preceded by the same incantation.

"When you put down a domino, you add up the dots at each end, aiming for a number divisible by five or three" Seymour took a deep breath. "If the combined figure is nine you get three points, allowing

31

you to move your matchstick three holes along this small rectangular board. And if the figure is, say, ten then you move it two spaces, and so on, until all 61 holes have been traversed and – god willing – we've won."

"Let's say there's a double five at one end. I play a three at the other. Adds up to thirteen. Right?" Captain Rehab had started to shuffle his fingers, only to stop when he realised there weren't enough. "So how many spaces do I move?"

"You don't move at all."

"But there's a three in thirteen. A one and a three."

"Yes, but you can't divide thirteen by either five or three."

Rehab's face sagged, weighed down by the incomprehensibility of it all.

"I don't get it. I just don't get it."

"Why can't you?" said Frank.

"Why can't you what?" said Seymour.

"Why can't you divide thirteen by either a five or a three?"

Recently, Seymour had even looked it up in the dictionary. It was called dyscalculia. The White Horse was on the brink of domino history (in the East Riding (East) area) with a team afflicted by numerical dyslexia. Only luck – and Seymour's unbeaten run of eleven games – had got them this far.

"Are we winning?"

The match had limped (with numerous altercations) to the halfway point, allowing Nellie to slip out from behind the bar with a tray of sausage rolls.

"I'm worried Rehab's brain is going to explode, but yes we are. Rather easily."

"Just The Ship to beat next month then?"

"Stan Clough's lot? Yes. Grudge match. Will you come?"

Apart from a few greasy crumbs, the tray had been picked bare. Nellie smoothed the wrinkles of her dress and dropped onto a chair alongside Seymour.

"Listen," she whispered. "Do you still play the accordion?"

There was an enormous cheer from Rehab's table. Dominoes were skittering across the floor in every direction.

"Yes, I do. When I can. It's a Gabbanelli."

"Well whatever it is, Harry needs a player on The Burlingtonian. Just weekends. Might be worth asking him. Oh, and before you ask," she grinned. "Yes, of course I'll be there."

"That's good….and thanks for the tip."

Suddenly everyone was storming the bar. "White Horse Winners" had been chalked on the darts scoreboard, and Rehab was wafting a double six high over his head.

"Six bloody holes. I moved six fucking holes to win, Seymour."

"Bobby Charlton eat your heart out," yelled Clinkers, whose nose (apart from its square of hairy brown skin) had turned an alarming shade of plum.

From his seat over in the snug, Harry Spanners looked up and raised a glass in triumph at no-one in particular.

"Cheers," mouthed Seymour.

"To victory," mouthed Harry, holding up his fingers in a Churchillian salute.

Although they'd rarely spoken, Seymour had a soft spot for Harry Spanners. Maybe it was that slight limp, or the face that was so comically veined it looked like a piece of Stilton. Or maybe the omnipresent sailor's cap and faded blue smock. Either way, he'd be chasing him about that job. A boat was a boat, after all, even if this one was on its last sea legs.

Ten minutes later he was home, tiptoeing upstairs nursing a familiar feeling of guilt-tinged dread. From Isaac's bedroom, he could hear the muffled pulse of a pop song. And as he fumbled in the gloom for his pyjamas, the floorboards started creaking like the deck of a rolling ship.

"You smell of beer," said Lucy, rolling away to face the wall.

"I've cleaned my teeth." There was no response. "I think we might win the league." Still nothing. "Sleep tight, love."

It was Saturday the next day, and Seymour stirred early. He'd that kite to finish for Mrs Cribbis and a suicidal curiosity to discover what was left of his 'Goodrun'. There was also nothing whatsoever to detain him in bed. Slipping into the room next door, he gently shook his son's shoulder.

"Really low tide, son. I'm going to see if there's anything to salvage."

Minutes later, the two were striding through the town's empty streets. Along the promenade, furious seagulls were squabbling over cold chips, and a procession of lorries was shipping the overnight catch away from the north pier in crates spilling with ice.

Abandoned by the tide, the harbour's exposed seabed looked smooth and glossy, and its motley population of marooned yachts and fishing cobles leaned drunkenly in every direction. Where Seymour's boat had once lain, only a confusion of indistinguishable bits remained.

Seven days, and fourteen high tides, had swept the rest of it off to Norway.

Even at this hour, a handful of local kids had gathered on the jetty to dangle bait into the muddy pools left around its ancient wooden foundations. While Seymour mourned his dinghy, Isaac hung back to watch, fascinated by the profusion of crabs they were pulling from the water on hooks baited with dead fish.

Along the edge of the quay, a line of coloured water-filled buckets was already alive with furious crustaceans, and the boy looked carefully in each one.

"Dad. Over here. Quick."

It was the last bucket which had seized his attention. There it was again. Amongst the knot of claws and feelers, a sudden flash of pink and white.

"Dad. Come on. Now."

As Seymour walked to join him, Isaac dropped to his knees and swirled both hands into the freezing water. After a few seconds, he pulled them out again; clamped tight around whatever he had caught.

"Show me," said Seymour.

As he unlocked his fingers, an alien shell emerged, speckled with sand.

"I think we've found grandad's teeth," said Isaac.

A small crab was sitting where Bill's tongue would normally be.

"I think you're right," said Seymour.

Chapter Four

Lucy had been awake when Seymour and Isaac left. As their voices passed under her bedroom window, she'd risen and examined herself in the full-length mirror. As a child, she had always been thin. Now her cheeks were hollowed into dark bowls, and the line of her ribs showed more relief than her breasts.

Passing next door, she slid her hand into her son's still warm bed. There was a battered copy of a Littlewoods mail order catalogue tucked down the side. When she tugged it free, the pages fell open at the photographs of women's underwear. Slipping it back carefully, she headed down into the kitchen, where the sun was already pouring in through a wide garden window.

A week had passed since the humiliation, and since then – apart from a few hours at the shop – she'd sequestered herself upstairs with her books, sliding downstairs only for tea and toast when she felt certain Seymour was not there. Recently, it had always been the same when her irritation flared. It was as if the anger plundered her strength, leaving her with nothing to bottle the lingering aftertaste of shame.

It was touching to see how hard Seymour tried. Every pot and pan had been washed and stacked. The sawdust which was usually heaped in every kitchen corner had gone. There were no offcuts of wood; no runaway nails, and the soldering iron – which was invariably glowing on the stove – had been spirited away along with the radio valves, and the random, ragged skeins of string.

From a dressing gown pocket, Lucy pulled a packet of Woodbines, and an old cigarette lighter. There was a pile of library books on the wooden sideboard (which Seymour had made) and she tilted her head to read the titles. Shackleton. Cook. Captain Scott. The Titanic. Books about the sea; and books about seafarers. Without thinking, she picked up the top volume and opened it. The pages were covered with technical blueprints and boat designs. And tucked into the middle, were a handful of newspaper cuttings about Francis Chichester, the old man who'd just sailed alone around the world.

She leaned back, closed her eyes, and took an immense lung-full of smoke. So far as she knew, Seymour had never read a novel in his life. The first birthday present she'd ever bought for him (just after the war) was a bound copy of 'Sons and Lovers' that had ended up under a leg of his father's dining table.

After that she'd deduced that (since he lost both with satisfying regularity) pipes and penknives were all he really wanted, and consequently (come Christmas and birthdays) all he ever got.

There was a clinking noise at the back gate. The milkman was swapping their empty bottles for full ones. From the corner of the kitchen, she became aware of another sound; music – a hymn – swelling louder as the voices grew in confidence. It was morning worship on the BBC Home Service, and despite herself, Lucy smiled.

Unless it was Christmas – when she deemed the service from Kings College, Cambridge to be a non-negotiable family moment – a functioning wireless ranked low on Seymour's list of domestic priorities. True, he had a weakness for the shipping forecast, but The Archers left him cold and the radio was a refugee from that dreadful man's junk shop.

If it worked, she was lucky and today she was lucky. While she'd been languishing upstairs behind drawn curtains, Seymour had fixed it, and now the ruddy glow from its dial illuminated the cruelty of her present dilemma. Although living with him was becoming intolerable, there was still space in her heart for a 42-year-old man who made kites.

The war hadn't helped. When it was over, apart from a few letters, there'd been no contact between them for over six years.

Once the threat of bombing had passed, Lucy's parents had retrieved her from a Pennine farm, and sent her back to school. Seymour, on the other hand, had been billeted with a family near Dolgellau until VE Day, at which point Mr.Pilbeam Senior had mailed him a train ticket home and a letter asking his son if he could speak Welsh.

"No, but my legs have shrunk," Seymour wrote back, enclosing a photograph of a wooden dinghy – a Firefly – skidding across the pewter waters of Lake Bala. "They must have been in the water too long," he added in a postscript.

Had Mr. Pilbeam looked closer – he didn't – he'd have noticed that the emaciated young man holding the tiller was his son. And that the sparkle on the water was matched only by the light shining in the boy's eyes; a glow which was still there six months later, when he and Lucy finally reunited.

"God," she'd said. "Is that you?"

"Yes. Bloody hell," he'd replied. "Is that you?"

It was January, and there'd been heavy falls of snow since Boxing Day.

"I've brought a sledge. Do you fancy a go?"

"Of course. And long trousers too. You're learning."

Under the light of a streetlamp, each of them was intrigued by the changes in the other. Both were dark-haired and wartime slender, with strong vibrant faces. But to Seymour (who sported a thick black moustache) it seemed like Lucy's entire being had become charged with restless sexual energy as if some dangerous force compelled her. And in Lucy's eyes, the very opposite appeared true of Seymour, whose languid aura of self-contentment had altered little since she'd reached out her hand at the boating pool.

38

"You look like a young Einstein," she said. "You've got the same nose and hair."

Seymour rocked awkwardly from foot to foot. He was wearing a thick black donkey jacket, and the snow rustled under the weight of his heavy studded brogues.

"Could you repeat that in front of my father?" he smiled. "He thinks I'm thick."

"And are you? Thick, I mean?"

"Maybe. But I made this myself," he told her, holding up a carefully-crafted fusion of steel and wood. "Fastest sledge in town."

"Can you get two on it?"

"Only me so far, but I'm game if you are."

"I've never been on a sledge before. Can I ride on top?"

Seymour could feel the skin on his entire face burning. "Just so long as you watch where you put your hands," he grinned.

It was true. There wasn't much she'd ever done in her short life which merited the description of fun. When she was eleven, her mother had presented her with a copy of 'Personal Hygiene For Girls' inscribed with the handwritten warning: "Know this, my darling Lucy. All Men are Fools". Inside it, were tips on how to air pantaloons by an open bedroom window, and more interestingly, what parts of her body she would be ill-advised to fiddle with.

By the age of fifteen, she'd discovered the parts (and D.H.Lawrence) and the fiddling had started with a vengeance. Every night, in the throes of her ecstasy – with her underwear positioned dutifully by a draught – she felt destined for a life of passion very different from the loveless one endured by her parents.

39

Bill and Olive were kind, and their detached, stone-built home – which overlooked a golf course – was comfortable and clean and cold in every way. In the corner of the lounge, was a piano on which Olive played popular classics with such thunderous syncopation, golfers on the distant first tee could hum along to every note. On the walls were hung countless mediocre paintings (by Olive) alongside bookshelves stacked with unopened biographies and obscure classics.

Every square foot of the house ached with frustration. Bill was a dutiful, toothless and dull town hall clerk who polished his war medals on Saturday and his work shoes on Sunday. Olive (in her own view) was a beautiful shopkeeper's daughter whose sweetheart had been blown to pieces; and who's undiscovered (and hitherto unidentified) talents were ebbing away in the company of a substitute.

Since the two rarely touched, it seemed unimaginable to Lucy that her parents could ever have had sex. And yet they had – at least twice – producing first Ralph, and then Lucy with a ten-year gap in between. "Apart from for us, do you think they ever did it?" she'd once asked her older brother. But by then, Ralph had left home and was selling used cars on a patch of waste land behind the Co-op.

"I wish we saw more of him," she told her mother. "Ralph, I mean."

"All men are fools," prompted Olive, pointing to a framed picture of Emmeline Pankhurst on the mantelpiece. "Especially your brother."

For a moment, looking at him now, she wondered if Seymour might be another fool. But the thought escaped as quickly as it had come. Like her mother before her, she'd reached the end of a long war consumed by yearning. All she wanted now was a dark, sensitive man; someone with his own teeth who looked like a film star; and maybe this boy was the one. So far, there'd been no-one else, and, in the new-falling snow, the promise of mischief was irresistible.

"So, where's this hill then?" she said.

"Walk this way," he replied, slipping one hand around her waist and pulling the sledge along behind them with the other.

Everyone in their town had heard of The Black Pudding; and nobody had a clue how it had acquired the name. All were agreed, however. In the right conditions, there wasn't a better sledging hill in Yorkshire, and the bloodstains locked into the ice were testimony to the many that had tried and failed to master it.

Starting as a broad concrete ramp, the slope ran fifty yards between iron railings, before turning sharply across a car park, down the steep grassy bank of a mill pond and then on across the ice. If the snow was packed, and the water was frozen, it was a half-mile and sixty seconds of bone-rattling madness which ended in a soft nest of bulrushes; or the local hospital.

"And how do we know the ice will take our weight?"

The snow was falling thicker now, and as Lucy peered through it, the streetlights came on revealing the hard, glassy surface of the ramp. Way beyond it, she could see the ragged disc of the pond, perfectly white, inside its dark ring of reeds.

"We don't. But we'll be going so fast we'll hardly touch it anyway," said Seymour. "Now climb on and let's do it."

Aiming its runners down the hill, Seymour pulled on a pair of woollen mittens and lay belly-down on his sledge. Clutching a broad wooden cross-piece, he splayed his legs out wide, and banged the toes of his shoes hard into the snow. Once he was settled, Lucy tightened the belt of her coat, and stretched out along his back.

"Hold onto my shoulders and keep your legs up all the time. OK?"

For a few seconds, they were both absolutely still; paralysed by sensations which neither had experienced before. Closing his eyes, Seymour savoured the cushion of Lucy's breasts in his back, and the warmth of her stockinged legs stretched out along his. Meanwhile,

41

Lucy could smell Seymour's hair ointment, and feel the soft rise of his buttocks against her groin.

There'd been nothing about this in 'Personal Hygiene For Girls', she thought.

"Ready?" said Seymour.

"God yes, I'm ready," she gasped.

"Sorry. I missed that."

"Yes, yes. Just look after me."

Lifting his toes from the snow, they were off; thundering perilously close to the left-hand railings as they neared the bottom of the ramp and span hard right onto the deserted spread of the car park. To make the turn, Seymour had rammed his right foot into the snow, steering safely away from a kerb, before picking his line towards the edge of the lodge.

At the beginning, Lucy had clamped her eyes shut, but now they were shining wildly with excitement. Every bump seemed to shake them tighter, and when Seymour leaned, she leaned too, feeling their direction change as the weight shifted between the runners, cleaving hissing sparks of ice onto their faces and backs.

Where the car park ended, the sledge lurched steeply downwards through thicker, softer snow. She felt thorns tearing at her legs, and in the thumping blackness she reached her arms right around Seymour's chest, and buried her face in the soft warmth of his scarf.

For a second, they were airborne. Then with a clatter, the sledge was down and picking up speed, and the only sounds were the chatter of skidding steel and the shouts of two young people screaming in triumph.

Nothing could thwart them now. They'd done it. And as the far bank screamed into view, Seymour slammed his left foot into the ice, causing the sledge to spin twice around before stopping – under complete control – at the furthest edge of the pond.

"Oh my god. Oh my god."

Lucy's heart was jumping, and she was laughing uncontrollably as she tried to stand. For some reason, one of her feet was much colder than the other.

"You enjoyed it then?"

"I lost a shoe. It was incredible."

"You lost one. I ruined two." Seymour's big toes were poking out through the end of his shoes. "Makes a change from my trousers, I suppose."

"We'll get frostbite."

"I'll find it. Put your foot on the sledge."

Both were standing awkwardly, and somehow Lucy's hand had arrived on Seymour's shoulder. Stepping closer, he put both his around her waist, and moved his head forward until their cheeks were touching……..

Twenty years ago? Really? Was it that long? Such an awful lot of penknives and pipes. Somewhere in between, she'd given up trying to connect her feelings then to her feelings now. People changed together (if they were lucky) or at different speeds. Or sometimes, they simply didn't change at all.

Lighting up a second cigarette, she stood at the window. Something was bubbling skywards from the gasworks and a bag of coal had toppled over by the gate. Suddenly, everything looked shabby and the radio had conked out. To her left was the large brick outbuilding where Seymour periodically liked to hide with the accordion he'd never told her about. Dusty cobwebs masked its solitary window, and there was a padlock on the door which looked new.

"I'm back love. You'll never guess what we found."

Seymour strode exultantly into the kitchen. It would be so easy to crush him, she thought, but her reflections had stirred a little tenderness.

"Go on. Surprise me."

"Shut your eyes and stretch out your hands."

"It's not an eel is it?"

Years before, he'd caught an eel in the harbour which had still been writhing four hours later.

"No, it's not an eel. Put out your hands."

When he was certain she wasn't peeping, Seymour pulled his father-in-law's teeth from an inside jacket pocket and placed them on Lucy's fingers. A pink crayfish had been artfully placed between the teeth.

"Ta-daaaaa. Breakfast."

"You absolute sod." Lucy hurled the teeth skywards.

"Can you believe it? They were in a crab bucket."

A few minutes later, they were sharing a cigarette together and Bill's dentures were simmering in a saucepan of scummy water.

"Best to boil them. You never know what goes into that harbour," said Lucy.

"You never know what goes into Bill's mouth either," chuckled Seymour.

"Isaac didn't come back with you?"

"He said he was meeting some friends."

There'd been a lot of that recently; moods and mysterious absences.

Two years earlier, against every expectation, Isaac had passed his eleven-plus, and was now languishing at the bottom of every set in the town's boys-only grammar school. Just a summer ago, on his yearly report, Isaac's headmaster had concluded that "this child grins well, but the rest is less satisfactory". Seymour had laughed. Lucy had wept. And another dreary week of domestic non-communication had followed.

"I think there's a girlfriend. He's carved the letter 'A' into his satchel and it's all over his exercise books."

"I did the same once. Except it was an 'L' obviously."

He took a sideways look at his wife. It was wonderful to be talking again. But she wasn't a girl anymore, and she was worryingly gaunt.

"I'm worried about him," she said, passing her husband the last of the cigarette. "I don't think he likes us. Or me, mainly."

"He's a teenager. We were teenagers once. Remember?"

"Whatever happened to that sledge? The one we flew down Black Pudding on."

"I've still got it. Out there, in the old stable."

"I so, so fancied you that day."

For the second time in a few minutes, she was beaming, and a rare flush of blood had appeared in her cheeks. It had been months since he'd seen her so happy.

"There was nothing left of the boat, sadly. Just mud."

Lucy didn't reply. She was stroking her lips again between her thumb and forefinger.

"I was thinking." He paused. Even though he had rehearsed all the lines, this was much harder than he'd imagined. "I was thinking that I might build one of my own. Not now necessarily. Just some time in the future maybe."

"I saw the book."

"It wouldn't cost much. It's just an idea. What do you think?"

"And what will I do? Where will I be when you're making it, or sailing it, or playing bloody dominoes with those fools in your pub?"

"There's another little thing," he whispered. Hopefully, she wouldn't hear him. "I've got a little seasonal weekend job on The Burlingtonian."

But by then, as always, she was long gone, and the radio – jolted by the slamming of the kitchen door – had stuttered back to life with the shipping forecast.

"*Sea area Humber....winds 1 or 2.....sea slight....weather sunshine...visibility good.*"

At last. The summer was finally here. The summer would change everything.

Chapter Five

As a child, Seymour Pilbeam had learned that the wind could disappear just as quickly as it arrived. In one moment, a furious rising swirl of leaves; in the next, a tell-tale sag in his line, that signalled the distant death of another kite. Early on in their marriage, he'd realised that Lucy's moods were similarly contrary, blowing out just as quickly as they'd blown in.

One minute, she'd be throwing plates. Five minutes later, she'd be asking if he'd remembered the Durex. Survival, he'd decided (privately), was like sailing a boat. Just so long as you kept a weather eye out for squalls, everything would be just fine. And, so far, even in the blackest times, Lucy's storms blew out eventually.

For the next two weeks, a happy calm prevailed, helped by a glorious burst of Mediterranean sunshine which flooded the town with heat. Some nights, after work, the couple met on the beach and swam out to the wooden rafts anchored offshore. On others, when Isaac joined them, they drove a few miles along the dunes, crouching around huge fires of driftwood until the sand was too hot for their feet.

"You should bring your accordion down one night and play for us," she said, one evening as they drove home under a pink sky.

"I didn't think you'd heard me," he stammered. "How did you know?"

In the back of the car, Isaac leaned forward. There was a hurricane brewing. There had to be.

"I'm not deaf, Seymour. Everyone within a mile of our house probably knows."

And that, it seemed, was that. No recriminations. No retreat to a lightless bedroom. Not even the hint of a sulk. Under the kindly spell of summer, harmony prevailed and Seymour's secret affair with a squeeze box was out. The following weekend, even his mother-in-law seemed to know about it.

"Let's hear this bloody organ then," bellowed Olive, from a deckchair in the garden.

"Three wheels on my wagon and I'm still rolling along," chorused Bill, for no apparent reason.

Between them lay an empty bottle of medium dry sherry and a half-finished glass of stout.

"You got any more of this?" pleaded Olive, from behind a broad, drunken smile.

"Some enchanted evening," sang Bill, who had a weakness for musicals his wife didn't share. "You may see a strangerrrrrr."

Both were deliriously happy. Ever since the debacle of the launch, Lucy's mother had lived in dread of her husband being spotted without his teeth; a possibility she'd held at bay by keeping him under virtual house arrest on a diet of tomato soup, pending the arrival of freshly-minted dentures.

"Christ. That could be months. Years maybe," he'd moaned.

"And you'll stay inside until they're here."

"There was nothing wrong with the real ones you made me take out."

"What was that? What did you say?"

"Nothing, dear."

As a concession, Olive promised to try him with omelettes, but then –
a miracle, indeed – a postcard had arrived from their daughter. The
teeth had been found, and under cover of darkness, they'd driven to
the seaside to retrieve them.

"Is it me, or do they taste a bit funny?" wondered Bill, after slipping
them back into his mouth. "What did you say once flowed into that
harbour?"

"Shit, grandad," said Isaac.

"What was that? What did he did he say, Olive?"

"Nothing dear."

After that, the sherry had appeared, and Bill had been allowed back
onto solids. Everyone seemed to have forgotten about the accordion
until breakfast the next morning, when Seymour – to his own surprise
– slipped it quietly into the conversation.

"I'm playing it on The Burlingtonian later. Just for practise really….
and hopefully a few tips. You'd be welcome to watch." Seymour
scanned the table anxiously across his bowl of porridge. "It'd be free.
You wouldn't need tickets. It's a lovely day."

Lucy stroked her lips and picked at some loose skin around her
thumb with a forefinger.

"Yes. On two conditions." Inwardly, Seymour breathed a deep sigh
of relief. His wife was smiling. "First no sails. And second, dad….."

"What?" asked Bill, who was making up for lost time with a fifth slice
of toast.

"Glue those teeth in."

By mid-morning – under a perfect blue sky – the entire town was
alive with the happy holiday bustle of summer. Striding through
it, on his way to the harbour, Seymour clutched his accordion case

tight, and savoured the clamour.

At the railway station, entire tribes of factory workers and their families were arriving for the trip they'd looked forward to since the last one. Three (sometimes four) generations tumbled into taxis, heading off to their favourite guest houses (hot and cold water in every room) while the machinery back home fell silent, and whole towns emptied for their annual week of peace.

Seymour loved to see the parents in their Sunday best, dragging fat suitcases and fractious children in new t-shirts, past shop windows overflowing with goods he'd only ever seen at the seaside. The joke soap that left your face black; the paper flags on sticks that would soon be fluttering on a thousand sandcastles; the X-ray spectacles and the comedy nylon wigs.

Above the town's two quays, Stan Clough's amusements were already humming with light and electricity. Somewhere deep inside them, hidden machinery clicked and whirred, creating warm rhythms of noise which crept out amongst the smell of fried food and fish and flooded Seymour with the same glow he'd felt there as a child.

Not that he'd visited the place often. Only twice that he remembered, and never with his father. Mills and factories might temporarily close, but dead people still needed boxes, declared Mr.Pilbeam Snr. Or words to that effect. Then, after Hitler had invaded Poland – and his mother had walked into a tram – the Yorkshire coast somehow lost its appeal.

"I can't believe you've never been," he'd said to Lucy, soon after their sledging adventures had graduated into something more serious.

"We normally only go to Llandudno," she'd replied. "Mummy prefers North Wales. She thinks the east coast is far too common."

A line of starlings watched him as he descended the wide crescent of steps at the head of the north pier. "It's not common," he thought. "It's the sea. It's people. It's bloody amazing."

50

Away to his left he took in the stone-speckled beach, tracing its curve along the wall of steep, chalk cliffs to the flashing dot of a lighthouse. In front of him, on a rising tide, the harbour was bouncing with craft of every shape and size. And beyond the sea walls, a sleek, white yacht – sails fully extended – was moving smoothly away from its own line of wake.

"Lovely day for a picture."

There was a tap on his shoulder. Seymour didn't even need to look.

"Hello Frank. You must be coining it in."

"Fifty-three in two hours. I'll be finished if cameras ever get cheap. Not that they will. What brings you down here?"

"The same thing as you."

A wooden gangplank was being wheeled alongside a large, cream-painted pleasure cruiser by two potbellied men in blue sweaters. A coil of black fumes hung over its funnel, and a woman with a loudhailer was urging trippers to get their tickets for one of the six daily cruises into the bay.

"Sixty passengers on each. Wow. That's a lot of pictures."

"It is a very lot of pictures," said Frank.

"How many pictures, exactly?" said Seymour. "Six times sixty?"

"I haven't a fucking clue," said Frank.

Seymour felt inside a pocket and pulled out a small, metal souvenir badge. It was one of the few tangible relics of his mother and although the print was badly faded – and he'd no memories of the trip – he could still make out a picture of the boat, alongside a motto that hadn't changed in a half century; 'All Smiles On The Burlingtonian'.

Looking at it now – dwarfing every other vessel in the harbour – it seemed incredible the thing could still float. During the war, it had

51

struck a stray mine on its way home from Dunkirk. Despite being holed beneath the waterline, she'd limped home – no hands lost – to a hero's welcome and a permanent place in the town's mythology.

Since then, rust had been trying to finish what the Germans started. Flaking, orange streaks ran down from its rivets; crumbling blisters of metal seemed to be bursting up along every rotten seam; and a look of faded neglect ran from bow to stern.

Lots of words came to mind when he scrutinised it, thought Seymour. Iconic; doughty; heroic. But sadly, seaworthy wasn't one of them.

"I hope you've been practising your sea shanties."

A rotund man with a red face limped across the gangplank and wrapped his arm around Seymour's shoulders. He, too, wore a thick blue sweater with the name of the boat stitched across his chest.

"I'm a little nervous, Harry," said Seymour. "Couldn't you just use the radio instead?"

"It's broken," replied Harry, with a hitch of his trousers. "Let me show you around."

It didn't take long. Below deck, there was a cramped bar next to a small toilet with a broken door. Up top there was a boxy wheelhouse and enough varnished benches for half of the 60 or so passengers. No-one ever complained when they had to stand. Most of them were too busy being sick to care.

"Where do I sit?" asked Seymour.

"You don't. You wander around and keep their minds off the swell."

"I've only ever played sitting down."

But Spanners had gone, dragging his bad leg to the wheelhouse as the first punters streamed on board. At a thumbs-up from his shore crew, Harry turned on the engine. Tremors rippled along the decking and a few flakes of ancient paint dropped into the harbour before the engine settled into a comforting palsy-like tremor.

Seymour took in the spectacle. The boat was crammed and as the boat slipped its moorings, he could see an iridescent patch of diesel into which something sticky was falling, like black snow.

"They're looking a bit worried," whispered Frank, whose orange jacket was already speckled with smuts from the funnel. "I think you'd better start playing."

By lunchtime, after three one-hour trips, Seymour was loving it. True, it had felt awkward at first – and it wasn't easy staying upright – but the customers were in a sunshine mood and the bar was doing a roaring trade. Under flawless skies, people had even sung along (although not always to what he was playing) and by lunchtime his pockets bulged with tips.

"You're good," said Harry, as the boat began to fill with trippers once again. "But possibly a bit repetitive. How many tunes do you actually know?"

"Six," said Seymour. "But I could play them in a different order."

At the end of the gangplank, a long queue was waiting patiently, and the entire pier jostled with holidaymakers driven off the beach by the incoming tide. From a quiet spot at the stern, Seymour rested his arms and watched the throng with a sense of dread.

Amongst the hats and sunburned faces, he could see his green-clad mother-in-law pushing an old metal pram. Alongside her, wearing a favourite canary-coloured dress, was Lucy. And just a few strides behind – preoccupied by a large cloud of candy floss – trudged Bill.

"Make way. Make way. Special guests of the orchestra here."

As Olive muscled to the head of the line, a few disgruntled voices were raised in protest, only to fall silent whenever their owners caught the steel in her eye.

"Dare I ask what she's pushing?" asked Frank.

"It's a dog," said Seymour.

"Of course it is," said Frank.

As the trio looked on, there was a weak yelp from the hood of the pram.

"There, there Arthur," hushed Olive. "We'll soon have you on board."

"I feel sick," muttered Seymour. "I need the toilet."

There were ten steel steps down from the deck which led to two doors off a dimly lit corridor. Behind the one marked 'Cocktail Lounge' Seymour found a tiny wooden bar with a beer-soaked floor and one small table. It had clearly been a busy morning. Above the counter – on a single wall-mounted shelf – just a few full bottles of Mackeson remained, and the one visible ashtray was piled high with stubs.

Unpeeling his feet from the lino, Seymour stepped back into the corridor drawn by a strange noise coming from behind the broken door of the toilet; a noise which sounded like a man trying to smoke, gargle and yodel at the same time.

"Uerrrrrgshhhhhhaaallwedooooowijjadrunkardkshaylor……"

Seymour prodded the door open with his foot. The smell of stale beer and tobacco came out.

"Ooohrayandupsherishes……"

Someone was slumped forward on the bowl with his arms dangling and his head swaying from side to side.

"Rehab," groaned Seymour.

There was another grunt, followed by a long, loud burp. One of the Captain's eyes appeared to be swivelling in the opposite direction to

54

its partner.

"Needed a seat. Needed to shit down is all," he slurred.

"Jesus."

"Hey but Taff, Taff, Taff. We showed them at the dominoes, didn't we lad. You and me. By God we did."

"Please tell me you've got nothing to do with this boat?"

With Seymour's help, the drunken sailor eased himself up into a standing position.

"I help out in the bar sometimes, that's all……."

Spanners must be insane, thought Seymour.

"…..and anyway, mark this. No bugger else knows the sea like me. No-one."

Somewhere above them, a man's voice was raised, followed by the deep vibration of the engine. Trip No.4. They were off. As the boat came away from its mooring, Rehab lurched into Seymour's arms.

"Just so long as I'm on board this vessel, nobody – no bloody body – has got anything to fear."

"All smiles on The Burlingtonian," thought Seymour.

Chapter Six

To the world at large, it was never very clear how the fire started. Or who was to blame.

For insurance purposes, Harry Spanners swore blind it was an electrical fault. And Frank from Snaps (who went on to make a few quid selling pictures of the rescue to a Fleet Street newspaper) secretly blamed one of his own discarded flash bulbs.

Nobody had noticed the blackened shape of Rehab slink away amongst the crowd, and the blaze had destroyed every trace of his presence in the bar (bobble hat, jacket, Swan Vestas and rolling tobacco) along with the 'No Naked Flames' sign, of which just a melted blob remained in the corridor where everybody agreed the fire must have originated.

To Seymour, with hindsight, the whole episode had a feeling of dread inevitability about it. Trying desperately hard to expunge the memory of Rehab's rolling eyes he'd climbed back into the sunshine and picked up his accordion. Every square inch of the deck was squeezed with people; some tilting their heads back under the warm sun; others looking out across the stillness of the bay.

Here and there, he could see a few sails, drooping uselessly, and further away, the silhouette of an oil tanker puffing south along the horizon. From the sharp end of the boat, he could see Frank hurtling towards him.

"Christ almighty," he blustered. "Do you know Rehab's down there running the bloody bar?"

"You hum it Frank, and I'll play along."

For a second, the photographer eyed him suspiciously.

"That's a joke, right?"

"One day you really must tell me how you got your nickname," said Seymour.

"Is that another joke?" said Frank.

Just as he had on the day's first excursions, Seymour started his session at the stern of the boat with a couple of wartime singalongs.

"Brilliant, Seymour," bellowed Spanners through the window of the wheelhouse. "They're loving it. You'll be headlining at the Palladium next."

As he weaved through the crowd, followed closely by Frank and his cameras, strangers clapped his back, and urged him on. Even to his own ears, the sound of the accordion – blended with the seagulls and the diesel chug of the engine – produced a pleasingly nautical sound. It had been lonely, learning to play in the outhouse, but here, in the salty seaside air, he was glad that he had.

He only hoped that his wife felt the same.

"The bar's run out of beer. What's the bloody use of a bar without beer?"

It was his father-in-law, Bill, squeezed onto a wooden bench alongside his wife, daughter and pram. A large piece of candy floss was dangling from his chin.

"You look like you've got a pink goatee," remarked Seymour.

"Bill. You're a bloody idiot," said Olive, ripping the sugary fluff from her husband's chin. "Buck yourself up man or bugger off."

Seymour hitched his accordion back into position and ran his fingers over the keys. Since coming aboard, Lucy had ignored him, and her jaw was clamped troublingly tight. When he followed the line of her gaze out to sea, there was absolutely nothing there.

"Lovely day for a picture."

Frank was standing in front of Seymour's mother-in-law, transfixed by the contents of the pram.

"A group picture with the mutt perhaps? Ready first thing tomorrow."

From what he could make out, a stocky black dog was either sleeping or dead in a nest of baby's blankets, surrounded by a flotilla of half-chewed rubber ducks.

"I don't know who you are," hissed Olive. "But this is no mutt. This is Arthur and, He's a bulldog of the very finest pedigree."

"So fine it can't actually walk," muttered Bill.

"What was that?"

"Nothing dear," he added. "Nothing important."

With a theatrical flourish, Seymour struck up with 'Ilkley Moor baht'at'. After just a few bars, almost everyone on the boat was singing; a full-throated swell of Northern vowels which rolled out over the rowing boats and fishing cobles that peppered the waters around them. Even Bill had been unable to resist, adding unexpectedly deft harmonies to the strange throttled whimper which now rose from the depths of the pram.

"Your Arthur. Fine singing voice," shouted Frank, who'd been unable to detach himself from the dog that thought it was a baby.

Olive closed her eyes and breathed deeply. An hour, they'd said, no more. It would soon be all over and they could drive home. It had never been like this in North Wales. Now look at it. Her own husband was singing a solo in a crass Yorkshire accent; her infantile son-in-law was playing a circus instrument for tips; and a small man in a dirty jacket was prodding her beloved Arthur.

"So why can't it walk?" asked Frank.

"It can walk," seethed Olive. "But it chooses not to."

"That's weird," said Frank. "My mum's just the same. And my dad."

It was at that precise moment – just as Seymour's mother-in-law grabbed Frank by his camera straps and tightened them around his throat – that Lucy uttered the three words which changed the entire day.

"What's that smell?" she said.

At first, it was just the people around her who took notice; each one sniffing suspiciously at the cocktail of seaside aromas which swirled around the ship. But within a few minutes, the singing – and Seymour's musical accompaniment – had been replaced by a spreading mumble of anxiety.

"I can't smell anything," said Bill.

"You've got candy floss up your nose," said Olive.

There were always smells at sea and not all of them nice ones. On a calm day, even the faintest whiff could drift for miles, often in strange combinations; a fisherman crisping his breakfast bacon and the rank tang of rotting fish; the ripe warmth of sewage and the oily sting of diesel. Sometimes, when they stood out alone – like fried onions – the effect was almost hypnotic, causing distant mariners to lust for hot dogs whilst gazing longingly towards a shoreline they could scarcely see.

But this one was different. Even Seymour knew that. From the back of the boat he'd watched Harry Spanners open the wheelhouse door to sniff the air. Something unfamiliar was swirling around – something sharp and acrid which didn't belong. And now Frank's hand was pressing into his lower back.

"Keep playing and keep smiling," he whispered. "And follow me."

Both could feel the eyes on their backs as they moved from the stern towards the centre of the boat. Nothing in the rhythm of the vessel had changed. Every rivet was still swivelling in its socket; and the engine was still delivering a steady ten knots through the sparkling millpond sea. It was just a freaky burning smell, thought Seymour; probably just someone torching tyres on the beach.

"Jesus. Don't you know anything a bit less gloomy?"

Having played five of his tunes, Seymour's finale was urging people to pack up their troubles in their old kitbags and stop worrying.

"I didn't ask for this bloody job, Frank," said Seymour, "I never expected to be playing in public."

"Fair enough. What else do you know?"

"Bread of Heaven?"

"That's Welsh isn't it?"

"Not really."

"Be honest. It's a bit Welsh. What was that first tune you played?"

"Away In A Manger?"

"That's the one. Perfect. Play it again, Sam."

For a moment, the mood brightened. Wafting his candy floss stick like a conductor's baton, Seymour's father-in-law had reactivated the floating choir and the sound of Christmas was spreading around the deck. Sitting next to Bill, he could see Lucy stroking pursed lips and staring furiously back towards the harbour. She looked skeletally thin.

"You alright love?" asked Seymour, as he and Frank pushed past. Suddenly, those plans to build a boat didn't seem terribly realistic.

"None of us are alright," she said, turning to him with a look of undiluted contempt. "There's something burning on this bloody tub."

There was no time for a reply. Somewhere beneath them there was a sudden, horrible bang, followed by the shattering sound of glass. From the stairs down to the bar – preceded by the same bitter smell – came a dark, ghost-like patch of smoke.

"Stay calm. Don't panic."

Harry Spanners had lurched from his wheelhouse, clutching a fire extinguisher and a torch. As the door rattled behind him, there was a dreadful pulse of heat, and another fusillade of breaking bottles.

"Put your bloody accordion down. Take these. Do what you can. Rehab's down there in the sodding bar."

Seymour, Harry and Frank were now alone at the top of the stairs. Everyone else had retreated to the ends of the boat where Olive, Lucy and Arthur appeared to be the only ones not screaming.

"Me?" shouted Seymour. "Go down there. You're kidding. I'm not even on the payroll."

A dark haze of fumes had settled over the entire vessel and the engine – which had been faltering – fell suddenly still.

"I need to make a Mayday call," explained Harry.

"But it's only August," said Frank.

"For the fucking lifeboat you thick sod." Harry's face had turned scarlet. "As soon as that's done, I'll join you."

"Come on then Taff," grinned Frank holding up his cameras. "There might be some money in this."

61

"Careful on these steps," said Seymour, who could hear the terror in his own voice. "They're roasting hot."

For the first time all day, the boat was silent. The only movement came from the gentle rock of the sea, and – apart from a few ancient, creaking ropes – there were no sounds to disturb the slip-slap of water on the hull. After their initial panic, the trippers had frozen; transfixed by the sight of the two men stepping down into the blackness of the hold.

"Thank you everybody for keeping calm." Spanners was standing on the bridge, speaking through a tin megaphone. "The lifeboat is on its way. Everything is under control."

High above the harbour, there was a sudden white puff of light, followed – after a half second – by a loud bang. A few moments later, another rocket went off, and cheering broke out among the passengers. In the choking darkness below, Seymour and Frank had heard the explosions too.

"Rehab. Rehab. Are you alright? We've come to get you."

There were no flames, but the air was so thick they were virtually blind. Within a few seconds, they were also soaking wet. Rust-stained water was cascading from a primitive sprinkler system, turning to steam as they felt their way along the walls.

"Rehab. Where the fuck are you, you dozy pillock?"

Up to their left, sparks were sizzling from a scorched wooden fusebox. Taking aim with the extinguisher, Seymour unleashed a volley of foam in its general direction.

"I'm pretty sure that's not what you're supposed to do," complained Frank, ducking his head from the shower of furious sparks. "Liquid and electricity. Didn't you not learn nothing at school?"

Seymour kept quiet. It felt odd to be corrected by a man who still thought the world was flat, but now wasn't the time. Not when there was a dead body to find.

"You check the toilet. I'll check the bar. There's nothing else down here. He's got to be in one of them."

"Unless he's simply melted," said Frank, examining the ruins of his outfit.

Holding the torch by his face, Seymour stepped into the nauseous gloom of the bar. Broken glass littered the floor, and a tangle of flames was still visible in a plastic ashtray which he blasted from point blank range. In its few furious minutes, the fire had destroyed almost everything. Even the old wooden top of the counter was gone.

"He's not in here," he shouted, dispensing a few more precautionary squirts of the extinguisher. "The fire's out though. Any luck in the bogs?"

"Nope," said Frank, tiptoeing into the ruins of the bar. "Not a dicky bird."

The two men surveyed the damage. Both knew people in the town who'd been saying The Burlingtonian was a death-trap for years. Now it would be months before the old boat took to the sea again. That's if it ever did. Over thirty years late, it seemed, the Huns had finally got what they wanted.

"I just don't understand it," mused Seymour. "He was down here half an hour ago and no-one saw him come out."

"It's a mystery," said Frank. "So now let's take a few pictures and scram."

In the days that followed, Seymour would always wish he'd said no. After all, they'd done nothing – and saved no-one – and their lives had never been at risk. Nevertheless, he'd stood frowning in the ruined shell of the bar clutching a fire extinguisher for the photograph.

"They'll be ready at 9am sharp tomorrow," chuckled Frank, blinking away tears from the flash.

A few moments later, they were out in the sunshine. Shielding his eyes, Seymour could see the lifeboat, surging towards them on a great crest of foam. Three of its seven-strong crew were already standing ready at the bow, and where the light caught its glossy blue hull, the boat seemed to blink in its own reflection.

"You're a pair of bloody heroes. Give us a kiss." Harry Spanners had been waiting for them to emerge. His voice dropped to a whisper. "Where the hell is Rehab? This gets serious if he's snuffed it."

Before either of the men could answer, they were mobbed by a crowd of cheering holidaymakers, jostling forwards with a handshake or a wildly planted lipstick kiss.

"Let's hear it for Seymour and Frank," yelled Spanners through his megaphone.

More whooping followed, and amidst the carnival atmosphere, almost nobody noticed the lifeboat roping up along the port side; or the charred outline of a man slipping quietly into the sanctuary of The Burlingtonian's wheelhouse.

"This is silly," muttered Seymour. Someone else had just stuck their lips to his cheeks. "We didn't do anything."

"Absolute rubbish. You were brilliant," whispered the woman.

Seymour leaned back to examine the passenger's face. "Nellie. Bloody Hell. Brilliant."

He hadn't seen her since the dominoes match. And he'd never seen her looking so dressed up, not even on match nights.

"I told you I'd come," she said, opening her face into a glorious smile. "Is it always this exciting when you unpack your organ."

"It's an accordion," said Seymour, feeling momentarily dizzy. "A

Gabbanelli, actually."

"You told me," winked Nellie. "You can maybe get it out for me at the pub some time."

There was another surge of passengers and Seymour found himself carried forwards to the back of the boat.

"I'll catch up with you later, Nellie. Sorry."

Somewhere behind, Frank was taking photographs of the lifeboat crew as they lashed a walkway across to the stricken vessel. Dozens of faces were following their every move, and a motley armada of rowing boats and speedboats had made its way out from the harbour to soak up the drama.

Only two people seemed indifferent to the proceedings. One of them was gently rocking a pram. The other was sitting, staring silently at Seymour, as the crowd turned away from him to assess their prospects of rescue.

"Small fire. Old boat. Calm sunny day," said Seymour, injecting a breezy tone into his voice. "We're fine. You're fine. There was never any danger."

With a faint nod of appreciation – lacking the energy to examine what she felt or why – Lucy closed herself down. Seymour was a good man, she knew that, so why didn't she feel proud? Why did she always feel ashamed and alienated by the things he did (or planned to do) and by the feckless people he liked doing them with?

Standing in front of her, Seymour could think of nothing useful to add. Long ago, he'd reached two firm conclusions. Firstly, that some people were like kites. Once they were up, they could soon come crashing down. And secondly, that loving his wife didn't require him to understand her. Just so long as she was there, nothing else mattered.

In all probability, everything that had gone wrong was his fault anyway.

"I've just been talking to the lifeboat crew."

Seymour's father-in-law had returned with news.

"They're taking passengers off in batches of twenty. Four trips should do it. Women and children first."

"And dogs?" asked Olive, who – despite the day's heat – was still ensconced in a green coat and hat. "What about my Arthur?"

Bill's face, which was already badly sun-burned, turned a deeper shade of crimson.

"Buffoon," she hissed. "You didn't ask."

Olive tugged herself up, removed the candy floss stick that was tucked behind Bill's right ear, and set off for the lifeboat. Just a couple of spaces remained, and the last few buoyancy aids were being issued to any woman who stepped forwards.

"How long before it comes back?" she boomed. "I'm not familiar with waiting."

A tall man with thick, dark hair stepped forwards. He was wearing a densely-knitted Aran sweater underneath an oilskin boiler suit and his wellington boots didn't appear to stop until his groin.

"It'll be around a half-hour, ma'am…."

The voice was velvety rich (quite possibly tutored, she thought) delivered calmly without a trace of the local vowels. Against every instinct, her irritation wilted.

"….meanwhile, we're doing everything we can to get you off quickly and safely."

 "And who might you be?"

"I'm the coxswain, ma'am. I'm here to look after you….."

There was a faint stirring in the pram, followed by a high-pitched cry and the squeak of a rubber toy.

"......and your grandchild," he added.

"It's not a bloody human," barked Olive. "It's a dog. And we exit this junk together. Or we don't leave at all."

"That's absolutely fine. If you leave the pram, there's room for you both on the first boat."

"Thank you. That's most gracious of you, Mr....."

"Clough, ma'am. Stan Clough," said the coxswain, extending an arm. "Please step this way. I'll carry your pet."

Olive walked serenely down into the lifeboat. Whatever resistance she'd been mustering had been swallowed in a bitter flash of memory. Something in the lifeboat-man's pitch perfect enunciation had reminded her of the boy who never came back. And when he eventually placed Arthur in her lap, she was weeping.

"Room for just one more," shouted the coxswain, stepping back onto the pleasure cruiser.

"Hello Stan," said Seymour.

"Hello Seymour," said Stan. "And hello, Mrs Pilbeam."

Lucy had stepped up alongside her husband.

"You know each other?" he asked.

Of course they did. Everyone knew Stan Clough. With two hair salons carrying his name (and three amusement arcades) he was simultaneously the town's brightest star and its biggest anomaly. Nobody really understood why he'd ever come back, but everybody agreed they'd miss him if he left again.

Stan was box office. Stan was interesting. And very few people who escaped this town ever gave it a second thought; unless of course – like Stan Clough – they had a rich father who also happened to be a local hero.

But it was more than that. Somewhere on his travels, Stan had changed. The boy who'd left home at eighteen had been overweight and monosyllabic. The well-dressed man who returned to inherit the family house and fortune boasted both a university degree and an accent that was as polished as the Italian shoes he ordered from Lucy's shop. He was also a very fine seaman.

"Yes. We've met," said Lucy. "I've met most of the feet around here."

"He sold me the boat," said Seymour.

"Is it alright if I sit with my mother?" Lucy either hadn't heard. Or she'd ignored him.

"Without question, Mrs P" smiled Stan. "Allow me."

"We play you soon," said Seymour, as his wife took the coxswain's hand. "Title decider."

There was no comeback from the lifeboat skipper. Before Lucy had even settled, the boat wheeled away in a flamboyant arc to the flutter of distant cheers.

"I've run out of film." Frank had resurfaced looking bored. "I'll never have to work again after this."

"Come with me."

The encounter with Stan had unsettled him. The man was good at everything. And unlike most of his own pub's wretched dominoes team, that probably included the five times table. Looking back towards the wheelhouse, he could see a soot-stained face grinning inanely through gleaming teeth.

"You should get your accordion going again before the lifeboat comes back," said Frank. "Pick up the mood."

The smiling visage in the wheelhouse was now putting what appeared to be a tumbler-full of whisky to his lips.

"What do you suggest I play, Frank?" said Seymour, irritably. "The chances are I won't know it anyway."

"What Shall We Do With A Drunken Sailor?"

In one swig, the figure emptied the glass and was now filling it again from a half-empty bottle.

"Very good question." said Seymour.

Chapter Seven

In a town where so little happened – or had ever happened – Seymour's deeds quickly assumed heroic proportions.

By the middle of the following week, people were saying he'd walked through chest high flames to pull children from an inferno; that his ravaged face would require years of plastic surgery, and that a medal of some sort was on a train north with a handwritten note from the Queen.

It was nothing Seymour hadn't quietly feared. Although he'd only ever worked for a tiny weekly newspaper, he knew what a good story felt like (especially one with pictures) and long before breakfast the next day, Frank was at Seymour's front door, clutching a fistful of glossy prints.

"Just look at them. They're amazing," gushed Frank. "We need to get down to your office. The nationals might even want them."

"Shhh. Keep your voice down," hissed Seymour. "Not everyone wants to hear all this."

His wife certainly wouldn't. When he'd finally got home the previous evening, she was already swaddled in bed. The only sounds had been coming from Isaac's radio, and for the first time he realised just how badly he smelled of burned plastic.

"Are you in there, son?" Seymour turned the handle, and eased open Isaac's door. "Just making sure you're alright."

"I'm fine. You stink."

"It's been a weird sort of day. Have you had any tea?"

"I heard. Yes. Close the door on your way out, dad."

For the rest of the night, he'd sat alone in the living room, listening quietly to a Charlie Mingus record between troubled snatches of sleep. When he woke up all he could feel was Lucy's disappointment dripping through the ceiling. On recent form, it would be days before she spoke to him again. Unless he could suffocate this story at birth, it might be weeks.

"I hear you're up for the Victoria Cross."

"They're for soldiers, you idiot."

Frank had fanned his photographs across the kitchen table. Outside, a soft dawn light was showing through the leaves of the garden's solitary sycamore tree.

"I don't suppose you'd just give them to me," said Seymour. "Forget the whole thing. I really don't want any publicity."

"Get lost, Seymour. This is my story too," countered Frank. "And anyway, you work on a newspaper. What's bloody wrong with you?"

Seymour groaned. For once, Frank was right. The news wasn't something a person could own; not even if you were part of it. Nor was it in any way controllable; or containable. He'd edited enough front pages to know that. With luck, a few lukewarm facts would reduce the story to what it truly was; just like he'd told Lucy.

Small fire on decrepit boat. Nobody dead. The end.

By the time they reached his office, however, Seymour's hopes of anonymity were gone. Around a dozen passing cars had flashed their lights; two policemen, a traffic warden and a dog-walker had insisted on a handshake; and an attractive lady at a bus stop had implied she wanted rather more.

"How do all these people know?"

"I've no idea," said Frank. "But she was bloody gorgeous."

"You're not married are you," asked Seymour.

"Never really even had a girlfriend. Not sure why."

There was a hiss of brakes. A lorry driver was waving through his open window.

"Just be careful what you wish for," said Seymour.

Normally, it was a sleepy little office. Normally, the biggest story might be a jellyfish invasion. But today, the place was already buzzing when they arrived. The previous week's pictures had been hastily cleared from the ground floor window; two telephones were ringing out on the reception desk; and an elderly man with a stoop was waiting for them as they entered.

"Knew you'd be here. Magnificent show." He was wearing a threadbare three-piece suit and a pair of half-moon spectacles. "Up school. Up bloody school."

It wasn't difficult to work out what Reginald 'Soapy' Latheron had done before taking over as editor of the town's ailing weekly rag. Everything he said (or the way he said it) seemed rooted in one of his previous unsuccessful incarnations.

Most recently, he'd been the headmaster of the local grammar school. Before that, he'd been a fighter pilot. And rather like most of his Spitfires, 'Soapy' appeared to be taking the paper down with him.

"Looks like the old gal could have gone to the bottom of the drink without you blighters." Seymour and Frank backed discreetly off. Soapy's halitosis had been known to clear a dance floor. "Bally first class. Prefect material. Heroes. Both of you. Without a shadow."

In the three years since Mr. Latheron had run the paper, sales had entered a death spin. It wasn't simply that there was never any news, there were hardly any staff either. The average age of its three reporters was 61, and (in a town where most people spoke slowly anyway) none of them could do shorthand. In the back office there were just two sub-editors (of whom Seymour was one) plus a handful of troublesome compositors who turned out on Wednesdays and Thursdays to set the paper in the galleys and run the presses.

There were few things Seymour loved better than the smell of warm ink and the weekly rumble of newsprint on print day. But Soapy's wayward tenure had seen circulation drop by half and most townsfolk only read it when it was wrapped around their chips.

"Mr. Latheron. Listen. I really need a word."

The three men had retreated upstairs to the editor's first floor office where a bottle of 15-year-old Talisker malt was holding down the Daily Telegraph racing section.

"You don't need to bally well say anything," said Soapy, easing his paunch under the edge of an immense leather-topped desk. "We're going to give this a proper spread. Front cover. Centre pages. The whole shooting match. Nothing less. Biggest story since the gerries tried to sink the bugger. Great show. Proper heroes."

"It's just that……," said Seymour.

Soapy had switched off and was writing furiously on a pad. Upside down, Seymour could make out 'Redcar.3.15'. The rest was gibberish.

"….. I was wondering if we could just keep it low profile, a couple of paragraphs on an inside page, maybe? To be honest that's all it's worth, and I really don't need the fuss."

"Commendable modesty. I like that in a chap." Soapy was still breathing heavily from the walk upstairs. "Wouldn't hear of it though. A hero's a hero in my book. One of the glorious few, eh? And anyway......"

Frank had spread his photographs across the editor's blotter. The shot of Seymour in the blackened bar had been artfully placed on top.

"......and anyway, I'm going to be writing the piece myself. A bloody proper job. What we in the RAF used to call....."

Easing his well-nourished belly back round the edge of his desk, Soapy rose to his full height, swept back his hair and hooked his spectacles in a waistcoat pocket.

".....the dogs bollocks. That's what it'll be. Now if you'll excuse me...."

It was a development which afforded Seymour a brief flash of hope. Even if the details were sketchy, most of the paper's staff knew Soapy's routine. At 11.30am (after a cursory news conference) he wrestled on his coat, bid adieu to his secretary, and vanished out of the front door. When he returned around 4.30pm – often minus sundry items of clothing – he was drunk.

It seemed inconceivable to Seymour that anything coherent could emerge from a brain so comprehensively pickled. And yet two days later, when he set out his paste, pencils and scissors, there it was on his desk. Fifteen hundred words; beautifully penned in ink (not typed) without a single crossing out, or any sign of hesitation.

There was no accompanying note; no message; and no explanation of how Soapy had come by his information. It was if the article – complete with magnificent flowing curlicues – had descended fully-formed from another age.

'Readers and fellow-residents,

For anyone who does not yet know, we are living in the presence of heroes. Just a few days ago, two of our finest citizens descended into the bowels of a blazing boat, packed with summer guests and rendered it safe from fire. Their deeds will never be forgotten. Their names will never be forgotten....'

Seymour's face was burning helplessly. It was a well-written story – far better than the real one – but everything about it was wrong; a fantasy; a communal fabrication willed into life by a town where nothing interesting had happened for years. But maybe that was the point. All Soapy had done wrong was construct the narrative people wanted. And what could possibly be the harm in that?

'......to many of us here, Mr. Seymour Pilbeam, 42, is a gentle local character who moved to the town around fifteen years ago. Married with one son, it was he who gave us our annual beach kite-flying competition, a far cry from the events of last weekend aboard The Burlingtonian, where – like Mr. Wallace Hartley on the Titanic – he continued to play his accordion even as disaster encroached......'

He'd read enough. Someone else could write the headlines. If it couldn't be stopped, he wanted no part in it. Pushing the copy onto his colleague's desk, Seymour fled the building. In a few hours, it would be out on the streets. And a few days after that, it would all be forgotten. For once, he was glad Lucy had withdrawn from circulation. With a bit of luck, she wouldn't even see it.

Outside, the pavements were packed with people flowing down to the shore. For days the sun had sat in a cloudless sky. Every guest room in the town was booked, and by noon the beach was crammed with windbreaks and deckchairs. Joining the stream of trippers, Seymour aimed for a long line of brick-built fishermen's lockups at the back of the harbour. Precarious mountains of lobster pots were piled alongside, and the air hung ripe with drying seaweed.

At the fourth door, Seymour held back to read an engraved brass plaque – 'Harry's Chandlery. Est. 1922'. Inside, once his eyes had adjusted to the gloom, his heart began to race.

75

From the pier, nobody would have guessed it. Every corner of the tiny store was crammed with the necessities of the sea. Snapshackles and swivels; carbine hooks and padeyes; gleaming new windlasses and row upon row of plastic fenders, perched like eggs, in a heap behind the counter. Nearby there were spade anchors and claw anchors, winches, rudders and centreboards, all fighting for space amidst the shelves of paint and the knotted heaps of multi-coloured rope.

Tenderly, Seymour picked a polished bow shackle from the wall and rubbed the metal between his fingers, enjoying the cold precision of the locking screw. There was rarely a day when he didn't find himself in this place; drugged by the smell of polyurethane; and secretly buying things which he had absolutely no use for.

Secretly, he justified it as therapy. There was no boat anymore, but the objects brought pleasure; they calmed him; and an hour inside a chandlery was the closest he could get to sailing in a space of abbey-like peace.

"Mind giving me your autograph?"

The voice was coming from a figure reclining in a battered lounge chair. There was a girlie magazine spread open across his knee.

"I haven't interrupted anything have I?" asked Seymour, switching his gaze from Harry's groin to a cluster of enormous wooden pulleys hanging from the beams above his head.

"I was bored," said Harry, folding up the magazine and shoving it under a pile of canvas sails.

"I don't want to know."

"They've been there since I was a kid; the pulleys, I mean. I don't suppose there's a boat left on the sea that still uses them."

"Beautiful things," said Seymour. "Would you mind fastening your belt?"

"Listen. I've lost The Burlingtonian. Forever, probably. Cut me some slack."

"You've got this place. It's not all bad. I'd swap you any time."

There were only a handful of maritime dynasties left in the town, but Seymour envied them all. Between the wars, Harry's father had opened the store to satisfy an almost insatiable appetite for the sea.

For wealthy anglers, there had been tunny to fight in the bay, and for the fishing boats, a bottomless supply of herring, haddock, cod and mackerel. These were people for whom the ocean wasn't a recreational amenity; it was a genetic requirement stitched so tightly into their lives that it could never be separated out. Not even Seymour's bogus Welsh ancestry could hope to compete with that.

"You're practically my only customer," said Harry, sadly. "The place is dying on its arse."

Seymour picked up a length of hemp rope and began tying its two ends together in a reef knot.

"Tell me about the fire," he said. "What happened to Rehab? Where the hell was he?"

"He was asleep in the toilet down below."

"But Rehab hardly ever goes to the toilet. And anyway, Frank had checked it."

"Frank had checked it. Say no more."

"We thought he was dead," said Seymour.

"He was pissed. Free drinks. Never a good time to refill your cigarette lighter."

"Shit. The clown."

"You won't say anything, will you?" pleaded Harry. "I've told Rehab to lie low while the insurance sniff around. In a week or two, it will all blow over."

"I hope so," said Seymour. "It's embarrassing enough already."

"Look on the bright side," laughed Harry, stretching out his weak left leg. "You've entered harbour mythology. They'll be telling this story for years after you're dead."

"Just so long as my wife doesn't hear."

"And if you want one of those pulleys, it's yours." Harry had levered himself up. His flies were still unfastened. "See you at the dominoes."

When he left, the light was blinding and with the tide fully out, the harbour floor looked ugly and misshapen. Where a small beck entered it beneath a wharf, two ancient bicycles and a parking cone were sinking slowly into the mud.

From nowhere, a cloud had settled over his mood, and – even in the sunshine – the town appeared scruffy and grey; peopled by dingy-looking strangers. In his pocket, he could feel the small metal shackle he'd bought at the chandlery, pressing guiltily against his thigh. Soon he'd be hiding it in the shed alongside his disgraced accordion and the parts for a boat that didn't exist, and probably never would.

Without thinking, he'd drifted south of the harbour, and was looking down on a large rectangular lake full of motorised boats. Two people sat in each one – a father and son mostly – and from the promenade he could hear their laughter as the coloured craft rocked and swerved like dodgem cars on water. A few steps further on, he was standing outside the lifeboat station, a drab brick shed with sliding blue doors, sandwiched between two rundown hotels.

Inside, he could see a figure tinkering with an aerial on the orange wheelhouse of the lifeboat. From a tiny side office, there was a crackle of radio static followed by a single sustained tone.

"That's it. Perfect," someone shouted. "One more for luck."

Seymour slipped through the doors, feeling the leaden weight of a moment he'd almost forgotten. In the cold shadow of the boat, he sat down on a bench lined with identical yellow wellingtons and let the wall take his weight.

He'd sat here before. Just a few months after they'd moved to the coast. Late spring was it? Around 1952? He couldn't be sure. Dates and birthdays had never been his thing. But he remembered his wife, and how glorious she'd looked then; and how his love for her – and their unborn child – had felt like a neutron bomb.

Everything was perfect. By day – while Seymour worked – she walked along the beach, with her hands clasped tightly around her belly. At night, in their first tiny bedsit, a salty breeze flowed through the bedroom and while his wife slept, Seymour strained his ears for the sound of the surf.

In the lifeboat station, there was a second sharp burst of distortion from a speaker somewhere. Two hushed voices were discussing something intensely – a problem of some sort – on the far side of the boat. Even now, all these years, Seymour felt the mean pinch of regret.

The first time he'd heard the rockets go off, he hadn't known what it was. But after that, he'd always be watching – in lashing rain if necessary – as the ancient tractor dragged the lifeboat out across the sands into the rolling spume. To be a lifeboatman; that would really be something. He'd had to ask. There wasn't a choice. And from what he remembered, his interviewer had at least been kind.

"What sort of experience do you have on boats?"

"None. But I've read a lot of books and I'm good with motors."

"So have you ever actually been to sea?"

"Not yet."

Seymour stood up and examined his surroundings. It had been a very short interview, a ludicrous mistake, and he'd never gone back. Near the entrance, mounted on the wall, there were two polished wooden panels; one showing the names of the lifeboat's coxswains stretching back well over a century.

Many of the surnames showed up time and time again, and at the bottom was the current incumbent; Stan Clough. Two entries above his was the name of the man who'd questioned him fifteen years before.

David Clough. He'd never realised. It had been Stan's father who turned him away.

Maybe it had all been for the best. Lucy had known nothing about it, and Seymour saw no reason to share his humiliation. Once the disappointment had passed, he'd contented himself with being a spectator, watching every launch whenever he could; following the boat with an old telescope until it was too small to see.

Whenever the rockets sounded, he'd be there. And when Isaac was old enough, his son came too; sometimes pulled from his bed in his pyjamas. Off they'd go; heads bent into the rain, rushing through the night to watch as the arc lights flickered across the sand and the lifeboat surged into action. But Lucy had seen enough. One morning, when they returned – limp with cold – she'd been waiting.

"This stops now," she'd screamed. "He's a ten-year-old boy. You're pathetic."

"He loves it. Just ask him. Ask him. Isaac. Tell her."

But the boy had said nothing. Without a glance at either parent, he'd torn off his dripping gabardine, and slouched upstairs to the sanctuary of his eiderdown.

"Never again, Seymour. He stays at home," said Lucy.

After that, he'd been to just one more launch. A fishing boat had lost power two miles offshore on New Year's Eve. Despite hurricane winds, the lifeboat had set out around midnight with its full complement of seven crew. When they returned five hours later – mission accomplished – there were only six of them.

By the station door, Seymour turned his attention to the second of the wood panels. Under the gold-painted words 'Volunteers Lost At Sea', there was just one single name.

'1963 – David Clough, coxswain'

Seymour stepped back into the sunshine. Despite the mid-afternoon warmth, he was shivering. He should go back to work, but there wasn't any point. The paper would already be on its way to the shops. Halfway home, he watched a newsagent tucking a fresh sheet into his billboard.

"You're Seymour Pilbeam, right. You'll love this. Take a look."

Suddenly everyone in town was Seymour's friend. There was no stopping this now.

'LOCAL HERO SAVES 60 FROM BLAZING SHIP'

"Great work, mate."

Seymour looked at the pavement and felt the shackle, icy in his pocket.

Sooner or later, he would have to do something. He just wasn't sure what.

Chapter Eight

It wasn't something she'd ever admit, but Lucy had enjoyed her ride on the lifeboat. As it circled away from the stricken pleasure boat, she'd felt something reckless in its power, and the throaty surge of the engine had sent a quiver up her spine. There was also something undeniably commanding about the coxswain; qualities which had largely (but not entirely) eluded her when she'd been measuring him up for new shoes.

"Warm enough, Mrs.P?"

The skipper had addressed her with a broad, tanned smile. He was wearing aviator sunglasses, and a weekend growth of stubble.

"I'm fine, thank you, Mr.Clough."

It had taken less than five minutes, but they were back. There was a swift, alarming cessation of noise; and a warm hand (placed awkwardly low) was steering her up onto the quay where a growing audience appeared to be watching her every move.

"Give me a moment," she said, reaching out for a handrail.

Everything seemed to be moving. Out at sea, she could make out The Burlingtonian, still paralyzed in a smoky haze. But when she tried to walk, she felt dislocated and dizzy, as if the ground was sliding under her feet.

"Mrs. P. Are you absolutely sure you're alright?"

The coxswain was still there. His right hand was still there, too; exactly where it had been all those years before. Without it, she felt certain she would fall.

"Just give me a moment. A couple of breaths."

"Take a minute. No hurry," said Stan. "Seymour's perfectly safe. I'll bring him over next time."

Behind the coxswain, she could see her mother, swaddled in her green coat and a few paces behind, stumbled Bill. His face was yellow, and there were trails of vomit down his lapel.

"I think it was the mussels," he dribbled.

"I think it was the beer," fumed Olive.

"Or possibly the whelks."

Lucy's head was spinning, and she felt horribly weak. Every puff of breeze had evaporated and in the clammy afternoon air, old memories were stirring.

"Go and finish what you've got to do," she told Stan. "I'm feeling much better."

"Are you sure? I could ring for a doctor."

"Absolutely sure. Honestly. It was probably just the diesel fumes."

Nothing in his eyes had given anything away. Perhaps it was only her who remembered. Sitting down on the harbour wall, she watched him hop nimbly back onto his lifeboat. Seconds later, it was thrusting back across the bay, roared on by the crowd massing on the quay. Nobody will ever forget they were here, realised Lucy. The only difference is that I'll wish that I could.

As it happened, a few days later, Lucy could recover no memories whatsoever of her walk back home. Although the fire itself remained depressingly vivid, her flight from it had been expunged as if the memory of one seaside humiliation – the sinking of Seymour's dinghy – was as much as her mind could contend with.

As she so often did, she'd retreated behind her bedroom curtains, emerging only for cups of tea and an occasional biscuit. Once, when she was certain the house had been vacated, she'd boiled herself an egg and pecked at the yolk. It wasn't something she'd shared, but her weight had been in freefall for months, and the funny spell by the lifeboat had not been the first.

Lying motionless in bed, with Emily Bronte and D.H for company, she could survive on crumbs. Anything more vigorous pushed her depleted reserves to breaking point, and her presence at work (or lack of it) was stretching the patience of her boss. Only the other day, there'd been a letter.

"We might only be a seaside shoe-shop, but we do now have the town's first X-ray pedoscope and I really can't do this alone. Please let me know what's going on."

Towards the end of the week, Isaac had sneaked into the bedroom. He wasn't her first visitor. While she slept, she knew Seymour sometimes crept in, leaving heavily sweetened tea and buttered toast which she nibbled on until she was bored. From the room below, she could sometimes discern the thin rumble of his electric train, but the accordion – for the first time in months – had fallen silent.

"Mum. How are you feeling?"

Isaac perched on the edge of the bed. He was wearing a faded denim shirt and jeans. Even in the half-light, she could see the summer was suiting him. His face was tanned, and he'd allowed wispy sideburns to creep down from his temple.

"I'm better, thanks. I'll be up later. Back to work on Monday."

"I just wondered if you'd seen this?"

84

From his back pocket, the boy pulled out a rolled copy of Seymour's newspaper, and began reading the front-page story. After a few lines, Lucy propped herself up, took the paper from Isaac's hands, and tucked it under her pillow with the letter from the shop.

"Everyone's talking about it. Dad's turned out to be a proper hero. Ha ha. I thought you'd be interested."

"I'm not. Not really. Have you asked him about it?"

"I haven't seen a lot of him, to be honest." Isaac shifted his weight uncomfortably. A vertical stripe of light had escaped from the curtains and fallen across his shoulder. "You know what the holidays are like? There's always so much other stuff."

"Like what exactly? Amusements and coffee bars? Girls?"

During one of their rare marital conversations, Seymour had wondered if there might be a girlfriend (the mysterious 'A') and then there was the shopping catalogue; and the crumpled tissues; and the lurching fear that she was losing the facility to communicate with (or even recognise) her own son. With a huge effort, she swung her legs from under the sheets and sat upright.

"You're much better than that," she said, softly. "Are you going to tell me who she is?"

"What? Are you serious? Like I'm going to take any kind of lessons from you – or him – on relationships. Or anything." Isaac was already halfway out of her bedroom. "What exactly are you two offering me anyway? Absolutely nothing. And what wrong with you? Why are you always in bed? Why does my dad play with trains? Why are you in the dark? Why don't you both just act fucking normal for once?"

"Isaac. Stop. Don't talk like that."

Lucy stretched forwards weakly, hoping for some contact. He was brandishing a paperback book snatched from her dressing table.

"Lady Chatterley? Bad language?" snarled Isaac, lobbing the book at his mother's feet. "If it's good enough for this twat, it's good enough for me."

She heard the door slam and fell backwards in a tangle of bedclothes. A swarm of motes rose through the sunlight, and a church bell somewhere rang twelve times; weakly as if it too, had been infected by the rare torpor of the heatwave. For the next few hours, she lay motionless – neither awake nor asleep – entranced by the stripe of light, as it inched invisibly across the wall like the hand of a clock.

Even if she trowelled deep into her memory, she wasn't sure if she could answer Isaac's question. There was no single point in her life, when she'd decided to retreat from it. What there had been was an almost infinite number of slights and setbacks, each one taking her further away from the magic that had glued her to the back of a boy on a sledge.

Back then, as she'd expected, the sex had been good. Perhaps it would have been good with anyone – and she was admittedly desperate – but there was no denying the sparks which flew between them. After four months of sporadic dating, they'd finally succumbed in his father's workshop where the contents of Seymour's trousers proved infinitely more interesting than his model boats.

Leaning back against a stack of half-finished coffins, she'd unbuckled his trousers, lifted her skirt and steered him in. A few seconds later, she was looking forward to getting home and finishing off the job properly. Seymour was passionate and his body had the tireless quality of a whippet, but his virginity ran far deeper than her own.

In the privacy of her own bedroom – while her mother practised her piano scales – Lucy's roving fingers had grown wise. It hadn't really mattered that Seymour lacked finesse, or that he'd clearly never given sex much thought. All that mattered in the beginning was a little inventive curiosity, and in that respect, Seymour showed himself to be a willing, if lethargic, apprentice.

"He's got a nice cock," she confided to a friend (failing to mention that it was the only one she'd seen), "He just doesn't know what to do with it."

Every month Seymour went to the barbers and returned – heart pounding – with his precious cargo of three Durex Fetherlite. And every month, she demanded to know why he hadn't got more.

"Because they'd think I was a pervert or something?" he complained. "It's scary enough buying those."

"You're 19, not 90. Three times a month isn't enough."

To supplement his meagre supply, he'd ransacked his father's cupboard drawers, finding several dozen rubbers (of unknown foreign brand and indeterminate age) which he showed to Lucy for her approval.

"You have got to be joking," spluttered Lucy, who'd never heard anything quite so disgusting. "Your father's condoms? I'd rather go into a convent."

"They're new ones; still in the packet. Look, they've not been used."

"Remind me. When did your mother die?"

"I'm not sure. Sometime before the war?"

"I rest my case. Buy a dozen next time."

From the kitchen below, Lucy heard noises; a knife on a plate; the metal lid of the bread bin slamming down. Isaac would be making a Marmite sandwich. In a moment, she'd hear his baseball boots scuffling past her window. For a second, she thought about pulling on a dressing gown, and going downstairs. Instead she pulled her knees up to her chest and rocked soothingly from side to side.

Seymour's father. Mr.Pilbeam Snr. The memory still made her retch.

After the war, she'd met him just twice. The first occasion had been in Seymour's miserable back sitting room. In one corner was a huge radio set. In the other, squeezed into a filthy armchair, was a small, balding man with a large head, wearing a tight, grey waistcoat.

"Did he tell you we're Welsh?" he'd asked.

Through a door in the corner, she could make out an old gas stove, a blackened aluminium frying pan and piles of unwashed crockery. The whole place stank of tobacco, and beneath that, the smell of something older; something worse.

"Have you come to play with his train set?"

"Don't dad. Please. This is Lucy. We've been seeing each other a while."

At the front door a few moments later, he'd pressed something into her hand. "Something to put in your mouth," he'd said. "You seem like a nice lass." When she opened it outside, she found a small piece of black toffee wrapped in old newspaper.

After that there was just one encounter before the wedding. Three times a month (or more if Seymour did what he was told) they'd slip into his father's workshop to make love. Entering through a door onto a narrow back alley gave them complete privacy, and – apart from this one occasion – they'd never been disturbed.

"Shhh. Listen. What's that?" Lucy was kneeling astride her boyfriend. She'd tugged her knickers to one side and her skirt was hunched up high around the waist. Only one of Seymour's legs was in his trousers. The other one was naked apart from a blue sock. "Someone's coming up the garden."

There was a rattling in the lock of the workshop door, and a flash from a torch fell through the window. By the time, it opened – allowing a hand to feel for and find the light switch – they were decent.

"I was just showing her my new box kite, dad."

Mr.Pilbeam's torch was still on and the full force of its beam was falling on Lucy's face.

"Hmmm," he grunted. "Just don't be using any of my rubber johnnies, that's all."

With that, he'd turned and left, slamming the door so hard it dislodged a drizzle of sawdust from the rafters.

"He's been watching us," hissed Lucy. "He probably always watches us."

"Don't be ridiculous. He didn't know we were here," said Seymour, whose voice sounded a lot less certain than his words.

Thinking about it later had made Lucy wet. It wasn't something she'd ever mention but the idea of being watched by other men – or women – excited her. And there were other things which interested her too, much darker possibilities, but none of them would have made sense to Seymour. And none of them would have involved his father.

"He's disgusting," she'd told him. "Revolting. He frightens me. And what's wrong with his legs?"

"What are you on about?"

"They're too short. They're ridiculous."

"You should tell him. He'd be pleased." Seymour was laughing.

"Why?"

"Because he thinks that means he's Welsh. And please. Don't be so hard on him," Seymour replied, adding sadly. "He's still my dad."

Since they had nowhere else to go, the couple's workshop trysts proceeded with caution and when the weather warmed, they'd take a bus out into the Pennines with a blanket, a picnic, and an armful of Seymour's kites. One time, they'd lain together, half-naked in the sun, watching a yellow one dancing hundreds of feet over their heads.

"Why do you like that so much?" asked Lucy.

Seymour sat up. His sunburned torso was speckled with grass and straw. There was a happy, unburdened smile in his eyes.

"Lick your finger. Hold it over your head. What do you feel?"

"It's gone cold."

"That's the wind. That's what I love. I love the fact that there's this invisible THING all around us, swirling and building and changing direction….and that I can make it visible with something as simple as that thing up there."

"Or a boat?"

"Yes. Or a boat."

Lucy had fallen silent. There was so much about Seymour she loved. He was strikingly handsome, for one thing. He was good-natured and funny. He was kind and he was enthusiastic between the sheets (not that they'd ever managed to find themselves in an actual bed) and yes, all things considered, she did love him. She was almost certain she did. But there were still some awkward questions; or one in particular. When did a boy become a man?

And what happened if he didn't?

"Lucy," said Seymour. The wind had collapsed, stranding his kite at the top of a huge oak tree. "Am I ever going to meet your parents again?"

That was a good question, too. It had been Lucy's fault (and she knew it) but the only time he'd met them had bordered on the surreal. It was a Friday evening and they'd been dating seriously for over nine months. Seymour's presence had been requested for tea at five, preceded by a glass of sherry at 4.30pm sharp.

"He's a man. You know what I think about men," Olive had informed her daughter. "It's high time we met. Just don't expect me to like him."

Her father had opened the door and Seymour had liked him from the start.

"You must be Seymour. I'm Bill. Olive's smaller half. Have a drink."

Bill was tidy and punctilious and rarely seen (in or out of the house) without a blazer and tie. Nothing about him was out of place, and he had an ex-soldier's instinct for natural hierarchies. In the presence of his wife, he was deferential and adoring. Away from her, he had an earthy sense of mischief, his future son-in-law immediately adored.

"You're bleeding," said Seymour.

"Am I?" asked Bill, pressing a crimson-spattered handkerchief against his chin. "Oh yes. Probably. Don't worry. Cut myself shaving. Usually do."

Two curling pieces of tissue paper were clinging to a fold beneath Bill's left ear, and the rest of his scar-crossed lower face looked like a tube map.

"Keep thinking I should grow a beard," he whispered. "Not sure she'd like it though."

For the two hours that followed, Seymour was in a daze. The house was clean and bright, and frighteningly well ordered. In the front parlour, light from a coal fire was flickering against a piano stacked high with classical sheet music. Hardback books lined the alcoves on each side of the chimney breast, and the walls were peppered with carefully spaced watercolours; mostly, it seemed, of mountains and lakes.

"They're all by my mother," explained Lucy. "She's very fond of the Lake District."

"They're very good," said Seymour.

"No. They're not. But it's sweet of you to say."

"And the books? There are so many. Are they all hers too?"

"All of them. I'm afraid dad only reads cereal boxes."

For tea, Olive (who had barely spoken) had set out her best crockery on a white lace tablecloth in the back-sitting room. After a starter course of bread and butter, she served up an enormous hot pork pie, slathered in rich white onion sauce.

"It's alright," whispered Bill. He did a lot of whispering. "I hate it too. Only once a week though, thank Christ."

"What was that?" said Olive.

"Nothing, dear. Lovely tea. As always."

"It's a family tradition," explained Lucy, "We have this every Friday evening. Always have."

Seymour looked at her with a growing sense of helplessness. It was quite easily the most disgusting meal he'd ever tasted. One more mouthful and he'd be sick. And yet Olive's plate was almost empty, and her husband's was not far behind.

"Under the table," whispered Bill, pointing at his feet. "Get rid of it."

Seymour bent down to look. A black dog was looking back at him. Hungrily.

"You know I'm not feeling awfully well, do you mind if…...?"

Olive rose, collected the plates in silence, and swept into the kitchen.

With a sly wink in Seymour's direction, Bill trotted after her to do the washing up.

"You can make up for it when she plays the piano," said Lucy.

"There was a dog under the table," he said. "It ate your dad's tea."

"I know. It ate mine as well."

An hour later it was all over, and Seymour felt drained. At a signal from Lucy's mother, they'd lined up on the sofa while she worked through her favourite Chopin sonatas. During the performance, Bill watched his wife's arched back with unwavering devotion. When it was over, she simply folded down the piano lid and went to bed.

"She likes you," said Lucy.

"How on earth do you know?" asked Seymour.

"Because she'd have told you if she didn't."

"I'd best be going upstairs too," winked Bill. "There's always half a chance on Fridays."

When Seymour finally emerged, it was still light. Beyond Bill's greenhouse, he could hear a last pair of golfers making its way down the fairway. To his right the cul-de-sac ran back up to the bus stop where a few early streetlamps were clicking on over the main road.

"Are you sure your mother liked me?"

Lucy had slipped on a pair of shoes and was walking with Seymour to the end of the lane.

"It's complicated. With all men, I mean. She doesn't think women get much of a chance. She's absolutely right."

"Why does she always wear green?"

"You've heard of Emily Davison?"

"Not really. No."

"She was the suffragette who threw herself in front of the King's horse at the Derby in 1913. My mum was there. She was a suffragette. She'd travelled to Epsom with Emily. She saw her die."

"That's terrible. But I still don't really understand the green outfits."

"Come on, Seymour. Don't you know anything?" Lucy bridled with irritation. "Green was one of the suffragette colours. It stands for hope. She's worn nothing else since."

In the murky light of her bedroom, Lucy stirred. A lorry had parked in the street, and she could hear two draymen rolling kegs of beer into the cellar of the club. One of them was telling a story about a stag party. The other kept interrupting with wolf whistles of disbelief. Although she badly needed the toilet, the men's banter had made her curious and the wandering train of her recollections had been lost.

Dragging herself to the window, she broke open the curtains. After a few steadying breaths, she pushed the catch on the sash and forced up the lower pane. One of the men, in a worn leather waistcoat, was sitting on the back of his truck smoking a cigarette. As the window moved, he steered his head in search of the noise.

"You asking me up there, darling?" he shouted. "What's the going rate?"

Two hours later, when Isaac knocked on his mother's bedroom door, there was no reply.

"Mum? I wanted to say sorry about earlier."

Apart from the muted clicking of the immersion heater, the house was silent. Outside, the cooing of a lovelorn wood pigeon had replaced the long-departed draymen.

"Mum? Are you OK?" Isaac eased open the door. "Is that you?"

There was a tiny figure bunched up in the corner, half covered by the curtain which had been torn from its railing. On the left side of the window, its surviving partner was flapping wildly in a chill current of air blowing straight from the sea.

Chapter Nine

"Well, it's so lovely to see you back. It really is."

There was an overpowering stench of shoe leather as Mrs. Eunice Bolt, the manageress of Havercroft's Town & Country Footwear (motto : 'You Should Be In Our Shoes') ushered her absentee saleslady through a back door.

"Sit down, sit down. We don't open for a bit. I'll put the kettle on," she fussed, adding with an undisguised hint of triumph. "It's a Russell Hobbs. First one in town."

Even in her weakened state, Lucy felt a smile invade her face. Since 1960, Mrs Bolt's numerous social distinctions had included being "only the third person in East Yorkshire to buy one of them new Minis"; a status she'd now enhanced with the breakthrough acquisition of a branded kettle favoured (she claimed) by the Queen. Still, Lucy wouldn't say no to a cup of tea. And she wouldn't be saying no to a chocolate bourbon either.

Normally she could walk from her back gate to the shop in a few minutes. Today, even with Seymour's help, it had taken her fifteen, and the effort had drained her. Nevertheless, she was determined to get through a day's work away from home. Ever since Isaac had walked into her bedroom she'd been drowning in her husband's attentiveness.

"Are you going to be alright? You're looking very peeky." Mrs Bolt was pouring Earl Grey through a strainer into two cups with matching saucers. There was no place for mugs in Havercroft's Town

& Country Footwear. "Mondays are normally quiet, mind. And I'll do the till."

Outside, along the promenade, a council wagon was scuttling from one overflowing waste bin to the next and for the first time in weeks, it was raining; squally horizontal showers obliging the men to perform their duties at a jog.

"Thanks. For the tea." Lucy had eaten two biscuits and could already feel the sugar clearing her head. "I'll be absolutely fine."

"You must be very proud of Seymour. The rest of the town seems to be."

"I'm afraid he thinks everything's been rather exaggerated," said Lucy. "He'll be happier when it's all blown over."

"We've not seen much of you since it happened. You didn't reply to my letter. I was worried."

Lucy swirled the dregs in her cup, drawn in by the soggy mass of leaves at the bottom. Mrs Bolt was a good woman; a kind woman, albeit a 62-year-old four times widow whose life had long been the subject of constant local speculation.

According to the known facts, her first two husbands died in car crashes; the third succumbed to septicaemia; and the fourth had suffered a massive heart attack after Germany equalised in the World Cup Final. Known facts, however, had never stood in the way of a spot of gossip. At the very least, according to persistent local rumours, the brakes had been tampered with on both occasions by an amorous local garage proprietor.

Lucy (who'd heard all these and other stories involving poison) looked a little closer at her tea. Four dead husbands, she had to admit, was rather a lot of accidents.

"I've just been a bit rundown. Some sort of summer virus. That's all."

Except that wasn't quite what Dr Turner had said. Not that she'd called him; or even gone to see him. Two days after collapsing (two days which she'd spent in bed) he'd turned up in her room and shoved a thermometer in her mouth.

"No temperature."

"No. I didn't think there would be."

"But you have difficulty sleeping?"

"Yes."

"You suffer from severe mood swings? You're anxious? Sometimes irritable?"

"You've been talking to my husband. Yes. Yes. Yes. Very."

"You feel weak sometimes, low on energy? Heartbeat and pulse irregular?"

"Three more yesses. Well done."

After that, he'd put his instruments away and opened the one remaining curtain. In the harsh light, Lucy scrutinised his profile, remembering the time – after Isaac was born – when she'd nursed such an all-devouring secret crush on this man that she genuinely believed frustration might be terminal.

"It's possible you may have an over-active thyroid." Dr Turner had pulled up a chair and was re-checking her pulse against his pocket watch. He was still fiendishly handsome, she thought, like the hero of a novel set in Cornwall. "It's beating faster," he said. "Maybe we should run a few tests and think about medication?"

"Was it Seymour who asked you here?"

"He's worried. He's got cause to be. Why are you in bed?"

"I'm unhappy, Dr Turner. I don't need any drugs."

"And how long have you been unhappy?"

"I'm not entirely sure I've ever been anything else."

Eunice had been right. Mondays were as slow as they'd always been. By mid-morning, just four people had been in; mums ducking out of the rain to buy school shoes for their kids. Although she had no real friends, there was scarcely a customer she didn't know, and – since the fire on the boat – everyone had made the connection to Seymour.

"Two celebrities in one shop," said one woman, who seemed far more interested in Lucy than shoes. "How's it feel to be married to a hero?"

"Let me know if you need any help," said Lucy. "We've got some size eights in the back."

By lunchtime she felt revived; happy that she'd made the effort; even happier that the shop was closed for an hour and that Eunice had disappeared for what she'd billed 'an exploratory date with a chap'. Over a fresh cup of tea, Lucy wondered if the 'chap' had heard the stories; and if he hadn't, whether someone ought to fill him in. And quickly.

Moving quietly through the shop, she entered the stock room. From floor to ceiling, three of the walls were lined with white shoeboxes. Across the fourth wall was a vintage leather sofa ('possibly the fourth Parker-Knoll in the town') into which Lucy collapsed with a deep sigh. "Everything has a reason." That's what Dr Turner had said before he left. "You just have to find it."

Lucy wasn't so sure. From where she was sitting, life felt like a sequence of incremental disappointments; stacked ever higher like the shoes. Maybe it only made sense if you knew where to look. Maybe there was only one box marked happiness which the blessed ones – people like Seymour and Eunice – had ransacked long ago.

Casting the question aside, she lifted a cardboard lid, exposing a pair of gleaming black brogues in a nest of tissue paper.

What was she doing in a seaside shoe shop anyway? At school, she'd been flying. There were no exams she couldn't pass, and seemingly no books she hadn't read. There was talk of her becoming a teacher – or a journalist – and every parent's evening ended with her mother's chest puffed out with pride. "Men are fools," she reminded her daughter. "Our time is coming."

And then she'd hurtled down Black Pudding.

After that, there'd been no planning. For the first time ever, her life had felt magnificently out of control. Not just the teenage sex (for which she was insatiable) but the deeper thrill of being wanted by a man with a passing resemblance to Heathcliff. Or at least to the Heathcliff she imagined at home after lights out when her hungry hands strayed south.

If she was honest, Seymour's love letters were a disappointment. A huge warning sign missed, she thought, sliding the shoes back into their space on the wall.

For Lucy, their correspondence had been an opportunity to embellish the grand romance she'd always wanted; the one which her mother had lost and still mourned. For Seymour, much as he tried, the words never matched the elegance of his joinery.

"Dad's just gone to the pub," he wrote at the end of his first awkward missive. "He says he'll get a pie for tea on the way back. Bet he forgets."

It sounded terrible now. But it hadn't then; not at all; not when the freedom and the fun obliterated every secret doubt. During those first few summers, they'd forged an unlikely alliance with Lucy's older brother Ralph; heading out to North Wales as a foursome (with his toothy girlfriend Vietta) in an enormous Armstrong Siddeley car; the roof strapped high with camping gear, and exhaust fumes pouring in through giant holes on the floor.

"It's probably best if you keep your feet up on the seats. Bit of a rustbucket," explained Ralph. "Might also be wise to keep the windows open."

On the way, Seymour had shown them the lake where he'd raced a Firefly during the war, and at Barmouth – during a baking August Bank Holiday weekend – he'd won Lucy a giant teddy bear in a kite flying competition.

"Where's it gone?" he asked the next day. The bear appeared to have vanished.

"I think I left it in the dunes," blushed Lucy. "I hope it wasn't looking."

Since their adventures in the workshop, Seymour's supply of condoms had improved, even if the technique still didn't quite equal his enthusiasm.

"They could probably hear you two in Cardiff last night," complained Ralph. "What did you put in his fucking tea?"

"Morning all. Did I ever tell you I was Welsh?" announced Seymour brightly, stumbling from his sleeping bag.

"You're a randy git is what you are," said Ralph, pointing towards a far corner of the field. "Tonight you can put your fucking tent over there."

A few hours later, Lucy and Seymour were unwrapping a fish supper on a bench overlooking the broad sandy sweep of the estuary. A steam train had stopped halfway across the bridge which linked the two sides. Steam was buzzing around its huge wheels.

"He's not like you at all is he?" observed Seymour, popping a chip into his mouth.

"Mum wanted a girl. She'd have kept going until she got one. Ralph never had a chance."

"He's alright though. He's got a car." Seymour paused to peel some dubious yellow batter from his cod. "But it's weird. I've still never heard his girlfriend speak."

"You've met my mum. You know what she's like. Ralph's dream woman is a mute."

Someone was knocking at the shop door. Lucy froze. She remembered turning the lock and pulling down the blind. Only Eunice had a key and she'd probably be choosing her fifth engagement ring by now. Out at the front, the noise changed. The handle was jerking up and down, and there was a squeak, like a gloved hand against rain-streaked glass. Lucy inched sideways on the sofa until she could see through a tiny gap.

"It's me. Seymour. Are you there?"

Quickly, she slid back again, hunching forwards with her hands between her thighs. There was more banging.

"I just want to know if you're alright. I'm worried about you. You're not well. You should be at home."

After five minutes, the commotion stopped. Lucy checked the electric clock on the wall. It would be another half-hour before Eunice returned from her mysterious rendezvous, and she suddenly felt weak with hunger. Next to the Russell Hobbs, there was an old biscuit tin dating back to the Coronation. Inside, she found an unopened packet of digestives.

Sometime around that Barmouth camping trip, she'd limped through her Higher School Certificate, and moved into a bedsit on her own. "Just because I passed it, doesn't mean I care," she told Olive. Whatever dreams her mother had been cultivating were shattered.

Within a week she'd replaced the lost hope of her daughter with a black bulldog puppy. And when that one eventually died, she replaced it with another. And then another. Nobody seemed quite sure how many there'd been. But they were all black and they were all called Arthur; a name they unknowingly shared with the boy who'd never got home.

"It could be worse," consoled Bill, whose hours at the golf club had suddenly increased dramatically. "At least our Ralph is doing alright."

'Our Ralph', as you put it, is a car salesman," snorted Olive, popping a square of dark chocolate into Arthur's open mouth. "A salesman with a girlfriend called Vietta. Vietta? I ask you. That is most certainly not alright."

But it would be Ralph who saved his sister. With his two-tone shoes and acrid cigars, Lucy's brother was a born salesman, and trade in his refurbished bangers was brisk. Needing a secretary to sweeten the books, he'd recruited Lucy. And when the cars broke down, Ralph wheeled in Seymour to get them back on the road. Apart from a few disgruntled punters, everyone was happy. The war was receding; people wanted fun; and finally, as rationing faded away, they had the cash to acquire some.

"I think we should get married."

It was a windy Sunday morning. They were in a coffee bar. Streams of people were filing away from a nearby church, pursued by swirls of the previous day's confetti. Lucy looked at Seymour, who was sipping a coke through a straw. He was wearing a tie.

"This year. Soon. I want to live with you. I want kids. And we've both got jobs now. We could afford it."

Somewhere deep inside Lucy's brain, something snagged; a thought, a warning maybe, caught on its travels and momentarily lost. When she reached for it – whatever it was – the thought had gone.

"Is this a proposal, Seymour Pilbeam?"

"I suppose it is, yes."

It wasn't the least bit unexpected. They'd known each other as lovers since the war. He was a good and handsome man. Even the sex (especially now she had a place of her own) was finally up to her quantity threshold. Without doubt, Seymour's love for her was wholehearted and strong. And under pressure, Lucy would have conceded that her feelings for him ran deep. She just wasn't sure how deep and, just lately, there had been a few moments of doubt.

Seymour still hadn't read a decent book, preferring Dan Dare in the Eagle comic to any of the romantic fodder she pressed into his oily hands. He was also spending large chunks of his mechanic's wage on miniature rolling stock for which she could muster no enthusiasm whatsoever. On the other hand, he loved the countryside, he bought her flowers, and he walked her home. In the end, did it matter that he'd flunked school, made kites and listened to Duke Ellington records? Nobody was perfect. Not even her mother.

"Yes."

"Yes, what?"

"Yes, I'll be your wife."

Two months later, on a magnificent summer Saturday, they were married in a small room at the back of the grime-crusted Town Hall. Apart from close family – and a bulldog with a tummy bug – there were no witnesses to the ceremony and the single surviving photograph captured Lucy in a knee-length cream satin dress, rigid with tension, her eyes burning behind a delicate silvery veil.

Alongside her, Seymour appears calm and quietly ecstatic in a suit tailored for a much bigger man. A pipe is clearly visible in the corner of his breast pocket.

"You're Seymour's father?"

The group had gathered for cold nibbles after the ceremony   at   a nearby snack bar where Olive had cornered Mr.Pilbeam Senior.

"I am, yes. Can you get a pint in here or what?"

"You're very short."

"Thank you. That's one of the nicest things anyone's ever said to me."

"Your son? Can he be trusted?"

"Honestly?" said Seymour's father, edging steadily towards the exit door. "Between you and me, I think he's a bit simple."

There was a commotion in the corner of the café. Arthur had been hiding under a table with a plateful of pork pies. After a glance at his subdued fellow guests, he trotted into the centre of the room and (rather spectacularly) regurgitated them.

"Stupid little dog," snapped Olive turning back to resume her interrogation.

But the clocks had struck 11, the pubs were open, and kick off was less than three hours away. Mr.Pilbeam had gone.

"Stupid little man," she muttered. They never saw each other again.

For the next few years, the newly-weds flourished. With Ralph's help – 'I know people who know people who know people' – they'd moved into a pre-fab council bungalow where a mood of happy chaos prevailed amidst the leaking roof, Lucy's books and Seymour's half-completed projects in oak, larch and pine.

For Lucy especially, their newly acquired intimacy was challenging. Seymour's boyish curiosity was entertaining, but his inability to finish anything was not. The man was a human Labrador, lolloping from one enthusiasm to the next. One week he was obsessed with organ music; the next he was tootling (without discernible promise) on a second-hand clarinet; one weekend, he was out testing his latest box kite, the next he was hunched over an electric train with a soldering iron.

"I'm thinking about making a loom," he'd said one day. "I could weave my own ties."

That hadn't happened either (thankfully) and apart from the trail of mess, only one theme endured amongst Seymour's many pipedreams.

Boats. Always boats.

In the tiny spare bedroom, there were boxes stuffed with designs for dinghies and yachts and whenever he could, he still slipped back to his father's workshop to make miniature sailing boats for anyone who still wanted one. But the numbers were dwindling fast and the old boating pond where he'd first encountered his wife, was fetid with neglect.

"I just don't get it," he complained to Lucy. "Boats don't go out of fashion. They can't."

It was around this time – eighteen months before Isaac was born – that Seymour bought a motorcycle; a 1936 Cotton with a deafening 500c engine which carried them out to the coast whenever the sun shone. Even the memory of it, fifteen years later, could make Lucy tingle.

On a motorbike, Seymour was transformed. With her arms tight around his waist, they sped together across the Yorkshire Wolds, leaning gracefully into every bend; feeling the tyres bite reassuringly into the bleached asphalt as the sea sped towards them.

They wore no helmets; the roads were deserted; and Seymour was fearless. On every trip, Lucy closed her eyes, remembering the first stirrings of desire she'd felt on a long-ago sledge.

For just a few eye-watering hours, it was as if all her husband's peculiar fascinations had been exorcised: exposing a man wholly in command of his world. Through his leather jacket she could feel the broad strength of his back and by the time they reached the dunes, each of them was hungry for only one thing.

Afterwards, Seymour would sit shirtless and watch the sailing boats slip out of the stone harbour, two miles to the north. If there was driftwood, he'd light a fire; and if he hadn't lost his pen-knife, he'd carve tiny human figures while Lucy lay back in the sun, wrestling with the same sense of dissatisfaction that now always followed sex.

"You know what? We should live at the sea," he'd said. A Union Jack was flying amidst the red roofs of the town clustered high around the distant quay. "A little spot like that. Perfect."

Along the flickering water's edge, a woman was building a wall of sand against the tide with her two young daughters. Crouching down in the surf, with his trousers rolled up, the girls' father was taking a photograph. All of them were laughing.

"I'm pregnant," she replied.

After that everything happened very quickly. If there was any discussion, she couldn't remember it. If there was any doubt, it was never broached. Within two months, they'd packed their belongings into one of Ralph's dodgy cars and followed it back across the Wolds on their motorcycle.

"I could stick on a side car when the baby comes. Imagine that."

"I was hoping we might run to four wheels not three," said Lucy, holding her bump as she straddled the pillion seat.

"My old Armstrong's still got four," winked Ralph. "Any decent offer considered."

"Sticking our heads in a gas oven would be cheaper," said Lucy.

"And quicker," said Seymour.

Neither of them knew much about where they were going. It was a traditional fishing town, they knew that. And in summer, it filled up with holidaymakers from the industrial North. They knew that, too. Years before, Seymour had visited with his mother, but apart from a souvenir badge, he remembered nothing. For each of them it was a blank page; a proper, new start; and their expectations were high.

For Seymour, the densely-packed harbour offered infinite pleasures; bright-painted trawlers rafted steady in pairs, while cranes disembowelled their fish; smaller clinker-built cobles, rattling under red canvas sails, and thirsting for the tide; the constant flow of lives built along the fragile line where the dark sea met the clay.

For Lucy, the broad streets, the clean air, even the old-fashioned shops – 'Huttons for Buttons' – held out contrasting promise of happy days ahead and at no time then, did she feel the small-town claustrophobia that would follow. Rarely had she seen her husband so energised.

As the town drifted into its long winter sleep, properties were emptying and Seymour had fallen in love with a large (if ramshackle) Victorian detached under the shadow of the town gasworks. On three sides, it was hidden by a jungle of garden. There was a coke stove in the kitchen, three bedrooms, two toilets and a filthy attic littered with the corpses of dead pigeons.

"They must have got trapped," said Seymour. "What do you think?"

What Lucy thought wasn't easy to express. The house itself had once been a magnificent merchant's home. She loved its affluent heft, its dark tiled floors, and the elegant curve of its banister rail. Outside there were sheds and shrubs, and a splendid old stable building with creaky double doors. But there were no uplifting views of the ocean. Out the back they could see a rusty gasometer. Opposite the front door was a workingman's club.

"The rent's cheap, I suppose," she smiled. "When we've cleaned it up, I'm sure it will be wonderful."

Finding employment had been just as easy. The local paper was looking for a handyman; someone who could service its ancient hot metal printers or ease open the office doors bloated by the seasonal damp; someone with a tool kit and an aptitude for solving problems on the cheap.

"I don't suppose you can write as well?" asked the editor (Mr. Latheron's predecessor).

"I've never tried, sir," replied Seymour, sensing a man who valued brevity.

"No barriers here, Pilbeam. Not if you're smart. None whatsoever. Start on Monday."

Three months later, on a stormy March night, Isaac Eric Pilbeam was born in a ground floor hospital room which opened onto a memorial garden. Lucy never knew it, but the rockets for the lifeboat had been fired at the precise moment the midwife cut the umbilical cord.

A few hours later, after the three of them had locked in a tearful embrace, Seymour rode his motorcycle alone through the town's wind-lashed streets. Shivering with paternal joy, he'd watched as the sky lightened, and the yellow-clad crew returned without loss. In that moment he felt as trouble-free as it was possible to feel.

He had a son and wife he loved in a town where he felt absurdly happy. Only one thing was missing, but that could wait....

There was another shake of the door. Lucy looked again at the clock. A cold cup of Earl Grey sat on the tea chest which passed for a table. Next to it was a half-eaten biscuit.

"It's me. Eunice. Let me in. Time to open up. Chop chop."

Lucy went to the front of the shop, raised the blind and swung the cardboard sign to 'Open'. Mrs Bolt's cheeks were flushed, and her breath stank of drink.

"Cockburns," she declared. "You can't beat a lunchtime mouthful."

"I gather it went well then," said Lucy.

"My god it went well. How are you feeling?" Eunice didn't wait for an answer. "It was brilliant, Lucy. Such a lovely man. Amusing. Young. Intelligent. Generous. We had four glasses of port AND a roast beef sandwich with coleslaw. Coleslaw!"

"Very nice," said Lucy. "Does he have a name?"

"He's a photographer. I'm pretty sure you'll know him?"

"I doubt it. I don't know anybody. Why? Who?"

"He saved all those people on the boat. Frank? Frank something or other."

"You don't even know his surname?"

"Not yet," said Eunice. "But he paid for all the drinks."

After that, for both, the afternoon dragged. Needing to make several important telephone calls (to her fellow widows) Eunice had vanished into a back office leaving Lucy out front to sell shoes. It was a rubbish job – the latest in a long line of them – but the two women had grown close and Lucy enjoyed her role as a surrogate daughter, almost as much as she savoured Mrs Bolt's dark take on marriage. To Eunice, men were like the things in their window. If you tried enough on, she informed Lucy repeatedly, you'd eventually find the perfect fit.

"Mrs P. How lovely to see you."

The bell on the door hadn't rung. It must be broken, thought Lucy. Wearing a long black coat, Stan Clough was shaking the rain from his umbrella.

"Filthy day," he said.

"Horrible," said Lucy, feeling unaccountably clammy. "But don't get settled. They've not been delivered yet."

No-one else in the town wore shoes like Stan Clough; hand-made and imported from Italy. Even in her own time at the shop, Lucy had sold him well over twenty pairs.

"In which case, I'll just talk to you." Stan had slunk deeper into the shop. "Last time I saw you was The Burlingtonian. You were feeling faint?"

"Yes, I remember."

She remembered something else too. Years before – when Isaac had been three – she'd taken him for a Saturday morning trim; back when Stan was still cutting hair and Isaac was so small he'd sat on a plank stretched across the arms of a huge chrome and leather-upholstered chair. It had been a sweltering August day and the salon floor lay buried beneath the furry grey clippings of the town's pensioners.

"Just shutting up," he'd smiled. "You're lucky."

His voice had surprised her. Years later, she could still remember the shock. Apart from Seymour's radio (when it was working) she'd only ever heard anything so cultured at the cinema. He even looked like a movie star; dazzling white teeth and a tailored blue Oxford shirt with the sleeves rolled up.

"I'm only filling in. It's my dad's business. Stand and watch if you're nervous."

She'd been wearing a blue polka dot dress, tight on the waist, with large white buttons right down the front. From the knee down, her

111

legs were tanned and bare.

"Have I seen you here before? I'm Stan. Stan Clough."

They were talking to each other's reflections in a huge mirror. To one side, behind the glass of a locked cabinet, Lucy could see boxes of Durex.

"I know who you are."

"I'm living away mostly right now. But it's a small town, I guess."

"Very," said Lucy, who had somehow found herself so close she could feel the man's heat as he levelled the silent boy's fringe.

"There. How's that?"

He was standing so close; their thighs were touching. Both of them were looking into the large mirror. She could see Isaac looking down shyly. She could see Stan's eyes widen as his hand slid across her buttocks, pushing the thin fabric hard against the naked skin beneath.

"Mum." Isaac was rubbing his right eye. "It tickles."

In her entire life – not before or since – had she ever wanted a man so badly; or so desperately needed to get a few minutes alone. Or, if necessary, with Seymour.

"Yes, of course. Sorry. How much do we owe you?"

A few minutes later, she and her boy had been out in the sunshine. A holiday coach had broken down nearby and its occupants were crowding around a park bench to eat their sandwiches. Behind her, the illuminated barber's pole had been switched off. She never went back inside the place again.

And then – almost ten years later – they'd met again at the shoe shop.

If he remembered that earlier 'moment' Stan had never said. Most likely, his memory was fogged by his countless other peccadilloes.

112

Almost every woman in the town had a story, and – thanks to Eunice – Lucy had heard all of them, none of which explained why their infrequent encounters always left her feeling emotionally violated.

"Listen, I think your son might have a crush on my daughter."

Stan had removed his coat and folded it carefully over the X-ray machine. "I didn't know you had a daughter."

"Separated. Alice. She's lovely. I share her with her mum."

'A' for Alice and the spiralling love doodles all over Isaac's schoolbooks. Of course. Of course. A for alarm, too. With a shiver she remembered the underwear catalogue hidden down the side of her son's bed.

"Are you sure? Is there a problem? He's a lovely boy. Really he is."

"So she says," smiled Stan. "And don't panic. That's how I know. She told me."

"It probably won't last the summer. These things never do," said Lucy. "A holiday crush."

"How old were you and Seymour?"

"I'm sorry?"

Two passers-by had squeezed their faces up against the window. Lucy could see their lips working and desperately hoped they wouldn't come in.

"That was intrusive. None of my business. Apologies."

From the back office, there was a harsh cackling noise. The two window shoppers had wandered away. Lucy sat down on one of the fitting benches.

"I met him before the war. I was just a girl."

"I was really sorry about what happened to his boat by the way.

113

There was genuinely nothing wrong with it that I knew of."

"He thinks you sabotaged it."

"I didn't. Cross my heart. I could help him if he still wants to get himself a boat."

"I'd rather you didn't."

Neither seemed certain where to take the conversation next. A chair had been pushed back in the next room. He remembered. The haircut. The dress. Isaac. His hand. All of it She was certain.

"Eunice – my manageress – will be out in a second. Your shoes should be here this time next week."

"Everyone knows Eunice," laughed Stan. "She attracts even more rumours than me."

"All lies, of course."

"Of course," said Stan. "Listen. Do you fancy a drink some time?"

"To talk about Isaac and your daughter?"

"To talk about whatever you want."

Lucy felt certain she was going to pass out.

"Alright then. Yes I do," she said.

Chapter Ten

"My mum knows."

"About what? I thought your mum was doolally?"

"I've written your initials all over my schoolbooks."

"Embarrassing."

"I know. I Love AC. Everywhere."

"You can't possibly even know that. We're 15."

"I know one thing."

"What's that?"

"I'd rather be with you than at home."

It had been an excellent summer, but it was nearly over. In a few days' time, they'd be back at their desks. For Isaac, that would mean the daily penance of the town's crumbling boy's grammar school; for Alice, the loveless dormitory of a boarding establishment in the Cheviot Hills.

The long August days had suited them. They were a well-matched couple. Almost every waking hour had been spent in each other's company, mooching around Clough's amusements, thumping their bottoms against the machines to dislodge loose pennies.

"Doesn't your dad own these machines?" Isaac had asked, his pockets swollen with coins.

"Him or some bank," said Alice. "But I really don't care."

Most days ended the same. By late afternoon, they'd head for the town's north beach to build cairns out of the dazzling chalk stones. If Alice had bought her dog – a recalcitrant beagle with one testicle – they'd roam further, stretching their long legs out along the edge of the tide until the clock called them back.

So far, they'd kissed but their hands hadn't strayed. Somehow, the right moment had never arisen, and a small (untested but fast-growing) part of Isaac was glad. Just before the holidays, two of his mates had been suspended for masturbating during a maths lesson. He'd actually seen the grey ooze in the curl of their fists and felt stung by envy.

Maybe there was something wrong with him. Or perhaps a little more practise was required. Back home in his bedroom – crouched over a Littlewood's catalogue – the sensations came freely enough, but nothing else did. And then just a few weeks earlier, there'd been an encouraging breakthrough.

It was the day before the disastrous boat launch. Uncle Ralph and Auntie Vietta had been invited over to watch. By early evening, everyone had gone their own way. Isaac's mother was in bed; Seymour was practising his accordion; Ralph had drunk himself into a coma; and the enigmatic (still mostly silent) Vietta was peeling off her clothes for a long, hot bath.

Isaac knew this because he was watching from inside a wardrobe. And now Vietta knew this because she had just opened the wardrobe door.

"Oh."

It was more than she'd said for some hours.

"I was in the bathroom. I heard you coming. I hid. I'm really really sorry."

116

Vietta stepped aside to allow him out. Two years before (wearing a bathing suit) she'd won Miss Skegness on a unanimous verdict. This time she was completely naked, and the verdict was just the same.

"You can watch if you like. You've seen it all now."

Isaac took one lingering forensic look and fled. When he examined the crotch of his pants five minutes later, they were wet, and a clear, sticky liquid was seeping from the end of his penis. At last, he thought. I'm a man.

Sitting on the beach with Alice now, he could feel the outline of the contraceptive in his pocket. He was pretty sure his dad wouldn't miss it. He was pretty sure he wouldn't use it either. Not this time anyway. Somewhere nearby, a car radio had been left on. He could hear the organ intro bleeding into 'A Whiter Shade of Pale'.

"I love that song," he said. "You can never get bored of it."

"How does your mum know it's me, if you only wrote my initials?"

Alice was wearing a short denim skirt, and a yellow t-shirt. Stretched out alongside, her dog was eating an abandoned toffee apple.

"Apparently, you told your dad. And your dad told her."

"Oh shit. He gets his shoes at her shop?"

"Exactly."

The nights were already closing in. Around dusk, they moved away from the beach, threading through back streets lined with guesthouses. Behind every window, people were watching their televisions.

After five minutes, they stopped outside an enormous balconied house overlooking the south bay. A giant monkey puzzle tree was flourishing in the garden. Its branches had been draped with coloured electric lights. Silhouetted in a wide first floor window, Isaac could make out the shape of a man hunched at a telescope.

"Is that your dad?"

"Yeah. He does that all the time. He loves to watch the sea."

"You'll have to ask me in some time."

"I will. I'm not sure when I'll be back though."

"Why did they split? Your mum and dad? Any idea?"

"Mum says he's a letch. But I've never actually asked my dad."

"Do you think he's a letch?"

"Probably. He is pretty gorgeous, to be fair…. if you like smarmy, rich ex-hairdressers."

"I sometimes wish mine would split. And then sometimes I don't."

"I can't help you with that," whispered Alice, leaning forwards for a kiss. "I'd better go."

"I'll write. I promise."

"Do. But keep it clean. No drawings."

From Stan Clough's house, Isaac could have found his way home blindfold. The town was criss-crossed by rows of identical Edwardian semis he'd navigated hundreds of times. Sometimes, he imagined everything in the town had burst out of the ground fully formed in just one night; the same bay windows, the same recessed porches, the same dreary people tending their lawns.

Now that the summer was done, he could feel a swelling tumour of impatience. At home, he didn't know who to hate the most, and at school his performance was in freefall. Hidden under a corner of his bedroom carpet was his end of term report; a litany of such elegant putdowns, he was secretly rather proud of it.

At the town's one level-crossing, he looped away from the looming gasworks, and cut through a series of back alleys until he was standing outside Johnny's Junk Shop. Cardboard boxes full of American hero comics were still piled up outside the door alongside a set of left-handed ladies golf clubs. Every minute or so, a man wearing combat trousers (and with hair sprouting from the bridge of his nose) emerged to carry something in.

"Are you still open?"

"What's it look like?" The man paused. His eyes were just visible over a picture of Batman. "Don't I know you? Ain't you Seymour's kid?"

"I am, but promise you won't tell him," hushed Isaac. "He says you're called Clinkers. Is that right?"

"Apparently so. Can't imagine why. What do you want?"

"Do you sell ink? Different coloured ink?"

After a rummage through Clinkers' stock, Isaac had what he wanted. With a little judicious mixing and matching, the 'E's', 'F's' and 'D's' on his school report would become 'B's; and every minus would be upgraded to a plus. The vitriolic comments from staff would be wildly at odds with his new grades, but Isaac was pretty confident – given the atmosphere back home – that neither of his parents would notice.

"You really won't say anything, will you?"

"You bought some ink. What is there to say?" Clinkers booted the last box back in through his door. "Want any ladies golf clubs?"

"Not really, but thanks for the magazine."

Five minutes later, he was home. At the gate he took a close look at his new bedtime reading before tucking it down the back of his jeans. The pictures were in full, glossy colour and the tundra-like expanses of dark pubic hair made him feel dizzy. It would be months before Alice was back in town. He might have worn himself away by then.

"Is that you? Mum was worried."

Isaac followed Seymour's voice to the long, rectangular brick stable and stepped inside. For years he'd steered clear of it. Ever since his mother had outlawed the swing which hung from the rafters, it had felt out of bounds – his father's sanctuary – and the place seemed altered beyond recognition.

In his memory, the walls were flaked with damp and crumbling lime mortar. Now they shone with dazzling white emulsion. Down its two long sides, half-planed timbers had been stacked and secured in neat piles. On its gable ends, shelves climbed up to the roof, overflowing with numbered cardboard boxes. Even the space above the joists was crammed. Looking up he saw ropes and oars and everywhere around his feet, the soft, orange underpadding of sawdust.

"I hear you've got a girlfriend."

Seymour was sitting with his accordion on his lap. He'd been dusting the bellows, and the vivid colours of its body had the look of an exotic bird. Every now and then, it emitted a deep, sad sigh.

"Jesus, dad. What do you do in here?" Isaac had picked up a bag full of galvanised nails. "Where did all this stuff come from? What's it for?"

"I thought I might try building a boat. Just a small one."

"You're mad. What kind of boat? You don't even know how to build a boat. Mum'll go completely spare."

Through the walls of the old stables they could hear a radio warming up inside the house. There was a loud click, followed by a jumble of music and foreign accents. Eventually, after a few seconds of chaos, a single, cultured voice opened up with the BBC news.

"I want a boat, Isaac. I always have. I don't understand why it's such a problem."

"I was there the last time, dad. That's why it's a problem."

"If that mast hadn't fallen down." Seymour carefully folded his accordion into its box. "She'd have liked it. I know she would. Look at her. It's what she needs."

"You're so wrong, dad," hissed Isaac, "And by the way, my girlfriend's none of your business."

All the joy had bled out of the boy's day. In the kitchen, Lucy was sitting in darkness, half-listening to the news. The only light was coming from a streetlamp, filtered through the sticky leaves of their sycamore.

"You must be hungry. Do you want some tea? I won't ask you where you've been."

"Don't," said Isaac.

For as long as he could remember, his mother's cooking had been a joke. Everyone else despised school dinners. He, on the other hand, couldn't get enough of them. At home, it felt like weeks since they'd eaten a meal together. And since the start of the summer holidays, he'd been living on hot dogs.

"There's a pork pie in the oven." Now that she said it, Isaac could make out the smell of burnt pastry. "Your granddad Bill's favourite."

"Since when? He hates it. He always gives his to that dog."

Lucy had retrieved a plate from the oven. Isaac was gawping emptily at the jelly oozing between the pink meat and the crust. Between his pants and his Levi's, he could feel the siren call of his new magazine.

"I'm not hungry, mum. I'm off to my bedroom."

Halfway up the stairs, he stopped. The radio had died, and his father was speaking in a low voice. Not for the first time, he crept back until he could hear what his parents were saying.

"You're going then?"

"I'll only be a few hours. I can't see what either of us will be missing." Seymour could see the fat turning opaque around his son's neglected pie. "We're never in the same room."

"You're really going to that pub."

"I'm going for a reason. I wouldn't go otherwise."

"Dominoes. That's your reason?"

"It's the last match of the season. I've told you. If we beat Stan Clough's lot from The Ship, we could win a cup. Is that really so dreadful?"

From the stairs, Isaac heard a door closed in anger, then the rattle of the garden gate. Leaping to his bedroom, he pushed up the sash window. Seconds later, Seymour came striding beneath his gaze.

"Dad. Listen. Please don't go."

If his father heard, he showed no sign of it. Quickening his pace, Seymour turned towards the harbour and slipped out of view. Somewhere inland a whistle was screaming across the town's windless rooftops.

At the closed wooden gates of the level crossing, he looked towards the sound following the dark onward speck of a train until it crossed in a jolting spasm of steel and steam. Seymour averted his eyes. When he reopened them, the engine was gone.

"Taff. Mate. We're going to be alright tonight. I know it. Secret weapon."

He'd reached the worn steps of The Ship Inn where Rehab was crushing a tab end under a familiar wellington boot.

"You reek like a box of mackerel. They won't let you in."

The last time they'd seen each other, the Captain had been hiding in the wheelhouse of The Burlingtonian. Since then nobody really knew where he'd been beyond the certainty that it was some considerable distance from a bath.

"I'm a fisherman in a fishing town. You should be used to it," sniffed Rehab. "Do you want to see my secret weapon or not?"

"What is it?"

"It's an abacus." Rehab gleefully flung open his filthy donkey jacket. A child's wooden toy was tucked under his arm.

"Brilliant," said Seymour, feeling the warm explosion of life as they entered the bar. "We may as well get the trophy engraved now."

The place was completely packed. Stationed around the crescent of the bar, a smoky crush of punters was waiting for fresh pints. Plates piled high with sausage rolls and hot pasties were being picked clean and returned for more. On every table, bowls of crisps fought for space with overflowing ashtrays and empty glasses, and high above the stew of smells, Seymour felt the comforting hum of expectation.

"You'll be needing this." Nellie was weaving through the room holding a freshly pulled pint of bitter. "Your wife not coming?"

"She's not feeling too well, no," said Seymour. Another half-dozen men had just forced their way in off the street. "Thanks for the pint. Must be weird to be on this side of the bar."

"You're my team. It's a big night for The White Horse, this. I wasn't going to let you down." Nellie placed a hand on Seymour's shoulder. "And don't worry, pet. Nobody else brings their woman to these affairs either."

Seymour hadn't really been listening. Through the pub's feature window, he could make out the two grey arms of the harbour walls, wrapped around a galaxy of green, red and white mooring lights.

"Phoenix," he said, suddenly. Nellie's hand still felt warm through his shirt.

"I'm sorry?"

"My next boat. I've just thought of a name. Phoenix. It's going to rise triumphantly out of that last disaster."

"I hope it does, love. I really do."

There was another surge, taking a table of drinks with it by the pub door. A single furious voice let out a howl of distress. Huddled beneath the trophy cabinet, he could see the rest of his team. Rehab had a full pint in each hand. Clinkers had a pint and a whisky chaser. Harry Spanners was hobbling to the bar for the next round.

"Oh god, I need to slow them down. See you later".

"Good luck," said Nellie, leaning forward to kiss Seymour on the cheek. "You're my boy."

There was a manic burst of whooping behind him.

"Get in, my son." For no apparent reason, Rehab was attempting to stand on a chair without releasing his two pints. "I've got a fucking abacus."

"How long have you all been drinking?"

"Seymour. Jah. Mein kapitain," said Spanners who (also for no apparent reason) was attempting to frogmarch back to the table with a packed tray of refreshments.

"Come on. Tell me. How long?"

"I've got an abacush," said Rehab.

Inside a wall-mounted cabinet, Seymour could see the dulled silver of the East Riding (East) Higginson's Bakery Domino League Cup. Fourteen years had passed since the name of the White Horse had troubled the town's decrepit engraver, and for the past five years (as witnessed by the dust) the trophy hadn't left The Ship.

"Rehab. Listen. Concentrate. You can't divide on an abacus."

The captain had immediately slumped back with a look of savage desperation.

"We're playing fives and threes." Seymour was speaking very slowly, taking great care to enunciate every word. "Remember? Just like the other times? We put down a domino at one end. We add its number to the number at the other end and what do we do.......?"

"....divide by five or three to find out many holes to move our peg along the cribbage board."

"Very good, Clinkers. Well done."

"I've got an abacush," said Rehab.

Seymour felt slightly sick. Every match night brought the same promise of public humiliation.

"First one up and back down the board wins."

"Top marks, Harry. Has anyone seen Frank? We're a man down."

"I've had it since I was a kid, too," said Rehab.

"You can't use it," said Seymour. "It's called cheating."

"Not even a teeny tiny bit?"

"Do you even know how to use it?"

There was a long pause during which Rehab attempted (with mixed results) to dock the rim of a beer glass to his mouth.

"Nah. Ain't got a clue."

Seymour took a long slurp of his ale. At the far side of the lounge – by the baize-topped competition table – two league officials were counting the match dominoes. Alongside them, he could see Stan Clough, sipping an orange juice. There were only five minutes to go. Two more people had just come in out of the night.

"Sorry, I'm late. I think you all know Eunice. Eunice Bolt from the shoe shop." No-one in the town had ever seen Frank with a woman before. "And before the match, we've got something to announce."

"We're getting married," said Eunice.

"Bloody hell," said Rehab.

"Fuck me," said Clinkers.

"Check your brake cables," said Harry.

"What was that?" demanded Frank, who was wearing white flannel trousers, and a navy-blue blazer.

"Congratulations" said Seymour, turning to Eunice. "Lucy seems lifted now she's back at work. Thank you."

"She's a lovely woman," said Eunice. "Just a bit delicate."

"GAME TIME, ladies and gentlemen. First players to the table pleasssse."

There was a crazed last skirmish for drinks. Within an hour – maybe less – it would all be over, and both teams were scrutinising the blackboard to see who would be playing who. As always, it would be the best of seven. Two games of doubles followed by five individual duels. Each of the pairings had been drawn from a hat. And Seymour had just been drawn against Stan Clough in the seventh and deciding game.

"No chance," sighed Seymour. "This lot haven't lost a game all season."

"We'll get you to that deciding leg, won't we boys?" said Frank.

"I need a whisky," said Rehab.

For years to come, everyone would say that they had never known a pub fall so quiet; or that dominoes could get quite so tense. After the doubles, it was honours even. 1-1. Seymour and Frank had won convincingly. Harry Spanners and Clinkers had been disqualified for swapping dominoes under the table.

"We'd have been alright if you hadn't dropped it," said Spanners.

"We'd have been alright if you hadn't passed it to their player," said Clinkers.

Apart from the clatter of the pieces, the bar was still. Behind the crowd circling the table, dozens more were standing on chairs, arching their necks to follow each chain of pieces. Whenever a score was achieved, the action paused while the referee advanced the player's peg along the cribbage board. When everyone was satisfied, play resumed.

Suddenly, everything seemed wearily predictable. First, Clinkers missed out on victory by a single hole (2-1 to The Ship) then Rehab suffered a mild nervous breakdown trying to work out whether fourteen was divisible by three (3-1 to The Ship).

"They won't do it," said Nellie, who had joined her team by the table. "It's our night."

A half-hour later, Frank and Spanners had crushed their two opponents, and the pub was exploding with noise. 3-3. As Seymour and Stan took their seats, a stampede of men dashed to the toilets, necessitating a brief delay in proceedings.

"Seymour," said Stan.

"Stan," replied Seymour.

"Quiet everybody," shouted the match official. 'Please. Some decorum."

Once again, the only sound came from the shuffling of the dominoes on the felt. When the twenty-eight pieces were still, the combatants selected seven and play began; with each man launching his peg on its trip up and down the board. Whenever their own dominoes offered no match for the number at either end, they drew from the pile and continued.

To an outsider, the game appeared bereft of skill; chance, and nothing more. To Stan and Seymour, it was a labyrinth of odds and possibilities; a test of memory and nerve which grew ever more complex as the draw pile shrank and their options narrowed.

After ten minutes, their brains were in overdrive. At one end of the chain there was a four: at the other a six. Only two dominoes remained in the pile. Each of the combatants was stranded just six peg holes away from victory.

"It's you to play," said Seymour.

"Yes, I know."

Stan opened his fingers. Inside was a four paired with a six. For a long second, he wavered, before matching the four of his domino to the four on the line. There was now a six at either end.

"Six's either end," intoned the referee. "That's 12. Four threes. The Ship's peg moves four and has just two holes to go for a win."

Seymour closed a fist tightly around his own last domino. It was a double two. He couldn't go.

"You to pick up then, Seymour," smiled Stan.

"Yes, I know," he replied.

Seymour's hand was hovering over the final two pieces. Both men knew what was hidden there. Both knew that one of them was a double six and that whoever turned it over had won. For the first time in the game, a stray voice broke the hush.

"Come on Seymour, lad. Come on."

Instinctively, he turned towards the noise. Out in the street, someone had thrown a bottle, triggering a fire alarm in a derelict chippie. Through the open front door of the pub he could see Frank and Eunice locked in an awkward kiss.

"Do him, Taff. He's yours. Come on."

Seymour put a hand over his face and turned over a domino. Every single eye in the pub, except his, watched it settle.

"White Horse plays double six," bellowed the referee. "Please. Please. That's twelve one end, six the other. Eighteen is six threes. The White Horse moves six. The White Horse wins."

There was nothing tribal in what followed. It was dominoes, not football, and everyone was happy to park their loyalties and ruin what little remained of the carpet. In the tales that sprang up later, it was said the pub served free drinks until dawn, but since nobody remembered how or when they left, the rumours could never be confirmed.

In any event, Seymour had shaken hands with Stan and drifted away long before proceedings got too rowdy. Out on the street, he'd slipped an arm around Nellie's waist and whispered goodnight. She felt woozy and warm and welcoming.

"I'm going your way. I'll walk with you," she said.

"No. You stay and celebrate. Let me know when you've got the cup engraved. I'll pop in."

"You were brilliant. Thanks. Don't be a stranger."

It was a short walk to Seymour's house, just long enough for his spirits to dive. From the outside, the place looked dead. Every window was closed and black. Even the back gate had been bolted shut.

Reaching his arm over the top, Seymour let himself into the yard. There was a dim light shining through the half open door of his workshop and the broken arm of a padlock was hanging loosely from the frame.

"Hello. Lucy? Isaac? Are you in there?"

Seymour pushed the door and watched it swing back against the wall. Nobody was inside. He took a step forward and froze. Under the light thrown from the single bulb he could see where a hammer had been tossed on the floor.

Alongside it – scattered in a tangle of tortoiseshell and chrome – lay the broken ruins of his accordion.

Part Two

'Phoenix'

1967-68

Chapter One

It was late October – after the leaves had turned crisp – that Seymour started looking for the wood. Any earlier, and the sap would have still been rising in the trees. Any later, and the short, damp days would have crushed his resolve. The anger that had propelled him for months was weakening. Only when the timber was cut and he could feel the resin on his fingers, would he be certain to carry this through.

"I think we should have turned left, or possibly right. Or we've passed it."

Captain Rehab was behind the wheel of a decrepit Ford Commer van. He was also behind an unwieldy map which was obliterating most of the front window.

"Most people don't drive and navigate at the same time," suggested Seymour.

"I'm better with charts," grumbled Rehab. "My dad said I was born with a compass in my head."

Seymour smiled. If the rumours were only half true, the bottom of the North Sea was littered with evidence to the contrary. Whatever, Rehab had in his head – on dry land, at least – it didn't appear to include a sense of direction.

"Definitely right maybe." Rehab's bloodshot eyes protruded over the top edge of the map. "Or left. What do you reckon?"

A chalk farm track ran straight ahead until it vanished in a coppice of old forest. Wherever Seymour looked, there were no sharp edges to the landscape, and the hills (such as they were) rolled out in a series of interlocking folds, freshly ploughed and patrolled by frantic packs of seagulls.

"It's all coming back to me now. It's the other side of those trees."

Seymour desperately hoped the captain was right. Ever since Rehab had heard his friend was building a boat – or thinking about it – he'd been talking about the farmer (and wood merchant) whose renowned timber had sailed the seven seas.

"How come you know this place?"

"My dad was a shipbuilder," said Rehab. "I grew up watching him."

"And my dad made coffins," he replied. "I grew up watching him."

There was a heavy thudding from the back axle where a dodgy weld was coming unstuck. Seymour bounced in his seat and looked across at Rehab's weathered profile.

"I've known you for ten years and you've never told me that before."

"You've never asked me anything before," said Rehab, bringing the van to a halt alongside the edge of a field shining with scattered flint. "Nobody ever does."

"Well, I'm asking you now."

Seymour could have listened for hours. The man's life was a revelation. Like Harry Spanners, the blue-eyed captain was a child of the sea; whose father had been a renowned master-builder; the architect of over one hundred wooden clinker-built sailing boats.

Along the entire east coast, his cobles (as they were called) had been prized by fishermen whose lives, and livelihoods, depended on them. In fifty years (until arthritis forced him to down his chisels)

Rehab's father had never once taken a day's holiday. And after his death, when Rehab was nineteen, the shipbuilder's remains had been floated out to sea in a burning wooden boat, watched over by a hundred fishermen.

"Some of those men had travelled down from Scotland just to be there."

"But you never picked up the tools after he was gone?"

"A bit. Here and there. I tried, but I knew I'd never be as good. I loved sailing them more than making them."

"So, all those stories about you are......?"

"Complete shite," chuckled Rehab. "Most of them anyway."

"What about this place? Do you still reckon you know where your dad got his wood?"

"And Captain Cook before him," winked Rehab, cranking up the engine. "Course I do."

Ahead of them, a break had opened in the trees. As the van pulled through it, they saw a knotted cluster of crumbling outbuildings gathered around a magnificent Georgian farmhouse. Two elderly sheepdogs were yapping at the feet of an elderly man in filthy blue overalls.

"Larch," said the figure.

"Yup." Rehab nodded.

"You look just like your father. He was a piss artist as well."

The farmer sniffed and climbed slowly onto the metal seat of an ancient tractor. Tethered to the back of it was an even older trailer.

"What is this place?" whispered Seymour. "It's like the farm that time forgot."

There was a choky roar from the front, followed by a filthy black explosion from the back.

"On the back," croaked the farmer.

Ten minutes later they were pulling up by the grassy edge of a wide valley. Stretched along its sides, Seymour had already seen what they'd come for; a dozen or so conifers, pointing skywards like pale yellow-green fingers. A pulse of excitement lifted him to his feet.

"You're smiling," said Rehab.

"So are you," said Seymour.

"He's found you one. Look."

The farmer was standing by a magnificent, solitary larch; eighty-foot-tall and arrow-straight down to the point where its trunk arched slightly allowing the roots to plunge deep into the flanks of the valley.

"I don't understand. Why here? Why not a perfectly straight one?"

"You tell him. You're the expert."

"You're building a coble, right? Like my dad?"

"I'm going to try to. Maybe with your help. That's the plan. Yes."

"The planks on the side of those boats are curved between the bow and the stern. They start high, they dip in the middle and then they rise again."

Seymour reached out his hand and ran it down the gluey flanks of the tree.

"So, you need a slightly bent one?"

"Exactly."

"And there's enough wood on this for an entire boat?"

"Two probably," said Rehab. "Happy?"

"Delirious," beamed Seymour.

The next time he saw it, the tree would have been transformed. Overnight, it would be felled, stripped of its horizontal branches, and sliced into planks by an enormous circular saw. For a few weeks, the timbers would rest. Soon after that (and perilously close to Christmas) they'd be turning up at his house on a lorry.

"I can't believe how thin he'll cut it," pondered Seymour as they drove home. "Half an inch or so? That's nothing."

"Most cobles were launched and sailed off the beach. By two fellas. Three at most. They had to be light," said Rehab, who was using both hands to wrestle the van out of second gear. "Getting cold feet?"

"I've always had cold feet."

"I'd turn the heater on," grinned the captain. "Only that doesn't work either."

It was a slow drive back to the coast. A sea fret had worked its way inland, dragging a thick mist across the hilltop roads. As darkness swallowed them (and Rehab's inner compass malfunctioned) the two men peered hopefully into the murk for signposts.

"These lights are useless. Where are we?"

"Dynamo's kaput, I'm afraid. No idea."

After that, the two men sat in silence as the road descended towards the orange glow of their town. Apart from a few late taxis, the streets were midweek quiet. Outside the Winter Gardens Bingo Hall there was a thrum of folk waiting for the last bus. Winter Gardens was about right, thought Seymour. The summer honeypots selling rock and plastic buckets had been boarded up for weeks and their owners had long cleared off to Spain with the swallows.

Through the frosted windows of The White Horse, Seymour could make out the blurred shapes of figures standing at the bar. It looked quiet in there, too. For a few weeks after the dominoes, the place had been turned upside down; a lock-in every night and a blind eye from the local constabulary. Or so he'd been told.

At Nellie's request, he'd made a glass-fronted wooden cabinet for the cup, along with a picture frame for one of Frank's snaps of the victorious team. There in the middle of it was Rehab holding a double six in one hand and the remains of a child's abacus in the other. It had been a good night, thought Seymour, a great night. But there hadn't been many since.

"Not seen you in the boozer much recently," said Rehab. The van had limped to Seymour's home and was parked under a yellow streetlight.

"No. I've….err….I'll get down there soon. Not sure why really."

"Annual Christmas fishing trip? Can't miss that."

"I'll do my best."

"New doms season starting shortly, too."

"Not for me, I'm afraid. I'm bowing out on a high."

"Really? We'll die without you."

"Six times three? Quickly. Come on."

"Nine?"

"You'll be absolutely fine. And thanks for today. I owe you."

Outside his back door, Seymour hesitated, key in hand. It had been a tumultuous few months and the summer felt like a dreadfully long time ago. In the moonlight, he could see the gleaming new padlock on his shed. Hidden inside – in a bag under the sink – were the remains of his accordion.

Nothing had ever been said about what happened.

Just a few years before, during a brief obsession with Benny Goodman, he'd acquired a cheap clarinet from Clinkers' shop only to find it smashed into useless pieces less than a month later. Then, as now, he'd assumed Lucy had simply snapped. Then, as now, there was no profit to be had from an inquest. If it was a phase, they'd get through it together. If it was more than that – if, as he sometimes wondered, it was an illness – well, he loved her whatever.

In any case, there was no going back to The Burlingtonian.

Thanks to Rehab's lighter (and the subsequent findings of a safety team) Harry Spanners was looking at a repair bill of £2,000. Short of a miracle, the scrap dealers were circling and Seymour's beloved Gabbanelli would be staying under the sink; in a thousand pieces, its fate never to be discussed. And in the meantime – until the wood arrived – some sort of life had to stumble forwards.

"I don't like the way we speak."

Lucy had made the declaration one evening, a few weeks before Seymour's secret trip to source his wood. Now that the summer was in retreat, she'd decided to work mornings in the shoe shop and spend the afternoons in bed. By September, Seymour thought the routine was really suiting her. Although still frail, her energy levels were up, and she was finally putting back a little weight.

"We sound common; coarse. I want us to be better. The accent in this town is rubbing off on our son."

"I've got a name," grunted Isaac. Despite his protests, Lucy was still serving reheated pork pies every Friday. "Most people have fish and chips for tea at the end of the week. Why can't we?"

"That's exactly what I mean. It's sepper not tea. Just like it's lench not dinner."

139

"Lench? Sepper? Dad. What's she on about?"

"Vowels. It's our vowels. Lench not lunch. Sepper not supper. Gep not gap."

Seymour raised his eyebrows doubtfully. For three nights running, he'd stayed up late putting the finishing touches to a new kite, made entirely of plastic and judging by the trees outside, the wind was building nicely.

"I thought I might go for a walk after tea if that's alright."

"Sepper," sighed Lucy. "And just so you both know…."

"What?" said Isaac, pushing a half-eaten pie to one side of his plate.

"I've signed up for elocution lessons. In fact, I've been to two already."

Seymour had known they were happening. For weeks, his own newspaper had been carrying adverts for classes at the town library. 'Learn To Speak Like A Royal' was the promise. Ten weekly sessions for an accent like Alvar Liddell's at the BBC.

Around the office, they'd even joked about them, conducting their tea break banter in regal tones until Mr Latheron (who was regal enough without tuition) put a stop to it. "Bad form, chaps," he'd informed the staff in a handwritten memo. "Cease forthwith."

Seymour looked again at the bending branches. It had been months – maybe years – since Lucy had been so, well, positive. Recently she'd bought two new dresses and was wearing a little make-up again. For the first time since the ill-fated launch, they'd even had sex; so rumbustiously in fact, that Isaac had refused to look at them for a week. And yet he still couldn't escape the feeling that everything she did or said now was a rejection.

"You don't have an accent, love," he said. "Neither do your parents. You've got a lovely voice."

"I sound northern. We all do. Listen to the radio. No-one sounds like us."

"If you ask me, it's pretentious," whispered Seymour.

"Dad's right," smirked Isaac. "It's a load of crep."

"Just because your father can't change, doesn't mean the rest of us are stuck."

"I'm not stuck. I'm me," said Seymour. But by then Lucy was gone, sending Isaac's plate skittering across the floor in a furious parting gesture.

Later he could never be certain how much that conversation had shifted things. After she'd decamped, he slipped out with his new kite, reaching the south shore with a half-hour's light still left in the day. Even if the damned thing didn't fly, the ozone would clear his head.

The cruising lights of a tanker were sparkling on the horizon. Two red orbs to the left of a green one. Starboard side showing. Whatever the thing was carrying, it was heading south. Seymour smiled proudly to himself. Somehow over the years, he'd taught himself all the international signs of the sea.

From its signature flash, he could calculate where and how far away any lighthouse was. From the sound of its horn he knew if a fogbound ship was in trouble or just warning you off. If anything honked, moved or blinked on the water, Seymour could tell its story just as clearly as the books piled high on Lucy's bedside table. None of his tales were novels, admittedly. But that didn't mean he was stuck. Not a bit of it.

Three hundred feet above his head, Seymour's plastic kite was struggling. As the wind strengthened, the material had become stretched, allowing one of its two cross-pieces to slip free. Between his fingers, he could feel the energy drain from the line as the crumpled bundle dropped into the sea. Brushing the rain from his face, he felt in his pocket for a penknife and sliced the cord.

The tanker's lights were gone, but the unfamiliar tug of anger he'd felt since his accordion's brutal death hadn't quite disappeared. Just lately there'd been a lot of bruising indignities. But this one was different. This one had really hurt.

Somewhere in the dark, the waves would be eating his kite. With a last glance in its direction, Seymour headed home through empty streets, slowing only to peer briefly through the darkened windows of the lifeboat station. Across the street, a lone drunk was emptying his bladder against a parked scooter.

"What yer lookin at pal?" he bellowed. "Do I owe you owt or summat?"

"You need elocution lessons," replied Seymour. "You could go with my wife."

"Go fook yerself, you dozy pillock." The drunk looked sadly down at the pavement. "Bollocks, I've pissed in mi shoes."

Seymour moved on. It wasn't his nature to be gloomy and he'd been lifted by the colour in Lucy's cheeks. Maybe things really were on the up again. Even the fire on The Burlingtonian had delivered an unexpectedly welcome postscript. At the end of September, he'd been called into the editor's office. It was 11.25am and a full afternoon card of racing was scheduled at Thirsk.

"Pilbeam, my boy. Pilbeam. Our local hero. This won't take long."

Seymour couldn't detach his gaze from Mr. Latheron's claret-coloured nose. One red light, he thought. A dinghy moving under power at night.

"You're smiling, Pilbeam. Good show. Happy in your lot. That's the ticket. How can I help? Quick snifter, perhaps?"

"You wanted a natter?"

142

"Ah yes, yes. Quite so." The editor's left eye was following the big hand on a wall clock. "Now you know the ethos here, Pilbeam. Strictly no barriers. Came here as a handyman? Graduated onto the sub's table? Correct?"

"Correct."

"Saved all those bally lives, eh?"

"It wasn't really like that."

"So how do you fancy a spot of writing? Eh? Eh? Nothing grand. I was thinking a weekly diary. Bits of local nonsense. Giant marrows. That sort of caper. Thought we'd call it 'Pilbeam's People'. What do you say? Yes? Yes. Of course, it's a yes. Good show. Must dash. Up school."

The following week, Seymour's debut column had appeared in the town's weekly newspaper. There was no fanfare and the writing was as solidly unmemorable as the subject matter; just a handful of routine plugs for local events alongside a personal plea to the readers for more interesting material.

"Got something unusual to share?" he'd written. "Then you too could be one of Pilbeam's People!"

The first contribution had arrived the next day; a potato crisp with a 'face' of the Madonna on one side. Seymour's heart soared. 'Pilbeam's People' wasn't going to change the world but the extra £2 a week might just change his. And even better still, it would get him out of the office.

"To be honest, I thought that spud face looked more like Sandie Shaw ...."

Soon after the fire, Seymour had resumed his lunchtime excursions to 'Harry's Chandlery.Est.1922', where – from the depths of his filthy armchair – the proprietor, Harry Spanners was reviewing the contents of his friend's first scoop.

"……. or maybe the Queen Mother."

Seymour was looking again at the enormous pulleys suspended from the ceiling.

"How much do you need to get The Burlingtonian ship-shape?"

"That's never going to happen. Two grand. Maybe more," sighed Harry. "Anyway, I've had an offer from a breaker."

"You can't do that. It's part of the town. In summer, it IS the bloody town." Seymour squatted on a low stool, resting his back against a shelf tottering with antique sailing books. "What if I used my column to back some sort of a fund-raising effort?"

"Sounds interesting. Go on." Harry's wheel-shaped face widened.

"I don't know yet. Something sponsored, maybe."

"You ever read this?"

Harry had pulled a mildewed hard-back from the shelf, just a few dozen pages long. The print was tiny, and the pages were rimed with damp. "The Coble; Britain's Forgotten Boat" There was even an author's signature and a date on the frontispiece. 'Harold Garbutt – 1885'.

"Garbutt? Your grandfather?" said Seymour. For an unsettling moment, he'd forgotten that 'Spanners' wasn't actually the family name.

"He built cobles. Just like Rehab's old man. He wrote that book. You know what a coble is?"

"Of course I do."

"Have you ever sailed in one?

Seymour shook his head. All his friends knew about the obsession. None of them knew how catastrophically inexperienced he was; and that practically everything he knew about sailing had come from

144

books. Or the side of a boating pool.

"Would you like to? Today? Now?"

Things moved very quickly after he said yes. Within a few minutes, he was pulling on waterproof overalls and wellington boots. Within an hour he was climbing down a greasy metal ladder on the harbour wall and stepping into the well of Harry's boat. Even before it had moved, Seymour felt himself on the brink of tears.

Everything about it was so beautiful. Along the flanks, its overlapping side planks glowed with fresh varnish. Around its deep and broad belly, the gunwales rose so elegantly they seemed to kiss where they joined to form the hard edge of the bow. Inside the hull, Harry had painted the timbers orange. There was virtually no metal; no plastic; no fibre glass, and the wood felt warm to Seymour's touch.

"It's beautiful," he said, stroking the curvature of its solid pine mast.

"We haven't got long. An hour before the tide drains the harbour."

There was a damp flurry of hemp as Harry hoisted the musty brown mainsail and waited for the wind to pull it into shape. Seymour looked up to see how the head of the sail was bound to the yard arm; and how the yard itself was slung to the mast allowing it to pivot with the wind. To his amazement, he knew all the terminology. Everything he'd ever read had stuck.

"Just do what I say."

Seymour lowered himself onto a thwart in the centre of the boat. Although the harbour was autumn-quiet, the light was poor, and in the open sea beyond the twin piers, white tops were showing on the swell. Despite his weak leg, however, Spanners was a man transformed.

With the tiller in one hand he felt the flow of the tide. Through the rope connected to the corner of the sail, he felt every twitching surge of the wind. It was as if his body had been tuned directly into the elements, allowing information to flow up one arm and down through the other.

Nothing he did was rushed. Everything he did was calm. There was no yanking or heaving, no drama. Harry's mastery, thought Seymour, was virtually invisible; something felt, not taught; something which alchemised delicacy into power, and grace into speed; something which, in that moment, Seymour knew he'd been looking for all his life.

"I'm going to shake the jib out. You alright to steer?"

Without hesitating, Seymour shuffled back and grasped the tiller. Behind them lay a broad white wake, and beyond that the harbour walls, already a half-mile away. When the bow rose and sliced through a wave, the boat shuddered. In the smooth troughs between, it seemed to gurgle with delight.

As Seymour watched, Harry attached the jib sail to the outward end of the bowsprit, jutting out from the front like a horizontal mast. It was ochre brown like the mainsail, but less than half its size.

"I'll take the tiller again, now. You pull it up. This could get tasty."

With both sails secured, the coble surged smoothly forwards in an explosion of spray.

"You're enjoying this aren't you?"

"It's beyond brilliant," said Seymour. His hair was thick with salt.

"We'd better head back or else we'll be stuck out here."

The wind had dropped anyway, and streetlights were coming on all over the broad clump of the town. Behind them, the two men could hear a trawler racing home to beat the tide. In the swirl of its wake, the coble corkscrewed angrily, narrowly missing the harbour wall as Harry nursed it safely back onto its mooring.

"Thank you. Thank you," said Seymour. The two men were carefully shaking out the sails and packing them away under the gunwales. "I can't believe how fast they go."

"They used to race them. From here right up the coast and back. Fifty mile or so."

"Not anymore?"

"Not for years. There's only forty or so sailing cobles left." Harry looked over at the trawler which had passed them. A forklift truck stacked with boxes was parked alongside it. "None of them are working boats."

"How difficult would be to resurrect that coble race?"

"Very difficult I should think. Why would we?"

"Because we could get it sponsored? Raise some cash? Save your tub?"

Harry had heaved himself up the ladder. The last of the tide was slurping away, revealing (amongst other things) the porcelain bowl of an abandoned toilet.

"That's not a bad idea," said Spanners.

"Could we do it?" Seymour's eyes were sparkling.

"I'm certain we could. Me and you could be a team."

"No need, Harry."

"What? You going to buy one then?"

"No, Harry. I'm going to build one."

It was almost exactly three weeks later that Seymour and Captain Rehab found themselves standing by a larch tree with a farmer and two ancient dogs. And it was four weeks after that, the wood was delivered to Seymour's home when he was out…

….and when Lucy was in.

Chapter Two

"Mr Pilbeam not in?"

There was a tall grey-haired man at the back door, speaking a sort of rustic twang. From the expression on his wind-tanned face, he'd clearly not been expecting a woman; and certainly not one in a half-open dressing gown.

"Mr. Pilbeam?" he stammered. "Oi've got his wood?"

Lucy peered around the stranger's back to where a skeletal, and similarly weather-beaten, youth was ferrying long strips of pale timber into their yard from the back of a truck. Rain was falling hard out of a filthy black sky. As he traipsed back and forth, two pensionable sheepdogs followed his every step.

"It's Mr. Pilbeam I want," said the old man, lifting the peak of his cap to reach an itch on his forehead.

"Yes. I've got that. I'm Mrs Pilbeam."

Now it was the tall man's turn to look beyond Lucy, as if his quarry might be concealed somewhere in the folds of her nightwear. From a distance, they appeared to be engaged in a strange and silent country dance.

"Do either of you have names?" she added.

The woodman's eyes returned to meet hers. Behind him, the last plank had been unloaded, and the youth was slinging a sheet of tarpaulin across the pile.

"No-one's ever asked us that before," he said. There was a dirty roar from the truck. Hunching his jacket over his head, the old man turned and hobbled towards it.

"Nice tits by the way," he yelled. The words were almost lost in the thickening rain. "Lucky fella that Pilbeam, wherever he is."

"Yokels," muttered Lucy, belatedly tightening her waistband.

As the lorry bounced away through the puddles, there were two loud explosions from its exhaust. Lucy looked thoughtfully across at the pile of wood, before heading quickly back to her bedroom. She was late, and she hated people who were late.

Thirty minutes on, she was striding across town, half-hidden by a giant umbrella. Since the summer, with every passing week, she'd felt a little stronger. Even Eunice, her manageress, had noticed. "You've got some of your bounce back, luv" she'd quipped. "Seymour must be hitting the spot."

Against her skin, she could feel the dangerous silk of new underwear. Although she rarely wasted her lonely afternoons in bed, Eunice hadn't been wrong. It had been fun reacquainting herself with the occupant of Seymour's Y-fronts. Sex was sex, after all, and (supposedly) they were living in the Age of Aquarius; if that actually applied when you were over forty-years-old, working in a seaside shoe shop and married to a man with a train set.

Eunice was certainly getting her fill. According to her daily gynaecological bulletins, Frank's 'thing' had to be the biggest in the town, and far away the largest specimen of her various husbands. "I've got a photograph if you're interested," she'd revealed the previous day. "Frank says he exposed it himself."

"I bet he did," said Lucy.

"And I should add," concluded Eunice, "There aren't that many 'things' in this dump I haven't seen."

Lucy giggled aloud at the memory and pressed on. If anything, the rain was pounding harder and ragged brown lakes were gathering in the potholes. When she passed the bus station, two double deckers lurched out together, clattering filthy water across the pavement. Apart from their drivers, both were completely empty.

As the buses swept by, she noticed a large crowd gathering outside the Spiritualist Union chapel for an afternoon of clairvoyance, old women, mostly. The town was full of ageing women; widows of sailors worn away by the sea. Or wives left behind when their husbands decamped to the pub and never came back. Lucy pitied them all.

Her mother was dead right. It was a man's town in a man's world.

At the end of the main promenade, she forked right under the shadow of a Victorian spire. Ahead, she could see the ugly bulk of the Titanic Hotel, fitted out – it was said locally – by the same design team as the doomed ship. Inside were two hundred cobwebbed bedrooms towering above a glittering labyrinth of chandeliered public spaces.

In summer, it stayed afloat thanks to the venerable few who liked their deckchairs warped and their soup the wrong side of hot. In the winter, a skeleton staff cranked up the tank-sized boiler and prayed for a miracle. Rather like its namesake, everyone knew the hotel was going down. With just a little luck, however, the skeletons would all get off before it sank.

Walking past its mole-ruined croquet lawn, Lucy climbed a wide stone staircase and entered the lobby through a revolving door. To her right was an immense, vaulted (and empty) dining room blazing with light. To her left, flanked by smoke-stained murals, polished double doors led into a mirrored lounge bar. There were no staff anywhere that she could see; just a lone figure hunched over an open fireplace set with balled newspaper and kindling.

"Stan?"

There was a grating sound and the flash of a match. Smoke began to curl around the wood, and a few sparks of coal dust crackled in the strengthening flame.

"All our local rag is fit for, I'm afraid," he said, rising to his feet. He was wearing American jeans (lightly faded at the knee), a white cotton shirt and woollen sports jacket. His shoes were pointed toe and light tan, Italian.

"Don't let Seymour hear that. He loves it."

"Really good to see you again."

The pair embraced and pecked each other lightly on the cheek. With his hand on her elbow, Stan led Lucy to a round table by the fire where a bottle of Taittinger was chilling in a silver bucket.

"It's cold enough in here already. I'm not sure we'll need the ice."

"It's your favourite though, yes?"

"It is now." Lucy took a sip, feeling her lipstick cling to the rim. "I'd have been happy with a snowball a few months ago."

It was their third meeting since the blaze on the boat. Each had taken place at the same hotel; twice in this same bar, and once (when there was still some summer heat left in the day) out on the overgrown terrace, hidden deep within the rambling shrubs of its borders.

From there, they'd been able to hear the ocean but not see it. And without asking, he'd ordered champagne, handing her the cork as a souvenir which she had secretly dated and kept.

"Eunice and Frank are getting married," she said.

"Frank? Do I know him?"

"Works for 'Snaps'? Orange blazer? Pictures ready at 9?"

"Ah yes. Frank," remembered Stan. "Brains of a cormorant."

151

Lucy laughed awkwardly. Conversations between them often started slowly like this. There was a squeaking sound from the bar, where a barman with long fingers was drying a wine glass.

"Everything alright with the champagne, Mr.Clough?" he asked. "Will you be requiring anything to eat?"

"Yes, and no," replied Stan. "And thank you. That will be all."

Most of the staff seemed to know who he was. The entire place seemed more like a home to him than a hotel and she didn't doubt that he was intimate with its sleeping quarters. Even if a fraction of the tales were true, she was consorting with a man for whom female company was a drug, in a dying hotel with virtually no witnesses.

And yet not once, in several hours alone, had there been any hint of impropriety. Whatever his agenda truly was, sex didn't appear to be on it, and the purpose of their meetings remained a mystery. Stan seemed authentically happy just to talk. Lucy, for her part, was consumed with curiosity for a man unlike anyone she'd ever met; a situation complicated by the fact that she'd met virtually none and slept with just one.

So far, she'd reached just one certain conclusion. Both of them appeared desperately lonely. And whilst it didn't quite explain her make-up (or artfully chosen knickers) what could the harm be in a little innocent fizz and chat; especially when nothing appeared to be deemed off limits.

"Do you mind me asking what happened to your wife?"

Lucy had put that question during their first rendezvous – outside in the hotel's garden – prompting an exaggerated intake of breath.

"Which one?"

"I didn't know there'd been two. Or is it more than two?"

"Just two," said Stan. "And I don't mind at all."

On the other side of a trimmed yew barrier, a lawn mower coughed into life. The gardener's hat appeared to be moving independently along the top of the hedge.

"The first time we were both very young. I was still at university. By the time I graduated we'd both changed. We were different people so we shook hands and called it a day. We're still good friends, by the way."

"And number two?"

"She walked out on me two years ago."

"Stan. I'm really sorry."

"We'd been married fifteen years. We've got Alice. We share Alice." Stan's voice had dropped to a whisper. "Turned out she was having an affair with my financial adviser."

"You didn't suspect?"

"She told me one day and left home the next."

"No chance of her coming back?"

"I don't want her back."

After that, the floodgates had opened; and the more they talked, the more they found to talk about. Stan had left home at eighteen, he claimed, with no intention of returning. By the time he was 21, he'd acquired an ex-wife and a first class honours degree in English; he'd also written two unpublished novels; and (somewhere along the way) discarded any trace of the accent he'd carried away with him from the seaside.

"I hated every brick of this place when I left. I hated the sound of it in my voice when I spoke."

"There's nothing wrong with it now," Lucy had told him, "I'd love to read those books some time."

153

"That's sweet, but they're really very poor. Back then everyone thought they were D.H.Lawrence. Randy old fraud that he was."

"Why did you come back?" Lucy was blushing.

"My father had drowned. I didn't really have any choice."

She remembered the funeral. Everyone remembered the funeral. Stan's father had died at sea and his body had never been found. When the cortege crept through the town, people were bowing to the empty coffin of a hero who'd sailed his lifeboat into a hurricane. They were also sneaking a look at the tall young heir dressed in black walking slowly behind the hearse holding a wreath of orange, white and blue.

"Nobody was quite sure who you were," explained Lucy. "You could have disappeared again after the service."

"I couldn't. Not really. I'd been doing supply at a boy's boarding school. I'd even been cutting hair again. We were broke. We had a daughter. We weren't terribly happy. And there was my dad's business."

"You could have sold it."

"That didn't feel like a choice. Anyway, I'd popped back occasionally over the years. I'd worked in his salons; got my bloody hairdressing certificates. And I didn't hate the place like I once did. It sort of crept up on me to the point where I actually quite liked it."

"And now you're on your own."

"And now I'm on my own," laughed Stan, raising his champagne. "And very, very rich."

After that first meeting, Lucy had walked home in a daze. After their second, she'd signed up for elocution lessons and retrieved the Littlewoods catalogue from beneath Isaac's bed. Suddenly, her son wasn't the only person in their house interested in the latest women's underwear.

Alongside Stan, she felt shabby and old-fashioned; inside and out. The man's company was like a blast of awakening wind. He'd travelled, he read books, he could cook, and he listened. That was the best thing, she realised. He listened. So wherever this was going – even if it was a bedroom somewhere – she was absolutely determined to go with it.

There was a dull clump from the fire. A piece of smouldering wood had rolled out onto the hearth. Beneath the deep bay window of the bar, a dark stain was advancing across the anaglypta where rain had broken through a rotten sash. Somewhere, a bell rang five times and a young girl in black slipped in to draw three sets of crimson curtains.

"I'll have to go pretty soon," said Lucy. The champagne had all gone, and she felt strangely weary. "They'll be wondering where I am."

"Seymour doesn't know?"

The girl had left the room without looking at them. A few minutes later, the barman returned with one large brandy.

"There's no rush for me, I'm afraid," said Stan. "Sure you don't want one?"

"Absolutely sure. Thanks. And no, I haven't told him. He's not your biggest fan."

"God, yes. The boat? Am I forgiven?"

"Beating you at dominoes helped, I think."

"He didn't beat me." Stan had stood up to warm his back against the fire. "I felt sorry for him. I let him win."

"That's not true."

"I'm afraid it is."

A snake of anger turned in Lucy's belly. She'd loathed Seymour that night; stinking of beer and his shoes splattered with who knows what. But a week later, when he'd shown her the cabinet he'd made, there was such simple pride in his face that she'd wilted. It wasn't a bad thing that he'd done. He didn't do bad things. Not really. But knowing this – if it was true – would destroy him.

"Could someone get my coat?"

On the hotel steps, the couple hesitated under Lucy's umbrella. It was dark, the building had no outside lights, and the rain was coming harder, pushed off the sea by a raw north-westerly wind.

"Will we do it again?" asked Stan.

"Of course. I hope so. But with Christmas and everything, it might be a while."

"That's fine. I'll pop into the shop some time."

There was another vicious squall of wind. Lucy tipped her brolly towards it for cover. An arm had curled around her waist, and a record player somewhere was pumping out Glenn Miller.

"I do remember, you know" said Stan, quietly. Lucy released herself and looked at him. "We got close once before."

"I don't think so."

"I cut your boy's hair. You were wearing a blue dress. I'm certain."

"It must have been someone else."

"With polka dots?"

Lucy's legs felt heavy. She could feel the warmth of his hand through her coat.

"I'm flattered. I always assumed I was one of many."

"You were."

"Look. I really do need to go."

"But you're not now."

There'd been an awkward kiss and Lucy was gone. When she arrived home, she was carrying sausage, eggs and potatoes, but had no memory of being in a shop. She felt dirty and numb and nothing seemed quite so clear any more.

She'd have done anything with him; absolutely anything. But there was something in his well-rehearsed calm – or his control – which blighted the picture; and that story about the dominoes…Lucy shivered in the dark shadows of their yard. Black lagoons of rain were pooling in the tarpaulin around Seymour's wood.

Through the window she could see her husband sitting alone at the kitchen table. Something must have distracted him. He'd looked up and laughed and Isaac had joined him with two cups of tea. Lucy felt herself shrivel in the cold. It was past six o-clock. She was late. She collapsed her umbrella and went in.

"Look at you. You're soaked. Where've you been?"

A half-dismantled piece of machinery lay in bits across the table. Seymour's ancient toolbox sat on the Formica top of the sideboard.

"Just some stocktaking with Eunice. I've bought you some tea." She held up a shopping bag.

"Not tea. Sepper," said Isaac. Lucy could feel herself smiling.

"And we've eaten," added Seymour. "Chips."

"With gravy."

"Listen love, we need to talk. Get that coat off. I think you'd better sit down."

Somehow, they knew. They knew. All she wanted was her bed and her books but there was no escape. Seymour had folded his arms across his chest and was watching her slip out of her wet shoes. There was a mole wrench on a chair and a bottle of white spirit in the sink.

"I'll make you a cuppa," said Isaac. "Sorry. A ceppa."

"What is it? What's going on?"

Seymour pushed an envelope across the table.

"You'd better read this."

For a few moments, the only sounds were the distant tones of the Home Service and the hiss of the kettle. Lucy put down the letter, looked up and met Seymour's sad eyes, allowing her own tears (of relief) to join the ones flowing down his face.

"When's the funeral," she said quietly.

Seymour's father was buried three days later in a Pennine graveyard choked with unloved headstones. Only five mourners braved the sleet to bid him farewell; Seymour, Isaac, the cleaner who'd found the corpse and sent the letter, alongside the last two relics of Mr.Pilbeam Senior's all-male outings to the rugby.

Lucy had stayed away. There'd been no arguments. She'd never made any secret of her views. Seymour's father had ceased to exist years before and his passing made no impact on her contempt. What was it he'd said? "Something to put in your mouth". He'd been a dirty, dark little man whose dirty, dark and lonely little life had ended in front of a crackling television set two weeks before anybody noticed.

She'd never stopped Seymour meeting him once a year at a pub somewhere (usually with Isaac in tow); just so long as nobody expected her to like him. Or care about him. Anything else ran the risk of exposing her to the dreadful thing that Seymour himself might become.

After the shock of the letter – and the confusion stirred by her afternoon with Stan Clough – Lucy had relapsed; disappearing back into her bedroom, with a note dispatched to Eunice blaming family tragedy for the need to take a break from duties. The funeral was out of the question. And the prospect of clearing out her dead father-in-law's house had made her physically sick.

"Don't bring a single thing back here. Not a teaspoon. Understand?" Lucy's voice had boomed downstairs from the dark of her sanctuary.

"We won't," replied Seymour. "You're absolutely sure you don't want to come?"

They'd given her a minute and then driven (without her) in silence to the funeral. There'd been no wake; just a few flimsy handshakes and a cheque for the undertaker; an unshaven fellow with a Midlands accent who'd delivered the coffin to the graveside in the back of a hired white transit van.

"A little respect would have been appreciated," said Seymour.

"Didn't know the fella," said the undertaker, who seemed satisfied by the contents of his envelope.

"Isn't that normally the case in your line of work?"

"S'pose. Cheers for the dosh."

"And don't you have a hearse?"

"Failed its MOT last night."

With a careless shrug, he'd disappeared with his money. What the hell did it matter anyway, mused Seymour? His father was lying in the oak coffin he'd built for himself forty years before; everyone had been paid and the cleaner who'd found the corpse had buggered off to catch her bus.

"That undertaker was wearing sandals, dad."

"Yes. I know. Just don't tell your mother."

There was a catch in Seymour's voice. The streetlights had come on drenching the gravestones in a weak orange glow.

"Are you OK? Are you crying?"

"He was my dad, Isaac. Crying's allowed. Just don't tell your mother."

By the time they reached the house, the town was deserted. Apart from a few early Friday night revellers, everyone was still washing away the week's work. Along both sides of his father's terraced street, every window looked dead.

"Jesus. This is spooky. Where is everybody?"

"The front rooms are for best," smiled Seymour. "That's why they're dark."

"What if it's completely dark in your dad's old place?"

"It will be. I've bought torches."

There were two steps up to the door. Above it was a glass panel engraved with the number one. Below that was a torn flier for a local Chinese restaurant flapping in the letterbox. Isaac pulled it free and slid a key in the lock, pushing hard against a mountain of old newspapers and bills. As it opened, a cat screamed out followed by a gust of rotten air.

"I'd forgotten about the cat," said Seymour, shining his torch into the tiled hallway. "That's probably what smells."

It had been years since he'd been inside. Not much had changed. The prevailing décor was still brown, and, in every room, the utility furniture stood where it had always stood, guarded by mantelpiece clocks that hadn't been wound since Seymour was a boy. Perhaps the sediment lay a little deeper; and maybe the door handles felt a little stickier, but it was still his house.

160

"You lived here? As a kid? Creepy."

"We had electricity then," said Seymour. "Most of the time."

Isaac was looking into the front room. A sofa and two armchairs were stationed around an Axminster rug. Inside a glass-fronted mahogany cabinet, three shelves were laden with Edward VIII Coronation memorabilia. Everything was clean, pristine and dust-free. Like a time capsule.

"We never went in that room much. Not after my mother was hit by the tram. The door was always shut."

At the bottom of the stairs, Seymour directed his torch towards the two doors on the tiny landing. Behind the one on the left was his parent's room; behind the other, his own. The toilet had been in the back yard. The only sink had been in the kitchen, at one end of a bleached, wooden draining board.

"Are you going up?"

Seymour shook his head. He'd seen enough already. There was nothing here for him. The smell was intolerable, and it wasn't just the cat. In the back room where his father had lived (and died) someone had thoughtfully removed the armchair revealing an ugly black stain on the carpet between the four indentations of its legs. Alongside the vacated space was a pile of old Radio Times magazines. Isaac had picked the top one up.

"Looks like he died watching snooker," he said. "What are we going to do?"

"House clearance? It's all junk."

"That's cruel. There must be something you want."

Seymour was looking intently out of the back-parlour window. Coffins hadn't made his father rich, but he'd never gone short. When a wartime bomb destroyed a neighbouring slum, Mr. Pilbeam

Snr had quietly bought the land but done nothing with it. So far as he knew, it was festering out there now, beyond the cluster of dismal brick sheds and the knot of dead brambles that hid the old workshop. A thick carpet of ivy had swallowed the entire building. Two rusty skylights were the only trace of it he could see.

"You might be right Isaac. Let's get some fresh air."

The scullery door was unlocked. Seymour was already through it. In the yard, he'd found a broken broom handle and was beating a path up through the weeds.

"Hang on, dad. Calm down. When did your dad last use it?"

"I've been thinking about that." Seymour was panting hard. He and Isaac had reached a green wall of wilting nettles. Behind it was the old door. "He packed in work ten years ago. Nobody will have been in since then."

"Listen. Why did mum hate him so much?"

"That's a horrible question." Seymour had started to tear at the thorny vegetation. "I don't know that she did. I don't think she ever knew him."

"Why then?"

"Maybe she didn't want me to turn out like he did."

"Which was what?"

"He liked his rugby, his beer, his darts; didn't have much time for me. Or for my mum while she was well. He was a simple, uneducated man. Not a bad man. That's just the way it was, then."

"And have you? Turned out like him?"

Seymour stopped and examined his bloodied hands. He thought of his brutalised accordion and his pile of seasoned larch. He thought of warm sausage rolls, Nellie's beer, and a coble surging past a breakwater.

"No. I don't believe I have. What do you think?"

"What I think doesn't matter. Not if she thinks you have."

"Yes, you matter. And I love her, Isaac. But I love her for what she is. Not for what she might be. Always have. Always will. Now come on. Let's take a look in here."

It was the sweet fragrance of pine which shook him the most. Every surface lay deep in its golden dust and their feet moved noiselessly through the sediment of ancient shavings. At one end, where a stack of shelves had collapsed, orange jewels of treacly sap blinked at them from a confusion of fallen timbers. At the other, three lidless coffins, powdery with grey cobwebs, stood side by side like giant Russian dolls.

"Hey dad. Is this yours?"

Isaac had pulled an old sailor's chest from beneath a workbench cluttered with pots and bottles and boxes heaped with rusty screws. The words 'Seymour's Stuff' had been neatly stencilled on the lid in white paint.

"Not that I know of."

Their two torches flashed inside together, as Isaac lifted the lid.

"Buried treasure. Brilliant."

At the top, there were four completed toy boats, and three half-finished ones. Further down, there were two kites, a box of beautifully painted toy soldiers, and a half-dozen scrapbooks carefully wrapped in a Welsh flag.

"I didn't put them here," said Seymour, "I'd no idea."

"They're full of pictures of boats. Hundreds of pictures of boats."

Isaac was flicking through the scrapbooks. Every page had been covered by photographs cut from newspapers and magazines. Pictures of legendary ships like Cutty Sark and the Golden Hind; pictures of family yachts and cutters, sloops and dinghies; brigantines and junks; each one dated and labelled in Seymour's cramped handwriting.

"My dad must have kept them. I really didn't know."

"He must have been more interested than you thought. Can I keep some of this?"

"Not even a teaspoon, remember?"

Seymour closed the lid and pushed it back under the bench. The boy had a toy yacht and a kite tucked under each arm.

"That wood back home in the yard?" said Isaac. "You're not seriously still thinking about building a boat. Please don't. Please let it drop."

But Seymour wasn't listening. Seymour had seen what was on the walls.

Chapter Three

"Is it alright if I have that calendar?"

Shortly after the funeral, Seymour had returned to his father's workshop with Frank. For several hours, the two men had stripped every tool from the racks which covered its damp-streaked walls.

The chisels alone had filled four fish boxes: the wood planes, another three. After that, they'd moved onto the saws. Tenon saws, rip saws, hack saws, coping saws and keyhole saws; followed by vices, mallets, hammers (claw, ball pein and cross pein), clamps, screwdrivers, drills, drill bits (masonry and wood), files, bradawls, squares, grinders and enough miscellaneous joinery to fill three hessian sacks.

"I feel like a grave robber," said Seymour, prising open a cabinet full of meticulously categorised brass screws.

"The calendar, Taff? What do you reckon?"

Pinned to the centre of a noticeboard, surrounded by curling receipts, was a photograph of a goose-pimpled Miss December 1958 clutching what appeared to be an enormous haggis. A blush-saving sash carrying the words 'Mike's Meats' had been carefully placed across the model's chest.

"It's ten years out of date, Frank. And it's horrible. Truly horrible"

"October's even better. See. Have a look. Bloody hell. Weird."

Frank had taken down the mildew-spotted calendar and was scrutinising every one of its twelve photographs; each of which featured a nude female festooned in offal.

"Take it, Frank. Please."

"Cheers, Taff. Eunice will totally love this."

Somehow, Seymour doubted it, but it didn't matter. With darkness falling, the two men heaved the last consignment of tools onto the back seat of Seymour's Austin 1100. An unearthly groan was followed by the clank of a silencer parting company with its mounting. Every cloud, thought Seymour. At least this way, Frank's prattle would be inaudible.

There was time for one last look around. Apart from a few pots of linseed oil and glue, they'd stripped the place. All that remained of substance were the unclaimed coffins and a chest marked 'Seymour's Stuff', and in a few months' time they too would be disappearing along with the rest of his father's old street; condemned, flattened and worthless; no longer considered fit for habitation.

"What about that chest?" asked Frank, briefly tearing his eyes from Miss October's.

"No room," said Seymour, tugging the car door shut.

It had been a relief to drive back without talking; or listening. With Christmas fast approaching, the roads had taken an icy turn and his threadbare tyres necessitated intense concentration. Across the Wolds, lines of early snow lay in the ploughed welts of the fields, and a few lost flakes danced in the cone of his headlights.

Lots of things seemed to be mutating, thought Seymour. Not just the weather. Over the years, he'd grown so attuned to Lucy's storms, he could watch them for days – and sometimes weeks – before they broke. Recently, however, they'd whipped up so suddenly, and with such ferocity, that he could no longer predict where they'd come from; or, more worryingly, when they'd end. And sometimes – to his much deeper mystification – the storms didn't come at all.

But there was something else. Seymour knew that he had changed, too. Perhaps it was the accordion, or his father's death, but a resistance movement was stirring. It wasn't that he wanted to hurt Lucy back. It was more the creeping realisation that nothing he craved was worthy of such ridicule; that nothing he did – or had ever done – was so wrong.

The larch had been an insane whim. When he'd seen the tree, he'd been overwhelmed and later, after the planks turned up at home, he'd wanted them to disappear. For days, he'd waited for Lucy to demand an explanation. But weeks passed and the timber had still not been mentioned; as if it wasn't there at all; rendered invisible behind the books and elocution lessons – and his wife's newfound preoccupation with her wardrobe.

Emboldened, he'd taken a midnight sledgehammer to the end of his outhouse and demolished an entire gable wall. With a few props, roof boards and plastic sheets he'd extended the building sufficiently to slide the timbers in out of the damp. Over a few days, without a single word from Lucy, he'd created a space big enough to build a boat in. All he was missing was the tools......but not anymore.

Two miles from the coast, Seymour saw the glow of the town and the distant flash of a lighthouse. Somewhere on the return journey, he'd lost the rest of his exhaust and Frank had dropped into a deep sleep. Winding down his window, Seymour felt the cold night on his face and reached in his jacket pocket for a pipe.

"Christ. It's freezing in here." Frank had stirred from his slumber. "What's that noise? What's that stink?"

"We've lost the silencer," shouted Seymour.

"You what? Can't hear."

"The silencer. We've lost it."

"Who was playing?"

"SILENCER. GONE. NOISE."

Frank shrugged and watched in awe as Seymour – using only his left hand – filled his pipe from a tin, tamped down the tobacco, and lit it first time with just one match.

"That's incredible. You didn't even let go of the wheel."

"And for my next trick," smiled Seymour, through a swirl of smoke. "Are you alright to walk back from mine?"

With one final shudder, the tool-laden car fell silent outside Seymour's house. A solo straggler was zig-zagging away from the club and the only clouds in a perfect night sky were coming from the gasworks.

"Listen, Taff. I think I've done something a bit stupid," whispered Frank.

"I'll try and act surprised," said Seymour.

"I gave Eunice a photograph of my todger."

"Just a bit stupid, you said."

"I'm frightened she's going to show it round town. Lucy hasn't seen it has she? At the shoe shop?"

"She's said nothing to me."

"Rehab? Spanners? They said anything? I'm dead if they see it."

"Not a word. Don't worry. What were you thinking?"

"I get dead bored in the winter. And I've got all those cameras."

Seymour could see a jet of steam emerging from the radiator of his car. Another problem to fix, he thought. Another mess in the kitchen sink.

"You going on the annual Christmas Eve fishing contest," asked Frank, brightening. "Only six days to go."

"I'm not sure. I'll be working till then, and I've got this to fix."

"Sod that. Course you are. It's only for a few hours. Quick pint after." Frank was struggling with his door. A wire coat hanger was protruding from the hole where the handle should have been. Seymour leaned across and tugged it.

"Thanks for today," he said. The door had sprung open. "And don't forget Miss October."

"No problems. See you on the 24th."

"And that photograph, Frank...."

"Shhhhhhh...."

"Let's hope Eunice doesn't feel the need for an enlargement."

"Fuck off, you Welsh git."

By breakfast-time the following morning, the tools had been secreted in Seymour's outhouse. With a single, withering look, Lucy had made it clear that the disposal of her father-in-law's meagre remains (and no less meagre assets) were of absolutely no interest to her. Not a teaspoon, she'd said. Not a teaspoon, she'd meant. If Seymour had retrieved a few memories, she'd no desire to know what they were. Christmas was stressful enough, without invoking the ghost of her decomposing father-in-law.

"Are you getting the tree tonight?"

Seymour scrutinised his hands and slid them guiltily under the table. The creases were lined with grease and dirt.

"Of course, yes. After work? Isaac? Do you want to come?"

"I'm seeing Alice. She's back from school."

"Just make sure you choose a nice one," warned Lucy.

Christmas hadn't always been tense like this. Seymour was certain of that. When they'd first been married – and money was even tighter – Lucy would glitter paint twigs and pinecones, creating festive tableaux with candles and tinsel. For years, they'd both looked forwards to the first snow, and although they'd never gone back to Black Pudding, Seymour's sledge was always ready and oiled.

And then somehow, the joy had given way to ritual – or habit – and Seymour's gleaming runners had turned to rust. Like everything in their lives, Christmas had slowly become an edifice teetering permanently on the brink of collapse; sustained not by invention and surprise but by the absolute lack of either.

For it to work for Lucy, everything had to repeat itself, year on year; the same Christmas balls and lights; the same food; the same music; the same inviolable bubble of silence for the radio carols from King's College, Cambridge. Just a few years before, he'd returned from the market with a tree she'd thrown straight out onto the street.

"It's too thick at the bottom….it's no shape…..and it's dropping needles already."

After she'd slunk to her bedroom, he'd recovered it. By the time he pushed the fizzing bare wires of the lights into a socket, it looked like every tree they'd ever dressed; with every flaw hidden, and every bauble in its predetermined space.

"You got a new one," she'd said the next morning. "It's beautiful."

It was a good thing they were both busy. At Havercroft's Town & Country Wear, Lucy was back working longer hours to cope with the seasonal demand. One half of the town's population, it seemed, would be getting corn plasters for Christmas. The other half would be getting new slippers.

"It's the same every year," she'd remarked to Eunice, over their daily chocolate bourbon. "People here must have cupboards full of them."

"I think a lot of people wear them outside as well as in, love," said Eunice. "Saves time. Less fuss."

There'd been just one brief glimpse of Stan Clough. Two days before Christmas, he'd dropped by to collect a pair of shoes. Lucy had been busy with another customer but the sight of him had made her bowels lurch. Whether it was lust or shame (or both) she simply wasn't sure. Either way, a smile and a raised hand was as close as they got.

"He left you a card," said Eunice. There was a disapproving tone in her voice. "It's the annual WI lunch later. You can read it when I've gone."

Later, Lucy curled up on the ancient stockroom sofa, and opened it with shaking hands. The picture was a Van Gogh; a vase of luminous sunflowers; and the message inside had been inked in an elegant, swooping hand. "See you in January, I hope. The sooner the better X."

After studying it carefully, Lucy hid the card under a box of Dr. Scholl's sandals. Without any tangible evidence, she'd begun to wonder if it all might fade away; or if her own imagination had conjured a relationship – maybe even a future – where there was neither. Now there was a card. And a message.

"You going to show me what he wrote or what?"

Lucy's eyes snapped open. She could smell sherry and cigarettes; and feel the warm bulk of her boss squeezing onto the sofa. Still only half-awake, she checked the time on the wall. She'd been sleeping for over an hour.

"And why are we still closed?"

"Eunice, I'm so sorry. It's so warm in here. I'm not used to working full time. How was lunch?"

"I'm not blind you know; not when it comes to men."

"You've lost me."

"Stan Clough. Listen, Lucy. I can see the attraction. But…"

"It was a card. That's all, Eunice. I won't be sending him one."

"Just be careful. That's all."

"I will be. We're just friends. He's good for me."

"And Seymour isn't?"

There was a clatter outside the shop; customers rattling for service. Lucy made a mental note of where she'd hidden the card and put on a smile.

"You've had four husbands, Eunice. Number five on his way. No lectures please."

It was funny, though (and slightly confusing) but for once, she was feeling mildly positive about Seymour. His tree this year had been an unexpected triumph; the train set had disappeared from the living room, along with most of his usual detritus; and she'd found him a beautiful new bone-handled penknife for Christmas.

At work, he seemed so infectiously happy it was difficult not to catch it. And while 'Pilbeam's People' was hardly 'Pickwick's Papers', the fact remained that her husband had become a writer and his weekly jottings had helped revive a newspaper that was down on its knees.

Every week his column seemed to winkle out a pleasing, new eccentric – like the Morris dancing dog or the vegetarian pork butcher– but it was his recent Christmas campaign which had really got people buzzing.

"If The Burlingtonian goes down, the town goes down," he'd declared, alongside a rallying call to the town's seasonally affected populace. "Together, we can save this historic boat from a slow death by acetylene......and, who know, we might even save the town as well."

Starting with the Christmas Eve angling competition, there was to be a series of fund-raising events, climaxing in a September revival of the long-defunct coble race. "We can do it," Seymour had promised in his final article of the year. "The whole world will be watching us."

If it was a slight exaggeration, no-one in the newsroom was complaining. Sales and advertising revenue were up, and 'Soapy' Latheron hadn't smiled so much since baling out of his Spitfire into a sewage plant.

Two days before Christmas (bad weather had scrubbed all the racing) the editor had even picked up his quill again to endorse Seymour's campaign with an editorial, heavily indebted to Winston Churchill. "This town will fight decline on its beaches; vanquish defeatism on its streets, and we WILL refloat our boat."

Seymour had laughed out loud when he read it. In a strangely troubled year there'd been very few moments of joy. If he and Lucy could somehow lurch through the holiday intact, he'd put it down as a score-draw. And if they couldn't, well, work would start on the boat on New Year's Day. Come what may, he was competing in that race.

"We're shut. Open again on the 28th."

Someone was banging a window. Lucy was in the back room locking up.

"Alright. Alright. Just hang on a minute," she shouted. "Please."

Switching the lights off as she left, Lucy emerged into a sharp, frosty evening.

"Oh, it's you."

"I thought we could walk home together," said Seymour. "I've finished too."

"Have you been drinking?"

"One bottle of wine between six of us. Soapy's gift to the editorial staff. Have you?"

The town's seasonal illuminations were flickering in a lacerating sea breeze. This year, the council had gone for a Disney theme, but the bulbs on Pinocchio had already fizzled out. Only the lights of his nose were still functioning, and it rose over the street like a large (and somewhat threatening) orange penis.

"Let's try not to fall out," said Seymour looking for Lucy's hand.

"Are you going on that fishing thing again tomorrow?"

"I am but I'll be back in the afternoon. Early as possible. It never lasts long"

A dusty black car was parked outside their house, and an ancient pram had been pulled into their yard. For years, Seymour and Lucy had gone to her parents for Christmas, and then suddenly the invitation had ceased. Now Olive, Bill (and Arthur) came to the seaside for three nights of gin, charades, and Naughty Peter; a card game which made Olive chortle so much she invariably wet her pants.

At the back door, Seymour poked his head into the pram. "Hello Arthur", he said. There was a moist snuffle, followed by what was quite possibly a fart. In the kitchen he could see two large suitcases alongside three hastily wrapped presents. Without looking he knew what they were. Every year, it was the same; a painting for each of them by Lucy's mother. Since 1962, he'd had four watercolours of Arthur, all of which had gone in the bin.

"Presents were never a big thing when I was a child," Lucy had once explained.

174

"Any reason why?"

"I think it was because Father Christmas is a man."

In the living room, Bill had lit a fire and Olive had found the Gordon's. With his back on all of them, Isaac was watching the television in the corner. A chunky green rocket was just about to blast from the top of a desert island.

"Thunderbirds. Brilliant," declared Bill, "Who's your favourite Tracy? Virgin or Scott?"

"Virgil" said Isaac, wearily. "You do realise they're puppets?"

"Happy Christmas everyone," beamed Lucy, leaning forwards to embrace her parents.

"You sound different. What's happened to your voice?" asked Olive.

"Sssssssssh," hissed Isaac, shuffling closer to the television.

"I can't see now," grumbled Bill, turning to Seymour. "Have you got any stout?"

"Elocution lessons, mum."

"Well, it's very nice. What time is Ralph coming?"

"Puppets?" Bill was looking confused. "I thought they walked funny."

"Oh, and who chose your tree?" said Olive. "It looks like a gooseberry bush."

Seymour felt drained. Every atom of spontaneity had gone. Even the conversations felt rehearsed. Soon, Lucy would serve a light supper of teacakes, crumpets and celery sticks, followed by mince pies from Higginsons. When the plates were cleared, they'd be joined for drinks by Ralph and Vietta. And long before midnight, unless Naughty Peter had already intervened, Olive would rise without a word, and head for bed.

175

"You've not been around much since term ended."

Lucy hunched up next to Isaac on the floor. She was clutching a large gin and tonic. An ugly man with an egg-shaped head was bouncing up and down on the screen. Strings were clearly visible rising from every joint of his body.

"I've been with Alice. I've been over at her place."

"You've been inside?" A prickle of anxiety ran across the skin on Lucy's neck. "What's it like?"

"Immaculate. Soulless. Cold. Leather sofas. Thick carpet. Colour telly. Lots of books. Great view. What else?"

"Did you see her dad?"

"Mr.Clough? Yeah. He took us for a Wimpy."

"Was that good? Was he nice?"

"It was a Wimpy, mum. And he was fine; a bit dull but pleasant. OK? Interrogation over?"

For Lucy, the next hour passed in a daze. When she resurfaced, supper had somehow been and gone and her hands were in a washing up bowl.

"Are you alright, love? You didn't eat anything."

Seymour was passing her the dirty dishes. There was raucous laughter from the sofa.

"I'm fine. Don't fuss. Leave me alone."

"Ralph and Vietta have bought Babycham."

"Three bottles," shouted Ralph. "And there's a big foaming glass for you."

"I'll stick to the gin, thanks," said Lucy, drying her hands on a tea towel. She felt dowdy and sexless, and she was still in her work clothes.

"Gin for me, too," said Olive. "And Babycham for Arthur."

By 8pm (as per the usual itinerary) the television was off; Bill was wrestling with a pack of cards and Isaac had turned his attention to the blushing pink void of Auntie Vietta's decolletage.

"What are you driving these days, mate?" asked Ralph.

"Nothing. My exhaust dropped off. You?"

"Lotus Cortina. Mark One. Proper little beauty."

"And how's the motor trade?"

"Good, thanks. Good. I'm looking to diversify. Bigger show room. Or property development. Make some serious money."

"You'll need land. That's not cheap."

"It's not. But keep this under your hat. We're looking to buy a couple of bombed out acres at the back of your dead dad's old place."

"Do you know whose land it is?"

"No idea. It's all through an agent. I thought you might know."

"I wish I could help you, Ralph, I really do. But why would anyone sell cheap?"

"Because we've not really said what we want it for."

"And if the poor sap selling it knew that you were actually a dodgy car dealer……"

"…. then the price would go up and I'd be stiffed."

"Don't worry," smiled Seymour. "Your secret's safe with me."

An hour later, it was all over. Olive and Bill were asleep; Lucy was having a bath; and Ralph and Vietta had retreated to The Titanic Hotel in a flurry of scent; depriving Isaac of the two things still keeping him awake. As Christmas Eve approached, Seymour was the last one up; scrupulously ensuring that his radio was tuned to the Home Service.

When he was satisfied nothing could go wrong, he stirred the embers and topped up his lilo. Beds were in short supply at Christmas, and his alarm was set for 7am. With luck, he'd be back well before the carols started. And if he wasn't (which, of course, he absolutely would be) all she had to do was turn the damned thing on....

It was so cold when he rose, Seymour could see his breath in the kitchen. Grabbing his fishing tackle from the shed, he tiptoed out across the yard under a sky-full of stars. Ten minutes later, he was walking up the north pier, gazing out across the ruffled calm of the moon-washed bay.

Twenty or so anglers were already stationed behind the seawall and as the light strengthened, their numbers began to swell. Seymour was pleased he'd made the effort. Ever since they'd moved to the seaside, he'd loved this event. Across four hours, a handful of locals battled it out to see who could catch the most fish.

There was no prize, and for the past four years, there'd been no fish either. What it always delivered in abundance, however, was banter, and the beers which invariably followed had made him feel part of something innocent and old, perpetuated by those good-hearted men of the sea whose company he cherished.

"This is amazing. We've never had such a turnout." In a pair of waist-high waders, Harry Spanners had arrived, clutching three different rods and a bacon sandwich. "There's a hundred people. Maybe more. Paying a quid each? It's your bloody article. It's brilliant."

"It's your boat, Harry," said Seymour. "That's what they're all here for."

"Whatever. Just keep your eye on Rehab. He's looking a bit smug."

Seymour ran his eye along the anglers squeezed down the full length of the pier. Captain Rehab had found himself a prime spot at the sea end of the quay where he was decanting clear liquid from a battered Thermos flask.

"You're up early," shouted Seymour. "What's in the bag?"

"Cheers," said Rehab, cheerily, knocking back his drink.

"The bag? What's in it?"

"Don't mind if I do," said Rehab, pouring himself a refill.

"Lovely day for a picture."

A familiar figure in a bright orange summer blazer was circling with his camera poised.

"Hello, Frank."

"Just two bob a picture and all of it for the restoration fund."

"All of it?"

Frank nodded unconvincingly. There was an ear-shattering blast on the foghorn. Half-stewed chunks of mackerel and lugworm were pulled hastily from rusty tins; a lethal array of shining hooks was baited, and after each man had hurled his line out into the sea, stillness returned to the competition.

"Anything doing, Harry?"

"Not a nibble. What about you?" As Harry spoke, his eyes remained locked on the tip of his fishing rod.

"I've had a bite," said Frank.

"Lying sod," said Harry.

"Yes I have," said Frank. "Frostbite."

As the end of the competition loomed, no-one had caught a thing. A parade of desolate faces stared emptily out at the sea. Even the seagulls had lost interest, and the only noise was a novice bingo-caller at one of Stan Clough's amusement arcades.

"Two fat ladies, eighty-seven."

"Here we go. Here we fucking go." At the end of the pier, Rehab was leaning back steeply and his rod was arched theatrically towards the sky. "It's an absolute bloody beast, whatever it is."

"Clickety click. Forty-three."

Like everyone else, Seymour put down his tackle and looked down over the sea wall. Something was coming to the surface at the end of Rehab's line.

"You've got sixty seconds," shouted Harry Spanners. "It only counts if it's up here on the scales within the time."

"Piss off, Spanners. You tosser."

"All the fours. Eight."

Rehab's hand on his reel was a blur. A large fish was now clearly visible on the hook.

"Ten seconds."

"Fuck you."

"Nine, eight, seven....."

"Yes. Yes. YES. It's a winner."

Rehab held up his dripping catch in triumph. There was weak flutter of applause from the packed audience of crestfallen fellow-competitors.

"What the hell's that?"

Harry Spanners had stepped into the clearing and was staring at the fish. The fish wasn't moving. The fish didn't look (or smell) like it had moved for a very long time.

"That, you sad loser, is my winning fish."

"That you boat-burning dipsomaniac, is a river trout."

There was a shuffle of feet as everyone tried to get a closer look.

"Bollocks," said Rehab, "It's a sea trout."

"It's a brown trout," said Harry. "Fiver on it."

"I'll tell you what it is."

"What is it then?"

"That," said Rehab, collapsing with laughter, "is all they had left in the fish shop."

"Lovely day for a picture," said Frank.

"Fuck off," said Harry.

An hour later, the lunchtime patrons of The White Horse could talk of nothing else. In a town which loved a yarn, the 1967 Christmas Eve Angling Festival had gained immediate entry into its hall of fame; and everyone (absolutely everyone) insisted on buying the Captain a drink.

"So nobody actually caught anything?" asked Nellie, passing pints in every direction.

"Not a thing," said Seymour.

"In four hours?"

"Nope."

"You'll stop a while though won't you?"

She was wearing a garland of mistletoe around her head and a short red dress which rode up around her thighs whenever she bent down for a bag of crisps.

"Got any cheese and onion, Nellie?" asked Frank.

"I think so, love. I'll have a rummage."

"I'll have some smoky bacon while you're down there," winked Harry. A dozen glowing faces were fighting for a look over the bar.

"Happy, happy, happy, happy Christmas," drooled Rehab.

"Lovely day for a picture," said Frank.

"Just so long as it's not one of your cock."

After that, Seymour's recollections faltered. There was a large whisky. He remembered that. Just like he remembered Frank storming off in a mood and Nellie circulating with trays of crab sticks and cockles, followed by a complimentary short for everyone who'd been in the fishing competition.

There'd been countless hugs and half-finished conversations and as the pub began to clear, he'd shared a cigarette with Nellie, and maybe – it was no more than that – he'd given her a Christmas kiss. Or did she kiss him? Not that it mattered. Because what happened next would never be forgotten; by Seymour, or anyone who witnessed it. Or, in fact, by anyone who didn't.

Suddenly, he was stumbling. There was cold air on his face, and the Town Hall clock was striking three. It was only five minutes home and he'd walked it a hundred times, but he felt drunker than he'd ever felt in his life. Something kept rising into his mouth, small rubbery pieces. Nellie's seafood, it had to be. He could taste vinegar in amongst the beer and somewhere in the mix, a hint of cheese and onion.

No longer able to walk, he rested his head against the cold glass of a window. Inside, a man in his underpants was watching his clothes in the tumble drier. A sign behind the glass said: "Laundrette. Drop Your Knickers Here."

"Thatshfunny", said Seymour.

"Happy Christmas," shouted the half-naked man inside.

Seymour opened his mouth to reciprocate, but it was the contents of his stomach which came out. Behind him, the clock rang again. Another fifteen minutes had passed. Be calm, be calm, he said to himself. The radio was set. He'd checked it. And not just once, either. It would work. It would work.

He didn't know how, but he'd made it to the back door. There was sick across his sleeve and shoes and now that he could focus, he could see sick on the door handle, too. As he stepped inside, light tore at his eyes. He raised an arm to his face, smelling stale beer (among other things) on his fingers. This isn't good, he thought. Really not good at all.

In the corner of the kitchen, Isaac and Bill were hunched around the radio. But the radio was dead, and the room was silent. There were no hymns; no carols; no heavenly voices. There were no lights on the dial and no tell-tale glow from its valves. Everything about it was as dead as the ghostly expression on his wife's face.

"Dad? Dad? Jesus."

"I'm so sorry. I'm so sorry. I'm so sorry."

"It's not the radio, dad."

"It's not? What then?"

"It's your two front teeth."

Seymour shrugged. He couldn't bring himself to look at Lucy.

"What about them?"

"They've disappeared."

Chapter Four

Seymour's tongue jabbed into the space vacated by his missing teeth. Everything in the room seemed to have frozen. Lucy sat down at the table. Tears were streaming down her face, and an intermittent crackle of East European voices was pouring from the radio.

"I don't understand," said Isaac.

"I've been shick," said Seymour.

"People don't lose their teeth when they're sick."

"Actually, I do," prompted Bill, unhelpfully.

And so Seymour told them everything; about the teenage sledging accident; about the capped teeth he'd nursed for years; about how he secretly glued them back whenever they failed; about his terror of dentists and his secret (much bigger) dread that Lucy might one day see him without them.

"I knew what your mother thought about teesh," he whistled. "So I never told you."

In the vacuum that followed, Bill looked at Olive, Olive looked at Lucy, Lucy looked at Seymour and the Russian National Anthem burst out of the radio at full volume.

"It's been doing that all afternoon," said Bill.

"Just tell me where you were sick," said Lucy.

Seymour wiped his hands on his trousers and examined the linoleum.

184

An owl was hooting mournfully in the garden sycamore.

"I asked you where you were sick?" Lucy's face was shining furiously.

"Outshide the laundrette," whispered Seymour. "On the pavement."

"Show me. Show all of us."

From a distance, they might have passed as carol singers; five individuals (and one pram) wrapped in thick, winter coats on an innocent jaunt for some head-clearing Christmas air. Except the 'baby' was a dog and the grey-faced man leading the way was looking for a puddle of his own vomit.

"It's there."

Seymour was pointing to a mess of half-digested crisps and crab sticks. Four people behind him leaned forward to look.

"Now find your teeth."

"You're joking, mum," said Isaac, tearing his eyes from the half-naked man with a white beard sitting alone inside the laundrette.

"Find them."

What followed was never mentioned again and although each shell-shocked witness was unable to forget, their collective silence allowed them hope that the memory might eventually fade away. But it was a forlorn expectation.

Seymour had found his teeth and successfully glued them back into place. However, his grisly party trick had obliterated much more than Christmas. Within the hour, Ralph and Vietta had checked out of their hotel and Lucy's parents were heading home with their dog and Olive's paintings.

For the next week, Seymour's wife was scarcely seen. Their gifts for each other lay unopened under the tree; Isaac unwrapped his presents alone in his bedroom; and on Boxing Day he'd materialised downstairs carrying a duffel bag.

"This is your fault, dad. I'm going to stay with Alice."

"At Stan Clough's? Please don't."

"Yes, at Mr. Clough's. They speak to each other there."

After that, the boy's house had fallen into silence. When his parents met on the stairs, they didn't look at each other. And when Lucy summoned the energy to dress, she never told her husband where she was going.

On two occasions, he'd found train tickets. On another, a cinema stub and a flyer for Julie Christie in 'Far From The Madding Crowd". Then on New Year's Eve, he'd ended up watching The White Heather Club on television alone as a thick band of snow swept in from the Arctic.

When it stopped, shortly after midnight, he'd waded out and opened the old stable. His father's tools glistened in their racks and his cargo of larch felt seasoned and dry. Apart from a few adventurous flakes of snow, the workshop appeared snug. More than that, he thought. It felt ready.

The following morning, wearing fingerless gloves against the cold, Seymour started to build his boat.

To be racing in September, he needed to be finished by July. To be finished by July, he'd have to steal every minute he could from his job and from what remained of his home life.

He looked at his hands and remembered his father. He looked at the tools and remembered the hours he'd spent watching his father. Hopefully, he'd inherited more than the old man's short legs. In the weeks ahead, Seymour would need all the skill he could muster. There were no formal plans for sailing cobles. No drawings, no blueprints, no designs. Guesswork and luck would play their part; local wisdom, too.

From the kitchen, he could hear the ascending note of a kettle. Lucy was making herself a pot of tea. Excellent, he smiled. Even if they weren't communicating, Lucy would be enjoying the spectacle of a world knee-deep in snow.

In the corner of the workshop, under a coil of discarded rope, Seymour saw the rusted end of a sledge runner and felt an irrational surge of hope. After the kites, and the wooden toys, he was finally on the brink of creating something which might last; onto which the wind would breathe and bring life. Yes, he and Lucy were a mess, but one day (he felt certain) she'd understand that he'd had no choice.

For the next few weeks, he worked alone.

After five days, he'd progressed no further than the single 20-foot length of timber which would form the bottom edge of his finished boat. Nobody would ever see it, but nothing was more important.

The ram (as it was called) would be the boat's spine; the gravitational centre from which everything else would slowly rise. If he cut corners here, he would fail later and so he crawled tirelessly around the stone floor in a pile of discarded sandpaper until every inch was smooth and he was satisfied that the real work could begin.

Next, he cut and planed the bottom planks – the floor of the coble – ensuring that each one overlapped in such a way that no water could ever seep through. Outside, the winter had set hard. There was newspaper talk of a coal famine and power cuts and across the Northern hills, dozens of stranded villages were praying for a thaw. And yet Seymour never once felt the cold.

Every hour in his workshop seemed to disappear in a sweltering fury of concentration. Seeking perfection, he plundered every minute he could from around the edges of his life; slipping home at lunchtime or working through the night until dawn, when he'd totter blinking out into the snow, sick with exhaustion; staring at his ruined hands.

Even when he slept, the boat followed him into his dreams; sometimes floundering on rocks, sometimes skipping across the waves. And since there was no escape from it, Seymour surrendered to his obsession. It was like a crossword with no clues; a landscape with no map; a place in which he was so frequently lost, he despaired.

In his panic, he pored over faded sepia photographs of Victorian fishing boats, scrutinising the curve of their planking under a magnifying glass. At the local library, he dug out dusty texts by long-forgotten shipbuilders, desperate for clues but finding none. Trial and error (many errors) had cost him precious time. Now every cut, every joint, and every blow of the hammer had to be meticulously rehearsed in his head.

But as skin and muscle gradually hardened, so did Seymour's confidence. Soon, he could wield a chisel like a wand, conjuring wood shavings that were thinner than paper. When he hit a nail, it plunged true and his saws bit deep with the confident snarl of his childhood, dispersing the same soft dust which now clung to everything.

By mid-January, an unlikely truce had broken out between Seymour and Lucy. They were sleeping apart but (provided Christmas was never mentioned again) some semblance of normality had returned. After two days, Isaac had returned home saying merely that Stan Clough's house was 'even more boring than here'; Seymour was writing his column again; and Lucy had resumed her duties at the shoe shop.

"I know exactly what you're doing," she'd said, after her first day back at work.

"Would you like to see?"

"Absolutely not."

And that had been it. Like Christmas, Seymour's 'secret' project had simply disappeared.

And yet, if anything, Lucy seemed perkier than she had for months. At night, if she left her bedroom door open, he would join her for sex, after which he'd return to his workshop, briefly curious about (but thankful for) his wife's mercurial appetites. Ever since their teens, she'd been hungrier than him. But this was different; harder and more knowing; shockingly so sometimes.

Maybe it was a good sign, he wondered, although it wasn't easy to see how.

"This doesn't mean I actually want you to sleep with me," she'd explained.

"What does it mean then?" said Seymour.

"It just means I want you to fuck me every now and then."

Perhaps it was as well, her door was usually shut. By early February, there'd been no let-up in the freeze and Seymour's progress had sagged. To prevent the larch from warping, he'd installed a paraffin heater, but the fumes weighted him down and his shoulders ached from the constancy of the task.

Grafting the curving bow piece – or forefoot – onto the ram had been a triumph but the effort had set him back days, and there were times now when he struggled to stay awake, let alone comprehend the inconstancies of his wife.

"You look knackered, Taff? Are you alright?"

It was deadline day at the newspaper and Seymour was floundering with his weekly column. As the cold snap ground on, funny stories had become harder to find; the barrel of seasonal goodwill was bare; and the age he'd spent staring at his typewriter had yielded nothing.

"Not really, Frank. How long have I got?"

"Two hours. Less if Soapy goes to the pub early."

189

"Shit. I've got a blank piece of paper here."

"I've got an idea."

Seymour groaned. Frank wasn't generally known for his ideas.

"Write about your boat."

"What do you mean?"

"Everyone knows you're building a coble in your shed," said Frank, brightly. "If it was anyone else, you'd be writing it up."

"Yes, but I'm not the news. So I can't."

"That's bollocks. You were the news when Rehab set fire to The Burlingtonian…."

"That was different."

"…..and now you're trying to save it again."

"It's boring, Frank. I'm sawing pieces of wood and banging nails."

"Make it interesting then. Let people follow the story. Trust me. We're a seaside town. People will love it."

It was almost impossible to believe. Frank had said something sensible.

"Have we got time? For this week's paper?"

"You get tapping. I'll take a few photographs. No problem."

Seymour's story was an instant hit. Within days, a trickle of donations began to arrive, alongside rambling missives from old seadogs scrawled on pages torn from musty logbooks; crinkled photographs and rusty tools wrapped in brown paper. And once again, weekly sales were up.

"You've got the Midas touch, lad." 'Soapy' was beaming over a congratulatory mid-morning glass of port. "Born to do this you were. Bloody well born to it."

"There's a slight problem," mumbled Seymour.

"Bah," growled his editor. "We're not a nation normally daunted by slight problems."

"I'm not sure I'll get the boat finished in time."

"Not finish? Catastrophe. Can't be so," spluttered Soapy. "Time off. Take it. Whatever you need. Just keep writing. Chapter and verse. Every jot and tittle or tattle. Don't miss a thing. Readers love it. Love you."

"I'd need a day a week. Maybe even more?"

"Take it, boy. And please call me Soapy," said Soapy, topping up Seymour's glass.

"Up school?" said Seymour, draining it.

"Ha. Damned right. Up bally school."

Two weeks later, on Valentine's Day, the winter finally slipped away and everyone in the town felt it go. Ice-locked cars were suddenly free; house windows were flung open to purge weeks of stale air; and crusty bergs of old snow slid free from north-facing roofs. It wasn't a heatwave, but the freeze had relented and, according to Frank, it wouldn't be back.

"How do you know?" asked Seymour.

"My budgie," said Frank. "He's quiet all winter and sings again on the first day of Spring. Always has."

"You've got a budgie?"

"I have."

"That's sweet. I didn't know. What's he called?"

"Well he used to be called Frank," said Frank.

"And now?"

"Now he's called Eunice."

That same morning, buoyed by the dazzle of warm sunshine, Seymour propped a card (and a single rose) outside Lucy's bedroom door before heading to work. When he returned, Isaac was sitting in the living room reading a comic. There was no sign of the card, or his wife.

"Where's your mum?"

"Elocution lessons."

"Did she say when she'd be back?"

"Too late for sepper. There's cold meat in the pantry. I had a sausage roll."

"No homework to do?"

"All done," said Isaac, scooping up his comic, and slouching upstairs.

Somehow, Seymour doubted it. Although his son's doctored school reports had fooled Lucy, they'd been blindingly obvious to his father. "Bone idle and surly" didn't seem to fit with a B+ in physics, any more than the B++ he'd earned for being "a persistently disruptive influence" in geography.

As yet there'd been no formal reprimand, but trouble was surely looming. Except it wasn't really trouble, reckoned Seymour, it was growing up. As a child, he'd been just the same. Kites, evacuation and Adolf Hitler had saved him from the plodding boredom of school. Poor Isaac had only his weekly comic, a Littlewoods catalogue and (when she wasn't at boarding school) he still had that Alice girl, too.

"It would be good to meet your girlfriend at half-term," Seymour shouted up the empty stairs.

The muffled beat of a pop song came back; the same tune he'd been hearing everywhere since December. You say yes. I say no. Or was it the other way round? Each time he heard of it he thought of Lucy, except there was far too much goodbye these days and nothing like enough hello.

"I'm back."

Seymour swivelled away from the melody into a wall of perfume.

"I can see," he said.

Framed by the back door, Lucy slipped off her shoes in a pool of melting slush. Beneath a caramel-coloured mackintosh, he saw a cashmere jumper, short black and white check skirt and cream-coloured tights. Around her neck, a silk scarf was secured by an agate brooch framed in gold. Everything she was wearing looked new; unfamiliar.

"You look amazing. You smell amazing."

"Thank you. And thanks for your card. It was very sweet."

In her stockinged feet, she moved to where Seymour was standing, put a hand on each of his shoulders, and kissed him once on the lips.

"You seem relaxed. Good class?"

Seymour slid his arms around Lucy's waist. Her body felt supple and warm.

"It was but I'm really tired," she said, detaching his hands. "I fancy a bath and an early night."

"We could watch a bit of telly together?"

"Go and play with your boat, Seymour. It's Saturday tomorrow. If you can tear yourself away, we'll watch something then."

Except they didn't see each other the next day; or the day after that. At night, in his workshop, Seymour turned up the heater and slumped into a faded deckchair. Under the one naked light bulb, his progress felt pathetic; little more than a raft of planks; less of a boat than his wife's bloody loofah. "I should have stuck to my guns," he mumbled to himself. "I can't write about this."

"Wake up, you dozy prick. We've bought you an egg butty."

Seymour untangled his legs, unleashing an onslaught of pins and needles. He could see daylight through the crack in the door and as the deckchair creaked, an empty bottle of whisky shattered on the floor. With his good foot, Harry Spanners kicked the debris against a wall.

"Great set up in here," he said, taking in the gleaming chisels, and the neatly stacked timber.

"I can't do it on my own, Harry. I'm giving up. It's too hard."

"You need lifting, son. You need a little inspiration."

"Can I clean my teeth first?"

"You've got five minutes. Me and Rehab are taking you for a day out."

A half-hour later, the three men sat side by side at the front of the Captain's van. Outside, the air was sparkling, blowing hard and warm from the west; sending the snow into retreat under a sky so bright it made them squint.

East of the town the coastline bulged sharply outwards, creating a spear-shaped peninsula which narrowed as they moved towards the horizon. On either side, they could see foam-flecked chalk bays cut into the gleaming rock and at road's end, a freshly painted lighthouse, out-shone by the winter sunshine.

"It looks like a giant chess piece," said Rehab.

"It looks like the whole world's been washed and hung out to dry," said Seymour.

"It looks like you two poets need a drink," said Harry.

Turning left before the lighthouse, Rehab drove down between head-high hedges to a patch of waste ground overlooking a sheltered cove. Somewhere out at sea, Seymour could hear the engine of a northbound trawler struggling against the swell. Inside the bay, however, the water lay flat, disturbed only by the head of a curious seal, staring at the trio as they threaded down the cliff path and found a place to sit on the shingly beach.

"I've packed my famous flask," said Rehab.

"And I've packed a few pies," added Harry.

"It's wonderful," said Seymour. "I've never been in winter."

When they'd first moved to the seaside, this cove had been their favourite summer hideaway. Nowhere made them happier or more certain they'd made the right choice. At low tide, life teemed in its magical rock pools. It was here he'd shown Isaac how to make a sea anemone cling to his tiny finger.

They'd caught blenny fish and prawns in their hands and raced hermit crabs across the seaweed. He'd lain in the sun with Lucy's hair splayed across his chest and his hand on hers. And once, while her head was in a book, he'd written their names in the sand circled by a giant heart.

Even now, in winter, it was a place of wild beauty; the water smeared with creamy foam and a line of eight wooden fishing boats hauled safely beyond the reach of the waves.

"There isn't another boat like the coble in the world."

Harry had found an old brine-bleached tree trunk and the three men were leaning with their backs against it, looking out to the horizon and sipping Rehab's coffee.

"Flat bottom. No keel. No weight. Easy for two blokes to get in and out of the sea."

"Just like a Viking boat, I heard," said Rehab. "How are you liking my brew?"

Seymour took a swig, and felt the alcohol burn in his throat.

"Bloody dangerous though," continued Harry. "You'd set off with a load of rocks in the bottom to keep it stable. And as you caught more and more fish, you'd chuck the ballast over the side."

"So why would that make them dangerous?"

"There's nowt under a coble," explained Rehab. "No keel. They weren't made like a pissy modern sailing yacht. They were made to slide up these beaches. You had to know what you were doing."

"And if you didn't," interrupted Harry. "They'd turn turtle."

"They'd go over?"

"Precisely. And once that happened…"

"….they went down."

Listening to their memories, Seymour was entranced. All the years he'd known these men, he hadn't known them at all. Away from the noise of the bar, they'd seen things; real things; real life stuff, hard-edged and scalded by tragedy.

Rehab's deep blue eyes, and his thinning white hair; Harry's vein-crossed face and his dodgy leg; his friends weren't dinosaurs or characters in one of Lucy's novels, they were the living, breathing conduit for something so old its origins had vanished without trace.

"I'm out of my depth here," smiled Seymour. "Literally."

196

"Listen. I was only seventeen when I built my first coble," said Rehab.

"I'm not saying I couldn't build one. But just not this quickly."

"It sank three days later, mind," added Rehab.

"But you could do it if we helped." Harry was handing out four pork pies. One each for Seymour and Rehab. Two for himself. "For fuck's sake, his family made these things."

"What? Pies?"

"Cobles," grinned Harry. "And both our families sailed them. We'd be a dream team."

"Yes, but why would you?"

"Honest answer? Because we miss it," said Rehab, pushing a large piece of greasy crust into his mouth. "So we wouldn't be doing you a favour….."

"……you'd be doing us one."

Two days later, the 'dream team' assembled for the first time in Seymour's workshop. Over the next few weeks, it would practically become their home. If Seymour worked through the night, so did Rehab and Harry. And if Seymour's newspaper work took him elsewhere, his two friends pressed on without him.

To everyone's astonishment, Rehab quickly emerged as the unspoken leader of their tiny band; displaying knowledge and an intensity no-one had ever suspected. When there was a problem, Rehab solved it. When there was a setback, Rehab urged them forward displaying such breath-taking attention to detail that even Harry (who'd known the Captain the longest) was stunned by the transformation.

"I don't get it. What are you on?" asked Harry.

"I was bored before. That's all," said Rehab. "Bored shitless."

By the end of March, the boat was taking recognisable shape. A set of makeshift frames had been attached along the length of the boat's solid spine to which the elegant curving side panels of larch could be fitted with copper rivets. Since each panel (or 'strake' as Rehab called them) overlapped its neighbour by less than an inch, there was no room for error. Nor was there any. No wood was ever wasted and every joint was always perfect; as if some hibernated skill had risen into their hands, undimmed by generations of neglect.

Sometimes, they worked closely as a threesome. Sometimes – for hours on end – Seymour was content just to watch, spellbound by the men's precision and by their feel for a task which relied on instinct as much as their technical prowess with a chisel.

Occasionally, the pair would stop, consult and make several knowing circuits of the boat with a pencil, marking places for trims or cuts. If it felt right, they pressed on. If it didn't, they stopped for a cigarette or a pipe of tobacco.

"What will you call it?" asked Harry, during a fag break in the fifth week.

"I've always fancied Phoenix," said Seymour.

"Because it grew out of the fire on my boat?"

"That and a few other disasters along the way."

It was never discussed, but Harry and Rehab knew what he meant. Over the years, Seymour had never disclosed much, but he'd said (and they'd seen) more than enough. Privately, they'd concluded long ago that his wife was a stuck-up piece of work and in Seymour's company, the subject was afforded a wide berth.

Around the bar at the White Horse it was different. In his absence, Seymour's friends (earwigged closely by Nellie) had given up trying to understand. It was like the poor bugger existed in two wholly separate worlds. In one of them, he seemed content. In the other, he virtually disappeared. And even now, Mrs Pilbeam was invisible.

There were no chance doorstep encounters; no biscuits; no cups of sugary tea. To avoid contact, she was using the front door and if he saw her around town, Rehab was convinced she'd no idea who he was. Only once had his two co-workers dared to test Seymour for some answers. After that, they'd kept their mouths shut.

"She gets tired easily," he'd barked. "And she's not a big fan of this."

And that had been it. No further questions were encouraged. Away from the hammering and the buzz of their saws, the main house seemed to hang in a pall of silence, and they were never once invited in. Every now and then, Seymour would slip away, only to return with the look of a chastised puppy.

"You alright, mate?" Harry had asked early on.

"I'm fine," said Seymour. "Let's crack on."

Without fail – every Wednesday morning – Frank would roll up with his camera to record their progress for Seymour's increasingly popular weekly column. Born out of desperation, it had grown to a full page of words and pictures chronicling the gradual emergence of a boat the entire community was slowly adopting.

Seymour's gunwales, gripes, strakes and thwarts had stirred the town's memory. Long-forgotten wooden boats were being hauled out of barns and lockups. Over thirty cobles had already signed up for the fund-raising race in September and a small museum was being mooted on the harbour to celebrate the town's fishing past.

"You've really started something here, lads," said Frank, as he organised the three shipbuilders for a front-page portrait. "There's even a bunch of people out on the street wanting a look."

As Easter approached, however, progress slowed. During the winter months, Rehab and Harry had survived on their cash handouts from the labour exchange. Four pounds and ten shillings a week wasn't much but it quenched their thirst and triggered some seasonal improvement in Rehab's maths.

"Buys me exactly six pints a day," he declared, tucking the cash into the back pocket of his filthy jeans. "A bit less, if I eat"

The return of spring meant there was serious money to be had; fish to be caught; and paying customers knocking on the door of Harry's chandlery. Haddock and holidaymakers had kept the community ticking for years. Unless you were young and could work through the winter storms, this was when the town's ageing workforce came out of hiding. It wasn't easy – tearing themselves away from Seymour's coble – but no-one knew how to rig a sailing boat or fettle a diesel engine like Harry.

And no-one knew fish like the Captain.

From April, every skipper wanted Rehab on their payroll. The man was a legend; a cod magnet. It was like he could see through the water to the places where the salmon and the sea trout ran. If he put down a pot, his lobsters would be the biggest, and in the summer he could fill a boat with dull-brained mackerel inside an hour.

"We'll do what we can when we can, Taff, but you don't really need us now. And we need the dosh."

Harry and Rehab were standing on either side of 'Phoenix'. For the third night running they'd grafted from dusk through to dawn. There was still a long way to go.

"Go fill your boots," said Seymour, shaking their hands. "I completely understand."

"See you down the Horse on Sunday lunch?"

"Of course. And thank you."

And so Seymour pressed on alone with furious intent. Now the strakes were in place, he could cut the internal ribs to give the boat strength, working not with larch but oak, cut from bent and ancient branches which mimicked the graceful contour of the flanks. For each side, he fashioned twelve curved ribs, and the work devoured him for almost a month.

Never had anything been so fiendishly hard. To fit snugly against the seven overlapping larch planks, each rib required seven matching notches which lined up so sweetly the wood squeaked. If he got it right, there wasn't a wave on earth which could crush her, but the effort ground him down and he desperately missed the company of his friends.

As Seymour's exhaustion bit, the days began to blur. Every waking thought now swirled about the boat, and his head rang with checklists and measurements. Twice a week he still trudged into the office to pen his column but as the desperation to finish grew, the quality of his work declined.

"I never dreamed how hard it would be," he told his devoted readers. "I'm beginning to feel like Captain Scott. So close. But still so far."

The fifteenth rib had taken him a day. The twenty-third took him three days and – as the night hours shortened – he could feel time running out.

"You alright, dad?"

Seymour had been scribbling in his notebook. It had been in his hand. But now the pencil was half-buried in wood shavings and he couldn't even remember closing his eyes.

"Isaac. Yes. Of course. Come in. I keep drifting off."

"Have you got any idea what time it is?"

"Not really, no." There was an old wind-up alarm clock on a shelf, but the face was covered in dust.

"It's ten o' clock," Isaac continued.

"Shit. Sorry. Morning or evening?"

"Does it matter? You live in here anyway."

It was only the second time his son had shown any curiosity. The first had been early on, when he'd looked in briefly to see his grandfather's relocated tools. Since then, he'd expressed no more interest than his mother.

"Do you want to see how it's going?"

Isaac shuffled around the narrow gap between the boat and the wall.

"I put the stern planking on next, then the gunwales. They're the flat bits around the edge. After that the rudder, the mast, the bowsprit, the varnish……"

"What the fuck's this?" Isaac was examining his fingers.

"Resin. You've touched a knot somewhere. It'll wash off."

"Great. Wonderful. Boat shit."

"You'll like it when it's finished. You'll like the sailing part."

"You'll never get me on it, dad. I promise."

Seymour didn't know what to say. Sequestered away from his family, he'd hoped that everything had held together; and that by eliminating it from their brief conversations, the boat had somehow disappeared. Whenever he'd seen Lucy their exchanges had been cordial and polite. Most evenings, they still ate together and on Saturdays, they even watched television as a family; most recently (and at Lucy's absolute insistence) an American sitcom about a hen-pecked man married to a 20th century witch.

"You always said you wouldn't watch American programmes?" Seymour had asked. "Everything from America was trash, you said."

"Did I say that?" Over the months, Lucy's voice had changed.

202

There was a glassily regal ring to it which Seymour disliked. "This is different."

"What changed your mind? You hate their accents."

"Just watch it," she'd insisted. "You'll see."

After a few minutes, Seymour's mind had wandered. If there was a message for him, he'd missed it. There was a pretty witch who wreaked havoc when she twitched her nose. There was a dull suburban husband. Apart from that it was just badly timed gags and canned laughter. Nothing about it even made him smile.

"It's not exactly D.H.Lawrence is it?" Seymour was halfway through the living room door.

"You're leaving? Don't go. It's really funny." For once she'd sounded more disappointed than angry. "And please, please don't go outside."

"I'll put the kettle on," he'd said. And he had.

Under the weak light of the workshop, Isaac was still trying to rub the sap from his fingers. Moths were banging themselves against a window laced in filthy grey cobwebs.

"If you help me, I'll finish it quicker?"

"And have mum hate me as well? No thanks."

"She doesn't hate me. I'm building a boat. That's not a sin."

The boy had picked up a hand-drill and was slowly turning the handle.

"Will it be ready for that race? I've seen all your stuff in the papers. Everyone has. I know what this is all about."

"It'll be tight, but I hope so."

"You don't even know how to sail one of these things."

"I'll have a few weeks to practise," laughed Seymour. "And I'll need crew."

"I'd rather die," said Isaac. "Don't even think about it."

It was far too late, and he was far too weary, to be upset. People said things, hurtful things. But people forgot them, too. And when the boat was under sail – when it was close-hauled under a blazing sun – that was when they'd understand. Until then, he could live with the sniping. None of it was exactly novel anyway.

Finally, the ribs were in place, and he could move on to the gunwales; the smooth wooden edges that ran from bow to stern. For months, he'd been dreading this phase of the construction. Crafting the ribs had been testing enough. But the gunwales required the oak to be cut and then physically bent around the bulging contours of the coble.

"It's simply not possible, Rehab," he'd complained over a Sunday pint. "It can't be done."

"All you need is a kettle," said Rehab, studying the head on his fifth pint of the day.

"A kettle? How many have you had?"

"Because once you've sat green oak in steam, you can practically knit with it."

It was another miracle. After a little experimentation, Seymour had rigged up a canvas tunnel with a kettle boiling on a paraffin stove at either end. When the tunnel was full of steam, he'd slid in a length of oak and waited – with disbelief – until it softened, and he could manipulate the wood like dough.

Seymour was consumed by excitement. Within a week, he had the gunwales in place. Within a fortnight, he'd flipped the boat over and fitted the stern plank and the bilge streaks to protect the bottom when she was beached. Turning it back once again, he'd laid in the flooring timbers and the four thwarts – or seats – crossing from one side to the other.

Every hour he could find, he now spent alone in his workshop. So long as his column was written, nobody at the paper seemed to mind. By mid-Spring, he'd abandoned any pretence of normal family life. Only when this was finished could he even think about mending all the things that he'd broken. Seeing how beautiful it was would help. It had to help. Because if a man could bend oak then surely anything was possible?

For the first time in weeks, Seymour took stock of the calendar. It was June already. The rudder and tiller were done; just the mast and the bowsprit left to finish; a week at most. Everything else (bar the rigging) was done.

Every square inch had been sanded and varnished until the grain stood out like black streaks of marble and on the iron-shod bow, one strake down from the gunwale, was a carved wooden nameplate with a single word picked out in white paint.

Phoenix.

On a warm summer's evening, Seymour pulled aside the makeshift gable end of his workshop and eased his boat out onto a trailer. As the sunlight caught the wood, it was transformed; from timber to gold; from nails and wood to something so powerful, so voluptuous it made him stumble.

Grasping the sides for support, he inched his way around. Everything about it was perfect; magnificent. To the touch, it felt like amber. And where the belly dipped away into darkness, it felt almost human. More than magnificent, he thought; a boy's dream which no-one could fail to be moved by. Not Lucy. Not Isaac. Not anyone. All it was waiting for was the wind.

Seymour looked at his arms, speckled with paint. He looked at his boat, unable to hold back the tears through a wild yelp of triumph as he hurtled in through the back door.

"It's finished. I'm done. Come and see."

He hadn't noticed that the kitchen was dark. Or that the sink was stacked with unwashed pots.

"Hello? HELLO?"

There was a light switch by the pantry door. He flicked it down and rubbed his eyes.

That was when he saw the white envelope propped up against a milk bottle containing a single dessicated Valentine rose.

Chapter Five

He'd never suspected, but Lucy had watched the boat grow. She knew how beautiful it was. And contrary to Seymour's low expectations, she was not immune to its appeal. On a handful of occasions – when she was certain he wasn't around – she'd let herself into his workshop; stepping gingerly across the velvet underlay of pine, drawn on by the deep contradictions of her love for him.

The last occasion had been just a day before her note. She'd heard that photographer fellow come and go (what the hell did Eunice see in him?) followed later by Seymour, lost in thought as he strode, head down, towards the newspaper office. A few minutes were all she'd need. Like everyone else, she'd read his articles; and like the entire town she knew the work was nearly done.

It had been a beautiful spring morning; scarcely a breeze and every sound seeming to travel on forever. Trainloads of trippers were pulling into the station. She could hear steam sizzling and the clamour of happy voices. She could feel the terrified clatter of her own heart. And as she pushed open the old stable door, a broad shaft of sunlight followed her in.

A few seconds was all it had required. Never had she seen anything built with such love. Every joint appeared perfect. To the touch, the wood felt like skin; and the way it swooped and rose between bow and stern gave it the appearance of a flower not a boat, a stitching together of petals not planks.

A guard dog was howling mournfully, stirred awake by a passing ambulance. Stepping quickly back into the yard, Lucy gulped in huge drafts of air; fighting the faintness and the worm of guilt which lay beyond. Trying to organise her thoughts was impossible. Just as it had done for months – years really – her head lurched between opposite poles. He loves me; he loves me not. The boy she'd met by a boating pool had made that incredible thing. But that was his dream, not hers. And to achieve it, he'd locked her out in favour of those half-wit companions.

He was a child. He'd always been a child. And she was a woman. She needed more. She didn't want a boat. She wanted a man. Just for once, she wanted a man. And yet the feeling embedded within that extraordinary creation had left her gasping. It was beyond expression.

It was like all the love letters that he'd never written. To her? No. Seymour wasn't capable of that. Was he? Never. Never. And even if he was, it had come far too late.

She was feeling better, calmer. Big breaths. Checking her handbag, and readying herself for work, she realised it had been a silly mistake. She shouldn't have gone to look.

She was sleeping with Stan now. Everything had changed.

"There's someone in the shop to see you."

It was the first week of January. She'd been in the stockroom thinking about Christmas. There was a sale on, but the constant stream of customers still couldn't push away the memory of Seymour stirring through his own vomit.

"Lucy? Hello? Are you with us? Your fancy man's out front?"

"I don't have a fancy man, Eunice."

"Well you might not think so, but I've been there. And he thinks you have."

208

The following week, they'd gone for a windswept stroll on the beach together. Finding time alone was no longer a problem. If Seymour wasn't asleep, he was working on his boat. And since he usually vanished without explanation, Lucy felt a similar lack of compunction. Not that her champagne-fuelled conversations with Stan were a sin. But with each successive rendezvous, that possibility was undoubtedly growing.

The elocutions lessons had been secretly junked, and they were quickly meeting two, sometimes, three times a week. By early February, they'd even managed to slip in a matinee at the cinema where they'd seen the heroine of 'Poor Cow' drift in and out of various people's beds.

"Have you ever slept with anyone else?" They'd taken a huge risk, but the picture house was deserted.

"That's none of your business." Lucy had felt every capillary on her face filling with blood. "I liked Terence Stamp though."

A few days later, they met again: for lunch at The Titanic. It was Valentine's Day, and a scattering of elderly diners was spread around the hotel's vast, and chronically under-heated, dining room. As usual, Stan and his partner had been ushered to an enormous bay window table overlooking the sea. The winter weather had broken, and the sands were frantic with stir-crazy dogs.

"You're quiet."

There was an unopened card and a Valentine rose in her bedroom back home. She wasn't in the mood for small talk.

"Did Seymour buy you a card?"

Lucy examined him calmly. There appeared no malice in the question. Stan's voice was kind, and in that moment, he looked extraordinarily handsome.

"I've never slept with anyone else. There's your answer."

"I didn't ask you that."

"Not this time. But that doesn't mean you'd stopped wanting to know."

"Does that bother you? Only having slept with Seymour."

"It didn't used to." Lucy picked up a knife and began rubbing at the tarnish with a napkin. "Now I think it does."

"Which bothers you most? Me wanting to know? Or you wanting to sleep with me?"

Stan reached into his pocket and held up a key. When the waiter came for their order, they'd gone. She wasn't surprised he had his own room. In a funny way, she'd always assumed (without asking) that he half-lived there. There were newspapers and books on a bedside table; net curtains and flowers in a Chinese vase; but the radiator was broken, and while Stan turned his back, Lucy slipped naked under the covers.

"Please don't talk," she whispered. "I can only do this if we don't talk."

An hour later, they were standing side by side in the tiny lift back down to the reception.

"Can I speak yet?" asked Stan.

"Sorry. Yes. This lift's not very reassuring is it?"

"What happens now? You seem very calm."

Lucy smiled and slid the cap off her lipstick. There was a hotel noticeboard on the lift wall. She was using the glass as a mirror.

"What happens now is we have lunch." She pursed her lips and quickly checked her hair. "And then we go back upstairs for more."

Walking home later, Lucy felt like her head might burst. She'd known it would happen. She'd stuffed a packet of Seymour's condoms and a spare pair of knickers into her handbag. She'd let herself go; made noises; sworn like an infantryman and when she'd parted with Stan she'd felt only elation. But as the gasworks loomed closer, her face burned, and her legs buckled with shame.

There was a brick alley which ran alongside the back of Seymour's workshop. She stepped into it and leaned against the wall. From her purse, she produced a dog-legged cigarette and a pack of matches from the hotel bar.

"Shit.Shit.Shit." The matches were damp but the last one caught, and she held the smoke in her chest until she felt dizzy.

The sex had been powerful, but (literally) anti-climactic. She'd felt liberated by Stan's all-action style; and he was bigger than her husband, but (to her surprise) she'd taken no pleasure from his size. It was different. Better than that, it was exciting. As a lover, Seymour was thoughtful but passive to the point of narcolepsy. All Stan wanted to do was fuck.

In the alleyway, she let her lungs collapse. Beyond the wall at her back was Seymour's boat. She took another long drag, trapping the fumes even deeper. A stray cat had joined her in the darkness and was rubbing its back on her calf. The purring felt like a mild electric shock.

"Will we do this again?"

Back at the hotel Stan had asked the question she'd been thinking.

"I'll lose my job," she'd said.

"It can be what you want it to be. It doesn't have to be this. But I'd like it to be something."

The dining room had cleared, and a damp log was spluttering feebly in the grate. Around them was a sea of white, starched tablecloths.

"Other than terrifying, I don't know what this is, Stan," she said, taking her coat from a cadaverous hotel porter. "But thanks for lunch, and for everything else."

With a flash of teeth, the cat had fled. Lucy stared after it. She could smell tobacco (or something) on her fingers which she freshened up with a dab of hand cream. Someone up the street was putting their milk bottles out. She took a deep breath and stepped out under the sodium lights.

"You look amazing," said Seymour. "You smell amazing."

There was a half-eaten sausage roll on the draining board. She slipped her shoes off and kissed him, feeling herself moisten as their bodies touched. She was insane; she couldn't. Two men in one day? Then he'd made some hopeless remark and the moment had passed. Up in her room, she'd quickly sort things out on her own. Who needed men anyway.........?

"I bloody well need men."

A few more wretched weeks had passed. Eunice Bolt had invited Lucy to her home for tea. As it always did in March, the bottom had fallen out of shoes, and she'd closed the shop early. On the mantelpiece, over the gas fire, were four framed photographs of her dead husbands.

"Yes. I can rather see that," replied Lucy, "You've not got Frank's willy on display yet?"

"I've ALWAYS needed men." Eunice was carrying a tray through from her kitchen. On it were two schooner glasses and a bottle of sherry. "And there's no room for a penis on my mantelpiece, thank you."

Both women had laughed, Lucy the loudest. It was strange the way her horizons were expanding. But it was pleasing, too. After years spent incarcerated in her bedroom, she'd emerged back into the world with a girlfriend, a bond unimpaired by their difference in age.

Not that Eunice looked like the older one. Out of her blue nylon shop coat – mast-thin in a fitted dress – she had the body of a teenager. There were no sleep rings around her eyes; no laddered tights and nothing ever seemed out of place. The moment she stepped out of her bungalow door, Eunice was on show. And she was still sexy in a way Lucy doubted she could ever be.

Killing husbands, she thought. It must be good for your skin.

"Would you like to listen to my new stereogram?"

"I'd love to." Lucy knew what was coming.

"Did I tell you it was the first stereogram in the town?"

"You did actually. Several times."

"Cheeky mare," chortled Eunice. "For that you get Cliff Richard."

Perched on four spindly wooden legs, beneath a reproduction print by Picasso, the stereogram dominated the room like an altarpiece. When she lifted the polished lid, there was a turntable on one side and, on the other, a compartment squeezed tight with long-playing records. Lucy rummaged inside and extracted a random fistful of albums.

"Did we miss out on the sixties, Eunice?"

"I think you did. But don't panic. They're not quite over yet."

"Charlie Mingus….Ornette Coleman….Vivaldi….Frank Sinatra…. The Beatles……This is quite a collection. You'd get on well with Seymour."

"I've only actually ever bought one record in my life. All those belonged to my husbands. Different sounds, different memories."

Eunice had found 'Summer Holiday' and dropped the needle on the outer edge. When the music started, she was smiling.

"We've seen it on the movies," she crooned, falling back onto the sofa. "Now let's see if it's true. This one's mine. Bit more sherry?"

An hour later, the two women had emptied the bottle. On the stereogram, The Shadows had stepped aside for Ella Fitzgerald.

"This was my second husband's favourite. Martin. My first one – Warren – he was a Mozart man."

"What were the other two called?"

"Norris and Peter. They're the ones who died in bed."

"You know what people say, don't you?"

"Peter liked pretty much anything, and Norris wouldn't listen to anyone but Bach." Eunice sat up straight. "They say I killed two of them. Maybe all of them? Right?"

"Something like that."

"Of course, I fucking well didn't. You've seen Frank. I'm just not very lucky."

"It's a lot of husbands."

"It's a lot of crap records."

"Are you bothered about the stories?"

"It's a small town. People need stories." The disc had stuck. Eunice stood up and bumped the cabinet gently with her hip. "They'll be talking about you now anyway. Not me."

"I don't think I can stop, Eunice…"

"He's a good-looking man, love. He's rich. He's charming…. dangerous."

".... exciting....and I've never fitted in Seymour's world."

"That doesn't mean you couldn't. Give him time. I never used to like Louis Armstrong."

"Time? We've been married forever."

"Listen. Men don't even start growing up until they're forty. Sometimes they never do. Look at Frank. Women are the grown-ups. We're the ones who take responsibility. Always."

Lucy snuggled her head against her friend's bosom, feeling the viral glow of alcohol circulating in her body.

"I'm bored, Eunice. I want something better."

"And Stan Clough? He's better?"

"I like the danger. I like not knowing where it's going. I've never had that in my life."

"It'll get messy love, it always does."

"I know." The two women were lost in darkness. The only light was the flicker from the radio dial. "But then what?"

"There's a bed here, when you need it. And you will. I promise."

"Thanks." In the blackness, Lucy found her friend's hand and squeezed it. "And you? What about Frank? Is that still serious?"

"We have our ups and downs," said Eunice.

"I can imagine," laughed Lucy. "I've seen that photograph."

As the days lengthened, her courage grew. In quick succession, there were three more encounters at the hotel. Any doubts about his methodology (the books in the hotel room, his familiarity with the staff) were quashed at birth, unworthy of closer scrutiny.

Stan was thoughtful. He asked questions. He'd read widely, and he listened when she talked about her marriage, her son, even her parents. There was a huge space, she felt, which he'd created uniquely for her within which she felt both appreciated and attractive; and within which she was determined to spend more and more time.

He was also pleasingly rich and the owner of a car where the air conditioning wasn't just a hole in the bodywork.

"It's beautiful. What is it?"

"It's a Jaguar. Mark X. 4.2 litres. Like it?"

"Did you warm the spark plugs up in a frying pan?"

"Sorry?"

"Ignore me. Just keep driving."

It was like they were outlaws. At pre-arranged locations, Lucy slipped quickly into the plum-coloured limo while Stan gunned the engine. Until they were out of town, she hid in the footwell, emerging only when there was no chance of being seen.

"All clear?"

"All clear." Stan looked across at his passenger. He was wearing leather driving gloves. "Stunning, as always."

It was true. She was spending increasing amounts of time on her clothes, even if she was spending less and less time in them. Stripping off in the back of a Jaguar wasn't easy but wrestling half-naked on upholstered seats more than made up for it. A long lunch break was all it took. And Seymour no longer even noticed where she was.

If she was late, he rarely asked why. If she was dressed up, he was complimentary, but incurious. A strange lull – like a ceasefire – had permeated the household. Every night she heard the same muffled voices from the workshop, but never once asked what he was doing.

Sometimes, to absolve her feelings of guilt, she even welcomed him into her bed, relishing the duplicitous sensations while they lasted; recoiling from them in horror at first light.

"I'll bring you breakfast in bed if you want?"

"No thanks. But I'll have a cigarette."

She'd watched him step naked from the bed. He looked stronger and still carried no weight.

"I think Isaac might be struggling at school."

"His report was good."

"I think there might be more to it than that."

"Please, please don't drag him into this."

Even if Seymour was right, she couldn't admit it. All this subterfuge only worked if she could despise him and stay unshackled by doubt. And so far, she was doing fine. The previous day, she'd kissed Stan openly in the lobby of the hotel. The day before that, he'd driven her home. Seymour's grinding obsession was making things easy. Gradually, she was losing all her fear of the consequences.

"We haven't talked for ages. Dad's worried about you."

"Like you care." Isaac's voice was edging deeper. She hadn't noticed that before. "You're as bad as each other."

It was a warm May evening. Lucy had managed egg and chips for the three of them. Seymour had washed the pots before slipping out to the shed.

"You'd tell us if you were struggling at school?" asked Lucy, ignoring the jibe. There was no response. "What about that Alice girl then? Are you still in touch?"

"That Alice girl?" snapped Isaac. "There's no point. She won't be home till summer now. She's gone on a school trip to Italy this half-term. Paid for by all the mugs who feed her creepy dad's machines."

"Summer isn't so far away. And I thought you liked him."

"I never said that."

That was something else about Isaac she hadn't noticed before. The older he got, the more he looked like Seymour.

"He bought you a burger once or something?" It wasn't a surprise really, but Lucy badly wanted her son to endorse him. "You liked his house? Colour television you said?"

"He's oily," mumbled Isaac, making his usual move for an exit. "What's it matter to you? Everyone in the town hates him anyway."

Over the next two weeks, there was no contact between Lucy and her lover. After a glorious early prelude, the town had been rocked by storms and on three successive days, Stan and his lifeboat churned out into the surf, returning each time with a clutch of grim-faced sailors.

On the third occasion, Lucy heard the maroons and struggled along the wind-pummelled north pier to watch. Beyond the packed harbour, there was no horizon – just steely grey skies and the frenzy of the sea. Huge waves repulsed by the walls slammed furiously against the bigger waves behind them. Every impact sent a tremor through her feet, and bubbles of seafoam were clinging to her ruined hair.

It felt incredible to be outside. After the exchange with Isaac, she'd reverted to her afternoons in bed, mired in agonies of doubt. She was fine now though. She'd got over it. Stan was a good man and Isaac was just a teenager growing up in a small-minded town where everyone resented success. Stan made her happy. He really did.

Holding tight to a flagpole, Lucy was enraptured. The scene was magnificent, awe-inspiring, a revelation. And more than anything, it was the noise which stirred her; the foul clanging of the halyards, and the tearing, tugging roar of the ocean. All those times, Seymour had crept down here alone – in the teeth of midnight storms – and finally, somewhere, a tiny part of her understood.

Away to her right, she could make out shapes and lights circulating where the waves met the shore. As she watched, a dark spot moving towards her became the rolling blue wedge of the town's lifeboat. She could clearly see the crew hunched inside the orange cabin, and when it passed, she was sure Stan had turned his head from the wheel to the navigation lights at the head of the pier where she stood.

When it had passed out of sight, she went to sit in a milk bar directly opposite the lifeboat station. In front of her was a sugary coffee and a Wagon Wheel. There was a jukebox on the wall playing a song she'd never heard about a man sitting on the dock of the bay. Outside the rain was still pounding, and the mirrored walls of the café were fogged with damp. It was 5 o' clock and. Eunice would have closed up and gone home.

"We're finishing now, love. You've been here ages. Are you done?" A teenage girl with cropped black hair was holding out her hand. Lucy drained away the last of her coffee. "You're a bit old to be in here anyway."

Lucy put her coat on and stepped into the rain. Down on the beach she could see men in yellow waterproofs guiding the lifeboat back towards its boathouse. From deep inside there was a husky cheer, followed by two more hip hoorays. Moving closer, Lucy could see a huddle of rescuers in a cloud of their own steam.

"Blimey. You're a surprise. A nice surprise." Stan had detached himself from his crew. He was still wearing rubberised dungarees and a thick blue knitted sweater. "Sorry about the outfit."

"I rather like it," she smiled, as he placed his hand behind her neck, drawing her close enough for a kiss.

219

"It can be arranged," he grinned. "Rubber next time it is, then."

"I heard the rockets go off," said Lucy, "I wanted to see. Is everything alright?"

"It's fine. A rudder failure on a sailing dinghy. We've towed it back."

"Will you be long?"

"Aaah. There's always loads of paperwork and the lads like a pint. Come to my house tomorrow afternoon. It's about time you saw it."

"Your house? No. I can't. Eunice would kill me. I need to get back full time."

"After work then? Just for a natter?"

"Only if you wear your waterproofs," whispered Lucy.

"You're on," said Stan.

The following day, the entire town emerged from hiding. Overnight, the wind swung up from the south sucking up a plume of warm Saharan air. By mid-morning, the pavements felt warm underfoot and Havercroft's Town & Country Footwear was doing steady business in ladies' sandals.

"You feeling better?" asked Eunice, averting her eyes from a bunion.

"It was just a blip. Everything's good now. Once again, thank you."

"We were quiet anyway, love. Not a problem. Not with me."

"If it's alright, though, I might just slip away thirty minutes early?"

Everyone knew Stan Clough's family house. Apart from the lighthouse, it was the most conspicuous building along forty miles of coastline. From a distance, it looked like a giant white wedding cake; three floors rendered in glass, each with its own wrap around balcony. To the rear, it was carefully hidden from its neighbours by

220

conifers. To the front, it stared straight out to the sea across a broad sweep of lawn.

For four decades it had been the subject of endless speculation and green-eyed curiosity. To some it was a triumph of art deco flair. To others it was a monstrous symbol of the Clough's dynastic vanity. In their dreams, its detractors prayed for the day the entire place washed away in a storm. But failing that, they'd settle for a good poke around inside. And since neither outcome was likely, disgruntled beach-walkers satisfied themselves with whatever they could deduce through pairs of binoculars.

It seemed strange to Lucy, knowing that she was about to step inside. Close up, she could see details that were invisible from the sands; the twin brass portholes in the porch; the school of oak-carved dolphins which framed the enormous front door; and the stucco frieze of interlocking shells dividing the ground floor from its upper tiers.

Finding a knocker (in the form of a brass lobster) Lucy rapped loudly and waited. She could hear slippered footsteps on wood. The door opened, and Stan drew her into a circular space bathed in natural light. Huge canvases – of shipwrecked sailing ships and frantic modern seascapes – littered the walls and parquet-floored corridors ran in every direction. In the centre was an old brass telescope on a wooden tripod.

"Do you like it? Can I show you around?"

"It's beautiful. It feels like there's more light inside than out."

Lucy slipped off her shoes and followed Stan into the living room. Two deeply cushioned sofas faced each other across a polished walnut coffee table scattered with newspapers. Along opposite walls, shelves of books rose from floor to the ceiling. There was a fireplace crafted from driftwood, ringed by a hearth inset with chalk pebbles from the beach. And filling the room with the distant blue of the sea, a fourth wall made entirely of glass.

"You can hear the waves," she said.

"All the time. I sleep like a baby."

"It must have been a wonderful place to grow up in."

"Not really. But I love it now."

"It's big for one person, though?"

"I've a cleaner," smiled Stan. "Let me show you the rest of it."

Over the next few days, Lucy spent whatever time she could steal in the house. Every detail seemed perfect; from its artful kitchen lighting to the levers which operated the plugs in the sinks.

There was no junk, no sawdust, no discarded soldering irons and better still; after the icy privations of hotel sex, Stan's mirrored bedroom had unlocked them both. During their frenzied contortions, Lucy made sure she could watch every detail in reflection. And when they were done, she threw open the double doors to crouch on the balcony, gazing out at the ocean wrapped in a sheet.

"There's a toy boat in a glass case downstairs," she mentioned one day, rolling up a stocking.

"It's not a toy. It's a scale model of a Victorian lifeboat. I made it myself."

"You made model boats when you were a child?"

"When I was a teenager, yes. Of course. Why? What's wrong?"

"Nothing. Nothing's wrong."

It was a strange irritation, but – as she so often did – Lucy buried it away. Stan had the sea in his blood. Boats were allowed. Seymour didn't. So they weren't. And anyway, there were other glorious distractions. Every visit to the house lifted her. If it was lunchtime, they talked or pulled books randomly from the shelves. If it was the

222

evening, they watched American comedies on Stan's huge television, their half-naked bodies stitched together and their eyes always on the time.

"I've never watched this stuff before. I always thought it was rubbish."

"Bewitched? Bilko? You're missing out."

"We don't watch telly on Sundays either. I don't allow it."

"I Love Lucy."

"Sorry?"

"It's a joke; a television programme. You could watch what you want if you lived here."

Lucy sat up. It was hard to define precisely what it was, but whenever she was at home now, she felt sick. Not that anyone had noticed. Exactly two weeks had passed since she first crossed Stan's threshold but so far, neither Seymour nor her elusive son had noticed her growing absences.

"Are you asking me to?"

"I don't know. What do you think?"

"I think you need to do better than that. Is this an invite or not? What about your daughter and my son?

"I thought that was over."

"He doesn't like you, by the way, my son; he says you're smarmy."

"Not terribly popular with your menfolk, am I?" laughed Stan, sliding his legs free of Lucy's. "Will you think about it? There's no hurry. We could work it all out."

"I'm really not sure," said Lucy, fishing behind the sofa for her skirt. "I'd better go."

The next day she was in work early. A sea fret had wrapped its mists around the town centre, and cars were crawling carefully through the fog; their yellow lights peering anxiously along the promenade.

"Up with the lark," chortled Eunice, arriving later to the rare double of a fresh brew and a functioning assistant.

"Short nights. I couldn't sleep," said Lucy. "Midsummer today, remember."

By midday, the vapours had melted to leave a perfect, blue sky. All weekend, the weathermen had been promising a July heatwave. Hopefully they were right. The town was long overdue a summer season without rain.

"Eunice. Listen. You once offered me a bolthole…."

"I did."

"Is it still there?"

"Of course it is? Always. What's happened?"

"Stan's asked me to live with him."

"And let me guess. There's something you're not quite sure about?"

"I've got to get away from that flipping boat. I don't know what happens after that."

Outside the shop an elderly man was fumbling with the door handle. Before he could turn it, Eunice flipped the sign over to 'Closed'.

"You'd be welcome," she said. "But one thing though…"

"Anything. What?"

"I can't cook."

During their lunch hour Lucy dashed home. Seymour would be at the paper writing his column. Isaac should be at school. At the back of the old stable, she pulled back the tarpaulin for one last peep at the boat. It was beautiful; and it looked finished; but it had killed them. Upstairs she packed quickly – a small, cardboard suitcase; enough for a few days.

It was just a break, nothing more, she repeated to herself; a separation.

Down in the kitchen, she pulled the letter from her bag, along with the last papery remnant of Seymour's Valentine rose. Looking at the envelope she felt a rush of doubt, followed by a profound sense of calm. Choosing the right words had cost her a night's sleep but in a funny way she'd been writing it all her married life.

When he got back from work, Seymour went directly to his workshop. Two hours later, he pulled his boat out into the sun; dashed into the house; and found what she had written.

"When did I leave this? Today? Yesterday? You've probably no idea. I could have disappeared weeks ago, and I'm not sure you'd have noticed. Sharing you with a wooden mistress doesn't work for me, so I'm moving out for a while. I'm not happy. I haven't been happy for a while.

I know that you know that so why do we never talk?

It's easier for you. You've always known what you wanted. Now it's my turn, Seymour. I want to be happy, and I have to find out how. I've left a note for Isaac in his bedroom and I'm staying with Eunice. X

PS We met over a boat and now we're parting over a boat.

PPS I'm truly sorry. You're a better person than I could ever be.

X Love Lucy"

"Dad. Dad. What's going on?"

Seymour turned his head to the sound of the voice. He was still sitting at the kitchen table, and the sun was long-lost behind the overgrown trees in the yard.

"Why has mum moved out? What the fuck has she done?"

He remembered now. Seymour saw the letter and remembered. He'd passed out. He'd slept. He'd been frozen. He'd walked around in circles. Whatever it was, or had happened, yes, he remembered. Through the window, in the rippling green shade, he could see his boat on its trailer.

Isaac had burst in like he usually did, chucking his school bag on the floor. Isaac had run upstairs. Isaac was down again clutching a piece of paper and yelling in his face. Yes, he remembered. He'd got a letter too.

"I don't understand," he whispered. "It's finished."

"I told you, dad." Isaac was sobbing, furious tears. "I told you not to build that boat."

"But it's finished. Look, out there. Just the mast and the rigging to go."

"You're mental. You're both completely mental."

"It's only a boat, Isaac." Seymour sighed. Suddenly all he wanted was sleep. "I think this goes deeper than that."

"You've got to get her back."

"I'll try. I promise you. It'll be fine."

"And listen. Listen. I can't stay here dad."

Seymour looked up sadly. "You're going to your mum?"

"You're joking. She's as bad as you. I'll stay with a mate."

"Alice Clough?"

"No. Somewhere. Anywhere." Isaac's arms had sagged to his sides and he sounded calmer. "But I'll come here for my sepper. OK?"

Two days later, Seymour rang the doorbell of Eunice Bolt's semi. Parked on the drive was a new MG 1300; the first he'd seen in town. Four dead husbands, he thought. She's done well for herself. Through the letterbox, he could hear the warm piping of a clarinet. When the door opened, Lucy was holding a piece of toast thick with jam.

"Seymour."

"Lucy."

"We're just leaving for work. It's our breakfast."

"You've got a Benny Goodman record on."

"Not me. Eunice. She says it puts her in the mood."

"What for?"

"Shoes, I suppose."

"I got your letter. We both got your letters. Isaac's moved out."

"I know. He's been to see me. He'll be fine. Give him a few more days."

"I want you back, love. The boat's done now." Seymour could hear himself gabbling. "Well, almost. And I know I've spent too much time on it. I just wasn't thinking. I just wanted it done. I just wanted it to be right. And it is. It is right. I'm sorry. I'm sorry. I love you. Please come home."

"I can't Seymour. It's complicated."

"We could talk then. Take a day off. Let's talk."

Lucy's attention had drifted out to the street where a newspaper boy was searching through his bag.

"Leave me alone, Seymour," she sighed. "Just go home and finish your boat."

"That's the point though. It is finished. I can give you all the attention you want."

There was an uncompromising blast of air as the door thudded shut. Behind him, Seymour heard the squealing of bicycle brakes and a far-too cheery whistle.

"Daily Express, mister?"

"Fuck off," said Seymour, turning sharply out of the drive towards his office.

It was a Thursday. Print day. He'd go home but not just yet. As he always did, Seymour stationed himself alongside the editor in the oily shadows of the machine room, waiting for the presses to spew out another week's helping of happenings.

On the front page, under the headline 'The Phoenix Rises', was Frank's latest picture of his boat. On the inside was the current tally of cobles scheduled to race in The Burlingtonian fund-raiser.

"Over forty now, Pilbeam. Bloody fine show."

"Thank you, sir."

"Ink and oil and hot metal. Can't beat the smell, eh? Must dash. Dead cert in the first race at Catterick."

Seymour watched him go, tucked a warm copy of the paper under his arm, and slipped out of the building. Just like they'd said, the summer was building nicely. A line of mangy donkeys was ambling past a queue at the ice cream van for one of 'Satronelli's 99 Full Cream Whoppers'. Somehow, he'd fix it. He'd stand by his promise to Spanners. He'd race the boat and then sell it. Or give it away. Either way, no more boats. Done.

Buoyed by the feeling that a corner had been turned, Seymour picked up his stride. There was a thin wisp of smoke in the sky ahead and a few streets from home he heard the bell of a fire engine. When he looked again, the plume had thickened and Seymour was running, head down, drawn on by the distant crackle of exploding sap.

"Seymour, lad. Fucking hell."

Somehow, Rehab was there already, forcing a path through the knot of neighbours transfixed by the sparks and the smell of burning timber.

"Shift yourselves. Out of the pissing way."

The two men kicked open the gate and edged into the yard. It was still there, exactly where he'd left it that morning. Except his boat was now engulfed in smoke; and its larch panels were buried in flames.

"She's burned it," said Seymour, turning away. "It's gone."

Chapter Six

In the long discussions which followed around the town's coffee bars and pubs, everyone was agreed on one thing. It was a jolly good job Rehab hadn't been drinking. Even on a quiet day, the Captain smelled like a ripe beermat, and in the presence of naked flames – so close to the local gasworks – the possible consequences were unimaginable. The whole town could have gone up, said some. If only, said the rest.

The extent of Rehab's heroism, however, was less clear cut. It was, after all, a very small fire. No lives had been at risk, and after Seymour left the scene, nobody actually witnessed what happened next. In the Captain's (unaccountably modest) personal account, he'd simply pulled down Seymour's makeshift tarpaulin wall and smothered the flames in an instant.

Only a handful of people knew the real story; that twelve months after starting a blaze on one boat he'd extinguished a fire on another. And only two of them had seen the empty can of petrol which had been mysteriously removed from the yard by the time the emergency crew arrived. _

"Honestly, it's not as bad as you think. Let me get you a bag of nuts…."

The Captain had found Seymour in the White Horse. It was Thursday – wages day – and the weekly lunchtime crush was spilling out onto the pavement. Huddled in the snug, Seymour was busily sinking down through a second pint of beer.

"Listen, you dozy pillock. I managed to put it out. That's got to be worth a double."

"Not interested," said Seymour, draining his glass. "Another pint when you're ready Nellie. And a large rum for the hero."

"Let's sup these and go back to yours," said Rehab, whose face was still coated in smudge. "We can fix it. All you've lost is a few weeks."

"My wife set fire to my boat. How the fuck can I fix that?"

Three drinks later, Rehab had given up the argument. And three hours after that, Nellie was steering Seymour gently home from the pub. Only Rehab was left inside, swaying beneath a smoke-blackened grin, his feet seemingly bolted to the floor.

"He'll be alright. He'll still be standing on the same spot when I get back," said Nellie, clutching Seymour's left arm with both her hands.

"You're a good woman. I'd have been alright with someone like you."

There were blackened footprints on the pavement outside Seymour's gate and the smell of charred timber still hung amongst the trees.

"What exactly happened?"

"Don't ask." Seymour detached himself and straightened his back.

"I could come in and make you a bit of tea?"

"You've done enough. I owe you," he mumbled, bending down blindly in search of Nellie's lips. "A thank you kiss, that's all."

"You take care. You know where I am."

Seymour had vanished under the shadow of his sycamores. Without a glance at the boat, he hurried in and threw himself on the sofa. Even when Lucy had been napping, the house had never felt so cold. Isaac's transistor was silent, the clocks were all stopped, and without the troubled breathing of his wife, the pulse of the place had gone.

It wasn't a house anymore, he thought, it was a mausoleum.

The next morning brought another flawless sky. With his mouth around the kitchen tap, Seymour flushed away the night's sticky crud from his teeth. Around dawn, he'd woken shivering and aching for a toilet. Still half-drunk, he'd stood in the yard splashing pee on the outline of his boat. Now in the sunlight, he could clearly see the singed tarpaulin and beneath it, whatever remained of his dream.

Pulling on his shoes, he stepped outside and turned back the canvas. Every square inch of the boat was covered in soot and in the dark well of the boat, a few curious fragments of blackened fabric appeared to be bobbing in a pool of filthy water.

Seymour's overnight torpor had vanished. With a hosepipe and sponge, he sluiced away the smoke stains to expose the worst affected sections. All the critical damage was concentrated around the midpoint of the coble where a handful of side planks had burned right through and a section of the laboriously steamed oak gunwales had completely disappeared.

After several circuits of the boat, Seymour had seen enough. Rehab was right. 'Phoenix' wasn't clinically dead. She could be resuscitated with a little love and labour; but not by him. That moment had passed. After one final survey of the damage, he leaned in to retrieve the sodden fragment of cloth.

He'd immediately known what it was. He just wanted to be sure. Not all of it had been destroyed. He could still make out a large 'L' and the red tail of a dragon. For years, it had hung around the kitchen. The indestructible tea towel, Lucy had called it; bought long ago by her mother at a Llandudno gift shop, now reduced to ashes but still contaminated by the unmistakeable stink of petrol.

Over the coming week, the blaze eclipsed the heatwave as the town's sole topic of conversation. It didn't matter that hard information was scarce. Facts were never terribly helpful anyway. Everyone felt the same; the whole thing was just so unbelievably sad. Not only had the poor man lost his boat in a suspicious fire; but now (apparently) his wife had started a lesbian affair with that husband-killer from the shoe shop.

"It's all just so bloody grim," Eunice had remarked, during a lull. Havercroft's Town & Country Footwear had experienced a recent surge in customers; most of whom were content merely to look through the window. "Even you must feel for him?"

"It is. And I do," replied Lucy, hiding her face from the rubberneckers.

"Anyone said how it started?" asked Eunice. Like the entire town, she was desperate for gossip. "Have you said anything to him?"

"We've not spoken. I wouldn't know what to say. I sent him a note."

It was true. Shortly after the fire, an envelope had appeared on Seymour's mat. Inside was a single slip of paper and two short sentences. *"I know you won't believe this, Seymour. But I am truly sorry. X Lucy."*

Seymour had tossed it to one side, uncertain whether it was a confession, an apology, or both. Either way, there'd be no reply. Lucy might have dumped him, but he was anything but alone. Every day since the blaze had seen a growing number of unsolicited letters from strangers. Most were merely expressions of support but amongst the cash and cheques (which he returned) were two vaguely indecent proposals, one of which boasted several intimate anatomical photographs.

There'd been a string of visitors, too. Frank had been the first, dispatched (with stentorious urgings from Seymour's editor) to find out how the town's revered boat-builder was coping 'in his darkest hour'.

"You might want to take a look at these," said Seymour, handing over an envelope adorned with hearts.

233

"Bloody hell," blurted Frank, fumbling for his reading glasses. "Eunice hasn't got one of those. Not that I've found anyway."

"They've got to be a wind up. If Spanners can even write, I'm blaming him."

"You've not been answering your door. Everyone's worried about you."

"I can see that." Another six letters had arrived that morning. "It'll be fine. I just need a day or two."

"Soapy wants something in this week's paper."

"I thought he might," sighed Seymour. "Do what you have to do. Just don't ask me to write it."

"Give him a quote at least," said Frank, taking one last close look at the photographs.

"Tell him, the race goes on without me. Tell him, this isn't about my boat it's about The Burlingtonian. It's about the town."

"Perfect. Just one last question."

"Go on."

"What's a clitoris?"

"Jesus, Frank. Why?"

"Well, Eunice says I need to work out where it is…..so I asked Rehab."

"And what did the Captain say?"

"He said it was a kind of fish."

"So, don't tell me, you went to Corky Brown's fish shop…?"

"Yes. Brilliant. Exactly."

234

"And what did Corky say?"

"He said they'd just sold the last one."

When the next edition of the town's newspaper came out, Seymour's profile had climbed even higher. On the front page (underneath the headline 'Boat Blaze Hero's Mystery Boat Inferno') was Frank's picture of the fire-damaged 'Phoenix'. On the inside, two more pages were crammed with pictures and stories retracing the year-long saga.

Just one key fact was missing; no-one had said how the fire started. 'One of those things' was the broad consensus and after a while, it didn't seem to matter anyway. Official figures would later reveal it to be the best-selling issue in the rag's 187-year history; a milestone which Soapy marked with a three-day sabbatical at York races to which no-one else was invited.

Meanwhile, as the summer drifted into July, Seymour's struggle with despair was compounded by the accomplishments of an elderly man in Portsmouth.

Every newspaper, every news bulletin, was leading with the same story. Alec Rose, a 59-year-old vegetable dealer, had just sailed around the world alone in 354 days, prompting 200,000 people to cheer him back into port. For a few lacklustre hours, Seymour flicked through his old sailing books, hoping for a spark that never came.

"A vegetable dealer. A fucking vegetable dealer," he said (although there was nobody there to hear). "And I couldn't even get my pissing dinghy out of the harbour.

It was around this time that a gleaming black Austin pulled up outside Seymour's front door. In the driver's seat, a tidy-looking man wearing a sports jacket adjusted his moustache in the rear-view mirror and stepped out. Stretched across the back seat was a large black dog.

"Bill. How lovely to see you. No Olive?"

"She's with Lucy. I've dropped her off," he said, a little awkwardly, shaking Arthur from his slumbers. "It didn't seem right not to come and say hello."

Together, they carried the dog into the yard where he lay motionless (and without shame) on his back.

"Is he actually still alive?" asked Seymour. Each of the dog's legs was pointing vertically towards the sun.

"I believe so," said Bill, wiping his brow. "I've never known a dead one that farts quite so much."

"I'm glad you've come," said Seymour, laughing. "Let's keep hold of our teeth this time."

Dragging chairs from the kitchen, the two men joined the supine bulldog in the sun. Every few minutes, the garden was flooded with the smell of suppurating meat.

"That'll be the gasworks," said Seymour.

"I doubt it," said Bill, prodding Arthur with his foot.

"Have you seen Lucy? Is she OK?"

"She's quiet. But she seems fine."

"I'm not sure I understand women."

"You, me and about five million others."

"The weird thing is that I still think she would have come round to the boat in some way. Does that make any sense?"

"Not really."

"She told me I couldn't make her happy, Bill. But that's all I've ever wanted to do."

Bill leaned forwards and stroked Arthur's shining flank.

"It's funny. Lucy's mother was the same. She always knew what she didn't want. That was the easy bit. All the anger and frustration – whatever – came from never really knowing what she DID want.... Just something better, she always said. And still says. I used to think all of that fury was code; and that what she really wanted was anyone but me because I'd lived, and he hadn't."

"I'm not sure I understand."

"I've always been satisfied with my life. I got back from the war. I was alive. That was always enough for me. Just being alive was enough. I got a steady job. I played golf; had two kids. And I felt no embarrassment about my love for Olive."

"But Olive wanted more?"

"Yes. But she didn't know what it was. Or how to get it. So she fought. And along the way, she ridiculed everything about me."

"But you stayed together?"

"And I still love her," said Bill, softly. "We're more alike than you thought."

"Lucy blames my father. She says his generation shut women out. She says I'm no better."

"She's probably right. Her mum would think so."

"So it's your fault for dodging a German bullet and mine for being a man?"

"Something like that."

A refuse wagon was working its way along the street. They could hear the hollow clang of empty dustbins being rolled back into place.

"The boat was nearly finished anyway."

"Is it ruined? Could you repair it?"

"There's no time, Bill. I'm done with it."

"You should think about that, Seymour."

"Because?"

"Because maybe the boat isn't really the problem."

"Alright Sigmund Freud, so what IS the problem?"

"Not the faintest idea, old man," chuckled Bill. "Good luck."

Towards the end of July, Seymour drifted back into full-time work. It was good to be busy again – no-one quizzed him about the fire – and since his return coincided with the town's annual kite festival, 'Pilbeam's People' had a heart-gladdening mine of material to explore.

In the fifteen years since he'd started it, the event had exploded. For three days, the skies above the town's twin beaches bobbed with colour. Kites shaped like bananas and dragons; kites the size of cars; kites which danced; kites which rose until they were visible only by telescope; kites which soared and kites which (despite innumerate artful tugs and exhortations) resisted every effort to get them airborne.

It had been Seymour's idea. But it was Lucy who really pushed it. When they first arrived at the seaside – when she was just pregnant with Isaac – they'd planned it together, sticking fliers on telegraph poles and bus shelters which nobody read. At the first one, they'd flown the only kite above a wind-raddled beach, bent double with laughter. At the second, they'd been joined by two elderly men with military kites purloined from the Normandy landings.

After that, for Lucy, the magic slowly dropped away. The more people who came, the less interest she had. For a few years, she pushed baby

Isaac along to watch but soon after that, when it was fully established as a town institution, she abandoned it completely.

"You take everything too far," she'd told him. "I liked it when it was just us two."

Seymour immediately severed all ties with the festival, secretly thrilled that it thrived without him. A one-day local jamboree had evolved into a three-day extravaganza drawing kiters from all over Europe. But every year, Lucy railed against its popularity. And when a stray kite crashed into their yard, she'd stomped out and torn it to pieces.

"I've not been to this for years," he told Frank, as they walked towards the North shore. "Perfect weather for it."

And it was. On this Saturday afternoon, a warm breeze was blowing steadily seawards across the rooftops. From a distance, the air above the beach shimmered with colour. As the two men drew closer, the colours fractured amongst countless kites, each one anchored to an invisible hand somewhere deep inside a crowd squeezed between the sea wall and the incoming tide.

"That's absolutely amazing. I'd no idea," gasped Seymour.

"Are you blubbing?" asked Frank. "You look like you are."

"It's the Welsh in me, Frank. We get emotional."

Three men were arguing at the water's edge. The tangled lines of their kites were dragging each one out of the sky.

"Bloody goldmine for some people this is," shouted Frank. "You should be on commission."

He had a point. Everywhere, the streets were choked with families flooding in from the station and the coach parks. Between them and the ocean lay a gauntlet of chip shops, joke shops, whelk stalls and pubs. If they made it to the seafront, Stan Clough's amusements had designs on the last of their pennies. If they made it to the beach, at least the kite festival was free.

"Who's the dodgy Punch and Judy man?"

A blue and white tent – resembling a canvas sentry box – was being erected for a performance in front of an audience of children. As the crowd grew, the perplexed face of a man with a purple (and hairy) nose appeared briefly in the tent's tiny stage window before ducking back out of sight.

"Sorry about the delay, kids. I've lost the crocodile."

"Hilarious," squealed Frank. "It's Clinkers."

A child had burst out crying, prompting a squall of high-pitched boos. From deep inside the tent there was a volley of expletives, followed by the sound of a case slamming shut.

"Shit, damn and bollocks. I very much regret to say……"

Clinkers' disembodied voice was struggling against the salvo of abuse.

"……that no crocodile means no show……sorry, kids."

It was no use. Nobody could hear him. As his face rose gently into view, an ice cream cornet was launched from somewhere near the back.

"To be honest, I'm not sure where the naffing truncheon is either."

The cornet had landed; just below the hairline, holding its position for a second, before sliding down along the wiry bridge of the entertainer's proboscis.

"Which of you little fucking twats threw that?" roared Clinkers.

In the uproar that followed, Frank and Seymour spirited the junk shop owner to a café overlooking the beach. Behind them, three dozen children had pulled his tent to the ground.

240

"We should have let them lynch you."

"Sod off. Forty brats. Shilling each. Two quid. Most I've made in a day for yonks."

"It's not on. People won't come again."

"I've had that gear in the back of the shop for years. I didn't know half of it was missing. I'll probably find the crocodile when I go back."

"And then you'll give a free show?"

"I will, Seymour. For you mate, anything."

"And give the money to The Burlingtonian?"

"Do I have to?"

But Seymour wasn't listening. Amongst the collage of floating kites, he'd seen something. Or he thought he had.

"I'll catch up with you later," he said, slipping out towards the beach, his eyes firmly locked on a vivid patch of green rising strongly on the wind.

He'd thought it was lost but even from this distance he knew what it was. After his mother's death, he'd saved one dress from her wardrobe. Years later, he'd stitched its viridescent silk into a kite, which flew better than any he'd ever made; flashing like emerald foil whenever it dipped across the sun.

Leaning down over the harbour wall, Seymour followed the line from the kite's twitching tail to a point in the crowd. The last time he'd flown it, he'd been a teenager. But who was controlling it now? Head by head, he scanned the blur of shapes, before cutting onto the beach down a flight of barnacled stone steps.

He could still see the green kite, directly above him. Once again, he followed its string down into the crush of faces, pushing on until he

241

was certain he'd found who was holding it.

"Isaac?"

"Dad?"

"You're flying my kite."

"Correction. We're both flying your kite."

For the first time, Seymour noticed the girl; slim, golden-haired, and seemingly glued to his son's side.

"This is Alice," said Isaac. "Alice, this is my father."

"Of course. Lovely to meet you." Seymour stretched out his hand. "Are you here for the weekend?"

"Boarding school. We've broken up early for summer; just got back today. I'm spending a couple of weeks with my dad."

"I saw the kite," said Seymour. "It's amazing."

"It's from your workshop. Remember? There was that old box of yours and I took it. You don't mind?"

"It's fine. It's fine." Seymour looked up. Even now it was still the most beautiful thing in the air. "I'm glad you did."

"I'll come back home at the end of the week, when the school hols start. Is that OK?"

"Brilliant," said Seymour, turning to Alice. "Hopefully, I'll see you again, too."

The waves would soon be touching the wall. A few kites had already been retrieved, opening gaps in the floating wall of colour. Walking swiftly away from the seafront, Seymour turned left towards the deserted main promenade. It was almost 4 o'clock. Only a handful of shops were still open. From the pavement across the street, he could see Lucy, standing outside the glass door of Havercroft's. She had her back turned to the traffic and she was searching in her bag for a key.

The summer suited her. It always had. She was wearing a short, sky blue skirt; her legs were bare and tanned; and he could see the outline of a bra through the fabric of her simple, white blouse. When she turned, Seymour slipped into the shadows of a bookmaker's doorway, feeling the old tearing rush of his love. A race was reaching its climax on the television inside and the commentator's frenzied shouts leaked out into the sunshine.

Lucy looked up trying to locate the source of the noise. She had a cigarette ready at her mouth and her eyes were sparkling. Seymour backed quickly through the doorway into the bookies. She's put weight on, he thought. She's got her figure back.

"Seymour. Seymour. My fine fellow."

A crumpled figure in a crumpled suit was perched on a stool in front of a black and white screen. The floor around him was littered with abandoned betting slips.

"Not now Soapy. Please."

"I'm hearing you've got filly trouble," the editor growled, fumbling in his pocket for a hip flask. "You can always talk to me."

"I'll bear that in mind,"

"A good crack of the whip. That's the best thing for 'em, Pilbeam."

He could still see Lucy through the window. She was checking her watch and scrutinising the road in each direction. On the television, another race had started and Soapy was scratching furiously on a piece of paper. Outside in the sunshine, Lucy was smiling widely. She'd put on her sunglasses and stepped to the edge of the kerb.

Someone was coming.

"It's going to win," bellowed Soapy, sliding from his stool. "I'm a winner."

Lucy was still smiling. She'd stubbed out her cigarette. She was waving. A taxi, thought Seymour. But then where would she be going?

There was a sudden, sharp squeal of brakes. Seymour hurtled outside.

"Not now, not now."

A double decker bus pulled up at the stop directly outside the bookies and a dozen passengers clutching rolled-up kites were streaming on board. When the bus drew away, Lucy was gone. The pavement was empty. The only things moving were the glowing brake lights of a Jaguar, as it manoeuvred around a cyclist before speeding silently out of sight.

Seymour's mind was racing. Something was wrong. No, it wasn't. Nothing sinister had happened. His wife – the woman who'd set fire to his boat – had got a lift with someone. A new friend, probably. And yet something undoubtedly felt awry; a feeling compounded by the way she'd looked in that skirt.

"What happened to you?"

A comforting figure in an orange blazer was striding jauntily towards him.

"Frank. Sorry. I'd got enough for my story."

"No problem. All's well. Clinkers found his crocodile."

"Frank? What kind of car does Stan Clough drive?"

"Same as his dad always did. A Jaguar."

"You sure?"

"Pretty sure," said Frank, "And another thing."

"What?"

"I've been to the library." Frank was grinning proudly.

"And?"

"And a clitoris isn't a fish."

It was a short walk to Eunice's house. Her car was standing newly washed in a pool of water and the forecourt glowed under its weight of crimson begonias.

"Eunice? Lucy? Are you in?"

No reply. Seymour hammered the doorbell again; nothing came back but the sweet smell of freshly baked bread.

"Lucy? It's Seymour."

Through the letterbox, he could see right down to the kitchen window. An elegant woman in a bathing costume was half-sleeping outside in the back garden.

"Sorry to disturb you." Seymour had slipped in through a side alley. "I thought you were someone else."

"I've made some scones. Would you like one?" said Eunice, slipping a cardigan around her shoulders. "I don't really get many guests."

"I'm looking for Lucy. Is she in?"

"I could rustle up some tea. It's from Harrogate. It's very nice."

"That's sweet. But do you know where she might be?"

Eunice stood up. She was an attractive woman, thought Seymour. Intelligent, too. Not the most obvious candidate for a match with

Frank.

"Listen, Seymour……"

"She does still live here, doesn't she?"

"You've got to understand. She's my best friend."

"Where's she gone, Eunice?" Seymour could hear his voice rising. "You have to tell me."

"She moved out yesterday."

"Where? Somewhere in the town?"

"That I won't tell you. Sorry. But I promised."

Eunice hadn't needed to say. Seymour knew exactly where to go.

Hitting the seafront at a jog, he turned away from the harbour towards the southern edge of town. Apart from a few early revellers the streets were quiet. In a few more hours, the pubs would be swinging. And after that, the town's one nightclub would be cranking up its weekly 'Disc-o-Date'.

"I should have gone to that with Lucy," thought Seymour, slowing to a walk.

He could see it now; the last house before the dunes; the wedding cake house.

The house that Clough built.

Seymour stopped and took in the sea. It made no sense. None. What was the difference between them? Stan Clough was born to boats. His father had died for the fucking sea. Money and boats; that was the difference. Money and class and charm and boats and bullshit. And sex.

Of course, there would have been sex. Seymour's guts churned,

246

recalling the times – recent times – when she'd turned on to him, more desperate than he'd ever seen her; pushing him away when she was done.

Without even thinking, he was walking faster, covering the last few yards to the boundary. Like everybody in town, he'd stood there before, curiously wondering. Now all he could see was the dark outline of a Jaguar car, and the two figures behind a huge glass window.

They were talking. They were holding champagne glasses. The man's hand was on her waist. As Seymour watched they moved closer to him, looking out together over the long shadow of the house to the advancing lines of white breakers.

Seymour ducked and turned, stumbling for home. He felt cold and tired and dirty and he badly needed any kind of a drink.

"Dad. What's happened. Are you alright?"

He'd seen them advancing towards him – arm in arm – just a few streets from The White Horse.

"I'm fine." Seymour composed himself and wiped his eyes. "Where are you heading?"

"I'm walking Alice home."

"I'll see you later on then."

"Dad? What do you mean? I said end of the week. Dad? What's happened?"

"Goodnight Alice," said Seymour. "Lovely to see you again."

Inside the public bar it was standing room only. Behind a table crammed with empties he found Captain Rehab checking the football scores in the Saturday sports pink.

"I didn't know you did the pools?"

"I don't," said the Captain.

"I didn't know you were interested in football."

"I'm not."

Seymour tried another tack. "Listen. How long do you reckon it would take to get Phoenix seaworthy?"

Rehab folded the newspaper and surveyed his collection of glasses for salvageable dregs.

"I thought you'd written that off."

"I had. But I've written it back on again now."

"You, me and Spanners? A month, say. Working flat out."

"In time for the race?"

"Easy peasy."

"I couldn't pay. But I'd keep you in drinks. And pies."

"Now you're talking."

"What about the trawler work? And Harry's shop?"

"It's a good cause. We'll cope," said Rehab. "When do we start?"

"Tomorrow?" said Seymour, hopefully.

"Better make mine a large one then," said Rehab rubbing his hands together.

"Coming right up," said Nellie.

Chapter Seven

The sun was low in the sky when Seymour left the pub. In one hand was a carrier bag containing four large bottles of Guinness. In the other was a pipe which he relit once he'd settled at the kitchen table with a chipped glass and a penknife to prise off the metal tops.

As the dark thickened, the only visible sign of life was a bowlful of glowing tobacco, rising and falling between Seymour's face and lap as he waited for his visitor. Halfway through the second bottle, he heard the gate open and shut. He felt calm and determined; and completely void of anger.

"What are you doing, dad? It's pitch black in here."

"Don't put the light on," whispered Seymour. "I've got a candle."

A smoky stub had been shoved into the neck of an empty stout bottle. Seymour struck a match and held it to the wick.

"Your mum bought me this pipe," he said. "The penknife, too."

"Why didn't you tell me, dad? Back there.Why did you let me go to Alice's house?"

"Because you wouldn't have believed me. You had to see it." Seymour flipped the top of a third bottle and slid it across to his son. "Did you speak to her? Was she alright?"

"Is that for me?"

"Don't tell me it's your first."

"She was quite calm really. I was only there a minute. I couldn't stand it."

"And Alice?"

"I don't know. She'll go to her mum's, probably."

"I'm really sorry. You'll work something out, I'm sure. With Lucy, too."

"Maybe," said Isaac, wrinkling his face after a long pull of Guinness. "But I knew something was wrong. More wrong than just you being a selfish knob."

"It's been pretty crap, to be honest. Perhaps we'll be happier."

"You're not angry?"

Seymour shrugged. "It wouldn't do me any good if I was."

"You should be angry. You should be steaming. All her fancy clothes and that weird behaviour? It wasn't the boat, dad. It wasn't you. It was her."

"It's complicated. I don't know."

"I feel shit. What are you going to do? What's going to happen?"

Seymour wriggled back in his chair. It was an old Windsor he'd repaired countless times, and its arms were held in place by duct tape and string.

"I'm going to finish the boat. Want to help? I'll still need a first mate, too."

Isaac stretched forward to tap his bottle against Seymour's glass.

"Just try stopping me," he said.

When the school broke for summer, Seymour tossed his son's annual report straight into the dustbin. There'd been far too many lies in

250

their house, and the multi-coloured ink wasn't fooling anyone. In a year's time, Isaac would probably be turfed out of school with no qualifications. Until then, all that mattered was keeping him happy; a task made considerably easier by the holiday mood which had prevailed since Lucy's departure.

"Is it alright if I try some cooking?"

Isaac's request (happily acceded to) had been a surprise to them both. After the discovery of one of his grandmother's ancient cookbooks – a tome that still listed sturgeon as a staple ingredient – he'd advanced swiftly from scrambled egg to steak pies. For the first time ever, the kitchen smelled of warm pastry not lubricating oil, and it was flour not sawdust that the few rare visitors would depart with on their socks.

Home-made tomato soup had displaced teenage angst. It was to prove a fortuitous blooming of hidden talent.

Encouraged by the fine weather, Seymour had dragged 'Phoenix' out under the sun. And as the wood dried, his spirits lifted. In the workshop, he'd unearthed sufficient spare larch and oak to repair the damaged sections. The two canvas sails had been ordered from a sailmaker in South Shields. An end was once again in sight. Only the masts and the rigging remained to be found.

"Don't worry about them," promised Rehab. "They're under control."

To begin with, Seymour resumed work alone, pulling a cover over 'Phoenix' at night when he was too weary to continue. By mid-July, Rehab and Spanners had joined him full time, and the garden rattled with the sound of cursing and satisfied merriment.

It was a happiness beyond easy analysis. The three men felt conjoined by a sense of mission which didn't need to be explained. Nothing less than perfection would do. There were no mistakes or miscalculations; no energy was wasted; no corners were ever cut, and every morning

251

Seymour's tools were re-sharpened and ready to go.

Nor were any questions ever asked about the fire. Now that the charred wood had been expunged, there was no reason to probe. In its place was a fully restored hull, sanded to perfection and glowing under a dazzling hide of varnish. Every joint had been sealed with mastic; thin metal strips had been nailed along the forefoot to protect it from the beach shingle; and beneath its polyurethane glaze, the grain of the wood had lifted until every knot stared out at them like a holy eye.

"We used to slap cow shit in all the cracks and holes," said Rehab, standing back to admire their handiwork.

"Fascinating," said Seymour.

Isaac watched it all through the kitchen window with a mounting sense of awe. Amongst his schoolmates, Captain Rehab was a town joke, an easy target for adolescent derision. But every night when their work had stopped, the teenager went outside to sweep the shavings, feeling diminished by what the three men had accomplished.

"*I never understood it before,*" he wrote in a long, rambling letter to Alice. "*But it's a magnificent thing and I feel ashamed that I ever took my mother's side against it. Hopefully one day, we'll sail in it together.*"

"*It sounds amazing,*" she replied. "*But I can't come back. Not yet. You know your mum's not the first, don't you? There's been so many I've lost count but my dad's written and he's unrepentant. What a mess. I'm so sorry. He's an arse. I really hope she knows what she's doing.*"

Seymour hoped so too. Now that the secret was out, Lucy had abandoned the subterfuge. After several, highly tactile public appearances, everyone in the town knew the identity of Stan Clough's latest trophy and all of them were broadly of one mind; that it wouldn't last five minutes and that (in these exact words or similar) 'poor Mr. Pilbeam deserved better than that pissy cow.'

252

Unlike Isaac, however, 'poor' Seymour had not picked up his pen. Nor was he likely to. Lucy was privately mourned, but it had never been his way to worry too far into the future. At long last, he had a routine and a purpose and a looming sense of achievement. Every day, the house rocked with the laughter of friends; the sun was still shining; and his son appeared as if reborn.

"How's school?" asked Rehab, during the final few days of construction.

Isaac looked at Seymour. Seymour was looking at something under the boat.

"I got a B++ in maths."

"Alright smartarse. What's twelve times nine?" asked Spanners.

"A lot," said Isaac.

"You should be in our dominoes team," winked the Captain.

"What's for dinner?" asked Spanners.

Isaac's blossoming culinary skills had found a perfect outlet. If the three men started early, he'd welcome them with full English breakfasts served alongside tottering heaps of fried bread. If their shift finished late, he revived them with fried pork sausages and chips pulled from a pan of molten lard. In between, he provided a ceaseless supply of tea, without which none of them could function.

"How many sugars, Cap'n?" he'd asked nervously, when they first met.

"Six."

"Six?"

"Six," said Rehab. "I can't stand it too sweet."

By early August – right on schedule – they were almost done. No detail had been overlooked. Strapped inside the hull was a pair of wooden oars and a boathook. The tiller handle had been finished in creamy white paint and the boat's name appeared on two carved blocks placed either side of the bow.

"So where are the masts?" asked Spanners.

"Just be patient," replied Rehab. "Trust me."

The same afternoon, a lorry pulled up outside Seymour's house carrying two long-dead – and very tall – Christmas trees.

"Perfect," said Seymour. "You're a genius."

"I always thought so," said Rehab.

For years, in an act of seasonal folly, the local council had erected trees at the sea end of the town's two piers. By Christmas, they'd usually been blown away. Those that stayed upright into January were thrown unceremoniously onto a tip from which Rehab (in a rare moment of prescience) had salvaged these two survivors.

"We've a week," said Seymour. "That's all. I need to get sailing this thing."

The trio wasted no time. Within a few hours, they'd stripped the branches and the bark off both trees. Working right through the weekend, they cut the masts down to length; fashioning a longer one to carry the main sail and a shorter spike to hold the triangular jib sail clear of the bow. By the end of the fifth day – a Wednesday – each pine pole had been planed, varnished and slotted into place.

"It's bloody brilliant," said Frank, squatting to take a photograph of the nameplate. "Will it float?"

The saga of Seymour's boat had been returned to the front pages of the local paper. Finally, it seemed the town was getting the happy ending it wanted. Seymour's editor had supplied its saviours with a large bottle of cider; and to mark its completion, Isaac had baked a cake, topped with a marzipan model of 'Phoenix' cornered by four candles.

"One candle for each of us," cheered Isaac, raising a glass. "Thanks for letting me help."

"Hold it there," said Frank, snapping off another picture. Two days later, the photograph was public property.

"Mr.Pilbeam Has Built His Boat" read the triumphant headline.

Underneath it was the latest news of a burgeoning regatta which was now just two weeks away. Over fifty craft were expected, along with television crews and huge crowds. To keep order, all police leave had been cancelled. To raise cash, volunteers would be patrolling the streets with collection buckets.

"Cheer up," said Spanners. "We've saved The Burlingtonian."

"Not quite," replied Seymour.

It was Saturday lunchtime and the three men (with Isaac) were tucked into a corner of The White Horse with the newspaper. A mood of weary anti-climax had set in and Seymour's thoughts had drifted back to Lucy.

"I'm skint," grumbled Rehab. "All the fishing boats are out at sea."

"You could sell your life story," suggested Isaac

"I could. But there's a small problem."

"What's that?"

"I can't remember any of it."

There was a flurry of laughter from the bar where Nellie was filling shelves from an ancient wooden crate.

"You mean you don't want to remember any of it," she chuckled.

"We're going to miss all this," said Spanners

"You haven't even sailed it yet." Nellie had come round to stand by their table with a tray of free drinks. "No more after these, mind," she said.

"The sails only arrived this morning…. the sea trials start tomorrow".

"Does anyone know a ghost writer," said Rehab reaching for a pint. "It's all flooding back."

At first light, the shipbuilders reconvened at Seymour's house with three hangovers and one dodgy van. After a plateful of Isaac's 'special' sausage sandwiches, they felt well enough to tow the boat down onto the sand where Spanners gathered them round for a survivor's lesson in the art of rigging.

"If you remember nothing else, remember this…."

Holding the main halyard in both hands, he hauled up the big sail and waited for the wind to pull it tight. As the canvas filled, the boat lurched fiercely on its trailer. Before it could crash over, Spanners released the halyard and the sail slid swiftly back down the mast under its own weight. In an instant, the boat was still.

"…. if the sail can't be dropped immediately, you're in trouble."

"I don't understand." Isaac was suddenly feeling very nervous.

"These boats are great in so many ways," explained Harry. "They're fast. They're strong. They sail well in light winds."

"There's a but?"

"But they've got no keel underneath so they can struggle in really heavy side winds."

"What do you mean struggle?" asked Isaac, suspiciously.

"If a big gust catches them – or even a big wave – they'll go over unless you can drop the sail quickly which means you never tie off the rope holding the sail up. You either keep it in your hand if the winds are light or loop it over a stanchion so you can easily flick it off."

"Jesus, dad. Did you know all this stuff?"

Isaac turned to Seymour. Seymour was looking pale.

"They're shitting themselves," said Rehab. "Well done. Great lesson."

"And what happens if it does go over?" queried Isaac. "There's a way of righting it surely?"

"Nope," said Spanners.

"Nope," said the Captain.

"Errrr. I don't think so," said Seymour.

"So we die?"

"Possibly. Or." Spanners had grasped the shiny pine mast. "You slide this out of its socket. You grab hold of it. And you use it as a life raft. Simple."

"Simple," replied Seymour.

"Simple," said Rehab.

"And one other thing. Always carry a knife."

It was a relief to get on the water. With a heave from Rehab, they'd easily crested the low-breaking waves and in those first few, tearful seconds, Seymour savoured the gentle pitch of the sea, unable to exclude the years of pain which had preceded it. Back on the beach, Nellie had turned up to watch. She was standing alongside Rehab, barefooted in the shallows; Isaac was whistling a nautical air, and Spanners was waiting calmly with his left hand on the tiller.

"I know what you're feeling," he whispered. "I've been there myself."

By midday, Seymour was in ecstasy. The winds had built slowly under a blazing sky; Spanners was a patient teacher; and the boat came alive as it tacked and turned, issuing deep noises of satisfaction wherever the joints tightened, and the timbers swelled in the salt.

When he felt they were ready, Harry steered back to the beach enabling Seymour and Isaac to press on alone, feeling their confidence sucking them ever closer to the wind until the sails were drum-tight and the vibrations ran down through the mast into their feet and hands.

"You made this. I can't believe it," gushed Isaac, wiping the spray from his face. "It's incredible."

For the next seven nights, the pair kept up their practise, sailing further each time; looking constantly for stronger winds and the black patches of ruffled sea which told them where the winds might be. Everything he'd ever read was making sense. He knew how to gybe. He knew how to open the sails and ride a following sea. Instinctively, he knew when to push hard and when to slacken off. After a time, he could even sense the flow of the tide, and gauge whether the breezes were swerving or building or simply fading away with the sun.

Nothing mattered for either but their presence on the water. Seymour's weekly column had resumed, but the work was undemanding, and the paper had surrendered itself entirely to the regatta. "Just write about your bally boat. Practise all you like," Soapy had told him. "After that, we'll see."

Isaac, meanwhile, was splitting his time between the amusement arcades (where he was happy to fleece Stan Clough out of a few shillings) and a part-time afternoon job peeling potatoes at a local chip shop. Other than that, he was down at the shoreline with his father, shaking out the sails until their speed built and the town shrank to nothing behind them.

"We're good at this," beamed Isaac, after their first week's practise. They were back home, and he was busily beating eggs together for pancakes.

"I think we might be," said Seymour. "But we won't really know that until we sail in some bad weather."

"I can't understand why mum wouldn't like it."

"Maybe it's too frivolous. Or maybe it's because I like it."

"Have you tried to see her?"

"I don't think I could."

That wasn't entirely true. Just once, he'd stationed himself outside Stan's house, watching their shapes through the windows. The next morning he'd gone back, without any explicit purpose, and trailed her to work. But both episodes had left him confused and exhausted.

"I got a letter," said Isaac, flipping a pancake in the frying pan. "I threw it away."

"Did you read it? Did you keep it?"

"What do you think?"

By the weekend of the regatta, there had been no further contact. After an age of anticipation, the town could only think of one thing. Everything else – including Seymour's travails – would have to wait until it was over. Every bed and every campsite had been booked out for weeks. Every road into the resort was choked by Friday evening and the weathermen were talking about the hottest September day since forever.

No-one had ever witnessed anything like it. From a simple boat race, the event had exploded into a full-blown festival of the sea. A circus and two fairs had appeared overnight on the outskirts; fire-eaters and acrobats and men in clown suits stalked the streets; there was even an oompah band on the steps of the police station.

From pickled crustaceans to caramelised onions; visitors encountered a different, glorious smell around every corner. Outside every chip shop and café there was a queue. Outside every pub, circles of short-sleeved men stood guarding glasses of flat beer, wondering where their wives had got to and whether they'd have time for another quick half. Or maybe even a pint.

Behind the doors of one of those pubs – The Ship Inn – Harry Spanners was trying to make himself heard. Around him were squeezed the skippers and crew of fifty-three sailing cobles. Almost all of them were strangers, up from the Suffolk shingles or down from the Scottish border ports and practically anywhere in between with a beach.

Most were older men, too, with deep blue eyes and faded fishermen's smocks. Only two of them seemed out of place. Looking younger – and considerably more nervous – than anyone else in the room, Seymour and his son had slipped in to stand quietly at the back. Harry caught Isaac's eye, winked, and dived into his briefing.

"Give order, please. A little hush."

He shuffled awkwardly on his feet. Lately his leg had been keeping him awake. The doctor had told him it was arthritis in the ankle. Like every half-crippled old salt, the sea was catching up with him.

"Thank you. And thank you for coming. People know me as Harry Spanners and I've had the dubious pleasure of organising this race...."

"Get on with it, you boring spaz. This place shuts in an hour."

Harry scanned the room furiously for the heckler. A bronzed face beneath a filthy bobble hat beamed back at him from the bar.

"Not me. Honest."

"Piss off, Rehab. You know what we're doing anyway."

An hour later, so did everybody else. At 1pm the next day – Saturday – every boat in the regatta needed to be out on the water at the entrance to the harbour. High tide was mid-afternoon, and the starting cannon on the north pier would be fired at 2pm precisely.

From thereon, the course was blindingly simple; six miles east along the peninsula shoreline to a marker buoy below the lighthouse, then six miles back to the starting point. If the wind was a moderate northerly, it would all be over in two or three hours.

"But listen, this is a celebration, not a serious race," explained Spanners. "Some of you have got bigger cobles, bigger sails and bigger crews. So please – please – don't take this too seriously. No barging. No cutting across. No dirty tactics. Yes, there'll be a prize for the overall winner but each of you – skippers and crews – will get a small commemorative trophy….and….and….and there'll be a lock-in here tomorrow night."

"Now, you're talking," bellowed Rehab, adding his hat to the others being thrown dementedly around the room.

"One last thing. Quiet please. Quiet. Be serious," said Spanners, waiting for the din to subside. "This is rotten luck after the summer we've had but there's a strong chance the weather will finally break tomorrow…"

There was an immediate hush. Rehab was busy pulling his hat from his beer. Every face excepting his turned to the speaker.

"….don't panic, it's not certain, but the forecast is for thunderstorms at some point in the afternoon, accompanied by some pretty dirty winds. And some bad visibility."

Seymour's hand went up at the back of the group. "Is there any chance it will be called off?" he asked.

"A very small one. We'll decide at midday tomorrow."

All the seadogs could feel something was brewing. By mid-morning on race day, it was still achingly hot, but for the first time since June, the air felt charged and an invasion of tiny black insects had swept through the town. The locals called them thunderbugs, but there'd been no rain and the only visible portent was a line of towering anvil-topped clouds massing way to the north of the white cliffs.

"Is it on? Do we sail?" Like Spanners, Seymour had come down to a harbour café for a late breakfast. Spectators were already beginning to swarm aimlessly around the seafront and a steady thump of music was pulsing from one of Stan Clough's arcades. "Horribly sticky, isn't it?"

"Yes, it's on. It'll just be a bit blowy," said Harry, squirting red sauce onto his bacon. "You don't have to do this."

"Oh yes I do," said Seymour. "Even if I never do anything else."

"I've bought you a little present. A thank you." Spanners reached down beneath the table to retrieve a polished wooden box. The lid was inlaid with mother-of-pearl in the shape of an anchor. "Open it."

"You don't owe me. That's ridiculous. I owe you."

"Open it."

Seymour stroked the lid before carefully easing it open.

"A concertina. My god, it's beautiful."

"Take it out. It was my dad's. It's been hanging round the shop for years."

There was a comical honk from the bellows as Seymour eased the instrument from its case.

"Bloody hell, Harry. It's a Jeffries. It's probably worth a fortune.

262

Why?"

"Because you've saved my boat you nit, and because……."

"Go on. Why?"

"Because I heard about your accordion."

There was barely an hour to the cannon. Seymour thanked Harry again and wandered out among the growing crowd. No-one seemed concerned by the darkening sky. Entire families walked arm in arm, kitted out in their weekend best; slacks and sports jackets for the men, carnival-patterned dresses for the girls. Wherever he turned, there was noise. Chart songs drifting down from the waltzers at the fair; garbled exhortations from a man with a loudhailer; a dog barking wildly at the sails beginning to flap around the sheltered mouth of the harbour.

Along the side of a short jetty, he could see 'Phoenix', bobbing on the flooding tide. Isaac was already there, fussing with the rigging between mouthfuls of a hot dog. Watching him, Seymour felt a stab of guilt. Everything had changed so quickly. Just a year before, his first boat had been moored at the exact same spot. He could still see his father-in-law's dentures sinking into the brine. He could still see Lucy's stiff back turned in flight towards home.

"We thought you might be here. Déjà vu, old boy."

"Bill. Blimey. What a lovely surprise."

"Not just me, I'm afraid," he whispered. "Full team's here. Couldn't keep them away."

A pram broke free of the crowd steered by an elderly woman dressed in green.

"Hello Seymour."

"Hello Olive."

"Arthur still going strong then?"

"He's not the first you know. We do change them when they die."
She sounded older, more fragile than Seymour remembered.

"But they're all called Arthur?"

"They are." Olive applied the brake to the pram and adjusted her
hat. "We don't blame you; you know. Not entirely."

"Oh. Listen. I don't know whose fault it was. But not today. Please?"

Bill had escorted Olive to a narrow bench on the jetty from where
they were inspecting the gathering fleet.

"Is that her? Is that your boat? The one you made?"

"Yes, it is. I'm afraid it's caused rather a lot of trouble."

"You should still be very proud," said Olive, adding quietly. "We miss
you; you know."

"We don't blame you either, you wanker."

"Hello Ralph. Hello Vietta."

Lucy's brother had arrived sporting a blue trilby and a three-piece
Windsor check suit. His wife's dress was the shortest thing Seymour
had ever seen.

"Coo-ee. Hello Isaac," shouted Vietta, flicking her leg back, and
blowing a kiss.

"Hello Auntie Vee," returned Isaac, blushing. He'd been looking up
at her from the boat for some time and concluded that she was not
wearing any knickers.

"We're here for the annual sinking," crowed Ralph.

"All men are fools," muttered Olive. "All of them."

264

"That's thoughtful of you, Ralph. How's business?"

"You tell me, you crafty bastard. I've just bought your pissing land."

"You found out then?" Seymour felt certain he was about to get thumped.

"Of course I fucking did. Your name was on the contract."

"You'd have fleeced me if you'd known at the beginning. It was a fair price."

"I would have. And, yes it was."

"No hard feelings?"

"Nah, course not." Ralph had removed his hat, revealing the incontrovertible first signs of pattern baldness. "'Cos I'll still do alright out of it you Welsh twat."

"That's good. I'm glad," said Seymour.

"So now go and give us a good laugh," said Ralph.

There was a loud boom, followed by a skyward explosion of seagulls.

"That's the one-hour signal. I'd better go. Thanks for coming. All of you."

"Take care," said Olive.

Seymour hurried down a rusty iron ladder and hopped into his boat. The wind was stiffening quickly, and he was sure he'd heard thunder.

"Auntie Vietta isn't wearing any pants," said Isaac, casting a hopeful glance back in her direction. "What's in the box?"

"Later," said Seymour, unhitching the warps. "Let's get this done."

It was an extraordinary sight. One by one, the cobles were assembling at the mouth of the harbour. Only the town's elders – in the heady days of the herring fleets – had seen anything comparable; boats painted in every combination of colours; massing together under a moving patchwork of maroon sails.

Aboard the biggest of them was a six-man crew and skipper. Only the smallest craft, like Seymour's, operated with two. But regardless of size, each had a name which evoked a lost age of the sea. Names like Gansey Lass and Girl Annie; Guiding Star and Free Spirit; Summer Rose and Three Brothers. No more than a handful were still working boats. The rest had been lovingly mothballed in the forlorn hope of occasions like this.

"I bet we look like Vikings," said Isaac.

For almost two miles along the town's north shore, spectators were crammed four deep to enjoy the spectacle. As well as the fifty-three cobles, another hundred vessels – from rowing boats to powerboats – had swollen the floating procession. Overhead, a television film crew hung precariously from a yellow rescue helicopter.

"I'm not sure the Vikings got quite such a good reception," said Seymour.

"Possibly not. But they'd have liked your sister-in-law."

There was a second roar from the cannon; then a cheer which ran through the crowd like a fuse. In the chaos which followed, the cobles locked together in a dense pack of crashing wood and canvas. Then, as each one found enough space, the pack broke apart. A line of sails was soon stretching out towards the lighthouse, heeling over in a wind that rumbled darkly from the north under a sky black with electricity.

After five minutes, Seymour and Isaac were languishing at the back of the field. Ahead of them the lead boat was practically out of sight and clear of the harbour, conditions had worsened quickly. Pushed up by the wind, the sea had grown choppy and white tops were breaking off the deepening swell, sending spray into and over their boat. At the three-mile mark, they were cold and saturated, and it had started to rain.

"We could go back, Isaac."

"No way. We can get warm when it's over."

"It could be worse, I suppose. And we're only going to have to make one tricky manoeuvre."

With the wind coming from the north, they could sail eastwards with the sails in their current position. It was only at the halfway point, when they turned for home, that things might get interesting, but secretly Seymour was becoming agitated. Both the rain and the visibility had deteriorated and the only other coble they could see was the leader heading back.

"Is there a prize for being last?" bellowed Isaac.

"I'm going to sail a little closer to the shore. It might be more sheltered there."

Seymour looked anxiously over his shoulder and pushed the rudder away from his body. He felt reassured by the solid presence of cliffs, but the waves were piling higher and it was tough to hold his course in the turmoil.

"Hold on, Isaac. Get hold of something."

For a few seconds, the bow rose sickeningly before slamming down into the spume between two enormous crests. Neither of them had expected the noise or the nerve-deadening chill. To keep the boat from capsizing, they were stretching so far out that their backs were almost touching the sea.

"What about making the sail smaller? Don't you put a reef in it or something?"

"I should do."

"So why don't we?"

"Because I don't know how to."

Seymour felt stupid and sick. He should have cried off when Spanners asked. These other sailors had years of experience. All he'd done was read a few books, and practise in the dead-calm of summer. He thought of what Lucy would say, and he felt sicker. After all these years, maybe she was right. He was a pathetic dreamer, barely half a man; that's what she'd once called him. Maybe she'd always been right.

"Don't worry dad. We're doing OK."

In the lee of the cliffs, the boat was sitting flatter in the water; the swell had eased, and they were making swift progress. Ahead of them, as the fret momentarily fractured, they could see the lighthouse flashing at the tip of the promontory. Somewhere below it would be the cluster of orange floats that marked the halfway point.

"Everyone else is on their way back. Lucky sods."

Away to their right, split up by miles of clear water, the rest of the fleet had turned and was racing home to the finish line.

"Who cares?" Isaac's wind-burned cheeks were glowing. "They're not sailing the boat that Mr.Pilbeam built."

"Look. There. Listen. We've found it."

A large bell had been crudely lashed to four buoys which were tugging furiously in the current. Once again, the weather was closing in hard and – at the exposed end of the peninsula – the wind had intensified horribly. Suddenly, every rope seemed to quiver; the sail cracked; and a spinning vortex of air turned them head on to a fusillade of sleety rain.

"We need to make that turn." Seymour was screaming, but the gale was screaming louder. "Just this one turn and we'll be on a straight run for home. OK? You OK?"

Isaac nodded. He was shivering; all the colour had gone from his face; and for the first time, Seymour realised they were both terrified.

"Let's get out of here dad."

"When I say ready about, drop the sail. Let it go."

The sky had turned black. Their only bearings were the comforting sweep of the beam from the lighthouse, and the graveyard clanging of the bell.

"Let's do it."

"Ready about," yelled Seymour, pushing the tiller hard away from him. "Drop the sail." As the boat came round, the full force of the gale struck. "Let go of the rope, Isaac. Drop the sail."

"I have let it go. It won't come down. Look." Isaac held up his hands. The ends of his fingers were white with cold. "It's stuck on that fucking box."

Seymour looked at the knot and Harry's beautiful case, but there was no time to reach either. He'd seen what was coming. Two huge waves were bearing down on them from different directions. The first tore the rudder from the back of the boat. The second swung them side on to the wind.

"We're going over. We're going over. Stay close to me."

There was no resistance from 'Phoenix'. Unable to steer away, she was poleaxed by a gust which flattened the boat, throwing its two occupants clear of the stricken hull.

"The mast. We've got to release the mast." Seymour felt in his back pocket. It was still there. Thank god for Harry Spanners. "I'm going to cut it free. Hold on to whatever you can."

Only the edge of the boat was still above water. The sails and the mast were the last things keeping it afloat. Working calmly, Seymour attacked the rigging with his penknife. Unless he could detach the sail, the whole thing would go down in minutes, but the canvas was saturated and heavy, and the deep swell made it impossible to see.

"You're doing great, dad," shouted Isaac over the roar of the wind.

It had taken scarily long, but Seymour was done. The sail was free, and the mast had sprung clear of its mounting. With a last surge of effort, Isaac released the hull and reached for the mast. When he turned back to look, 'Phoenix' had gone. The only clue that it had ever existed was a box bobbing by his shoulder.

"It's sunk. It's made of wood. It shouldn't sink," cried Isaac.

Seymour couldn't take his eyes off the space where the boat had once been.

"It's the best place for it," he said, lashing the mast to the marker buoy with the remains of his rigging. If they kept talking (about anything) they'd stay alive. If they stayed alive, they'd be rescued.

"Get as much of your body out of the water as you can."

"I'm just so cold, dad."

"Someone will notice we're missing. We're going to be alright."

"The sail wouldn't come down. That was my job." The waves were coming at regular intervals, lifting them up as they passed through. "What was in the box anyway?"

"A concertina. Harry gave me it to replace my accordion."

"What happened to your accordion?"

"You know what happened. Mum smashed it up."

"She didn't dad." Isaac's face shone ghost-like in the fleeting cone of white light. "It was me who did that. It wasn't mum."

Seymour's mouth opened, but the words were torn away by the wind. In the lull which followed, both heard the distant boom of a horn.

"You have to know this too," gulped Isaac.

"What? What?"

"I can't hold on. I can't hold on. I can't feel anything in my fingers."

Isaac fell backwards off the mast. Holding on with his left hand, Seymour dragged the boy's face clear of the water. A second horn blast broke through the storm; louder and longer than before.

"Come on. Just a few more minutes."

If they were both tied to the buoy, they couldn't slip off. With what remained of his strength, Seymour secured the boy's arms using the last tattered remnants of rope.

"I've got to tell you, dad." Isaac's voice was fading. "Mum didn't burn the boat either."

"I can't hear you," Seymour pressed an ear against his son's mouth.

"I torched the boat. Not mum. Me."

"We're going to be alright, love. We are. Hang on."

"I just wanted things to be normal," said Isaac. His eyes were closed, and his head had fallen forwards onto his own arms.

"I know you did. We all did. It's fine. It really doesn't matter."

The horn was close now, and Seymour could hear the throb of an engine.

"Stay awake. Come on. Wake up. Isaac. Stay with me."

Someone was shouting. Lots of voices were shouting and a dark shape in the mist was acquiring bulk and colour.

"We're over here. Quickly. Follow the sound of the bell."

Now Seymour could make it out, the orange and blues of the lifeboat. He could see the spotlights on the cabin; and, as the clouds began to lift, he saw the familiar outline of a tall man in yellow waterproofs holding a megaphone.

Part Three

'Gratitude'

1968-70

Chapter One

The town was no stranger to unusual maritime mishaps. For several summer seasons, a wedge-faced man named Wallace Hartley had led the local orchestra, before boarding a ship which sailed straight into an iceberg.

The doomed musician's violin (like Seymour's concertina) was recovered intact. The doomed musician himself, however, never drew breath again. Mr. Hartley's icy fate had subsequently earned him both a plaque and a place in local folklore; honours for which Seymour Pilbeam now seemed inescapably bound.

It helped that the helicopter film crew had captured every moment; and that a spate of worldwide gloom had put television news editors on alert for any kind of tonic. An epic father-son rescue (from a boat which had been mysteriously incinerated) was simply too good to resist and on Stan Clough's colour television set, Lucy devoured every frame.

She'd known the regatta was coming. Like everyone else, she'd felt the excitement build. She'd watched the bunting go up along the promenade. She'd seen the 'No Vacancies' signs appear in every boarding house window. In quiet moments at the shoe shop, she'd even picked up the local rag and followed her husband's weekly boatbuilding diary, from the mystery of the fire to Phoenix's recent sea trials with Isaac.

"What do you feel when you read that stuff? Honestly?" asked Eunice, during one of their bourbon biscuit breaks.

"I'm interested," she replied. "But I don't know that I feel anything different."

But Lucy wasn't as immune to pride as she'd imagined. On the day of the race, there'd been a presence in her ribcage that was more than simply the heat. Cars and buses had been streaming into the resort all morning. From Stan's balcony, she could see the cobles milling around the harbour entrance. And later, through his telescope, she'd spotted the silent smoke of the starter cannon, followed moments later, by an angry crack of cordite.

Even with her own untrained eyes, Lucy had sensed the weather changing. It was more stifling than it had been all summer, and a mountain of cloud was moving in swiftly from the north. As the procession of sails stretched out towards the lighthouse, she'd watched the sky darken and wondered which of the boats was carrying Seymour and Isaac.

She could never tell Eunice, but it was impossible not to be moved. Seymour had built his boat, against all the odds. Looking out across the white-flecked rollers, she wondered what, if anything, he felt for her. Like everyone in the town, he probably blamed her for the fire. But he clearly still felt something, or else why had he been following her all summer?

"Do you still love him?" Eunice had never been one to let things go easily.

"Yes. Of course," she'd answered tetchily, but without hesitation. "Do you still love all yours?"

She knew what people thought; that she was an arsonist and an adulterer; just like she knew that only half of the rumours were right. Isaac had struck the match, not her; she was certain of that. A few weeks before, she'd even written to him, spelling out her suspicions and promising never to tell. There'd been no reply, and – on reflection – she was happy that Seymour and their son were reconciled; and that the boat which had driven her out had somehow drawn Isaac back in.

Above the wet-slate rooftops, there was a low thud of thunder. Inky grey lines of a rainstorm had blanketed the fleet. Within seconds, the summer had disappeared. Pellets of hail were pounding against the windows; the air temperature had collapsed; and in the broiling clouds over the lifeboat station, there were two sudden flashes of light.

For the next hour, Lucy followed events through Stan's binoculars. She watched the lifeboat being dragged out across the sands. She tracked its course until it was swallowed by the rain and she counted the returning cobles, until finally – as the storm blew out across the North Sea – the only thing left on the water was the rolling orange and blue of Stan and his rescue crew.

Grabbing a mac and a brolly, Lucy raced to the sea-front to watch the lifeboat come ashore. Hundreds of people were there already, pushed up tight to the water's edge, every eye trained on the tractor backing out into the surf for the lifeboat. In the back streets, a police siren was wailing, and the blue lights of a waiting ambulance shook in the rock pools of the retreating tide.

"He'll be alright. They'll both be alright."

Lucy turned. A man she vaguely recognised, wearing an orange blazer, was screwing a lens onto his camera. She had a sudden (thankfully brief) flashback to a picture of a man's penis which Eunice had been showing to customers in the shop.

"I'm Frank, remember? You've gone a bit pale," he said, holding up his camera. "I'm here to get some snaps."

With that he was gone, heading for the scrum of people climbing out of the lifeboat. She could see Stan clearing a pathway through the cheering crowd. Behind him, two figures draped in blankets were running through an arch of back-slapping holidaymakers. Flashbulbs seemed to be exploding everywhere, illuminating the shell-shocked faces of her husband and son.

"They were lucky. Another half-hour in the water would have killed them."

It was almost dark when Stan returned. There'd been a report to write (as always) followed by a few necessary beers with the other volunteers. Back home, standing at the drinks cabinet, he'd filled a large tumbler with Irish whisky. In two swallows it was gone.

"You OK, or do you want a top up?"

Lucy's taste for champagne hadn't faltered since their first date. Every week, the bin men took away a dozen empty bottles, but like everything else in the house, she never once asked where they came from. Like so many things in Stan's life, the place was a mystery.

People arrived every day with boxes; jocular van men filled the fridge with meat and fish, and since Stan did all the cooking, there was no reason for her to get involved; or to ask. She felt comfortable and relaxed – she felt looked after – but it was his home. And it was his money.

"I've had enough, thanks," she said.

She rarely drank to excess but tonight the bubbles had dislocated her. She felt sleepy and argumentative.

"He lost his boat again too, poor bugger." Stan walked round to the television and turned up the sound. A news reporter in a blue waterproof jacket was midway through an over-excited account of the day's events. "Listen to this. Seymour's a local saint. He'll be walking on water next."

"They'll recover it though, surely?" asked Lucy.

The onscreen reporter had stuck a microphone in Seymour's face as he stepped into the ambulance. "We're fine. We're both OK. My son's as tough as old boots. We just need a couple of hours by a hot fire. Thank you. And thanks too to the lifeboat. Those people are amazing. Goodnight."

"Useless sod," said Stan, switching channels.

"I'm going to bed," said Lucy.

It had been a strange few weeks. As she stripped and washed, the day's events seemed entirely in keeping with an endless summer of strangeness. When it began, she'd been practically sharing her bed with a boat. Now she had a mirrored wardrobe stuffed with beautiful clothes; drawers full of extravagant underwear; and a man who was as good-looking as he was generous.

Maybe the house was the best of it. Every minute there filled her with joy. When the sun shone (and Stan's staff had done their chores) she'd spend her afternoons stretched out in a padded deckchair, watching dogs chase balls on the beach. When the sun went hiding, the house was so warm she stalked its wooden floors naked, secretly hoping (as she once had with Seymour) that someone might be watching.

For the first time in months, she was reading regularly again, pulling first editions and leather-bound volumes from the wall of books which covered one end of the living room. Someone had bought wisely. Work by Camus and Nabokov nestled against poetry by Larkin and Cummings, and when her morning shifts at the shoe shop were done, Lucy grazed amongst them, selecting books at random into which she could disappear for hours.

"They're amazing. They must be worth a fortune."

Stan had got home late bearing flowers and chocolates. Lucy was waiting for him at the door in a silk dressing gown.

"I'm afraid the summer months are always like this," he said, passing over the bouquet.

"They're lovely. Thank you. You don't have to apologise."

"Anyway, what's so amazing?"

"This collection. It's better than a library."

"Is it? I've never really looked. Alice's mother bought most of them. She was the book person, not me."

"But you did an English degree. You've written two novels?"

"I was never really a very serious student. In one ear out the other, I'm afraid."

"All the same, I'd love to read them."

"I'll dig them out some time." Stan held up his hands in mock horror. Each of the finger ends was green. "I need a quick wash first."

It was the same almost every night. Lucy knew why. She'd been to see what he did. Once the amusement arcades closed, cash from the machines was scooped into buckets. Behind the double locked door of a squalid oil-scented office, Stan counted pennies and sixpences into filthy cotton bags.

During the summer, he spent his evenings circled by tottering columns of coins. Once the figures added up, the cash headed home in the boot of his Jag. Everything he ever bought was paid for in notes; a bizarre existence, she thought, for a man with a cultured voice and a serious education.

"Have you ever thought of selling up? All those silly machines and flashing lights?"

It was the first time she'd challenged him. They'd been driving home – drunk – from a rare dinner party.

"It's the way my dad it," he'd said. "What else could I do?"

The following weekend, Stan took her on a midnight tour of his empire. She'd stood watching dreamily as he turned the lights back on inside the sprawling arcade which ran like a neon corridor from the seafront right through to the town's main shopping street.

While Stan flicked switches, she dropped a penny into a machine to make a policeman laugh. The doll's eyes swivelled murderously as it rocked from side to side. Lucy turned away from its stare and slid a coin into an old glass-fronted cabinet. A ball bearing appeared in the bottom and she flicked a lever which sent the ball round and round until it vanished into a slot marked 'No Win'.

"It's a swizz. Does anyone ever win?"

The whole place had lit up. Tacky damp-streaked paintings of Hollywood stars lined the walls and every garish strip of backlit plastic hummed with electricity.

It stinks, she thought. Seaside rock and stale smoke. Just like Stan's laundry.

"I usually do alright," he grinned. "You ever been on a dodgem car?"

"I've never been in an amusements before…."

As Stan led her to the dodgem track, the arcade's loudspeakers burst into life. Two cars had been wheeled out, each sprayed in fluorescent purple sparkle.

"…….and I've never driven a car."

"Really? It's simple. Slip your shoulder through that strap. Push the pedal to go. Turn the wheel to steer."

A hit song by The Equals was thumping through the deserted amusements; 'Baby,Come Back' were the only words she could decipher. There was a brief fizzing of sparks over her head and Stan was barking instructions which she couldn't hear. Lucy dabbed her right toe on the accelerator and the car sped forwards into the side wall.

"Ouch."

"Steering wheel. Use the steering wheel."

"I caught my bosom in this bloody harness."

Lucy span the wheel until her car came under control. For the next few minutes, she followed Stan around the metalled track, growing in confidence with every lap. After three circuits, she manoeuvred sharply and slammed hard into his dodgem, pounding him another twice before he had time to recover. When Stan eventually caught her up, the music – and the session – had stopped.

"Admit it, you enjoyed that?"

"Very therapeutic," she laughed.

"Why don't you come and work with me? We'd be a good team. I need someone."

Lucy looked across the pinball machines and the one-armed bandits to where a faulty light was flickering on a cross-eyed painting of Marilyn Monroe.

"Can I think about that?" She already knew it was a no. "Working at the shop is good for me. I'd be a recluse without it."

Eunice had told her much the same often enough. Lucy's instincts were solitary; a preference complicated by the feeling (shared with her mother) that life had somehow let her down. And anyway, if she was honest, Stan's business repulsed her.

The whole enterprise didn't fit with the image she had of him and the less she knew about it the better. For some time, she'd been choosing her walking routes around the town to avoid even a glimpse of his arcades; and after the bizarre joyride on the dodgems, it was rarely mentioned again.

To everyone's relief, the glorious summer had resumed after the distraction of what was now referred to locally as 'Seymour's regatta'. In the warm weeks which followed, the town had split into two camps; those who felt the event had been ruined, and those who were already enjoying its silver lining.

Advance hotel bookings for the following summer were up; Harry Spanners had started restoration work on The Burlingtonian; and a second race was being openly mooted in the letters section of Seymour's paper.

At the shoe shop, Lucy heard it all. In the pulsating early days of her affair, she'd thought about giving the job up. But as the leaves began to fall, she was spending more and more time there. Her former scorn for tittle-tattle had softened and she no longer cared whether customers liked her or not. Being romantically sandwiched between a playboy and a saint made her an object of curiosity; she understood that. Just so long as they didn't judge, and they didn't ask any questions.

"Actually, I think they feel sorry for you," said Eunice. The annual panic-buy of slippers was yet to start, and the two women were filling the stockroom with furry footwear. "I think they know where it's heading."

"And where's that?"

"You're too clever for him. He wants a cage bird. Not a Jack Russell."

"Oh thank you very much," laughed Lucy. "Not bad coming from a Rottweiler."

"A beagle then. You're too wayward for him. You won't be trained. It's right what people are saying. It won't last."

"What about you and Frank anyway? What happened to the wedding? You'd said August."

"It'll happen. Eventually." Eunice lit a cigarette from a pack she kept concealed in a wellington boot. "To be honest, it got pushed aside while you were living with me."

"I enjoyed being in your house. It was fun."

"You should go and see Seymour." Eunice held out the smoking tab. "You should see how he's getting on."

"Too late," said Lucy, examining the filter before sucking hard on the cigarette. "I already have."

It was just once. Two weeks after the regatta, she'd found herself being pulled towards her old house. She'd heard a radio over the wall – jazz of some kind – and when she walked around the back, the gate had been half-open.

Seymour was humming to himself behind it, his lips pressed together to mimic a trumpet. The effort had made Lucy smile. Involuntarily, she'd eased the gate wider and stepped through to find him blowing an imaginary horn.

"Louis Armstrong?" she smiled. "Or Miles Davis?"

"Dizzy Gillespie actually," said Seymour, dropping bringing his arms to his sides.

"How are you? Your column hasn't started again in the paper."

"I didn't know you read it."

"I don't. Not really," said Lucy looking around at the knee-high weeds and mounds of mouldy wood shavings. "Only when it gets boring in the shop."

"Thanks for the compliment. I'll make some tea. Take a pew."

There were two garden chairs in the sun. Lucy slid on her sunglasses and sat down. When Seymour returned with a tray, neither knew quite where to start.

"I'll go first," said Seymour. "I owe you an apology."

"You? Me? I think that's the wrong way round."

"I thought it was you who'd try to burn my boat…"

"I was the most obvious suspect."

"….and I probably resented you for that more than…. than….you walking out on us. But it wasn't you. And I'm sorry."

"Did you guess or did Isaac tell you?"

"He told me. Out in the storm." Seymour felt cold again and his hands were shaking. "He thought we were going to die."

"And have you forgiven him?"

"Of course. Of course. Poor kid. It was all my fault – our fault – anyway."

"I thought that's why you'd been following me."

"I knew you'd seen me. I wanted you to."

"And now, in a way, I've followed you."

"Yes." Seymour averted his eyes.

"Will you build another one?"

"If I don't, will you come back?"

"Let's not do this, Seymour. I just wanted…."

"Would you come back? Do you miss us?"

"I miss what we were. I don't miss what we'd become. I miss Isaac."

"But not me?"

"Would he see me? I know he wouldn't want to see…."

"Stan Clough? No, he wouldn't," said Seymour, sadly. "But he'd definitely see you."

It was calmer after that. Seymour made fresh tea, and they pushed their chairs into the late afternoon warmth. When she left, two hours later, she was intrigued by how amicably the time had passed; and how easily her husband had adapted to life without her.

On the Town Hall clock, she could see it was almost seven. Stan would be watching re-runs of 'Bilko' with his copper-stained fingers around a glass of 20-year-old Talisker. When she got back, he'd pass her a flute of champagne. They'd have sex (recently he'd favoured the kitchen table) and he'd cook a meal. Later, he'd ramble through the day's news (dodgy staff, cheating customers, and lifeboat repairs) and slowly her brain would close down; much as it did when Seymour flew his kites.

With Stan's house in sight, she diverted onto the beach and slipped off her shoes. Two young boys were shivering in their trunks behind a wall of sand. Apart from them, and a man trudging alongside an old black labrador, the strand was deserted. At the steps up to Stan's garden, she sat down to brush her feet and retrieve a tired-looking black and white photograph from her handbag.

It had been taken at this exact spot. They'd been coming down together and a man in a bright-coloured jacket had ambushed them at the bottom with his camera. Seymour was wearing sports jacket and pressed dark trousers with turn-ups concealing his trademark brogues. Lucy had stepped out in a calf-length cotton dress and a sleeveless blouse. In between them, the tiny shape of Isaac was stretching his hands up to be held. And when she looked now, she could see the Clough property on the cliff behind their backs.

They had been happy. The photograph proved it. The photograph radiated happiness. They'd been handsome too. Seymour with his easy smile and his sleek, black hair; Lucy, forever bristling with restless elegance, and both so thin they needed extra holes on their belts.

286

Tucking it carefully away, Lucy tried (again) to pinpoint where it had all gone so wrong. When they first arrived at the coast, life had exceeded her low expectations. The house was a mess, but Seymour had worked hard and for once, he was finishing the things he started. There were handmade coffee tables and cots. They'd prowled the auction houses. They'd painted every room. They'd filled it with pictures (and kites) and transformed an overgrown yard into a paved garden full of pots and flowers.

During their first winter (before Isaac was born) Seymour had bought ice skates and they'd learned to skate on a nearby frozen mere. The following summer, it felt like they'd landed in paradise. Every day, she pushed the pram proudly along the promenade and for the next few years, the distractions of motherhood drowned the nagging fear that Isaac wasn't the only child to be living under their roof.

Lucy tucked her hands between her thighs to keep warm. The nights were closing in fast. The streetlights would soon be coming on at four, bringing with them the old, exhausting questions. When did mild irritation become resentment? And how soon after that had resentment mutated into outright contempt?

Lately, she'd found herself thinking about the moment Stan Clough drifted his fingers across her thigh. Twelve years on, she could still smell the Brycreem and see the patterns on the salon wallpaper. Nothing had ever been quite the same after that. Not because of Stan himself; not then. It was just the feeling; that feeling. It was a like a light coming on in a secret room she'd locked.

Behind the door was a lonely teenage girl clutching 'Wuthering Heights' on the bus to Haworth. She was going to write. She was going to teach or paint or dance. She was going to change the world. All those half-cooked dreams; forgotten. And when that light finally came back on, Seymour had been the first thing she could hurt.

Lucy climbed the last step off the beach and shut the photograph back in her purse. Lights were blazing in every room of Stan's house, and she was aching for a drink. It was strange the way she'd ended up with the randy barber, but maybe it was for the best. Both were damaged goods. Together, at least, they couldn't hurt anyone else.

She met Isaac during the following week. After a flurry of notes, they'd agreed a time and place; Toppings Ice Cream Parlour, a venue so wedded to the 1950's, they refused to put The Rolling Stones on their juke box.

"You used to bring me here for an ice cream sundae."

Isaac slid into a mirrored booth opposite his mother. Between them lay a shiny expanse of stained yellow Formica.

"I did. And it was the first place I ever had a real coffee."

"Really? We should have the same now then."

Lucy opened her purse and handed him a ten-shilling note. There was a series of clunks from the juke box, followed by the hiccupping voice of Buddy Holly.

"I'm glad you saw dad. Did he tell you I'd set fire to the boat?"

"He didn't need to."

"I didn't want him to go on thinking it was you. It wasn't right that he ever did."

"I wanted that boat in hell. Just like you did. I knew why you'd done it. I wanted to do it myself. But….but it just wouldn't have changed anything."

"Because of Stan Clough?

"Don't Isaac. Ssshh. Please." The girl behind the counter was staring at them. "I didn't come here for a fight."

"All that time you treated dad like shit, what were you really doing?"

"All those hours he spent in that workshop what the hell was I supposed to be doing?"

Lucy removed her leather gloves and placed both hands flat on the table.

"Banana milk shake? Peace offering?" she smiled. Isaac had gently placed his own hands on top of hers.

"And give us a couple of bob," he said. "I'll bang some music on."

There had been no contact with Isaac (or Seymour) since. As the days shortened, the town was slowly shutting down. Notices appeared in shop windows – 'Back at Easter' – and the coach parks fell silent. To Lucy it felt like a plug had been opened somewhere allowing all the colours to drain away. Even Stan's amusements wound down. For five days a week his business went dark. By October, his only customers were kids and his machines had usually swallowed up their pocket money by Sunday lunchtime.

After a summer of solitude, Lucy had a companion again. Every weekend, she and Stan went dancing together in the crumbling hotel where they'd first shared a bed. There were wild shopping trips to London from which she returned dripping with jewellery. There were drives to the Lake District where long wet walks invariably ended at secret country pubs with blazing log fires downstairs and bedrooms already booked.

"How do you know all these places?" she asked him. They were sitting at either end of a large foamy bath in a hotel by the lake at Windermere. The electric blanket had been switched on in advance when they arrived.

"Misspent youth," said Stan.

"Everyone seems to know you though."

"I'm not a monk." Stan grabbed Lucy's legs and pulled until her chin was submerged in bubbles. "But I've never been happier than this.

Never."

The whirlwind stopped abruptly after four weeks. The remnants of a hurricane had arrived from the Caribbean, and the town was hammered by storms. For three successive days, the lifeboat had been dispatched in terrifying conditions, returning safely each time, mission accomplished. Nobody could remember weather like it, and Stan's courage was the talk of the town.

"He's quite the man right now," said Eunice. "You seem to collect local do-gooders."

"It's terrifying, Eunice. I never think he's coming back."

"It's still a bit of mystery though."

"What is?"

"That he does all this stuff, makes all this money, and he still hasn't got any friends."

"Yes, but he seems to know everybody, everywhere."

"That's not quite the same is it?"

Lucy hadn't needed that pointing out. At the weekly dance, they sat alone and the few dinner parties they'd attended always felt like business. It wasn't a lack of social finesse. Stan's wit and charm were unmatched and yet they were rarely asked back and they never entertained. Unlike Seymour, he simply didn't fit in; or didn't want to fit in. Once a week, he played pub dominoes but only because his crew expected him to, and all his serious drinking was done at home.

By nine o' clock most evenings, he was usually too drunk for sex and the only company he seemed to value was his own. It was fine when they were away, but by early November the glamour trips had given way to cold, wet days spent looking at the sea. If he was in, Stan read the Daily Express and gaped at the ocean through his telescope. The excitement all felt horribly spent. In their three months together,

290

Lucy realised, she had never seen him open a book.

"We've got company next week," he announced, over the noise of uncoordinated gunfire.

There was a cowboy film on the television. Two men were shooting each other in the street.

"Anyone, I know?" said Lucy, surprising herself with the edge in her voice.

"Alice. It's half-term. Her mum needs me to take the reins for a couple of days."

"Do you want me to make myself scarce? You know she'll hate me."

"I doubt that," said Stan. "She's a Clough."

The coxswain had timed her visit carefully. Since the Middle Ages, the town had staged a beach fire competition. After dark, rival teams built burning pyres of driftwood along the tideline and waited for the sea to come. When the waves arrived, the fire which burned the longest was declared the winner.

Lucy had always loved the occasion too. When Isaac was a toddler, she and Seymour had brought him to watch the piles glowing down the blackness of the beach; intrigued by the pagan crackling of the wood and its hissing battle to stay alive. She hadn't known then that Stan had done it since he was a boy and that – like everything else – he only ever did it to win.

On the evening of the competition, Stan collected his daughter from the railway station. She was wearing a blue duffel coat and carrying a small case. When she entered her father's house, Lucy was waiting nervously by the bookshelves.

"I hope you don't mind," she stammered.

"Not at all. I'm used to it. How's Isaac? Or perhaps you don't know?"

291

Lucy studied the girl closely under the bright pendant lights. She was tall, like her father, with kind eyes which swam in a warm, intelligent face. It wasn't difficult to imagine how a teenage boy might fall in deep.

"I don't see him a lot, but he's well. And he's taken up cooking."

"Has he?" Alice chuckled. "That's hilarious."

"You didn't know? I sort of assumed you'd know more than me."

"I don't; haven't for ages. It wasn't working out. Not with school and everything. So it really isn't your fault and like I said, I'm used to it."

"Used to it?"

"Time to go, ladies. Chop chop."

Stan was shovelling them towards the front door, clutching an armful of coats and hats.

"Talk later?" whispered Alice.

"I think maybe we'd better," said Lucy.

In the blackness of the beach, two dozen teams were preparing their fires. Figures loomed out of the darkness clutching battered wooden fish boxes, and torches flashed across the sand seeking anything that might burn. The fires would need to be lit shortly and the incoming tide was clearly visible in the weak light falling from the promenade.

Stan dropped a bag from his shoulder and eased out its contents.

"Logs and kindling? Is that allowed?" asked Lucy.

"No-one's ever told me that it's not."

"Dad doesn't do losing. You should really know that by now."

"He lost the dominoes."

"I threw the dominoes. You knew that."

"That's a lie. It still doesn't make any sense. Why would you?"

"Because I could?"

A ripple of flame was spreading down the beach. Urged on by a raw sea breeze, over twenty fires were roaring. One by one, as the first low band of breaking waves arrived, each blaze faded away until only Stan's defiant pile was left, glowing weakly, but clearly, above the foam.

People were already drifting from the beach. Behind them, the Clough family fire had succumbed, and the water was swirling with blackened fragments of wood.

"It's no wonder people hate you in this town, dad," said Alice. A few boos were echoing out along the street.

"It's all in good humour. Nobody's bothered really," said Stan.

Back in the living room, Lucy drew the curtains across the French windows, while Stan headed to the fridge for champagne. The smell of burning timber had followed them in off the sands.

"We stink," said Alice. "I'm going to wash and change."

When she resurfaced, Lucy was into her second bottle. Alice's father had vanished to the study.

"We're not eating?"

"Doesn't look like it. Your dad's obviously not hungry."

"I've still got lots of clothes here. I should move them to my mum's really."

"Stan says most of the books are your mum's. It's a wonderful collection."

"They are but she doesn't want them. Bad memories, I think. Do you read much yourself?"

Alice migrated to her father's collection of drinks, shook a bottle of Chianti and drained the remnants into a glass.

"I've been hoping to read your father's unpublished novels."

"Good luck with that," said Alice, looking around for a corkscrew.

"Because they're not very good?"

"Because they don't exist. He told my mum the same story. And god knows how many other women as well."

"If you're trying to hurt me......."

"I'm not. I promise." Alice had joined Lucy on the sofa. Both were feeling the alcohol. "But he's a git and you know it. You must know it. You just don't want to admit it." She took another long slurp of wine. "Did he tell you he was a brilliant Oxbridge student too?"

Lucy nodded. Her head was starting to spin. She felt certain she was about to be sick.

"Listen. He got thrown out of Manchester after a year. He's a dunce, a serial tax dodger and an incorrigible moody perverted lecher but I do get it. You're not completely insane. He's charming, reasonably funny and he's probably very good in bed but...."

"I think you've made your point," said Lucy.

"Top up?" said Alice, reaching for the champagne.

Lucy would have gone that night if she could. Upstairs, she heard Stan clatter into the bathroom and slump wetly onto the toilet seat. If he noticed that she'd slept apart, he didn't say. Two days later, with a sympathetic, parting kiss, Alice headed back to school. Since the beach fire competition, Stan had rarely been seen.

"Maintenance work," he told her. "This is when everything gets taken apart and serviced."

"And you can't pay someone else to do it?"

"Money, money, money," said Stan. And with that, he was gone.

Lucy's sense of desperation wasn't unique. After Bonfire Night, the weather had taken revenge for a record-breaking summer. For days, the sea ripped in from the east, tearing chunks from the coastline in an endless black storm. During its few feeble hours of daylight, the town spluttered into life for just long enough to count the cost; the caravans torn from crumbling cliffs, the boats crushed against the harbour wall and the fine crust of salt which clung to everything.

During the second week of the onslaught, a man was washed into the sea trying to rescue his dog from the waves. The rockets had been fired, but Stan had deemed it too dangerous to launch the lifeboat. Two days later, the dog-walker's corpse had drifted up on the beach in front of the coxswain's house, but no one was attributing blame.

"He'd have been dead within seconds anyway," was Rehab's view, and everyone in the rain-lashed bars and pubs concurred.

Nevertheless, the tragedy had taken its toll. Stan was unsettled and bored and his unexplained absences were growing longer. There'd been one brief moment; one happy weekend; when Stan had come home with a lump of cannabis – "it's everywhere", he said – and together they'd smoked two clumsily-wrapped joints before giggling their way out of their clothes.

Alice had been right. The sex was good. But it wasn't good enough. And it probably never had been.

On Christmas Eve, Eunice Bolt broke off from mixing herself a snowball to answer the doorbell. It was just after lunch and a few stray flakes of snow were beginning to settle.

"Lucy?"

"I know. I know. I'm sorry. Can I come in?"

"You can. But only if you don't mind listening to the carols from King's."

"On your fine stereogram?"

"What else?"

"Does it work? Properly?"

"Of course it does."

Lucy picked up her case and stepped into the warmth.

Chapter Two

"Does anybody else understand women, cos I don't?"

Seymour gathered a long deep breath. Lately, Frank's peregrinations about his love life were growing increasingly surreal. A few months back there'd even been talk of sending him to night classes in biology.

"What now, Frank?"

The usual hard core of drinking companions was huddled around the fire of the White Horse. Outside, the streets were silent. After a week of relentless snow, the temperatures had crashed again. It was March and the entire, weary country was frozen; closed for business.

"It's Eunice. I've found that other thing; the you know what."

"The fish?"

"Fuck off, Rehab."

"Go on. Finish the bloody story."

"Well last night, she asked me where her vulva was?"

"And what did you say," asked Seymour, with a sinking feeling.

"I told her it was parked outside on the drive next to my Vauxhall."

For a few minutes it felt like the pub might collapse. If Frank was winding them up, it was the funniest joke ever. If he wasn't, well maybe a whip-round for night school wasn't such a bad idea. Seymour looked around at the knot of smiling faces. It had been a long and strange winter; but a quiet one.

Now he was finally ready for a sea change......

Back in December, there'd been no domestic arguments about the tree. He'd won the annual fishing competition and his teeth had stayed firmly attached to his gums. Apart from Christmas cards (hers with a single kiss, his with two), there'd been no contact with Lucy and the holiday had proceeded without stress.

On Christmas Day, he'd even been invited for a private lunch at the pub with Isaac. "I can't have you two spending the day alone," explained Nellie. "The place is shut to customers. We can eat in my kitchen."

She might have added that (at 46), Nellie had spent most of her adult years running a pub single-handed; and that the proximity of a desirable unattached local hero was impossible to resist. Even when Lucy was around, she'd liked Seymour and (not incorrectly) she'd deduced that Seymour rather liked her. A turkey roast, followed by Morecambe and Wise, was the least she could do.

"We really appreciated that," said Seymour, stepping back later into a warning swirl of snow. "Thank you."

"Mistletoe kiss?" said Nellie. Her breath smelled of warm sherry.

Seymour turned back and puckered his lips. "Yes. Of course. Happy Christmas,"

"She fancies you," said Isaac, a few minutes later. "She so fancies you."

The following day, Seymour had ignored the weather forecasts and driven over to see Olive and Bill. Across the Wolds, a thick frost clung to the endless lines of hawthorn, and the landscape was utterly still. "We'll not be late back," promised Seymour. "When this starts to come down, it won't stop."

At his in-law's front door, he knocked; and then knocked again. From inside, he could hear Olive assaulting her piano. He wasn't sure, but it sounded like Arthur might be singing along.

"Come in, come in. Quickly." Bill was clutching a glass of beer. "Pray Jesus she'll stop when she knows you're here."

There was a violent crescendo of noise, followed by the slamming of a piano lid. Olive swung round on her stool and the three men lowered themselves deferentially onto the sofa.

"You've not been sick yet this year then?" asked Olive.

A freshly lit mound of coal was struggling in the grate. The room felt icy and Olive was wearing a thick, green coat.

"I'm using stronger glue," smiled Seymour. "And a happy Christmas to you too."

He'd enjoyed the hours that followed. For all the sadness that lay in their past, they were kind and thoughtful people. On the flyleaf of the cookery book, they'd bought for Isaac ("Foreign Food Made Easy") Olive had written: "Don't worry about school. Follow your dream." And when Seymour gifted them a kite, they'd seemed genuinely pleased.

"You know she's moved out, don't you? You know she's left that man?"

"I didn't know that, no," said Seymour.

Outside, the December darkness clamped hard around the house. Inside, the fire was making very little headway and its feeble flickerings were having to circumnavigate a large dog.

"We've not seen her. We wouldn't go near that man's house. She rang us from a payphone on Christmas Eve. She's back living with that Eunice trollop."

"I didn't know that either."

Through the living room window, Seymour could see the snow was falling steadily; big flakes snagging ominously on the glass.

"She sounded alright," volunteered Bill. "She asked if we were seeing you."

"She's tough. She's your daughter. I'm glad you told me."

"What will you do?" Olive had finally removed her coat. Beneath it she was wearing a green cardigan, a green skirt and green stockings.

"A new start maybe? I don't know," said Seymour, quietly. "Somewhere else, perhaps?"

"Are you two sure you don't want to wait until tomorrow?" asked Bill. Seymour and Isaac were getting ready to leave. The yellow lights of a council gritter swept past in a rattle of salt. "There's some pork pie left in the pantry."

"We'll be fine, grandad. We're fully tested in life-threatening conditions."

"Take care of each other."

Olive and Bill were huddled in their own doorway. For the first time, Seymour was struck by how content they looked. And how much in love they really were.

"Thanks for the book." Isaac slammed the passenger door in a cloud of snow. "Did Seymour tell you he'd got a girlfriend?"

An hour later, he was still chuckling as they crawled through a blizzard towards home. By midnight, there was still twenty miles to go and the snow was piling against the windscreen faster than Seymour's wipers could clear it. Occasionally, when it stopped, they could see a smooth track stretching out in the yellow beam of their lights; a narrow white band rolled across the vast silence of the wind-whipped fields.

Wherever there was a gap in the hedge, spear-like drifts were pushing across their route and as the road rose back onto the hills, Seymour's wheels began to spin. To keep moving, he tried swinging the car from side to side, knowing that to stop would be fatal.

"The front tyres are bald. They're not giving us anything."

"What is it about you, me and bad weather? How far to the top?"

"Another half-mile. We're going to have to go up backwards."

"You're joking?"

"There's more tread on the back tyres and…..we haven't got a first gear."

"That too is a joke?"

But Seymour had already started the manoeuvre. Ahead of them on the left was a broad patch of hard standing blown clear by the strengthening wind.

"I'll turn the nose into that and reverse back out and up the hill. You'll need to push me to get the thing moving."

"And then what?"

"And then you jump back in, kneel on the back seat and tell me where the road is."

"But the lights will be at the back, pointing downhill."

"Trust me."

To Isaac's surprise it had worked. Yard by painful yard, they reversed up the hill. Behind them the snow filled their tracks so quickly that the headlights illuminated a world without any trace of their presence. Nothing would come this way for hours. And if they stalled, Isaac realised, nobody would know how they'd got there.

"It's stopped. Look. The moon."

Atop the flat breadth of the escarpment, the road had levelled out. For the first time in hours they could see clearly. Ahead of them, the route looked passable and it was downhill all the way home. Nursing a stiff neck, Seymour swung the car round and headed for the distant lights of the harbour. Somewhere round here was the farm where he'd sourced the wood for his coble.

A lifetime ago? Or just fifteen months? Whichever it was, something had to change.

"What did you mean back there when you said, 'new start'?"

"That? Nothing. Tired Christmas talk. I didn't mean anything. Ignore me."

But that wasn't quite true. In late November, after endless delays, the sale of his father's land had finally gone through. A few days later, Ralph's money appeared in Seymour's bank account and since then he'd thought of little else. Even now, with the snow once again piling in off the sea, he couldn't quite dislodge it from his mind.

"I won't be hanging around in this dump when I leave school."

"Let's talk about it later when we're less knackered," said Seymour.

They were home; an epic trip, but they'd made it. Isaac was already racing for the warmth of his eiderdown.

"Will you go and see mum now she's moved out?" he shouted.

"I don't think so. Why?"

"Because, I don't think you should."

And he hadn't. In a year of extremes, January swept in without mercy. Every golden memory of the previous summer was driven out by an Arctic snap which quickly turned into a way of life. According to Frank, it was the end of the world. According to Rehab, the real culprit was a Polar Aertex.

"Vortex, not Aertex," interrupted Spanners. "They make shirts out of Aertex."

As coal supplies dwindled, the fire in the White Horse snug had become a daily forum for highbrow weather-related discussions. Keeping warm had become the town's single most important preoccupation.

"Bollocks," responded Rehab. "Shirts are made out of nylon."

"I like cotton shirts best," said Frank. "Nylon makes my back sweat."

Back in his workshop, Seymour was building sledges again. For the first time since 'Phoenix' he'd picked up his father's old tools, turning out toboggans which he manufactured – without charge – for anyone who asked. At his son's insistence, he'd even restored "Lucy's sledge", sanding out the damp stains and polishing its runners to a lethal sheen. Together with Isaac he'd carried it out to the seafront where, for the first time in local memory, the steep snowy ramps down to the beach had sheeted over with ice.

"You're mental," screamed Isaac, jumping onto his father's back before careering down icy concrete.

"Your mum and I did this once on a frozen lake," yelled Seymour.

"I don't believe it," Isaac yelled back. "My mum? Never."

To his closest friends, it seemed like the real Seymour was back. In secret, he was teaching himself how to play the concertina. He was also going days without giving Lucy a moment's thought. By February, the White Horse had reached the winter darts league final, and (as a spectator) he'd been to every match.

"Darts aren't my thing," he told Nellie. "But I'll go along to check on the maths."

It was just as well he did. Rehab's ability to land a dart on a pinhead was stitched into local legend. Unfortunately, it was matched by the panic which blinded him whenever a number swam into view.

"It's simple," explained Seymour. "You start with 501 and every number you hit is taken off that until you're down to a number you can finish with a double."

"I know all that. I'm not fucking stupid."

There was a murmur of dissent from the bar. As the holder of the East Riding (East) Higginson's Bakery Domino League title, the White Horse had been selected as the venue for the final. Two hours before the first dart, it was already packed.

"We have this tutorial every week. You've got a mental block."

"Alright smartarse. What's 27 off 419?"

"392."

"And what's 58 off that?"

"Another five billion years of evolution and you'll get there," chortled Spanners.

"Listen. You chuck 'em. Seymour'll count 'em," added Clinkers, whose skin graft had turned blue (as it usually did) with the onset of cold weather.

There was a blast of freezing air from the door. The team from The Ship stepped through. No one had been surprised that Stan Clough's local had reached the final. The only surprise was that their star player (and skipper) hadn't been seen since Christmas. According to Frank, he was being investigated by the Inland Revenue. According to everyone else, he'd got another woman.

"We'll batter them without him," whispered Spanners, carefully unpacking his three darts from their box. "Fly true, my beauties."

Barely an hour later, it was all over. After Rehab's first dart buried itself deep into the hand of a sleeping pensioner, there was no way back for the White Horse. Unsettled by the sight of so much blood, the home team's game had collapsed, handing the title to their oldest rivals.

"That was such a shit rebound," cursed Rehab, after the ambulance had gone. "Stupid old get. He was sitting too close."

"The food's been good though," said Frank. And it was.

At Seymour's request, Nellie had given Isaac an entire day in her pub kitchen. As the post-match inquest began, platters of pastry nibbles had begun to circulate, followed by more exotic fancies, pairing anchovies with cheese and smoked salmon with chunks of tinned pineapple. For townsfolk weaned on battered fish it was a revelation. Every plate had been pecked clean, and the humiliation of a 9-0 whitewash had been quickly forgotten.

"Lads," asked Frank, prodding uncertainly at a small mushroom. "What's a vol-au-vent?"

"Eunice'll probably know," said Rehab. "Ask her to show you her button."

By midnight, Seymour and Nellie were the last two in the pub. A few sodden beermats had been tossed hopefully on the fire and every table was piled high with beer glasses.

"Leave it," said Nellie. "Let's have a nightcap upstairs."

"Are you sure? I'll come back in the morning to wash up our plates?"

"A quick brandy, love. That's all. It's much cheaper than coal."

Seymour followed Nellie up a steep staircase to her flat over the pub. After the smoky noise of the bar, it felt like a feminine oasis. Green floral pattern carpet, and matching wallpaper, covered the floor and walls. Bottles of scent and women's magazines were scattered across the sideboard. Feeling much drunker than he'd realised, Seymour collapsed into the sofa. Straight ahead, through an open door, he could see a rose-coloured light glowing in Nellie's bedroom. Between him and the fire was a drying rack festooned with the landlady's smalls.

"Oh god, sorry. I'll move these."

Seymour's eyes followed Nellie's pants hungrily until they were lost to view.

"Just a small one," he stuttered, feeling unaccountably nervous. "I'll stoke up the fire."

Nellie joined him on the sofa and passed over a full glass which Seymour examined suspiciously, realising that Nellie's thigh was pushed up right against his. He took a sip. And then another. And then another. She was right. It was the warmest he'd felt for weeks.

"Isaac's a good cook. He'd be wasted in a town like this. Ready for another?"

"Bloody hell, Nellie. I've hardly started."

"It's been a long day," she sighed, reaching for the bottle.

As she sagged back down again, Nellie swung her legs over Seymour's lap.

"Don't worry. I'm not after your body. It's my veins."

There was an uncomfortable pause. Seymour could feel the brandy worming down through his chest. Better still, he could feel Nellie's calves pressing into his groin.

"I've come into a bit of money. I'm thinking of moving away."

"You can't do that. What would we do?"

"I've got boring, Nellie. I need an adventure. I think I might need one last boat. Something that stays afloat longer than five minutes."

"Just you? Or is a reunion on the cards?"

"Definitely not that. But with Isaac, hopefully…depending on what happens at school."

Nellie had allowed her head to fall onto Seymour's shoulder. The smell of her scent was so overwhelming, he felt faint.

"I'd miss you," she slurred. "You're the only decent bloke in this place."

A long-forgotten part of Seymour's body was waking up. "I think I'd better go."

"Sleep with me. We don't have to do anything. We can just share a bed."

"You're joking?"

"Try me."

"I've only ever slept with Lucy. And Isaac sometimes when he was a baby."

"Listen. It's freezing out there. We don't have to have sex. And my electric blanket's been on since seven."

Seymour laughed. "It's tempting, and I'm really fond of you. But…."

Nellie pulled herself upright and straightened her hair. "It's alright, love. I'm not hurt. And the offer won't go away…"

"I'm flattered. Honestly I am."

"…..and neither should you."

It was just as well he was busy. For the first time in months, there was a rhythm to his life which suited him. After the regatta, Seymour had doubted whether he'd ever work for the newspaper again, but the winter had imbued his weekly column with rare purpose.

When the ploughs broke through to snow-trapped villages, Seymour and his notebook travelled alongside with food and supplies. When the electricity failed, it was Seymour who campaigned for swift repairs. And when a snowman was spotted dressed in an England football strip, it was Seymour who got its picture on the front page.

Within a few days, front gardens all over the town had sprouted fancy dress snowmen of their own. Within a week, there were, by conservative estimates, some 2,000 snowmen dressed as anything from Fred Astaire to Father Christmas, and (in one unfortunate incident involving a large courgette) as Errol Flynn.

For a second time, the national media poured into the town. And then, just as swiftly, both they – and the snow – disappeared. Around late March (when Frank had cracked his infamous vulva-Volvo gag) the temperatures swerved upwards; Clough's amusements began to jingle again and one by one, the snowmen tiptoed sadly away.

Whenever Nellie's midnight offer snaked into Seymour's thoughts, he forced it away. Apart from one aside – "I wasn't joking" she'd whispered the next day – there'd been no practical opportunity to review his decision. People did silly things when they were drunk. He wasn't likely to be alone with her again. And in any case, Seymour's attention had just swivelled in a worrying new direction.

"There's been a letter from school."

Seymour was watching Isaac pour gravy over a plate of toad-in-the-hole. Since Lucy left, they'd both put on weight and the pantry was full of ingredients he'd never heard of.

"Are they making me head boy?"

"It says that you've been missing classes." Seymour scanned down the letter. "It says that your attendance has been 'sporadic to the point of negligible'."

"I don't even know what that means."

"It means you might as well not bother going."

"Suits me," said Isaac, pushing a large piece of pork sausage into his mouth.

Two days later, Seymour and Lucy greeted each other awkwardly outside the office of Isaac's headmaster. The morning staff meeting had just ended, and a procession of pipe-smoking men in gowns and mortar boards was splintering off in search of children.

"Are you well?" Lucy had broken the silence first. "It's been four months. You look well."

"I'm fat, that's what I am," said Seymour trying hard to pull in his stomach.

"My mum couldn't cook either. You can blame it on her."

"We had something called beef bourguignon last night." Seymour's hands had fallen to his waistband. "He might be a lazy dunce, but he's a fantastic cook."

"He could cook for me and Eunice if he liked."

"Give him time, Lucy. He's sixteen. He'll come round."

There was a creaking of old hinges. The face of an elderly secretary had crept around the office door along with an unlikely whiff of liniment. "He'll see you now," she said.

The meeting hadn't taken long. Without a radical change in attitude, their son was on course to fail every one of his 'O' Levels in June. At best, his behaviour in class was merely disruptive. At worst, he was guilty of fomenting widespread teenage unrest. The school's preference was for Isaac to stay at home until his exams and then leave.

"Is this our fault?" asked Lucy.

309

"Our fault?"

"You're surely not blaming me? He's unteachable. He tried to start a bloody riot in the playground."

"You're the one who left. You're the one who had the affair."

"And you're the one who spent more time with his boat than his son."

It had been a shock, for Lucy most of all. Seymour had always suspected Isaac's formal education might be a short one. As a child, he'd been much the same. When a wind was blowing, the world inside his classroom window could never compete with the dazzling possibilities beyond it. And still couldn't.

Lucy, on the other hand, had nourished high hopes; projecting her own disappointments onto their child; grooming him relentlessly for a school where he'd felt wretched from the moment he arrived in his grey shorts and his crimson barathea blazer.

"You might be right," said Seymour. "But I've always accepted him for what he is."

"He's throwing away his chance."

"He's found something he can do. We should celebrate that. And anyway….we're a good team now. Me and him."

Isaac never asked his father what the headmaster said, and Seymour never told. There had long been a tacit agreement between them anyway. In a few months' time, Isaac would flunk his exams and be free. If Lucy advised him differently, she'd be wasting her time.

The town's cafes and restaurants were clamouring for seasonal staff. By Easter, Isaac had swapped his classroom for a kitchen and his school cap for a toque. Nowhere served anything too fancy – savoury ducks were about as exotic as it got – but the tips from punters were good; he was learning; and, more importantly, his dad had fully recovered from the sinking.

It was The Burlingtonian which had completed his rescue. In the depths of winter, the refit had stalled. Engineers had downed frozen tools; skilled carpenters had walked off the job; and with the season fast approaching, Harry Spanners had turned to Rehab for salvation.

"You started the fucking fire," he pleaded. "You owe me, you twat."

"Charming." said Rehab. "How much?"

"Free drinks whenever you're on board…."

"Not enough. I'd be better off on the lobster pots."

"…..plus five percent of the take."

"Done. So long as you find one more recruit."

Seymour had needed no persuading; nor had his editor. After the regatta, the battered pleasure ship had become a symbol for local resilience. Everyone read the Fleet Street papers. Something called a package holiday was catching on fast and in its fight against the Costa Brava, The Burlingtonian was to be the town's first line of defence.

"That boat saw off the bally Krauts in the war," roared Soapy, firing an imaginary machine gun across the heads of his staff. "Now we'll see off the bally Spaniards."

"I'd like time off to get her ready for the season," pleaded Seymour.

"Of course. Of course. It's your patriotic duty. And it won't be time off. You can write about it as well. Double bubble. Just the job. Up school"

So it was that Seymour, Spanners, and Rehab were reunited in the clanking bowels of the town's stricken icon. For several weeks, they toiled together, often knee-deep in rusty bilge water, knowing that Easter was fast approaching and with it the first wave of work-weary visitors. When the weather was fine, they scraped rust off the hull and scoured the deck planking with wire wool. And when rain lashed across the harbour, they stripped out the burnt panelling from the bar and repainted the smoke-stained toilets.

"I'm back fishing the second this is done," moaned Rehab, during a mid-morning fag break. "I'm knackered. I need the rest."

"Understood," said Spanners.

Every job seemed to create a new problem. Beneath layers of ancient paint, the ironwork dissolved in their hands and fifty-year-old mahogany fittings crumbled into dust. At night, when they stumbled home, their joints ached, and their faces were black. But as the weeks slipped by, the load began to ease.

From the beginning there'd been spectators, shouting encouragement from the quay; volunteers; local people of all ages – children and pensioners – giving up their weekends to lend a hand. Thanks to 'Pilbeam's People', the trickle soon became a tidal surge.

The funnel was repainted in deep red. Fresh varnish was slapped on the doors, portholes were polished; salt was scraped off the windows and wooden benches; and as the air warmed, the old boat took on a gleam it hadn't known since she was launched.

"We did it," said Spanners. "I owe you both."

"Care to put a figure on it?" said Rehab. "Lost earnings et cetera?"

The three men were crowded in the wheelhouse. Through the window, they could see the final coat of white paint going down on the railings.

"First paying passengers this weekend?" asked Seymour.

"I was hoping you might play that concertina I gave you?" wondered Spanners. "A few shanties for the relaunch?"

"And I was hoping you'd ask."

"You could do it all summer if you wanted….provided you learn a few more tunes."

"I don't think so," said Seymour.

A large seagull had landed on the wet paint where it was furiously examining its feet.

"That sounds ominous," said Rehab banging on the window.

"I'm thinking of packing in my job. I'm thinking I might go away for a bit."

"Where? You don't know anywhere else."

"I've got enough money for a year or two. I thought me and Isaac maybe. You both know why……"

"I'll tell you what you need," said Spanners. "You need a new boat."

"I couldn't build one. No thanks. Not after the last time."

"Did I ever tell you I had a boat?" Rehab had been patting his pockets and produced an unopened half-bottle of rum. "Last seen in Kyle of Lochalsh twenty years ago, where you catch the ferry to Skye. Beautiful little 25-footer. Wooden hull. Two cabins. Tidy little galley. Might need a bit of work. Snug as a bug it is. Or was. I can't imagine the state it's in now."

"I didn't even know you'd been to Scotland," said Spanners.

"Lots of fish back then." Rehab took an enormous swig and burped loudly. "I was young, too. I did it for a couple of years, but it never really worked out. Never really finished that boat either. Had to piss off down here sharpish in the end."

"What happened?"

"I'd been mucking around with my skipper's teenage daughter. That was one thing."

"And the other thing?"

Rehab winked and tossed the (empty) rum bottle into Seymour's lap.

"I steered her dad's trawler into an oil rig."

There was a sound of massed cheering from the deck. With a final desperate wrench, the seagull tore itself free and fled with a squawk.

"I think we're finished," said Spanners.

The three men stumbled out blinking into the Spring sunshine where a posse of paint-splattered volunteers had burst into a rendition of 'Rule Britannia'.

"It looks amazing. It's never looked better," said Spanners. "I couldn't have done it without you two."

Captain Rehab was striding across the gangplank. Just before the quay, he turned with a lupine grin and raised a filthy hand to his forehead.

"My friends, I salute you both but now I need to get rich. The sea is calling."

"That boat, Rehab," shouted Seymour. "The one in Scotland. What was it called? You never said."

"A name that you are uniquely qualified to appreciate."

"And that is?"

"Gratitude," said the Captain. "Now, farewell."

There wasn't a spare ticket to be had for the first sailing. As the tide filled the harbour, Spanners took his place at the wheel, fired up The Burlingtonian's venerable diesel engines, and steered her alongside the north pier where (with one hour still to go) a line of excited passengers was being entertained by a local church band.

Harry's shore crew looked as peerless as their boat; each in a new woollen gansy; knitted in ribbed blue by the proud ladies of the town's Women's Institute. Standing amongst them, clutching a polished wooden box, Seymour found it impossible not to smile. The boat was truly magnificent. Multi-coloured bunting stretched from one end to the other and under the day's breezy skies, the paintwork was so dazzling, he had to look away.

"I hope you've expanded your repertoire."

Frank had arrived with his cameras. He was wearing a plain white shirt, but no orange jacket.

"Eunice has decided I'm too old for that now. I've set up on my own."

"I'm glad, Frank. And yes, I've learned a few more tunes."

"She'll be along later with Lucy, if that's OK I got them a couple of tickets."

There was a deep hoot followed by two black coughs of smoke from the funnel. People were boarding in single file, racing for the best seats and pulling out warm jackets as the cold watery air hit them. The shore crew were releasing the warps and tossing them aboard. Seymour unboxed the concertina and started to play; a little nervously at first but then, as The Burlingtonian eased out into the bay, with a swelling of unexpected pride.

"Who's on the bar? Please don't say Rehab," asked Frank, between rolls of film.

"My son's doing it. Isaac."

"He's not eighteen. He can't."

"No. But he won't set fire to it and can you see any police?"

"Fair enough," said Frank. "You're brilliant on that thing by the way. Everyone loves it."

315

Seymour loved it too. Although he missed his Gabbanelli, the warm piping sound of the concertina felt right for the open sea. Unlike that first season, two years before, he was playing sailors' music; shanties and reels which swirled around the deck before being wrenched away by the salty wind.

Over to his left he could see the long chalky band of the cliffs and the lighthouse, flashing even on this sharpest of April days. Phoenix was buried somewhere over there under fathoms of water. He wondered what it looked like now or if it would ever be found. He thought about the rescue, and he thought about Lucy, huddled under a blanket at the front of the boat with Eunice.

He'd watched her find a seat, and their eyes had met, but he wasn't expecting a conversation. If there was a time and place, this wasn't it. At the halfway point of the trip, Seymour joined Harry Spanners in the warmth of the wheelhouse. Through the glass, they could see fishing boats chugging for the buoys which marked their lobster pots.

"I know what you're thinking," said Spanners. His face was glowing with contentment.

"I am, yes. I miss it."

"Want to take the wheel for the return leg?"

"What about the music?"

"Bah. I'll put some Vera Lynn on. They'll love it."

The two men swapped places. Seymour clutched the top pair of spokes on the wheel and turned it gently to the right.

"Ease back the throttle a bit. That's it. Beautiful."

In a smooth, foamy arc, the boat came round and headed back towards the harbour. Through his feet and hands, Seymour could feel the deep heartbeat of the engine. Behind them a thinning line of smoke stretched horizontally back to the headland.

Up at the bow, Isaac had squeezed in between Eunice and his mum. The bar was closed; they were chatting; and although he couldn't hear what they were saying, Lucy had placed a hand on Isaac's shoulder. He saw smiles, followed by laughter, and he was glad.

"I'll take her this last bit into the harbour. Did you enjoy that?"

"More than you'll ever know," said Seymour.

Hundreds of spectators were waiting along both piers for the cruiser's return. Spanners span the wheel, pulled back the throttle and nudged her into position for the next trip. A long queue was already lining up as the first passengers streamed back onto dry land. From the gangplank, Seymour watched Lucy heading off towards the town centre. Goodrun, he thought briefly, before she was swallowed up by the day's trippers.

"Seymour?"

"Nellie? I wasn't expecting to see you. What's up?"

Something was wrong. She could hardly speak. Something terrible was wrong. He put his arm around her and pulled her head onto his chest. Somewhere over towards the north beach, he could hear a siren.

"It's alright. I've got you. Take your time."

"It's Captain Rehab." She was weeping uncontrollably. "Oh God, Seymour. I'm so sorry."

"Breathe, Nellie. Breathe. What's happened?"

"He's gone. He's gone. The silly old bastard's gone."

And that was when Seymour saw the flashing lights in front of the stall where Bill once bought his pink candy floss, and where today, two men in uniforms were carrying a body into the back of their ambulance.

Chapter Three

Everyone was agreed. The police and the council could huff and puff and stamp their feet, but Rehab was going out Viking-style, just like his father. As a concession, his body would be incinerated first (at a licensed crematorium) before the ashes were returned into the hands of his friends. From that point on, however, he was heading back to sea on a flaming coble. No arguments.

"To be fair, from a safety point of view, it's perhaps as well we're not the ones burning the actual corpse," mused Frank, when the funeral planning committee convened in Nellie's snug.

"Because?" asked Spanners.

"Because he was probably 90% rum, 8% brandy…"

"…and 2% fish and chips," added Seymour.

Frank spread his arms high. "Kaboom," he laughed. "Farewell to the human Molotov cocktail."

"90 + 8 + 2, that's 100 if you're listening up there," said Seymour mournfully.

A month of paralysis (and tears) had already drifted by since he died; a month of conjecture and rumour which was ended when the coroner declared that "Jansen Fallowdown (aka Captain Rehab) had drowned in a tragic accident complicated by the significant long-term presence of alcohol". Death by 'misadventure' was his official verdict. Another tragic piece of rotten maritime luck was the town elders' world-weary alternative.

"Jansen Fallowdown? He kept that bloody quiet."

"I still can't believe it," muttered Spanners. "I genuinely thought he was indestructible."

No-one would ever really know what had happened; not in the forensic detail the inquest (and his mates) had been forlornly seeking. There'd been no witnesses, and the Captain had been dead for several minutes before the alarm was raised and his limp body dragged from the sea.

"Much-loved fisherman dies in freak tragedy" was Soapy's headline in the local rag, over a story which contained the very few undisputed facts.

After raising a toast with Harry and Seymour on The Burlingtonian, Rehab had headed out alone in a small motorboat to lay his lobster pots. The sea was lively, but the winds were light; nothing that would have troubled a man who only came alive in a Force Nine gale.

Twenty minutes north of the harbour, he would have slowed down the engine. Turning from the wheel to toss the first creel overboard, he'd have watched the rope slither out until a brightly coloured marker buoy was bobbing on the surface, before moving onto the next drop. After that, everything was pure guesswork.

When the lifeboat crew arrived, they found Rehab's motorboat spinning around in solitary circles. There was nobody at the wheel; just a tight rope running down into the water at the stern which appeared to be dragging something. When the line was pulled in, Rehab's sunken body was at the end of it.

"So he lets go of the wheel to chuck a lobster pot in," said Seymour. "And as the rope runs out, it wraps around his ankle and pulls him overboard?"

"Yes, but why didn't he just climb back in. It doesn't make sense," said Spanners.

"Because he was drunk?" wondered Nellie, who was listening at the bar.

"Jansen Fallowdown though," said Frank, trying to steer the conversation out of its loop. "I wish I'd bloody known that."

"Because the rope got wrapped around the throttle and made his boat speed up?" said Seymour wearily.

"And when he pulled on the rope, his boat went even faster?" asked Spanners. "So he couldn't get back on board?"

"Yes. That's what the coroner thought. Yes."

"I don't buy it," said Spanners.

And so it went on.

The few indisputable truths, however, were that Rehab was dead; that his ashes were safely ensconced in Harry Spanner's chandlery; and that his midnight farewell had been scheduled for the last Sunday in May; long enough for word to spread, and late enough (hopefully) for a starry night and a flat calm to mark the Captain's final voyage.

When it came, it was both those things. Long before dark, the beach was packed. Children dodged between the legs of grizzled trawler men. Well-burnished stories and anecdotes passed freely around dense clusters of mourners, illuminated by roaring braziers. And as the light faded, the crowd pushed towards the water's edge to watch the passing of a legend.

It had been agreed before; no speeches and no songs. Everything felt epic enough without ceremony. When the time came, Harry and Seymour, and a handful of the Captain's fellow-fishermen, steadied the boat until the inrushing water could carry its weight. At the last moment, under the sky's fading streaks of light, Harry reached over and positioned the urn inside a small bundle of kindling.

"I've put a bottle of Courvoisier in with him," he whispered to Seymour. "And a pair of his old wellies."

One match was all it took. Slowly at first, and then fiercely, the flames spread along the length of the coble. Yet another burning boat, thought Seymour ruefully, as he waded back onto the beach where he turned to watch the bonfire edge further and further out to sea.

Behind him a few people had started clapping. A breeze was stirring off the land and the crackling vessel seemed to shrivel faster until it was no more than a white smudge. When it faded away completely, everyone was cheering; a glorious, rich farewell which rang out until the horizon was black again and the cold dots of the stars were the only things they could see.

"Nine tomorrow morning at Rehab's digs?" said Spanners, as the incoming tide drove people back towards their homes.

"Reluctantly, yes," said Seymour.

It was strange the way they'd put it off. All the years they'd known him, nobody had ever seen where the Captain lived; partly because he moved so often; but mostly because they were never invited. Up until his death, he'd been living in a room over a sweet shop owned by an elderly couple with no kids.

"He was an ex-miner; won the pools; came to the seaside with his wife," Rehab had told them. "I'm happy there. It's like I'm the son they never had."

"Lucky them," Frank had noted.

The next day, standing outside their friend's half-open bedroom door, Seymour and Spanners were stricken by doubt. Watching from the gloom of the landing, were the captain's grieving surrogate parents, each of whom was sucking a sherbet lemon.

"Tha can goo in, lad. It's nobbut a bed and a few bits. He nivver seemed to ha'much."

321

The former pitman's face was still so coal-pocked, he was virtually invisible at the top of the stairs.

"He liked wine gums though," said his wife, crunching hard on her sweet. "Liked the real stuff, too."

Seymour pushed gently on the door, found the light switch and stepped in. There was a single bed under a large sash window looking down on a yard. The bed had been made with perfect hospital corners and an ancient teddy bear with an eyepatch was sitting on the pillow.

Along one wall was a pair of shelves carrying two neat rows of first edition books. On the floor beneath them, a metal sea chest, marked 'J.F' contained his few neatly-folded clothes. Facing the shelves, separated by a well-travelled Indian rug, was an old walnut sea desk with brass handles. On the top of that, a large closed bible squatted alongside a fountain pen and a booklet of tide times. Underneath the desk, several rolled up charts had been squeezed carefully into a Victorian umbrella stand.

The only personal item they could see was a framed colour picture of a light-haired girl standing on the deck of a car ferry. Behind her was a large waterfront hotel; and beyond that a distant ridge of snow-toothed mountains. The ferry was called simply 'CUILLIN'.

"Bloody hell," gasped Spanners.

"We're in the wrong room," said Seymour. "There's no empty bottles."

"Tha's not," said the ex-miner. "It was allus like this."

For the next ten minutes, Spanners and Seymour respectfully examined the captain's few possessions. In a case beneath the bed, they found a brass telescope; his skipper's license; and a handful of salt-stained logbooks. On the shelves, every book was a true-life ocean adventure and every page wore the signs of constant reading.

"He was the real deal. He wasn't a joke," said Seymour, reverently replacing the volumes exactly as he'd found them.

"Have you seen this?" Spanners had opened the leather-bound bible. A single piece of lined notepaper had slid from its pages onto the rug. "I didn't know he could even write."

"Is it private? Should we be reading it?"

"It's like a set of last wishes." Spanners scanned the note and passed it to Seymour.

"This is amazing," he stammered. "He's left me his boat."

"And everything else goes to the Shipwrecked Mariners," said Spanners looking around. "The books and the telescope will be worth a few bob."

"He only told me about that boat a couple of weeks ago." Seymour was looking again at the photograph of the girl. "What the hell am I going to do with it?"

"You've been telling everybody you wanted a change," said Spanners as they stepped back out onto the street. "Now you've fucking well got one."

After that – Seymour decided much later – everything seemed to happen like he was in a pre-scripted film; as if Rehab had somehow laid down an invisible trail which would lead him (and Isaac) north to look for something that might not even exist.

Isaac had been the easiest part. The Captain's death had badly rattled him, stripping away any lingering interest in his exams. By mid-June, he'd sat the last one; his school blazer was in the dustbin; and he was settling down to a summer dropping battered haddock into bubbling fat. Seymour's proposition, when it finally crystallised, felt like the answer to a question he hadn't even asked.

"He's left you a boat? In Scotland?"

"If it hasn't rotted away, yes."

"And you're asking me if I want to come up there with you?"

Seymour's eyes widened, feeling his heart bounce with expectation.

"When do we start?"

"How does next week sound? After we've told your mum."

The following day, Seymour heated up his spark plugs and pootled off to see his brother-in-law. They'd need a half-decent vehicle to get past Hadrian's Wall, let alone the mountains on the other side of it. After the chicanery over his father's land, the least he could do was buy it from Ralph. Four hours later, he was on his way back through the terraced streets of his parent's hometown at the wheel of an odiferous white van.

"One lady owner. Practically new," Ralph had insisted, on a tour of his car showroom.

"A lesbian, presumably?"

"Are you having a laugh?" Ralph looked genuinely horrified.

"There's a porno girlie mag in the glove compartment."

"You're probably right then," said Ralph.

"….who smoked Woodbines?"

"Actually, now you mention it, he did look sort of butch."

Seymour wasn't going to argue. The money filling his wallet had once been his brother-in-law's and despite appearances (he still dressed like a spiv) Ralph had always played it straight, with Seymour, at least.

"Listen. That land I bought off you. I'm going to have to knock down your dad's old workshop. Is that alright? Nothing in there you want?"

"Not a thing," said Seymour, remembering his chest full of toys and his nights of half-naked teenage confusion with Lucy.

"Vietta's up the duff by the way," grinned Ralph, tossing over the keys.

"Congratulations," said Seymour, dropping them. "Is it yours?"

"Ha ha ha. Any problems with the van…….. call somebody else."

By the time he was back at the coast, Seymour felt reassured. It had run well and there was more than enough room for both his dad's old tools and the mountain of tinned food, camping gear, cooking apparatus and crockery which Isaac was conscientiously mustering in the kitchen.

"It's like Everest base camp in here," said Seymour, examining the labelled wooden crates and old army kitbags, all ready and packed for the off.

"I'm not sure about some of your choices," sneered Isaac, holding up a flaccid hot water bottle.

"We'll be fighting over that in a few months. We don't even know where we'll live. We might be back in a week."

"You've really no idea whether this boat is still there?" asked Isaac, tucking the rubber bottle into a rolled up sleeping bag.

"None whatsoever."

"Brilliant. Absolutely brilliant. I can't wait."

"Neither can I," said Seymour.

The anticipation was fierce. Both men had lost themselves in their mission. During the day, they scoured the shops ticking items off endless lists. During the long midsummer evenings, they packed and repacked the van until they were certain that nothing they'd need on the journey was out of reach; and that anything they couldn't shoehorn in could safely be left behind.

For Seymour, however, the process was wrought with quiet pain. Piece by piece, he was disconnecting himself from a town which seemed reluctant to see him go. At the newspaper his resignation had been accepted on condition that he supplied a monthly article chronicling his progress. The landlord of his house by the gasworks had waived notice, insisting only that it be cleared and cleaned upon vacation. Even the sweet shop couple had sent round a month's free supply of Sports Mixtures. Only two major issues, and one day's prep, were still outstanding.

"Mum now. Pub this evening. Leave first thing tomorrow? Alright?"

It was a humid afternoon and they were walking down the main shopping street. Ahead of them, Seymour could see Lucy hovering outside the shoe shop. She was looking up at a large black cloud drifting towards them from the south beach.

"I think I know what you're going to tell me…"

At Isaac's request they'd found a table at Toppings Ice Cream Parlour.

"…..you're going on some sort of trip. Right? Everyone's talking about it. I'm not deaf."

"We're going tomorrow. We're going to Scotland." Seymour could see the colour leaking from his wife's face. "That sailor who died – Captain Rehab – he left me a boat. And that's where it is. Up in Scotland."

"I don't believe it. Another bloody boat. What's wrong with you?"

"Not just him. Us," said Isaac, watching the waitress carefully as she placed three raspberry ice cream sundaes on their table.

"It's more than just a boat." Seymour looked helplessly at his floating berg of vanilla ice cream. "It sounds daft…. weird, maybe…. but I really think Rehab wanted me to go up there."

"For a week? A month? A year? Forever? How long?"

"We honestly don't know mum."

"We might even be back in a fortnight," said Seymour. Lucy was staring blankly at her son. "There might be nothing there."

"But if there is?"

"Either way, mum, it won't be forever. We're both stuck in this town. And you're the one who's always hated it most here anyway."

Lucy leaned back and closed her eyes. Isaac was right. She had loathed the town, their house, their life; just like she'd loathed Seymour's boats and his half-baked friends. Whenever she'd woken up, it had been there, always waiting; contempt, unmediated and raw.

"I did. That's true. Maybe I've mellowed," she smiled, calmly. "I'll certainly like it a lot less without you two in it."

For the next hour, while Seymour and Isaac ran through their plans. Lucy forced a smile to stay on her face. It wasn't easy, but it wouldn't help anyone to show what she really felt. She was envious – that was the truth of it – but as much as she could, she professed enthusiasm, hiding her sorrow behind a wall of maternal concern.

"Toothpaste? Toilet rolls? Tin opener?" she asked.

"Yes, No. Yes. We'll get some tomorrow," said Isaac,

"Will you write? Call? How will I hear?"

"We're going to Scotland, not Saturn,"

"As soon as we've got any kind of address, I'll let you have it. I promise."

The café had closed, and the three of them were standing awkwardly on the pavement under a giant fluorescent ice cream cone. Seymour opened his arms and drew both Lucy and Isaac into a group embrace. Rain was beginning to fall heavily, and shoppers were hovering in doorways for shelter.

"I'll look after him. I promise." There was a rumble of thunder. Seymour pushed forwards to kiss her cheek. "You take care, too."

"I will. I'd better go."

Lucy fumbled in her handbag for an umbrella. A black coil of rainwater was already running along the kerb thick with discarded fag ends. She turned once, offering a weak half-wave, and headed into the deluge. Every shred of daylight had melted away and the road was flickering blue and red with reflected neon.

Half-running, half-walking, Seymour and Isaac plotted their route home through the back streets in silence. By the time they were standing in the yard, a wide band of creamy light was pushing the rain out to sea. Trails of vapour were rising off the stone flags in the garden.

"I know what you're thinking, dad."

Isaac had unlocked the old stables. The innards of a decrepit valve radio drooped from a soggy cardboard box amongst a clutter of their discarded furniture. A few bits of Christmas tinsel had somehow become trapped in the rafters.

"She hasn't got anyone else, Isaac. Only that man-killer Eunice."

"She left you. She slept with my old girlfriend's bloody father. We're going tomorrow."

Seymour picked up a worn leather suitcase. Inside it were the last few pieces of his electric train set. A mint boxed Hornby Dublo model of the Mallard with three Pullman coaches and five yards of track. Everything else was already gathering dust at the junk shop.

"I can't have been easy," he said.

"Just go for a pint. Just go and see your mates." Isaac had detached the case from his father's hand and was pushing him towards the door, "But we're still going tomorrow. Hangover or not."

It was gone seven when Seymour peeked through the window of The White Horse. Along the main artery out of town, what passed for a rush hour (two extra buses) was long gone, and a patchwork-pink sunset flickered in the afternoon's puddles. Inside, he could see just two people. One was a solitary customer in a green army greatcoat downing his pint and fastening his buttons. The other was Nellie, distractedly polishing the horse brasses with an old cotton shirt.

"G'night Seymour," said the man in the ankle-length coat, careering out into the fresh air. "Don't do anything I wouldn't do."

Seymour held the door and watched him step blindly onto the road. Something about his face was vaguely familiar, but he'd no idea who he was. Ever since the fire on The Burlingtonian (not to mention the doomed regatta) it had been the same. People in the town felt like they knew him; like he was part of the town's blighted furniture.

Before Rehab's death, he hadn't minded; he'd been proud even. But now the Captain was gone? In the weakening light, the stranger had made it to the opposite pavement where he was wrestling with the door of a vandalised telephone box. Isaac was dead right. Everyone was ready for a break.

"You coming in or what?"

Seymour swivelled to his right. He could smell Brasso and the landlady's curves were outlined in the doorway against the glow from the saloon bar.

"Blimey. He looked like he'd had a few." Seymour followed her in. Even though it was June, a fire was blazing strongly beneath a large framed picture of a toucan.

"His divorce just came through," explained Nellie. "His wife got the kids. I threw him out at 3. He was back again when we opened at 6. I told him, just one pint. So, he's had it, he's drunk it and he's gone to ring and tell her he loves her."

Seymour smiled. Unless it was in their dreams, nobody messed with Nellie. "Fires in June?" he said. "What's going on?"

"Look around. There's nobody in. It's dead. And if there's nobody in, it's freezing in here."

In an alcove next to the fireplace, two darts hung limply from the bullseye of a cork board. Alongside it was the wooden cabinet Seymour had once made for the East Riding (East) Higginson's Bakery Domino League trophy. Apart from Frank's photograph of the victorious team, the cabinet was now empty.

"Shame we couldn't hang onto it," he said.

Nellie poured two large glasses of rum and stationed chairs within touching distance of the hearth.

"I doubt we'll even enter this year. It just doesn't feel right," she said. "Cheers."

"We're going away tomorrow. Me and Isaac. I was hoping to say goodbye to a few people."

"You're going ahead with it then. I never thought you would."

"It's like they say in the films, Nellie," chuckled Seymour. "There's something I've got to do."

"Rehab's so-called mystery boat? I heard. We'll miss you."

"Where is everybody?"

"Nobody's really been in for a while. You can imagine why," said Nellie, sadly. "Summer's always dead away from the sea front though. I don't even bother opening some nights."

For an awkward few minutes, their conversation stalled. Outside on the street, they could hear the drunk bellowing into the phone. Inside, the only noise came from the crimson embers collapsing deeper into the grate.

"This is the second fire in this building I've stared at with you," mumbled Seymour.

"It is. Last time you made it upstairs. This time your trousers are steaming."

"Very funny."

"No, really. They actually are steaming."

Seymour looked at his legs. A weak mist was circling around his thighs.

"We got caught out in the rain. They'll be dry soon."

"If you don't die of pneumonia first."

There was another awkward pause, during which the landlady stood up and smoothed the wrinkles in her dress down over her hips.

"Listen, erm, Nellie….I don't know how to say this…."

"I'm listening, whatever it is."

"The thing is….the thing is this….."

"For god's sake, Seymour. Spit it out man."

"Well, the last time we were together like this….I was…..Well, I was just wondering if you were joking."

"I don't tell a lot of jokes. Not as a rule. Not even at Christmas."

Nellie had put down her empty glass and sashayed to the pub door. Watching her, Seymour had a sudden uncomfortable flashback to the magazine (still) in his glove compartment.

"Not sex. I don't mean that. Or nudity."

"I know exactly what you mean," said Nellie, turning the key. "And I know exactly what I said."

"Also…also…I've got to be home before Isaac gets up tomorrow."

There was a click, followed by a fluorescent buzz. The lights behind the bar had been dimmed.

"Just a mature grown-up platonic sort of between the sheets cuddle?"

"If that's OK?"

"Of course. Absolutely fine. You're a gentleman and as it says over the front door, I'm a lady."

"You are. I am. Thank you. Thank you."

"But first things first," grinned Nellie.

"What's that then?"

"First, let's ease you out of those wet trousers."

"I'll put the guard round the fire," said Seymour.

Chapter Four

Neither of them had spoken for over an hour. As the mountains wrapped around their van across Rannoch Moor, the two men sat in silence. Apart from his years as an evacuee in Wales, Seymour's horizons had rarely budged from the North Sea, meaning that Isaac's solitary school trip to the Lake District, qualified him as the duo's most seasoned traveller. Nothing in their lives had prepared either of them for what unfolded beyond the canyon-like streets of Glasgow. And consequently, they regarded it with speechless awe.

Hereabouts, the road dipped into an enormous valley, squeezed tight by overlapping peaks which were still blotched in the shadows by patches of snow. Meltwater thundered in furious peaty spouts between boulders which – Seymour guessed – must have been tossed from the tops he was craning across the steering wheel to see.

Not until the road arched down to the coast, where it swooped between ancient silver birch and the white-brushed blue of a sea loch, could either one of them dare intrude on what they were witnessing.

"Fucking hell," said Isaac.

A young deer had broken cover from the woodland to their right. Before Seymour could even brake, it had leapt across the road into a thick jungle of roadside bracken.

"Your mum would have loved this." said Seymour.

The pair had stopped just once since leaving home at dawn. In a state of scarcely contained ecstasy, they'd motored north, putting the sepia hump of the Pennines behind them before Isaac insisted on a toilet break somewhere around the Scottish border. There, crouched over a furious Primus stove, he'd coaxed a meal out of eggs and stale bread to mark his first new country after England.

"Any idea what time it is, dad? I mean is this breakfast, dinner or tea?"

Seymour looked at the cloudless sky. The eggs were glorious. Further down the road lay the voluptuous curves of reiver country, and beyond that, the Highlands and the western sea.

"None whatsoever," he laughed. "Best meal ever, though."

It was late afternoon before they'd seen that first deer, by which time Seymour's stint at the wheel had extended to ten hours. Skirting north under the black bulk of Ben Nevis, the road had shrunk to a single lane which weaved uncertainly up through a maze of glens and forests before ascending again over a barren wilderness of ice-scoured granite, exposed here and there amongst the treeless heather like the flanks of ancient, fossilised whales.

Inside both, the adrenalin was spent.

"We need to find somewhere for some sleep," whispered Seymour, shaking his arms in turn to tease out the ache which had crept into his shoulders.

The highway had plateaued, but it was a grim and lifeless place and Seymour hunched forward again, driving his right foot hard to the floor. For a second time, the cab fell silent, but it was exhaustion, not exhilaration, which muted them. After another few miles, they passed a pub, slowing just enough to see that it was closed, before pressing down into a steep-sided river valley thick with berried rowan trees.

"Over there, dad. Looks perfect."

Where the stream passed under a stone pack bridge, there was room to park the van alongside a circular patch of turf. Charred stones marked the presence of an old fire ring, and the grassy banks were littered with kindling, swept down in the winter floods. Within a half-hour, their tent was up; a blaze was roaring; and Isaac was spearing luncheon meat to grill over a carefully marshalled heap of golden embers.

"Have you noticed?" said Isaac, leaning back out of the heat. "It's still light."

"It must be ten, maybe eleven o'clock."

"Cold though. I might be borrowing your hot water botty later."

Isaac rubbed his hands together and rolled blackened potatoes from the fire, exposing the scorched, soft flesh before scattering it with crisp cubes of meat and melted cheese.

"God, that's good," grinned Seymour. "My two best meals ever. On the same day."

The red taillights of a lone car were shrinking away towards the north. Neither of them had heard it pass.

"It's like fish and chips. Always tastes better outdoors," said Isaac, scraping his potato skins into the flames. "What time did you get in last night?"

"What time?" Seymour was relieved that his face was glowing already. "Not late, I don't think. I didn't really notice."

"You weren't too sad, though? Saying your goodbyes?"

"No. I wasn't. Not really. It was good. Really good. A sort of one-off, I suppose."

"Do you think we'll ever go back?"

"Of course I do. Why wouldn't I? We've come to find a boat. We're not running away."

335

"You might not be," said Isaac.

The fire was still alive when Seymour woke the next morning. Pulling the tent flap aside, he watched Isaac fill a kettle from the river, before impaling four rashers of bacon on a freshly whittled skewer.

"You've helped yourself to one of my penknives," said Seymour. His breath seemed to crackle in the frigid valley air. "You'll be smoking a pipe next."

They were on the move long before the sun cleared the mountains. As they pulled away, Seymour could see a thin line of smoke in his mirror rising to meet the still blue of a perfect June morning. There were only eighty miles left to go, and their route now followed the line of a broad tidal channel, separating their road from a distant purple-heathered shoreline sprinkled with thatched white cottages.

"I think that's the Isle of Skye." Isaac had been scrutinising a road map for several minutes. "Please don't burst into song."

By mid-morning, they'd stopped only once; to brew tea by a stone castle perched on a sea-wrapped rock, enraptured by the squat black trawlers and by the oystercatchers fussing impatiently amongst the kelp.

"Have you seen how clear the water is?"

Seymour leaned out over a jumble of weedy rocks. Three feet below the surface, he could see a young sea trout holding its position against the tide.

"It's like glass. Or ice. It's like it's a completely different substance to our murky rubbish back home."

"Feels like ice, too." Seymour was watching his fingers ripple just under the surface.

By midday they were there. Ahead of them, they could see the compact knot of slate roofs and single-storey bungalows tumbling down to the water's edge where the road ran out in a broad concrete ramp, lapped by the incoming tide.

Down the village's one main street, there was a garage, a chemist and a bar – The Peat Shovel – and where the asphalt met the sea, a small general store selling everything from fresh clams to square, white loaves of ageing bread. Even the one hotel, a four-storied Victorian folly, managed to fold harmlessly into the shoreline with its silvery roof angled hopefully towards the sun.

"It's stunning," gasped Isaac, climbing down from the van.

Every house seemed to be gazing across the sound; and beyond that to the soaring bulk of the island. Looking back at them – over the gyrating black currents – was a sister village where a car ferry appeared to be detaching itself from the shore. As they watched, there was a sudden explosion of turquoise water followed by the thump of a diesel engine. Five minutes later, it was in front of them, sliding its flat keel into position on the ramp.

"They make it look so easy," said Seymour. "I'm going to have a word."

A hydraulic steel platform was being lowered until its landward edge was clear of the water. Two warps had anchored the ferry on either side, and a handful of lorries was edging out across the platform onto the wet concrete. When the last one was off, a man in a blue jumper began directing the solitary waiting tractor up onto the empty deck.

"Did you ever know a fisherman round these parts called Rehab? Captain Rehab?"

Seymour had tiptoed down across the seaweed, watched by two curious locals on a park bench.

"Never heard of him, pal."

337

The ferryman's accent required close concentration. Seymour moved a little closer and tried again.

"Or Jansen Fallowdown?"

"Never heard of him either," he repeated. "But you could try Candunk."

"Candunk?"

"Yeah. Candunk. He knows everyone. Ask at The Refresh," said the sailor. "He's usually up there bible bashing."

"The Refresh?"

"That's what I said. At the railway station."

"And these ferries," asked Seymour, shielding his ears from the boat's horn. "Was there ever one called 'Cuillin'. C.U.I.L.L.I.N Or something like that?"

"There was, but I'm not sure when. I'll tell you who might know."

"Candunk?" said Isaac.

"Spot on," beamed the sailor. "Is he a mate of yours too?"

Seymour and Isaac left the van by the ferry park and walked back along the main street to the station. For trains, just like cars, the village was the end of the line. Only the toughest of travellers pressed on and out to the Hebrides. The rest were satisfied with a night of prayer at the village hotel; prayers issued in hope that the clouds (which had invariably dogged them all the way from Inverness) would eventually lift.

And invariably, it must be said, they didn't.

It was a wooden station building with ten chimney pots, and a rotten timber canopy. Alongside the single track, a diesel train was vibrating impatiently while boxes of ice-packed fish were stacked inside its line of wagons. Halfway along the platform they could see a large maroon sign, swinging over a glass-panelled door.

"Refresh? Refreshment Bar?" said Isaac, reaching for the door. As he opened it, a huge red-haired man in a filthy T-shirt staggered out, clutching his nose. "And let's try not to sound remotely English."

"I'm Welsh, remember," grinned Seymour. "If in doubt, call me Taff."

"Yes, Taff," said Isaac, bulldozing his way into a wall of tobacco, music and noise.

There was just one square room with a bar along its far side serving drinks to around fifty men, all of whom appeared to be shouting. The only light came from two soot-streaked sash windows overlooking the platform.

Squeezed onto a tiny stage in the corner (although it was scarcely audible) a frail-looking man with a large accordion was murdering the Scottish country songbook. Everyone else appeared to be clutching a beer-glass in one hand, and a whiskey tumbler in the other.

"Hey Jimmy." One of the rosier-cheeked drinkers was yelling in the face of the accordionist. "Gi' us a blast of The Bluebell Polka."

"Right you are Jimmy. Coming up."

"You're a good man, Jimmy. That's beautiful. I love that. Can I buy you a wee drink?"

In the cacophonous rumble of the bar, Seymour couldn't be sure if it was a new tune or merely a continuation of the old one.

"Is everyone in Scotland called Jimmy?" asked Isaac.

From outside there was a whistle, followed by a second more ill-tempered blast. Before the train had even slithered away, the station crew were pushing in to join the melee.

"You alreet there, Jimmy?" someone shouted.

"Piss off," shouted someone else, although why and at whom seemed unclear.

There was a huge, unexplained roar of laughter, accompanied by the sound of a breaking bottle. Somehow, Seymour and Isaac had been pushed up to the bar, where a blonde-haired girl was washing glasses in a bucket of lead-coloured water. Every square inch of the counter was covered in empties.

"What can I get you?"

"It's a bit early for a drink," said Seymour. A grubby hand was reaching over his shoulder. Somehow it was holding onto four empty glasses at once.

"It's 11.30 on a Friday morning and the last train's just gone. Up here, this is the weekend. If you don't want a drink, you're in the wrong place."

"We're looking for someone we think is called Candunk?"

The girl picked up a tea towel. She seemed calm, despite the clamour for more alcohol; her accent shrewdly moderated by the need to be heard.

"You get used to the racket," she said. "They make a lot more noise than trouble."

"And Candunk?"

"He a Weefree. He doesn't drink. He tries to stop other people drinking."

"This is getting weird," said Isaac.

"Free Church Of Scotland. No drink. No gambling. And don't hang your knickers out to dry on a Sunday. We call 'em Weefrees. Little minds."

"But he's real; he exists?"

"He works on the harbour; looks after people's boats; does a few odd jobs and repairs. Wears an old green tweed jacket. Pockets full of prayer books. You can't miss him."

"Much obliged," said Seymour, turning to leave.

"You haven't asked us why we're looking for him," said Isaac.

"Would you tell me if I wanted to know?"

"I would, yes."

"Well, that's alright then."

"So do you want to know or not?"

"Not really, no."

A man carrying a guitar had joined the accordionist on the tiny podium. Three of the strings on his instrument were missing; an impediment which passed without comment from his audience.

"Is it ever quiet in here?"

"When we're closed."

Isaac grinned. The girl was attractive, he thought. Tall with lacerating blue eyes and a kind clear-eyed smile which ensured that even when she was talking tough, she didn't actually sound it.

"I'm Isaac by the way. This is my dad, Seymour. He's Welsh."

"And I'm Celeste. Well Mary actually. But I've always been known as Celeste."

"Mary Celeste," said Isaac. "I get it. Funny."

It didn't take long for them to find him. Between the station and the sea, clustered around a small jetty, a concrete wasteland of beached boats and crumbling sheds ran from the edge of the town to a headland of yellow gorse. Amongst the sprouting willow herb, sodden heaps of timber fought for space with rusting cranes and caravans. Just a few corners showed signs of recent activity: neatly piled nets and upturned hulls, glossy with new paint. Mostly, the place was a bomb site.

"Can I help you two wee fellas?"

A short man wearing turned down wellington boots had emerged from what looked like a portable toilet. It was impossible to tell whether he was middle-aged or old. And even from a distance, Seymour had never seen a thicker (or a redder) beard.

"We're looking for someone we think is called…."

"Candunk," said Isaac.

The man removed a piece of chewing gum from his mouth, eyeing it suspiciously for a second, before putting it back.

"You've found him. And if you're looking for the Lord, you've found him too."

"We're here for a boat."

"Lots of those," said Candunk. "Only one God."

Now that they were close, it was clear that the man's facial hair had passed beyond the capabilities of any mortal barber. Above his eyes, a single cheroot-like brow filled the space between his eyes and his hairline. From the ears down, vast sideburns had conjoined with a ginger beard to obliterate the man's entire lower face, down to his Adam's apple. Only the sharp arête of his nose was unimpeded, sitting up like a pink bird in a nest spun from copper wire.

Seymour looked away, feeling faintly nauseous. "Let me try and explain," he said.

A few minutes later, they were following Candunk towards a large corrugated iron warehouse, built with its back against a steep, mossy outcrop of granite.

"No-one's been in here for years," he said. There was a sliding door, the height of two men, half hanging away from its runners. "The RAF kept a torpedo boat in it during the war for a while. Pretty much since then it's been a glorified tip."

"But there's a yacht in here?"

"Last time I looked there was."

Together, the three of them had heaved the door back along its track. Somewhere in the gloom beyond it, shards of roof were falling unseen.

"I put it in here myself. Twenty or so years ago. Me and the fella that built it."

"You knew Rehab? Jansen? You were here back then?"

"I dinnae know a Rehab. Or Jansen? Jonah we called him. Decent sort of fella, for a blasphemer. Tall. Liked the lasses. Liked all the lasses. Hell of a fisherman. He gave me a tenner. Told me to keep an eye on the boat. And then he was gone. Never saw him again."

"That has to be Rehab," said Seymour. "It just has to be."

"It's weird though." Isaac had moved deeper into the warehouse, sidestepping slimy puddles of old rain. "Why did he build a boat and then just disappear?"

"None of my business," said Candunk. "Like I say, he just vanished."

Amongst the mildewed boxes and rusty fridges, as their eyes adjusted, they could make out a large boat held upright by two wheeled trestles.

"It's there, dad."

Seymour stepped towards it. A crumpled black tarpaulin was dangling from the stern.

"Here, here. Isaac. Give us a hand with this."

Both were moving quickly now; fumbling frantically for a reward they had never expected to claim.

"I've got it, I've got it." Standing on an oil drum, Isaac had reached one corner of the cloth. "You grab the other corner and pull."

There was a horrible, slithering rattle as the tarp came free.

"Torch, torch," yelled Isaac. "I can see something."

"I've got a lighter. Any use?"

"Perfect. Just don't set fire to your beard."

Candunk snarled and threw it up to Isaac who flipped open the brass lid and span the small wheel against the flint. Even in the sparks, he could make out a word – a name – painted on the back of the boat.

"Come on. Come on. Come on."

At the third attempt, the wick took. Isaac moved the oily flame closer to the transom and wiped away at the grime with the sleeve of his shirt.

"What's it say?" Seymour could feel a pulse thumping in his neck.

"It's the name of the boat, dad. It's amazing."

"What name? What's it called?"

"Gratitude," said Isaac, leaping down to join his father in a clumsily ecstatic embrace.

"Praise be," said Candunk.

It took another two days to bring the boat back into the sunshine. By that time – even in the dank half-light of the warehouse – Seymour had learned a great deal about his legacy. It was a magnificent 28ft single-masted yacht with a painted wooden hull, and a deck crafted from slender strips of teak.

Despite two decades of neglect, the hull had survived extraordinarily well. In the perpetual damp (and cold) only the paintwork appeared to have really suffered. Most of the sea-resistant caulking – squeezed into the joints between the timbers – would need replacing but from its external appearance, Seymour felt hopeful; grateful even.

"Can I go into the cabin now?"

The trio had transferred the yacht onto a mobile gantry; a space had been cleared on the quayside lot; and Candunk had pulled 'Gratitude' free with the help of a reluctant tractor.

"They must have felt like this going into Tutunkhamun's tomb," said Isaac.

A ladder had been secured to the transom. In the dazzling June light, Seymour felt buoyed by the boat's condition. Two months of graft, he calculated. After that – providing the engine was repairable – she'd be in the water. Reaching up for the handrail, he heaved himself into the cockpit. In front of him was the door down into the cabin. For the first time he felt uneasy. Rehab must have been the last person to close it.

"I'm going in," he shouted, "Torch on."

Backing carefully down the steps, Seymour circled his light around the galley (a spotless two burner gas stove) into the wedge-shaped sleeping quarters beyond. Despite the tendrils of damp, and a thin layer of black dust, a sense of naval order prevailed. Dominating the central cabin was a fixed, polished table with padded benches on each side. To his right – opposite the cooking area – was a desk.

Seymour stood over it; ran his fingers across its smooth walnut surface and slowly lifted the lid. Inside there were charts, navigation instruments and a single photograph protruding from the pages of an old hardback book.

"What's it like? Found anything?" yelled Isaac.

"I've found Captain Ahab," smiled Seymour. "It's a copy of Moby Dick."

Seymour slid the picture free and held it in the square beam of light falling from the open hatch. It was a familiar scene; a wind-blown young woman and a ferry called 'Cuillin'; a distant ridge of snow-topped hills; and the unmistakeable façade of a white-stuccoed Edwardian hotel.

"Who is she?" Isaac had climbed down into the cabin. "That was taken here, over by the ferry ramp. Definitely it was."

"I've no idea. We found the same picture in his room back home."

"Did he ever have a girlfriend?"

"Not that we ever knew." Seymour pulled back two sets of tiny curtains. White flight flooded the living quarters. "He never really said very much about himself."

"Everything's so tidy. It's like he was here yesterday."

"It's magnificent. I just wish it didn't feel so sad."

There were no further clues to be found. Outside, perched on a large capstan, Candunk distributed the contents of his tartan-patterned Thermos flask.

"Nice coffee," said Isaac.

"Rehab had a flask just like it," said Seymour.

"It's tea, not coffee," said Candunk, fishing in his overalls for a pair

346

of reading glasses. "Let's have a look at this snap."

A little way along the quay, two men were untangling a nylon fishing net: shaking out the knots before settling it carefully in the well of their boat.

"She's bonny," he said, passing it back quickly. "But I can't help you. I don't know her."

"You sure? Take a longer look."

"I'm certain. I was never that interested in girls. The ferry was from round here though, right enough."

"Can I ask you something?" Seymour pocketed the photograph and tipped his dregs into the sea. "Candunk? That's quite an unusual name."

"It's not my name. Duncan's my name. It's just that when I was a kid…."

"It's alright. You really don't have to tell us."

"….when I was a kid, my friends would come round and ask, 'Can Dunc play?' and my mum would say 'No. Duncan cannot. It's Sunday and Duncan's got his bible studies.' And then they'd say, 'Can Dunc play later then?' and she'd say 'Listen, you fecking unbelievers. It's not Can Dunc play it's Can Duncan play and the answer's still no.'"

"So it stuck," said Isaac, feeling an unexpected surge of pity.

"It did, but it didn't matter." Candunk had packed away his flask. "Cos when all this hair started to grow, everyone stopped calling for me anyway."

They saw a lot of his whiskers in the glorious weeks that followed. It was Candunk who found them a caravan with two bedrooms; and a draughty view north to the green swarth of Raasay and the ocean beyond. It was Candunk who fixed Seymour up with paint and parts and power. And it was Candunk who quietly rebuilt the engine; decoking its calcified jets; replacing its perished seals and gaskets; and flushing clean its sclerotic veins until it purred like a new black heart.

Most of the time, however, Seymour was content to work alone; bare-backed under the sun; feeling his face and his hands take on the same wind-burned patina as the trawler men who brought him fresh coffee each day or the ferry captains who now greeted him as one of their own.

Perched on its metal gantry, 'Gratitude' was being reborn. Inch by painstaking inch, Seymour was returning it to a state of perfection; too busy to ask himself why or what he would do with it when the work was finished.

In a haze of dust, he forged on; a blur of chisels and sweat. By mid-July, the hull above the waterline had been painted a deep and flawless blue. Two weeks later, he was applying the final varnish seal to the deck; the keel had been shot-blasted and every length of rigging replaced and tightened until it squeaked. Rehab and Spanners had taught him well. Nothing escaped Seymour's ferocious scrutiny.

Every trace of rot had been eliminated; bulkheads had been strengthened; gas cylinders discarded; even Rehab's old sails and moth-chewed mattresses were sacrificed on the perpetual bonfire which smouldered on the quay and which he stoked constantly with deadwood and sawdust.

In a village starved of novelties, local interest had been stirred. Almost every day, a rotating clutch of spectators gathered to watch Seymour at work; most of whom refused to leave without a lengthy conversation regarding the price of clams. Without discernible effort, both the father and the son had been adopted. On Saturdays, Seymour had even started playing his concertina in the station bar, receiving no more attention than the elderly accordionist who appeared to have vanished inexplicably without trace.

"Fell off the ferry," said the blue-eyed young woman behind the bar when Seymour asked.

"Is that a joke?"

"Or pushed," she'd grinned. "We're a tough audience."

Isaac too had found his niche. Within a few days of arriving, Seymour's son had secured work scrubbing turnips in the kitchen of the waterside hotel. Shortly after that (when an under-chef was sacked for streaking naked through the guest lounge) he'd been placed in charge of starters.

Every morning, at the town's impromptu fish market, Isaac could be found haggling for clams and bulk-buying fresh mackerel. When the tide was low he went scouting for mussels; and when the first train chugged into the station, there was always a box of fresh melons marked with his name.

For both, it was a hard but happy routine blighted by just one thing: or rather, several billion things, each one no bigger than a pinhead. On humid summer nights – when the peat began to sweat – the skies filled with black clouds of midges driven insane by the proximity of human blood.

No-one in the town – however long they had lived – was immune to their bite. Unless a hard wind was blowing, they fell on any exposed flesh without mercy. During the day, the smoke from Seymour's bonfire kept them at bay. But around dusk, even the inside of his caravan seethed with ravenous swarms from which the only protection was a nylon stocking pulled tightly over each of their heads.

"This is insane. We look like the Kray twins," cursed Isaac, as they readied themselves for a Friday night dash to the station bar.

No-one understood why, but only The Refresh seemed to offer any sanctuary. Along the platform, squadrons of midges hovered in expectation of a meal. Behind the bar's substantial door (having sprinted from their homes) drinkers pulled off their masks knowing that no midge had ever crossed the portal and lived.

Some said it was the whisky fumes which kept them out. Others thought it might be the folk music. Or the Jimmy Shand records. Either way, it was a damned good reason to drop in for a dram. And another billion reasons more to stay for a second.

"Is it like this all year?" Seymour was standing at the bar, examining his hands. They were covered in small red bites. In the morning he'd be scratching them till they bled.

"They're not without their good points," said Celeste, filling two dimpled pint glasses.

"Such as?" asked Isaac.

"They keep the English away."

"Until the autumn when it's too wet to come anyway?" laughed Isaac, trying desperately to establish eye contact. "Correct?"

"Correct."

Isaac took a long swig from his beer. No-one had ever questioned his age. In The Refresh, you got served if you could pay.

"You should show her the photograph, dad. You've tried everyone else."

That wasn't quite true. Early on, Seymour had half-heartedly played Poirot before concluding that he was wasting his time. No-one in the town seemed to recognise her. Or if they did, no-one was saying. A one-night stand? A friend? A relative, maybe? The girl by the ferry could have been from anywhere. All the picture proved was how little he'd known the Captain. And how deeply he still felt his loss.

"There's no point." The beer, as it usually did, tasted of gun-metal.

"Show her the bloody photograph, dad."

350

Seymour pulled a white envelope from the breast pocket of his jacket and slid it across the bar.

"This is fun," said Celeste, drying her hands on the back of her jeans. "You want me to look?"

Seymour nodded wearily. The girl scrutinised the photograph.

"Thank you," she said. There was a crack in her voice and her hands had fallen to the counter for support.

"You know who it is," said Isaac.

"Just tell me again who you are. And why you have this photograph?"

"You really do know who it is?" Seymour's eyes were burning.

"I certainly should do," said Celeste. "Although she doesn't look much like that now."

"Who the fuck – sorry – is it?" blurted Isaac.

"It's my mum," she said, ringing the bell for last orders.

The following Wednesday, shortly after breakfast, Seymour boarded the 8.23 bus (at 8.57) clutching the barmaid's handwritten instructions. "Don't improvise," she'd said. "Or we'll never see you again." At its ninth stop the bus pulled up outside a simple white church walled in by a hedge of late-flowering rhododendrons.

"Is this the right spot?" Seymour asked the driver.

"How would I know?" he replied, wrestling the gearstick into first and closing the doors. "I don't know where you're going."

Seymour peered again at his note. On one side there was a map, showing the church and a track running away from it towards the sea. He looked up, shielding his eyes from the dazzle of a cloudless sky. There was an unmarked post – just where Celeste had said it would be – and a gravel lane threading through the heather in the direction of the shoreline.

He set off. For the first mile or so, the only sounds were his feet and a skylark. Gradually, however, as they were replaced by the groan of the sea, he turned again to the girl's scribblings. 'Look for the abandoned peat cuttings and take the left fork in the track. You're almost there.' Checking again, he could see piles of dried turf topped by a broken, rusty shovel. A few steps on, the dirt road split and he followed the narrower arm to the top of a steep incline where he stopped and held his breath.

The house was small, just a single storey croft with one window either side of a red-painted door and two glass panels admitting light through a metal roof. Between it and the sea lay a patchwork of cultivated plots, and where the field ran out, a wall of black stones had been piled high against the winter storms. From what he could see there was no power, and the only thing moving was a woman clipping rosemary in a herb garden.

Perhaps sensing his presence, the woman turned and waved him down.

"It's Seymour, isn't it? My daughter was here yesterday," she said, cheerily. "I'll put the kettle on."

Seymour followed her in through a garden of strange delights; past stones painted in bright colours and gorgeous configurations of flotsam wrestled into sculptures of birds or fish, with seaweed for feathers and shells for scales. Inside, almost everything had been reclaimed from the wild clutter of the sea.

Candles, hundreds of them, littered sideboards and ledges made from driftwood and tea chests. There was a drowned-looking sofa and a keel repurposed as a table, with four sawn-off oars for legs. Only the ancient gas cooker and the paraffin lamps looked as they should do. Even the girl in the photograph had gone; survived only by the force of her presence and the story he was dying to hear.

"Celeste brings me anything I can't grow or catch or pick from the rocks," she said, handing Seymour a chipped enamel cup. Her accent was a rich broth of the glens.

"It's got milk in it," he said, without thinking.

"I've a goat. And a boat. And books. And a radio I run from a car battery. So, I don't really need people. Not strangers, anyway. Don't talk much either. You're one of the first I've seen in a long time. I'm Jane by the way. Let's go back in the sun."

The white trunk of a tree had been propped up on breeze blocks facing out towards the breaking sea. There were barnacles where the bark had once been and something oily-dark was moving along the shoreline.

"It's an otter," she said. "Looking for crabs."

"I found this photograph," said Seymour. The creature had tilted its head in the direction of the stranger's voice. "Your daughter thinks it might be you."

She took the picture, studied it for a few seconds and handed it back.

"It was my camera. We'd just come across from Skye and my dad was doing Saturday shifts on the ferry. 1950. Maybe earlier. It was a long, long time ago. Celeste tells me he's died; and that he left you his boat?"

"I'm sorry," said Seymour, not really knowing where to begin.

"I was 21. I think he was about the same. No-one really knew where he'd come from. He was suddenly just there, in the town, and he was so different. Dark-haired, lean, a little mad and a lot dangerous. Ridiculously handsome, of course. Never said much, unless it was a joke. A bit James Dean. He seemed to know everything about boats and, of course, every skipper here wanted him on their crew. Just like every girl like me wanted him in their bed."

Seymour smiled. Nobody would ever understand how good it was to hear all this.

"He'd changed a bit at the end," he said.

"How so?"

"Long white hair and a broken nose. Not what you'd call sexy, but still slim and still dangerous and still handsome, I suppose. Captain Rehab, we called him."

While the woman laughed, Seymour studied her profile. A lifetime spent grafting under the sun had scorched her face, but she was still yellow-haired and beautiful.

"I knew him as Jansen, but for a joke the fishing lads called him Jonah. Everyone had a nickname then. Once he'd screwed everyone else, he finally worked his way round to me. Except with me, for some reason, it was different. With me, it got serious. At least, for a while it did."

"Were you still with him when he bought that boat?"

"Built that boat. When he built that boat, yes." She'd twisted on the bench until she was looking directly into Seymour's eyes. "That thing was his passion. For two years, he poured all his money and spare time into it. And then it was finished. It was ready. We were going to sail away together to Bora Bora; somewhere hot with no midges and have lots and lots of babies. And then suddenly he was gone. Never came back. Never saw or heard from him again."

"No letters? No explanation?"

"No letters. But I didn't need an explanation."

"What then?"

"My father was a weefree. Like Candunk. Desperately strict. In those days the ferry couldn't even sail on Sundays. Someone had told him we were sleeping together. He went round to the Refresh, pulled Jansen out into the station and beat him half to death with a fence post."

"The broken nose?"

"I suppose so, yes." There was a second otter now, dragging the carcass of a dead fish to its mate. "My father told me what he'd done. He told me he'd kill Jansen if he ever saw him again."

"Bloody hell. No wonder he liked a drink."

"Did you know that his boat never got in the water?"

"I guessed." Seymour shook his head. "He called it Gratitude. Any idea why?"

"I never knew that." Two parallel tears were running down each of her cheeks. "I'm not sure what he had to be grateful for."

"You, maybe? He kept your photograph."

"There was never anyone else after Jansen. Not a nun thing. It just never happened. Thank you for coming."

"I'm putting her in the water next week, said Seymour. Jane's eyes widened as she listened. They had the same gleaming intensity as her daughter's. "It'll be the first time she's ever sailed. You should be on it. Will you be?"

"I promise," she said. "Now go and catch that bus."

It was the most stressful week of Seymour's life. With Candunk at the controls of a crane, 'Gratitude' had been scooped up and lowered into the sea. Every gurgle had seemed like a leak, and every train had been met in expectation of the new sails which were coming from Portsmouth, along with the champagne due in from a vintner in Perth.

With twenty fours to go, everything was set. He'd fired up the engine for the first time. He'd hoisted the virgin sails and christened the kettle; he'd even slept alone in the aft cabin, pushing away strange dreams about Rehab roasting a howler monkey on a desert island. When he rose on the seventh day (a Sunday) the winds were blowing from the south; steady and true without the slightest hint of rain. All Candunk's grim prognostications had been misplaced.

"No sailing on the Lord's day," he'd warned. "Ezekiel. Chapter Eleven. Verse Five."

Seymour hadn't checked the quotation. For some time, he'd harboured serious doubts about Candunk's familiarity with the scriptures. Instead, he'd stood with Isaac and watched as Jane walked towards him along the water's edge, arm in arm with Celeste.

"You're here. You've come."

"You made me promise. And I've thought of nothing else all week."

"I should warn you that the last time I tried to sail a new boat with an audience…."

"…..the mast fell down and my grandad's teeth went in the sea," said Isaac.

"And the second time….."

"It sank."

"Third time lucky," said Seymour. And ten minutes later, they were off.

It was a heavenly day for a sail. For three hours, they cruised west across calm waters, propelled by a soft, steady breeze still warm from its long journey up from the equator. There was no need for charts. Seymour navigated by sight alone, threading calmly between the islands of Scalpay and Skye towards the old stone quay on Raasay and the flat top of Dun Caan beyond.

After a mile, it was as if they had been born to it. While Seymour held the wheel, Jane trimmed the mainsail, instinctively tightening the sheet until the boat heeled, forcing Celeste and Isaac up from the galley to lean out over the chattering broken water until their faces exploded with laughter.

"This is the best thing ever," said Isaac.

"Hold on tight," shouted Seymour. At a wink from Jane, he eased 'Gratitude' tighter to the wind. The sails snapped, and an exultant quiver seemed to run down into the keel. "This one's for Rehab."

"And for Jansen," yelled Jane.

"But hopefully not Jonah," screamed Isaac, who'd just realised how steeply the boat had tipped over.

As they turned towards their mooring, the boat rose even higher in its own surf. There was an instant pulse of speed, followed by a sizzling effulgence of spray and then just as quickly, absolute silence.

"You've sailed before."

They were out of the wind now. The boat was still. Across the sound, a range of black-fanged mountains was shaking off its overnight cloud. While Seymour secured it to the quay, Jane lowered the sails and stowed the sheet lines in perfect folds.

"Everyone knows the sea round here," she said.

Isaac and Celeste were soon passing up glasses of fizzy wine from the dark of the cabin, alongside trays piled with smoked salmon sandwiches and a steaming, hot bowl of fresh mussels.

"This quay was built by German POW's in the First World War," said Jane. "They were digging iron out of the island for the British to turn into shells which the British then fired back on the Germans. The food's great, by the way."

"So they were sort of killing themselves? That's horrible," said Celeste. "You've never told me that before."

"More booze anyone?" asked Isaac.

They were back by mid-afternoon. During the return trip the wind had pivoted, requiring the four to don warm jumpers as the yacht surged ahead of a cold northerly airstream. Traces of early snow were showing on the high tops and the shipping forecast was predicting a week of gales and high seas.

"Twenty years late but worth the wait. Thank you."

Seymour and Jane were taking extra care to secure the boat. Isaac had already headed for The Refresh with Celeste to wash a weeks-worth of whisky tumblers.

"We can do it again. You're a better sailor than I'll ever be. And he built her for you, not me."

"Come for tea some time. There's more I can tell you."

"Let me take a wild guess." Seymour was dropping extra fenders between 'Gratitude' and the harbour wall. "Rehab was Celeste's father?"

Jane smiled. "Something like that. Yes. He was gone before I was sure. Probably saved his life. If he'd come back my dad would have killed him."

"Captain Rehab? Mary Celeste? Just a coincidence."

"Nothing more."

"And does she know?"

"There wasn't much to tell before. But I'll tell her now. Now that the story has an end."

Seymour gripped her hand as she stepped from the boat. It was Sunday, deathly quiet, and only the ferry was moving, furrowing hard against the tide towards the island. Somehow it felt to him like a circle had just been completed.

"I'm sleeping on board now," he explained. "Isaac's still in the caravan."

"See you soon?"

"Of course," he said.

Seymour watched her go; slipped back into the boat's living quarters; and turned up the heater. It had been an exhausting day but that wasn't the reason he was desperate to be alone. The previous morning, the postman had dropped off another letter and it was there now; waiting to be read behind the copy of Sons and Lovers he'd ordered from the Highlands mobile library.

Filling a glass with flat leftovers, he lay back on his bunk and reached for the thick wad of correspondence hidden under his pillow. He was warm; Count Basie was oozing from the radio; and he'd nothing to do until he'd read every single line of Lucy's letters once again.

And if he was still awake after that, he'd have another try at D.H.Lawrence.

It was going to be a long winter. Not much else to do.

Chapter Five

June 28, 1970

Dear Seymour,

I got your card this morning. Thank you for letting me know that you've both arrived safely, although your address sounded slightly alarming. 'The Blue Caravan, Kyle of Lochalsh, Scotland'. Are you absolutely sure? And was I meant to read anything into the picture on the card? A very large bearded man in a kilt with a hungry-looking buzzard on his arm? It looked rather <u>threatening</u> to me and since your message was so short, I found myself looking for hidden meanings. Too much imagination I suppose, but am I the buzzard, by any chance?

Maybe if you write a little more next time – ??? – you can fill in a few gaps. How was your trip? Have you found what you're looking for? Do you think Isaac might write to me? Has he settled? Is he working? How is the Scottish weather and the food? What are your plans? Obviously, I understand your feelings towards me, but I'm still his mother and, whoever's fault this is, it's awful being so far away.

Not that I'm feeling sorry for myself. Just after you left, Eunice shut the shop and took herself to the Costa Brava for a fortnight with Frank, so I've had the house to myself. In the mornings, I've taken to strolling along the cliff top towards the lighthouse. It's four miles there, and a 43 bus back with a pot of tea at Headlands Café in between. In the afternoons, I've been happy with a deckchair in the back garden although I've lost my appetite for reading recently. Mostly, I just watch the clouds.

Ralph and Vietta send their regards. Obviously, I've told them what happened. He was over here on a test drive – an Austin Maxi? – and we went out for fish and chips as a threesome. You knew she was four months pregnant, didn't you? And she's still wearing miniskirts??!! Ralph was on good form though. He told me all about your father's bit of land. Why did you never tell me? I knew his house was worthless so I'd been wondering where you'd got your money but didn't want to ask. Ralph says there are still no hard feelings. He's going to make a packet anyway. He says he's sold it on to a supermarket chain and ordered a Bentley! He also says he kept a sledge of yours he found in the workshop. For their child? I expect you'll be quite pleased?

Two days after you left, I went back to our old house to collect my last few bits and pieces. It was kind of you to put them in boxes. Thanks for that too. Being there alone was pretty horrible and I couldn't wait to get back into the daylight. The garden looked lovely though. We did a good job there between us. The aubretia has gone wild and the leylandii have finally hidden the gasworks!

Just before I left, I looked into your workshop. There was a sack in the corner containing the remains of your accordion. Do you remember that clarinet you once had? When Isaac was younger? Before everything else? Well, I owe you a confession? I'm sure you always knew that it was me. I think I hated the noise of that even more than your boats. You were never easy to live with. But looking back, I don't think I could have lived with myself either.

Anyway, I've been writing this outside, the sun's just gone in and that stain at the bottom of this page is a drop of rain! Do take care of yourself and our son. And if you find the time, it would be lovely to hear a bit more of your circumstances.

Kind Regards

Lucy

P.S. I've quite enjoyed writing this. There were so few letters between us when we were courting.

P.P.S How was your farewell 'do' at The White Horse?

P.P.P.S. I'm not really the buzzard am I?

July 15, 1970

Dear Seymour,

Thank you for your letter which arrived yesterday morning. I was beginning to think your 'blue caravan' might have been blown into the sea. The weather here has taken rather an ugly turn. But then Frank got out his road atlas and reassured me it takes three days for a letter to get up there, although when I asked him exactly where 'there' was, he seemed rather vague. Still, they had a great time in Spain 'despite all that garlic', says Eunice.

How are things with you and my boy? Exciting, by the sound of it. Everyone is talking about your articles in the paper here. According to the front page this week, your finding that old boat is bigger than the moon landings. If my mother hasn't assassinated him first, you'll be getting an invite for tea with Edward Heath next!! Would you go??

Olive and Bill are well by the way, unlike Arthur, who's been seen by the vet three times already this summer. I'm not sure how mum would cope without him. I've never understood why, but their dogs have stopped my parents from killing each other. Both asked me to send on their good wishes. After what happened, I think they love you more than me.

Eunice cooked me a paella last night. It's a fancy rice dish with peppers and prawns. Horrible. Frank joined us and we shared a bottle of wine or 'vino tonto' as Eunice insisted on calling it. Since they got back, she's talked of nothing else but Espana, and how she's going to sell up the shop and move there to learn flamenco dancing after they've tied the knot next Spring. All <u>Frank</u> really wanted to talk about was your old friend Mr.Rehab, and the boat which you've found.

362

I can't imagine how special it must have felt and (even though you know what I think about boats) I was moved by the way you described the discovery for the paper. Everyone else I know felt the same emotions. You're a good writer. Something else about you that secretly makes me jealous!!

Please don't kill yourself repairing it. I know what you're like. Get Isaac to help. At least ask him to cook you some decent food. And next time, tell me more about his job in the hotel. What are his prospects? How much is he getting paid? It was lovely to get a card from him, although it said very little and his spelling is still atrocious. And no, of course I won't forget his birthday.

In answer to your questions, yes, I am eating properly. Eunice has seen to that. It's just that I can't put on any weight. I'm also working full time now and looking around for a flat to rent, somewhere with a spare bedroom and a bay window where I can sit and stare at the sea. I really don't want to live with Eunice and Frank in Tossa de Mar and I need somewhere on my own.

You're right when you say it wasn't all bad in that house, but it wasn't what I expected when we first decided to move to the coast. I know it was all we could find, and I know it was quite grand in some ways, but it always seemed so dark. To be honest, and I'm not blaming you, I always felt like a prisoner in it. Sorry. You'll probably stop writing if I start talking about 'all that' and I probably wouldn't blame you.

It's my coffee break at work now and Eunice is restocking the shelves with jellies and flip flops. I can't tell you how many we sell. In summer, this place is a little goldmine even when the weather is as rotten as this. Hopefully, it will calm down for the kite festival.

One last thing on the subject of midges. Mum says that she was up in Scotland for her honeymoon and found that eating lots of Marmite kept them away. Kept Bill away too, probably!! Let me know if they sell it at your local shop.

Thanks again for writing. I'm not daft. I know you don't have to.

P.S Everyone has gone car mad. Frank is buying himself a brand NEW !! Ford Capri. Eunice has decided he stashed away a fortune from those seaside snaps over the years. She also thinks he was moonlighting for a Fleet Street newspaper. And you used to tell me was a bit dense. Maybe he's not so daft after all?

P.P.S What will you do when the boat is finished?

With love x

July 28, 1970

Dear Seymour,

As it's rather late in the evening, I'm going to start this now and finish it tomorrow. I've just come back from the harbour and wanted you to know how <u>incredible</u> the kites have been this year. The weather was perfect and according to the man providing the commentary, there were even a few entrants from France.

In the official programme (which I'll put in the envelope) there's a page on the history of the event which talks about you (and very briefly, me). And next year there's going to be a 'Pilbeam Cup' for the highest-flying kite of the festival. It's all got very big and very serious. Did you know? Have you given permission? I feel very proud.

On a less happy note, mum's beloved Arthur has died. Dad says he weighed almost four stone at the end and the cause of death was 'multiple organ failure following prolonged inactivity'. Please don't laugh. This weekend they're going to take the wheels off and bury him in his pram on the edge of the golf course.

Dad was quite tearful when he rang last night. He was remembering how Arthur used to run onto the putting greens and make off with the players' balls. But obviously, that was before he lost the use of his legs. Please break the news to Isaac gently. I know he was very fond, as we all were.

It's the next day now. Nothing but blue skies. I've been thinking a lot about what you wrote. Actually, I'm not jealous of you. That was the wrong word. Yes, there are things about you that I envy, but jealousy isn't what I feel. Half the time, I don't know what I think anyway but I'd be happy to try and put things on paper. People don't talk about serious things until it's too late but with the written word there's no shouting or falling out. Just so long as you do the same? I've done and said some terrible things but not all of this is my fault. And I hate the fact that Isaac thinks it is.

The view from your caravan sounds incredible. Are there really deer outside? Are you sure your 'wild cat' wasn't just a runaway moggie?! It's good that you've got one of the locals to help you, but your adventure has made me realise how sheltered I am. It was always me reading books about faraway places but it's everyone else who's going to them. So how did that happen?

Anyway, I've found a flat. It's a holiday let on the first floor of a lovely old Victorian terrace, but the landlord has given me it for £30 a month, provided I stay till Christmas. Nothing about it is very grand apart from the outlook. The kitchen smells of gas, and the small bedroom hasn't even got a window. But once I've put a table and chairs in the bay window, I don't think I'll want to go anywhere else. No deer for me, just the boundless sea. All I need now is some cheap furniture from that man at the junk shop with the disturbing nose.

Did Isaac get my birthday card? There was a five-pound note in it, and it would be lovely to know he'd received it. What does a seventeen-year-old boy do up there anyway? Are there any girls? Or youth clubs? I heard yesterday that his old crush Alice has dropped out of her posh girls' school. Eunice had caught some whisper (you know what this town is like) but nobody seems to know why. I'm sure Isaac still blames me for their break-up. Hopefully, she'll prosper somewhere. She was a bright girl.

Anyway, I'd better dash. The clock has crept around to 8.30 and Eunice is on a WI 'mystery tour' to York, so I'm opening the shop.

Sorry this is all such a jumble of words. I'll try much harder in my next one!

P.S. Frank has just told me why that man is called Clinkers. Disgusting. Surely that CAN'T be true.

P.P.S. You still haven't said what you'd do when the boat is finished?

Lots of love xx

Lucy

August 20, 1970

Dear Seymour,

Thank you for your letter. You sound so happy. When you write, I can imagine that I'm there although your sea sounds very different to mine. Blue not brown! Dolphins not beer bottles! Not that I'm complaining. Eunice gave me an old sofa and I got a few other bits and bobs from your friend's creepy shop. I've even got a little transistor radio, so I can listen to 'Book At Bedtime' and watch the sun go down.

I was sorry to hear that you'd given up on the photograph you found. I can't help but think Mr. Rehab WANTED you to find it. Why else would he leave the same picture in two places? The answer must be up there somewhere. You should definitely keep looking but you're right about not mentioning it in your articles. Until you know who she is, it wouldn't be proper.

My mum was very interested in the story too. She's been terribly low since Arthur passed so I spent two nights there last weekend. She said the photographs show how easy it is for people to hide themselves and that sometimes what you see might all be a gigantic act. Dad was at some golf club do, so we shared a bottle of sherry and talked until midnight and I'm beginning to realise how similar we are.

She told me she didn't just lose her boyfriend on the Somme; she lost her childhood. She says that every passing year has made her more bitter that she was left to grow old in a man's world while her sweetheart could 'live' in his teens forever. I think a lot of women of her generation feel the same. I think that's why she's always worn suffragette green. But we were a bit weepy and drunk and I didn't really grasp it all.

To be honest, I think I always disappointed her. Growing up, I could feel her anger and she was forever willing me to 'BE SOMETHING'. The trouble is, I never worked out what that SOMETHING was and I'm certain that's why I was always so envious of people who had passions. Like you, perhaps? I just don't know. But it was lovely to talk to her properly, and in a funny way, I think she and dad are happier than they've ever been.

I was relieved to hear that Isaac had got my cash. It's brilliant that he's spending the money on a decent sharp knife. You and I never had anything like that. I can remember you used to sharpen the carving knife on the corner of the house. I was even joking the other day with Ralph about your spark plugs in the frying pan although I hated it at the time. Sometimes I lost my temper because you seemed so blind to my moods. Sometimes, shouting felt like the only way through.

It was sad in a way to leave Eunice. Over the years, she's been such a good friend. She even gave me a record player as a flat warming present, along with a selection of her ex-husbands' favourites. I was listening to Benny Goodman last night when I couldn't sleep. You'd have been proud of me. I'm so sorry about your clarinet. Do you think Isaac might ever send me a letter?

I'm going to stop there. Reading this letter back, it contains an awful lot of question marks. After what's happened, perhaps that isn't surprising. Don't take too long to reply. Whatever comes next, this correspondence has been good for me. Yes, there are lots of questions but I'm finding a few answers too. Are you?

Whoops, there goes another question.

Lots of love xxx

[signature]

P.S. I've enclosed a jar of Marmite and some of my old silk stockings!!! Don't tell Isaac they were mine!!

P.P.S I've taken your advice and booked in to see the doctor.

September 10, 1970

Dear Seymour,

It's the morning after your boat regatta and the street cleaners are out removing the balloons and the streamers and the chip papers which are blowing around outside. Most of the pubs stayed open late last night, and there are abandoned glasses everywhere. I can see them now from my window on people's garden walls or tossed in plant pots!

I wish you could have been here yesterday to see the spectacle. Everyone was talking about you. It was truly an amazing day. It was even better than the kites. I don't think I've ever seen anything like it. There must have been sixty cobbles – cobles? – in the race, only this time the weather was perfect; everybody got back safely; and there were crowds like you wouldn't believe.

In fact, it was a very good job the tide was out. I don't know where people would have stood if it wasn't. Both beaches and the harbour were packed and there must have been another hundred boats in the sea at the same time just watching. And thanks to your friend, Mr.Spanners, I was a VIP guest on the poop deck of The Burlingtonian.

Every one of the boats was beautifully turned out. All the paintwork looked fresh. Some of them had hoisted long coloured streamers. Some of the crews were even wearing fancy dress. The only negative thing was that one boat was missing; "the boat that Mr.Pilbeam built" (as everyone says round here).

Did I ever tell you I used to sneak in to look at it when you weren't there? I couldn't believe that the boy I'd met by a boating pool was capable of something like that. I still can't really. It was like a miracle in wood. With all my heart, I wish I'd behaved differently, and I can't imagine how you felt when it was lost. It was like there was a war between my admiration and my resentment. Sorry. Sorry. Sorry.

On a lighter note, Frank is now living with Eunice, complete with a singing bird which is driving her NUTS!! To get her own back, she's signed up for a 'learn Spanish in a month' correspondence course which is driving ME nuts at work!! We're not a shoe shop anymore. She says, we're a 'ropa de pueblo y campo'!! Anyway, Frank wants to send you an invite to their 'do'. Will you come?

Thank you for your letter. I don't know if anyone up there has a camera but perhaps you can send me a few photographs. I have a mental picture of you in your paint-spattered shorts with your shirt off, frantically swatting away insects. Mr. Rehab's boat sounds almost finished. Who does your laundry? Where do you eat? Where will you sail it?

You asked me how I knew about Alice and her school. I might be wrong, but it sounded like you were really asking 'am I still seeing Stan?' If you were, I suppose I can understand but the answer is <u>NO I'M NOT</u>. It was Eunice who told me. I've had no contact with that man for months. Nobody else has seen him either.

Anyway, back to the regatta. I forgot to mention that the money raised this year is going towards a big bronze sculpture of a fisherman. Apparently it's been in the pipeline for years but here's the best thing! The face is going to be modelled on your friend Mr. Rehab. So, all in all, whoever that man was, he's ended up leaving quite a mark.

Do keep writing. I can't tell you how much good this is doing.

Love xx

Lucy

P.S. Mr. Spanners told me your nickname was 'Taff'. I never knew. Your dad would have liked that.

P.P.S. I saw the doctor and he's taken some blood samples.

September 22, 1970

Dearest Seymour,

You found her!! You solved the mystery!! What an incredible story. But how sad that Mr.Rehab never got to know he had a daughter, and what a lonely way for the girl's mother to live out her life. Your account read like something out of a book. It really was that gripping.

Have you realised that **NONE** of this would have come out if your friend hadn't drowned? The mystery photographs, the boat, the life in Scotland, the girlfriend and the child. All of it would still be locked away. You must have realised because you said in your letter that you 'were tired of secrets'. Well that's good because I'm tired of secrets, too.

I've thought such a lot about Celeste's mother since I got your letter. Maybe it's my own mum's fault, but I've always resented the way men still feel they can up sticks. It's not right that they've got their pubs and their football teams and their jobs and that women are left piecing together a few scraps. Just like it wasn't right the way your father treated your mum. Or my dad forever at the bloody golf club.

Oh, dear this is all so serious but now that I'm living alone, I've had time to reflect and maybe I was jealous after all. Even when we were kids, you had dreams. You were forever making kites and cutting out pictures of boats. That wasn't a bad thing because I had dreams too except yours were tangible because you were a boy and mine were stuck in story books because I wasn't. Does that make sense? It does to me.

There were so many things bound up in my hatred of that boat. I was wrong when I accused you of never growing up. It was just that

I had nothing like that of my own and I was desperate to build an alternative. I wanted to sound different, look different. I wanted a life D.H.Lawrence might write about. Like Jane in her windswept croft. Not Lucy blocking out the stink of the gasworks.

I understand that none of this excuses what I did. But I think finally I understand why I did what I did. You can call it a protest, if you like. You'd forgotten me. There wasn't a place for me in your dreams. Stan felt like a way out; a chance for me to set a few rules. But honestly – no secrets – it was none of those things. He wasn't a way out, he was a fraud, and I bitterly regret every second I spent in his company.

Two days later: I've been thinking whether to tear up everything above. In the end (as you can see!!) I've decided not to. Whether or not you ever come home, I think it's important to clear the air. And it's a clear, beautiful morning again here. I sat and watched the sun rise out of the sea at about 6.30, reading again about your first sail in 'Gratitude'.

The Scottish islands sound magical and Jane must be a remarkable woman?! Will you see her again? How close is Isaac getting to her daughter? If my maths is right, she's at least three years older than him? Hopefully, he's not getting too distracted. It sounds like he's making real progress in that hotel. Please ask him again to WRITE. Not seeing him is punishment enough and his silence is simply cruel.

I love to think of you living on that boat, by the way. I imagine you waking up with a smile after a night rocked by the tide. I can hear the kettle blowing and I can see you sitting on the deck wafting the steam off your mug while you check your various wires and whatnots to make sure everything is exactly as it should be. It's funny that both of us wake up and look out at the sea, except my sun rises and your sun sinks.

Do be careful if you sail alone. Please! I know you will. All those books you've read won't turn you into a sailor overnight. Does the ship to shore radio work? Is there a life raft? Do you have charts?

A horn? PLEASE BE CAREFUL. You won't believe it, but I wept when you lost your boat last year.

I think I'd cry for ever if I lost you.

Must go. The town is stirring, and I promised to test Eunice on her Spanish declensions if we're quiet.

Lots of love xxx

Lucy

P.S. I was touched that you are re-reading all my letters back from the first. I hope this one doesn't put you off?

P.P.S. It's been a bad few weeks for pets. Frank's budgie has gone now. Personally, I suspect foul play, but Eunice swears blind it was a virus.

October 14, 1970

Dear Seymour,

Is everything alright? Where are you? There was no letter this week and I was looking forward to seeing that black postmark from Inverness and finding somewhere quiet to digest all your news. Eunice told me not to worry. She saw something on the TV about floods on the east coast line. But that made me more worried because if the weather has been bad, I keep imagining you out on that boat somewhere all on your own.

I've also been running over and over my last letter, thinking maybe I disturbed you and if that's the case, let's try and set up a telephone call somehow. Eunice has a telephone at the shop. There must be a public box nearby. If we heard each other's voices and talked about some of these things, it would surely be better. Was I too strong? Words on the page are so easily misinterpreted.

So PLEASE, PLEASE WRITE. At least, just let me know you're safe.

Xxxx

October 16, 1970

Dear Seymour,

Still, nothing. I don't really know what to do. Your column didn't appear in the paper, but when I called the editor's office, he told me that you've stopped now that the boat is finished. I even found the number of that hotel where Isaac is working, but nobody rang back. I'm not even sure they wrote down Eunice's number. The person I spoke to was virtually incomprehensible.

I'm going to send this anyway. Hopefully it will cross something from you coming south. You're a good person so I know you wouldn't be staying quiet just to hurt me. There simply has to be another reason. Perhaps my last letter never even got to you?

If I've still not heard by the weekend, I'm going to the police.

Xxx

October 20, 1970

Dear, dear Seymour,

I knew that there'd be a simple explanation, but if it wasn't for Eunice I'd have called out the search parties!! She kept telling me I was being ridiculous and looking back on the past week, she was absolutely right. As you well know, I've got a vivid imagination. It doesn't take much to put me on edge.

You'd said before that Jane had invited you to her cottage. I should have realised that's where you were. Sorry for being a worrit. You must have felt like a pirate, anchoring your boat close enough to row ashore. Can you really sail it on your own? It's so hard not having any idea of the geography. I bought an Ordnance Survey map but it doesn't help.

It seems daft to say that I felt jealous, but I did. In my head, Jane is a sultry 45-year-old Celt with perfect skin. A sort of sandy-haired Scarlett O'Hara who's lived like a nun for twenty years and who's now desperate for sex. Did you sleep on your boat? Or has she a spare room for guests?

Your driftwood fire on the beach together sounded incredible. I didn't know seaweed exploded when it got hot. I presume you told her how Mr.Rehab's remains were sent back to the sea. Did you know I was in the crowd that night? All those details must be very difficult for her to comprehend. There's so much about that man we will never know. Like, was there ever another woman in HIS life? Anyway, it was a big relief to hear from you. Your words were very sweet and reassuring and I'm thrilled if you think mine have been the same.

It seems wrong that you're apologising to me, though. Both of us were selfish, but only I was cruel.

Other news. I did get one letter during your RADIO SILENCE! It was very short (and I presume you held his pen to the paper!!) but Isaac has finally broken cover. You didn't tell me he'd been working shifts on the fishing boats. How strange that he loves the sea just like you. I could feel the excitement jumping off the page. He says he's made a friend who dives for clams which Isaac buys for the restaurant. He also mentioned that Celeste girl a couple of times, too????

For the first time in months, I had to have a lie down after I'd digested it. I understand why you went to Scotland, but I hate not being in your lives. Just like I hate the feeling that I don't deserve a place in your lives. I'm not a bad person, Seymour. I'm an ill person.

The tests came back and it turns out I've got an overactive thyroid. No, I'd never heard of it either, but the chances are high that mum had it too. Mood swings. Palpitations. Bad tempered irritability. Low energy. Insomnia. Reduced sex drive. Apart from the last one, does it ring any bells? The doctor says it can be treated, so there's nothing to worry about.

He said I'll be a new woman and I was tempted to say that the old one wasn't ALL bad, but then perhaps she was. He also told me I can't use the condition as an excuse. Thank goodness, the town stocks and the ducking stool have gone. Seemingly, everyone here knows that I was an unfaithful wife....

Please don't scare me like that again.

With much love. xxxx

Lucy

P.S. Isaac needn't worry about the thyroid thing. It's yet another one of life's curses which mostly only affects women!

November 15th, 1970

Dear Seymour,

The house plant is beautiful. Thank you. I knew you'd remember my birthday. I just wasn't sure whether you'd acknowledge it. Did you use morse code to order it? Or semaphore? Either way, the greenery looks glorious in my bay window but now that the heating in the flat has packed up, I just hope it can survive the winter.

The pictures you sent were even better. In colour, too. Who took them? Where were you sailing? Isaac looks incredible. His face is shining with happiness and your boat is beautiful. I'm examining it now, and I can see the love you've poured into it. Seeing Jane and her daughter was really interesting? They've both got the same Scandinavian eyes and they look so slim and natural and at ease with the world. Not dowdy and provincial like me.

No picture of you? You told me you'd grown a beard and I'd love to

375

have seen it!

How did being 45 happen? It only seems like 45 minutes since you were sledging me across that frozen lake, and lately I've been horribly conscious of time passing. Can you believe it's five months since you left? Five months since I heard your voice? You're right to say that we're not teenagers, and that we don't need to write every week, but I'm struggling a bit now and I'd love you to come back.

The nights have closed in horribly here and it must be worse in Scotland. Eunice looked it up in the Encyclopaedia Britannica and you're only getting eight hours of daylight. That's terrible. Please come home.

Yes, I am feeling much better, thanks. And it's really nothing serious. Please don't worry. I'm eating properly and filling my bra for the first time in years, and Frank asked me yesterday if I was pregnant. Not quite at ease with the world but getting there!

Only a short letter this time. We're stock-taking at the shop tonight. People have started buying their winter slippers already and we've not even had our first frost.

One last thing which is difficult but should be heard from me. Stan Clough's amusements have all been shut down, likewise his hair salons. According to the paper, the Inland Revenue are after him for years of tax evasion, but the local gossip is that he'll never be found. Overseas somewhere, probably. Or drowned.

It seems poor Alice came out of school because the fees weren't being paid. Also, the storms last month took away a huge section of the cliff below his 'wedding cake house'. For a while, it looked like it had survived but last night it slid into the sea. Eunice tells me the beach has been packed all day with people sifting through the wreckage. Good riddance to all of it.

I can't believe you've finished 'Sons and Lovers'. I'm going to have to test you on it when we meet. If there's a mobile library, try 'Madame

Bovary' by Gustave Flaubert. You'll know why when you've read it.

Wrap up warm. Are you still living on the boat?

Lots and lots of love

Lucy

P.S. They need a new coxswain here for the lifeboat???

December 12th, 1970

Dearest Seymour,

It feels like it has been raining forever. The sea from my window looks like mud and it's so cold in here now I can see my breath. As it always does, the townsfolk have gone into their burrows. Sometimes, we go hours between customers. Nobody much is out at all, apart from the lorries repossessing all the machines from the amusements.

Thanks, as ever, for your letter. Your cabin sounds snug and it's wonderful that you can play your concertina in the pub. Yes, I felt sad that you're staying up there through the winter, but why would you come back here? We don't even have a house and I understand that all this will take a little longer.

If the news about Stan Clough set you back, it wasn't intended to. I only told you so you knew how little he meant to me, and how ashamed I am. More and more dirt comes out about him every week. He had another wife in Leeds, according to this morning's rumours. My only consolation is that I saw the light and escaped just in time. For the umpteenth, but not the last time, I was a fool, an unhappy fool.

Your description of the winter light up there made my neck tingle. What will Isaac do now the hotel has closed the restaurant? Can he still keep his room there, or will he move back into the caravan? I assume you've still got funds from the land sale. Or are the odd jobs you're doing for that man on the harbour enough to keep you going?

Is there anything I can send? Luxuries? Basics? Blankets? A copy of 'Wuthering Heights'??

I'd be lying if I said I hadn't slumped a bit recently. It's partly the medication, I think, but Eunice talks of nothing but her fifth wedding, followed closely by her endless speculations regarding Frank's secret 'fortune'. At least my mum and dad are finally in a good place. They've been to see me in the company of their new dog, a Jack Russell which they'd spotted sleeping rough on the golf course. And guess what? Mum was wearing a red coat! Don't ask me why, but it was lovely to see them so happy.

As always, they asked about you. Secretly, I think they're hoping that one day we'll get back together again but I've told them not to expect miracles.

Another reason I've been low is this flat. Your friend Harry came to fix the boiler but it's still very cold and unless I renew my contract for another six months, I'll be out in two weeks.......Boxing Day, in other words. Eunice is insisting I move back in with them but I'd rather sleep in a bus shelter. Being alone has helped me think things through, and the town is full of empty holiday lets so I'll be fine and once we're into January there'll be light at the end of the tunnel.

Do let me know if there's anything you need. Isaac has gone quiet again, but he's a teenager. Just so long as he's happy and well, and it sounds like he is.

The rockets have just gone off at the lifeboat station. Still no new coxswain??!?

Don't stint on the gas.

Lots of love

Lucy

December 17th, 1970

Dearest Seymour,

It was incredible to hear your voice. My heart is still banging. When the phone rang in the shop, I was half-asleep in the stockroom. Eunice was out on one of her sherry lunches, so there was only me to pick it up. Why didn't we think of that before? Perhaps you needed to be ready. I completely understand that.

You sounded different. I don't know how or why. And it wasn't just the echo on the line either. You sounded wiser. Or stronger, perhaps? But next time, if there is one, remember to get a bigger pile of two pence pieces. It was hell hearing the pips. We'd only just got started.

I am fine. I promise you, I'm fine. But who knows, by the time you read this I might have told you all my news in person. And you won't need any coins for the phone box after all.

I'm coming to Scotland, Seymour. I really am.

It was hearing your voice that did it. I always thought it was me who was the romantic but I was completely wrong. You're the romantic, not me.

The lease on the flat has expired. I've handed in my notice at the shop and I'm packing my thermals in between jotting down these random lines. Please don't try and ring to stop me because I'll be on my way and the shop will all be shut up for Christmas.

If it doesn't work out, I'll come back and train up to be a teacher.

I'm just not sitting here alone on Christmas Day wishing I was somewhere else.

Wish me luck. I've never done anything like this before.

Xxxxxxxxxx

Lucy

December 20th

Perth. 11.13pm. I've never seen snow like this. It's taken two days to get here. I'm exhausted, and I'm spending two nights at a little hotel before travelling on. Most of the trains have been delayed anyway but the girl at the Post Office said this postcard should get through. Am still hoping to be up there on the 24th. No idea what time. Hope you like the card. The man with a buzzard? Remember? Please, please be there. xxxx

Chapter Six

By Christmas Eve, the blizzard hadn't let up for eight days. Only the ferry was immune to it, shuttling between the town and island where the snowline had crept down from the mountains to kiss the sea. Nobody had seen anything like it so early in the winter. And when the clouds periodically broke, Seymour felt as if his entire world was being attacked by a bitter, white mould.

Shortly after breakfast, he slid open the hatch of his boat and surveyed the weather. Several more inches had accumulated on the deck. Two sleeping bags and a blanket had failed him overnight (even with his clothes on) and the kettle was taking forever to boil. Spindrift was snaking across the quay carrying with it the smell of burning wood. For lots of reasons, something had to be done.

"Candunk. Oy. Candunk." Seymour's friend was hunched over a brazier stacked with burning logs. He was wearing a long black coat, and his whiskers were flecked with ice. "Bad timing but I need to get her out of the water today."

"Sometimes faith looks stupid until it snows. So sayeth Noah in the bible somewhere."

"I'm pretty sure he said rain, not snow," said Seymour. "And it was an ark not a sleigh."

"Heathen sassenach," muttered Candunk. "I'll get the crane."

Two hours later, the job was done. Neither man could feel his fingers, but 'Gratitude' was back inside the warehouse, safely lashed to a rusty cradle.

"I was going to spend the winter in her," said Seymour, checking the underside of his boat for damage. Apart from a few barnacles, it was perfect. "But I can't now."

"It's in the right place," said Candunk, disappearing back out into the snow. "You'd have been dead by January."

Seymour picked up his bags and peered doubtfully into the storm. Candunk's footsteps had vanished and in the yellow beam of a streetlight, the flakes appeared to be falling upwards. Nothing he'd left on the boat was needed until spring. The charts, his concertina, a few books and Lucy's letters were all that really mattered anyway.

Stamping the snow from his boots, he stepped out across the waste land which separated the quay from the station platform. A huddle of people was already gathering under the canopy for news. Only one train had made it through all week and the roads were impassable.

'Blocked at Strathcarron." An elderly woman he didn't know had yanked his arm accusingly. "Nothing now till the fucking 28th. My turkey was on that train."

Everyone had their own reasons to be desperate. Food was running low; every fishing boat was harbour-bound, and The Refresh was no longer selling doubles. Seymour felt in his pocket again for the postcard from Perth. Somewhere along the way, the ink had run, but the words were still perfectly clear; and perfectly terrifying.

A bereft-looking Christmas tree had been propped up in a fire bucket by the waiting room door. Through the window of the bar he could see Celeste passing pints into a sea of hands. Further up the platform, there was a sudden shift in the atmospherics. One by one, heads were turning inland, looking up to where the line entered a deep cutting; and where a green light was pulsating beneath the dropped arm of a signal.

Two men in uniforms, still clutching their whiskies, were pushing their way out of The Refresh. The sound of an engine was clearly audible above the wind, and a postal van had skidded its way into the station car park. As the train heaved into view, there was a cheer. Two engines coupled together behind a snow plough had somehow hauled five carriages from the North to the Irish Sea.

Nobody was hanging about. If anything, the blizzard was coming harder. One end of the platform was no longer visible from the other, and boxes of food, beer kegs, and sacks of coal and mail were being hauled swiftly undercover. Seymour looked down at his feet, happy to be distracted by the slow loss of sensation in his toes.

"I like your beard. It suits you."

There was an anguished noise. A man staggered bottom first out of the bar, hitched his trousers up, and staggered back in again. "Shut the fucking door, Jimmy," someone bellowed.

"The West coast, you said. Not the Wild West."

Seymour tore his eyes from his shoes. She was wearing a knee-length camel coat with a hat pulled down over her ears. Her eyes were shining with mischief.

"Say something then. I'm your wife, remember."

"It's the middle of winter. You came."

"I'd noticed," she laughed. They were the only two people left on the platform. The railway line had been reclaimed by snow. "But I'm not going back."

Seymour stretched forwards and folded Lucy into his arms. Each of them was wearing so many clothes, their bodies felt stiff but as their cheeks touched, he felt the warmth of her skin and allowed his lips to brush hers for a brief kiss.

"You've not brought much luggage," he said, stepping back sharply. She was carrying a large black leather shoulder bag and a small overnight case.

"I wasn't sure if I'd be welcome."

"I just can't believe it," said Seymour. A council snowplough was labouring down the main street pursued by a gang of chortling schoolboys. "You'd better follow me."

With their arms linked together, Seymour steered Lucy through the thickening gale. In an instant, everybody had disappeared. Over in the sound, even the ferry had stopped running and a wall of snow driven on a rising northerly gale was making it impossible to see.

"I wasn't expecting this," grinned Lucy. "I was expecting midges."

After five minutes they reached a windswept patch of flat land overlooking the flickering lights of the town and the sea beyond. In the failing light, Lucy could make out a large caravan behind a drift which had partially hidden the door.

"Listen. I've been living on the boat until today. I've not been in this for months." Seymour had pulled a shovel from his coal bunker and was frantically scraping away the snow. "It might be a bit of a dump, that's all."

"I'm loving it already," said Lucy, tailing him into the caravan before shutting out the storm. "And since I've chosen to be here…." A curtain of snow had slipped down her neck as she slammed the door. "…. you've got no need to worry."

Later that night (unable to sleep) Seymour still couldn't believe what had happened next. Without a word, Lucy had gone back into the snow to fill a bucket with fuel. She'd drawn the curtains and fired up the cooker. She'd opened cupboards and found dried macaroni and baked beans and by the time Seymour had breathed life into the small pot-bellied wood burner, they had warmth and light and they

384

had food.

"That was good," said Seymour.

"It really wasn't," said Lucy. "But I haven't eaten for thirty-six hours."

"Have you been cooking more? On your own? You look well. You've changed."

"Have I? Maybe a little. I feel well that's for sure." Lucy took a serious look at her new surroundings. They were sitting in a small living area with a gas cooker and a sofa that became a bed. There was also a separate bedroom and a small cupboard masquerading as a small bathroom. "It's all so tidy," she said. "I can't see any tools."

"I still don't have a watch either." Seymour pulled back a curtain. The caravan was quaking in the wind and the daylight was almost finished. "But it's usually dark at three."

On a shelf between a handful of sailing books there was a small radio. He reached up and turned it on, adjusting the channel dial until the carols were clear.

"My god, it works," said Lucy, drawing closer to him."

Flames were licking the glass of the stove and the space between them had filled with celestial voices. From yet another hidden cupboard, Seymour produced two glasses and a bottle of cheap brandy.

"Happy Christmas tomorrow," whispered Seymour.

"I hope so," replied Lucy.

After the carol concert they talked until they were too weary to talk any more. First, Seymour told Lucy that Isaac was back at the hotel, catering for the few Christmas regulars who'd braved the weather; and that his job came with a permanent room he rarely used because he was living in a council house (as a brother not a lover) with Celeste.

385

"They're incredibly close," Seymour explained. "But it's nothing more. Not yet."

"And Celeste's mother?"

"She's marooned in her cottage until the snow can be shifted."

When it was Lucy's turn she told Seymour that she'd been terrified of his reaction; that her mind was finally clear; and that (although she knew she'd said it on paper) she wanted to apologise again for "the whole, stinking mess".

"I didn't help, did I?" asked Seymour, sadly.

"You were thoughtless. I was bad."

"You don't seem bad now."

"Will we see Isaac tomorrow?"

"I'm having lunch at the hotel with Celeste. His treat. His cooking. "

"Let's make it a table for three," said Lucy.

By late morning on Christmas Day, the fight had gone out of the storm. A few cars were moving again, and the clouds had pulled clear of the peaks. The air temperature had slumped overnight, and the caravan windows were patterned with ice. Once it was scraped clear, Lucy gawped at a landscape which bore no resemblance to anything she had ever seen. "Magical" was the best description she could muster, looking again and again across the bitter circle of the sea to the ragged white crests of mountains beyond.

"Do you want to see the boat?" asked Seymour. Lucy nodded, and followed him along the edge of the harbour. Out in the channel, a cormorant was struggling to keep its footing on a snow-capped buoy. "She doesn't look like much out of the water."

Inside the hangar, Lucy walked twice around the hull, desperately trying to summon up the right words to say. It was strange, she realised, but Seymour's boat no longer felt like a vague obstacle to something she'd never defined. It felt like a gateway.

"Of course, if you're still here in spring……" Seymour let the thought hang. "We'd better go. I'm starving."

"Keep trying me, Seymour," said Lucy. "You shouldn't give up."

"She's really not like the other boats," said Seymour. "I won't."

When they finally sat down in the hotel restaurant, twenty or so diners were already attacking their prawn cocktails. Each of the men was wearing a lounge suit; and the women were dressed as if for a dance; long dresses and heirloom jewellery. Only a handful had succumbed to the hats they'd pulled from crackers. People were mostly eating in silence, gaping at the view between mouthfuls, indifferent to the Christmas soundtrack and the cheery exhortations of the staff.

"Celeste, this is Lucy, my wife. Lucy, meet Celeste."

A tall girl rose from a round table by the window. She was wearing jeans and a tired-looking silk blouse she'd left open at the neck. When she smiled (which she did most of the time) her lips parted on the most beautiful teeth Lucy had ever seen.

"I'm guessing that you're Seymour's surprise Christmas present."

"You could say that," said Lucy. "It's a long story. You don't mind, do you?"

"Not at all," said Celeste. A door into the kitchen had been opened spilling raised voices into the dining room. "Everyone's a bit hungover. Service might be a little slow."

Lucy looked around. She'd eaten in a place like this once before. She remembered the radiators clunking and the draughty windows. She could hear Stan Clough rattling his room key and ordering another bottle of champagne.

"Mum? Are you OK?"

She'd been lost for a second. A hand had locked around her wrist, but the voice wasn't Stan's. It was familiar and calming and it had stifled the grinding clatter of cutlery.

"Mum? What are you doing here? This is the best."

"Isaac?"

Her head cleared quickly. He seemed taller and older and there was a shadow of fuzz around his chin she'd never noticed before. When they embraced, he seemed stronger, too.

"You're wearing tartan trousers," she laughed, feeling a secret surge of relief. "And a white tuxedo."

"Non-negotiable, I'm afraid. Embarrassing. Hardly anyone turned up this morning. Too much snow. Or Scotch. Or both. Either way, I'm the youngest head chef AND head waiter ever so get ready with a big tip." Isaac turned again to Lucy. "I don't know what's going on, but this is brilliant."

"It's Christmas. It felt like the right thing to do."

"Will you stay? You can have my room here? You probably couldn't get back home if you wanted to. Not for ages." There was an irritated harrumph from the kitchen door. "I'll see you all later. Don't blame me if the turkey's dry. I normally do starters, remember."

There was a lot to talk about, and plenty of time to kill between courses. When Celeste wasn't asking about her father, Lucy was asking about Jane, and when the pace slowed (which it rarely did) Seymour couldn't take his eyes off his wife.

"My mum won't mind being cut off," said Celeste, rolling a grape between her fingers. "She cut herself off years ago anyway."

"Was it a shock, finding out?" asked Lucy. "About your father?"

"It was fantastic," said Celeste.

By late afternoon, they were the only three left in the restaurant and snow was tumbling again through the dusky streetlights. Carrying a tray with four black coffees and a box of chocolate mints, Isaac emerged from his duties smelling of custard.

"I'm only working here till New Year's Day. They won't need me after that until Spring."

"What will you do till then?" asked Lucy, feeling drained by three hours of conversation.

"There's a bar on the station. The Refresh. I'm going to introduce them to solids."

"It's a watering hole," explained Celeste. "This is practically the only day of the year it shuts, apart from Sundays."

"Baby-sized bridies," beamed Isaac.

"Or chunks of haggis on a stick," said Celeste.

When they strolled back to the caravan, Seymour and Lucy appeared content in their own silence. The only sound was the squeaking of the snow underfoot, and the caravan was too cold for anything but an early bed.

"I like her," said Lucy, fumbling for a light. For the second night running, the water was frozen in the van's pipes.

"He's happy," said Seymour. "Sleep tight."

The duration of Lucy's stay was never mentioned again. In the weeks and months that followed, their lives simply merged in a series of small, scarcely noticed increments and both found it easy to fill their days. Since arriving, Seymour had earned a reputation as a craftsman, and there was always joinery work to do in a town where every door was swollen shut with damp.

To give him space, Lucy moved out of the caravan into Isaac's vacated room at the hotel. She bought 'new' clothes at a Hogmanay Bring & Buy Sale which she adjusted to fit (time was never an issue) and when the weather allowed it, she was happy to explore alone; catching the ferry across the sound as a foot passenger; revelling in the clarion air and the unyielding skyline of mountains.

Every evening, they ate together in the caravan, unfolding the dining table in a window dominated by the sea. There was no rota and no timetable. Each of them took turns to cook, and during the long, dark evenings, they talked about their day or listened to the radio or played cribbage until the shipping forecast, after which Seymour would escort Lucy back to the hotel.

"Would you like to come in?" she asked around the middle of January.

"Only for a nightcap," he'd replied. "I'm not ready for anything else."

At the weekends, their routine shifted. On Saturday evenings, Seymour played his concertina in The Refresh, where a famished hush now fell whenever Isaac circulated with his mysterious nibbles. Lucy had stayed away to begin with, feeling the old furies rising, until – at her husband's insistence – she'd ventured inside to see what she was missing.

Sitting quietly by the tiny stage, she'd seethed quietly. "Where are all their wives?" she'd asked Seymour later. But despite herself, Lucy had grown used to the bedlam. The music was good, and every scarlet face was its own story. Whenever she could, she caught up with Celeste, lost in admiration for her energy. The girl was a whirlwind; a force of nature; and the whole bar seemed to revolve around her smile.

Gradually, as the roads cleared, Lucy found a little work of her own. None of it was paid. She had enough funds to last until the summer and (during a bout of staff flu) she spent three mornings a week helping at the tiny school, reading stories to children fascinated by her accent.

"You sound like the Queen," one of them had said.

"Ssssshhhhh," said another. "She IS the Queen."

"Don't tell anyone," whispered Lucy. "But you're right."

By early March, she'd attached herself to the mobile library; a converted fish merchant's van, choked with books which smelled of kippers. Every trip was a revelation, taking her inland to tiny hamlets, shrouded in wood smoke or around the coast to pastel-painted ports where ladies queued to swap one Mills and Boon for another and where the questions were almost as predictable as Lucy's sales pitch for the classics.

"Have you got any Barbara Cartland?" was one common refrain.

"Who is D.H.Lawrence?" was another.

"You'd love him, I'm sure," Lucy reassured them. "Just imagine Mills and Boon with dirty sex and longer sentences."

One day, the library had followed the bus north, turning left down a track until it ran out overlooking a small cottage in a bay where an attractive woman in her forties walked up from the garden carrying a plastic bag.

"You're Jane," said Lucy, pulling out a wooden fish crate jammed with paperbacks.

"And you're Seymour's wife."

"I went through a Daphne du Maurier phase when I was a teenager," said Lucy. "I always dreamed of living like you."

"That's funny because I always dreamed of living like someone like you."

"I don't think you'd swap. Not if you knew. It hasn't been easy."

"Your son has a father. And whoever said it was going to be easy?"

By April, the snows had retreated, and daffodils were showing around the curtilage of the caravan. Although the wind was still raw, there was warmth wherever shelter could be found, and the town had rediscovered its rhythm. The trains and the trawlers came and went; the shop was full of fresh vegetables; and the queue for peak-time ferries crept further and further up the ramp.

Shortly after breakfast on Good Friday, Seymour asked Lucy to prepare for a short trip. Two hours later, a white van packed with camping equipment crossed quietly onto the island and threaded north towards a black line of mountains, still rimed with snow. In the passenger seat, Lucy was wrestling with an old linen-backed map.

"Where are we going?" she asked.

"It's a mystery tour," grinned Seymour.

"I think they printed this map to fool Hitler. All the roads are in the wrong places."

Seymour looked across at his wife. He had always loved her. But at that moment, he didn't believe he'd ever loved her more.

"I went on a drive with Rehab once. He kept telling me he was lost and I remember thinking what an imbecile he was, except he wasn't lost. It was you and me who were lost."

There was a lorry stacked with timber heading towards them. Seymour pulled into a passing place and wound down the window. A few mud-black sheep stared down at him from the flanks of a nameless hill.

"They say there's a Viking princess buried up there somewhere," said Seymour. "She'd sailed here from Norway. Never got home."

"I'm not sure where home is any more," said Lucy.

"Join the club," said Seymour.

They took separate rooms on the first night at a frigid hotel, built alongside a much older bridge which spanned a furious tumble of meltwater. In the last spark of light, they walked upstream alongside spinning pools, drawn forward by a range of mountains which rose up like a giant spider, before stumbling back to a cheerless bar and a shared bathroom where the tap water ran brown.

"It's early in the season," said Seymour the next morning after a breakfast of damp cornflakes and pungent, stewed tea. "It'll get better."

"Hot water would have been nice," said Lucy.

On the second day, the road skirted closer to the mountains before running out at a broad, sandy cove, backed by a soft cordon of grass. While Lucy gathered driftwood, Seymour pitched the tent and fired up the cooker to warm tinned soup which they drank quickly under threatening skies. Later, when darkness fell, the wind eased and the clouds cleared exposing a crescent moon, and a rash of shooting stars. Hunched up close to the fire, their faces glowed orange.

"Jane and Celeste told me about this place. I was going to come on my own."

"I only ever went camping with you in Wales that once. It wasn't something mum and dad ever did." Lucy leaned back, brushing sparks from her hair. "I've never been much good at having fun"

"You seemed to be having fun in my dad's workshop."

"I was good at that," laughed Lucy. "You weren't too bad yourself. Just a bit slow on the uptake."

Down on the beach, a rogue wave was breaking apart in a hiss of wet sand. Seymour's arm had looped gently around Lucy's waist. Their hips were already touching.

"Listen. Don't go mad. But I want to sail back to Frank's wedding…."

He'd said it. There was no turning back.

"What? WHAT?" Lucy had pushed herself to her feet.

"Calm down. Let me finish."

Seymour took a deep breath. He knew he had to go on. Goodrun. Phoenix. Gratitude. It all came down to this.

"I want us to do it together. I want me and you to sail back together for their wedding. It's what Rehab would have wanted. I think you'd be brilliant at it. And if it doesn't work or if you're seasick or the weather's bad, then we'll abandon it……but at least we'll have tried."

"I don't even like boats. Or the sea really. You know I hate boats."

"I think that's what you think."

"So, what do you think?"

"I think you hate – or hated – what boats meant to me."

"And now?"

"And now I think you'd love it. Just like I knew you'd love this."

"So, this was all a test? Is that what you're saying?"

"I'm saying we need an adventure. That's all."

There was a dull thump from the fire. A large branch had burned through the middle and collapsed into the embers.

"How long would it take?" Lucy had sat down again. She sounded composed, curious.

"About four weeks."

"And how far is it?"

"Approximately 539 nautical miles," said Seymour, fighting a powerful instinct to laugh.

"Oh Jesus. When would we set off?"

"We?"

"You."

"Well, if the wedding is on June 21st...."

"Midsummer's Night? Yes."

".....then we'd leave about four weeks before. And you definitely said 'we'."

"I must be mad. Stark staring certifiable. Insane. Deranged. Bonkers."

"You're not," said Seymour. "And you won't regret it."

Chapter Seven

They had a month to prepare. Not a single day to be wasted. By late April, the boat was back in the water. While Candunk overhauled the engine, Lucy and Seymour caught the train to Inverness, returning with purpose-made warm clothing and waterproofs fit for a serious voyage.

In the evenings they agonised over charts, identifying places where they could berth; measuring out the distances between them; and familiarising themselves with a route which secretly filled each of them with dread. Every day seemed to yield a new list. Medicine, tinned food, fan belts, storm sails, emergency ropes, spare pulleys, thermal underwear. Nothing was left to chance. Everything was checked and itemised and squirrelled away on a vessel already bursting at the bulkheads with provisions.

"This is serious, isn't it?" asked Lucy. There was less than a week to go and the table on the boat was strewn with pencils, rubbers and brass dividers.

"It's the best time of year," said Seymour, carefully avoiding the question. "We'll have long days, hopefully good weather and…."

"Hopefully?"

"……and we finish the moment we get scared. I promise."

On the first of the four days that remained, they practised. The winds were light; the rigging had been checked; and, with a practised touch, Seymour released the warps, turned on the motor, and eased

'Gratitude' out into the current. For the next six hours, the sails came up and down; they tacked and gybed; each taking their turn on the sails and the wheel, until they felt confident in their skills on both.

"We didn't fall out," gasped Lucy, once the boat was safely back in its berth. "With each other, I mean. Not the boat."

"But did you enjoy it?"

Lucy swept a salty cord of hair back from her face. "Honestly?" she said. "Let's say, pleasantly surprised."

The next morning, a cold front dragged down Arctic winds which lashed the town with freezing rain. For almost 48 hours, Lucy and Seymour were confined to their boat. The hotel room and the caravan had already been quietly abandoned. They slept together now, huddled in a scrum of eiderdown, alert to the halyards writhing against the mast; constantly remembering new things they still needed to source. A hand bearing compass; bobble hats, insect repellent, a bailing bucket and disinfectant. And if it could be found (they were not hopeful) a bottle of suntan lotion.

With just one night left, they walked quietly up to the station, and slipped into The Refresh shortly after 6pm. Candunk was waiting for them at the door.

"He leadeth me the quiet waters by," he said. "Psalm 23."

"Let's hope you're right," said Seymour. "Thank you for being the guardian of Captain Rehab's boat."

"I won't come in, obviously. But I'll be thinking of you both."

"Listen, Candunk. I want you to have this book."

"There is only one good book, laddy, and I've got dozens at home."

"It was Rehab's. I found it on Gratitude. Moby Dick. He must have been reading it when he lived up here. There was a quote marked in pencil. Look, see. Here." Candunk took the book and held the opened page under the light from the bar. "Read it," said Seymour.

"*I know not all that may be coming, but be it what it will, I'll go to it laughing.*"

"It's perfect isn't it?"

"Listen, what happened to him on this platform was wrong."

"You knew?"

"Of course, I knew. Everyone knew. It brought shame on us. The girl's father was a local pastor. Half the men standing through that door now saw what he did."

"Is he still alive? Jane's father?"

"He was drummed out of the church; collapsed and died a year later. Heart attack, they reckon."

"By which time, Rehab – Jonah – was long gone, never knowing he had a daughter."

"That night he was beaten, I gave him the money to get away," said Candunk. "He was a good man. He'd have stayed if he'd known about the wee bairn. I know he would."

The two men shook hands warmly. There was a roar from the bar. Isaac had warned them that something was brewing. As they stepped in, a stray cork flew over their heads, followed by a full-throated splurge of accordion from a record player somewhere.

"Very funny," shouted Seymour. "That's the music from Captain Pugwash."

It was Friday night; the bar was packed; and both the drink and Isaac's 'McCanapes' (as they'd been branded) were going free for an hour. Seymour took in the bright, throbbing faces, realising how many of them he now knew by name.

"To the intrepid adventurers. Hip hip hooray."

Isaac, Jane and Celeste were raising a toast at the bar. Another fifty or so glasses chinked their approval. From the open door, Candunk was watching proceedings behind his nest of facial hair.

"God bless 'Gratitude' and all who sail in her," he roared.

"Hey Duncan, stranger, do you no fancy a wee dram?" someone shouted. But Candunk, his book, and the moment, were all gone.

"This is so sweet, thank you everybody. Thank you," said Seymour, steering Lucy to their huddle of friends.

"You should make a speech, dad," said Isaac. The Friday night racket was reaching its perennial crescendo. "Not that anyone would hear it."

"We're leaving first thing, so we'll not stop. Just one quick glass and we'll slip away."

"Don't forget to call. Or write. There's a phone here at the bar."

"We won't," said Lucy. "I might be back in a week anyway."

"Still time to change your mind, Isaac. We could squeeze you in somewhere."

"I'd be a gooseberry, dad. And I'm really happy here." The last tray of 'McCanapes' had triggered a minor ruckus over by the fireplace. "Maybe next time. Maybe when you get back, we could all sail to St.Kilda or something."

"I'd like that," said Seymour.

"I'll reserve judgment," smiled Lucy.

"You might like this, too." Jane pulled a folded photograph from her purse. "He'd have been about 23 or so."

It was the picture of a tall, young man standing alone on the town quay. He was wearing a fisherman's smock and a broad, toothy grin. In the background was the skeleton of a half-finished yacht.

"Rehab? My god. He was so handsome. He looks just like Celeste. And that must be 'Gratitude'? This is amazing. Is it for me? Can I take it?"

Jane nodded. "Say hello to his statue for me. Tell him I'll be there to see him some time. Tell him I'm long overdue some maintenance."

"We'd better go," said Seymour. There was a flurry of arms and damp cheeks. Isaac was wiping his tears away with a beer towel; Celeste was drunkenly hugging Seymour; and Lucy had been pulled into a parting embrace by Celeste's mother.

"Don't lose him," whispered Jane.

"I'll try not to."

"And don't you ever EVER hurt him again."

It was still dark when they rose and quietly detached themselves from the quay. Both had slept badly but by first light they were chugging south towards Mallaig in the company of a lone gull driven half-mad by the smell of fried bread.

Over the next three days, helped by soft winds and long, warm days, they made swift progress. When the wind was on the nose, they motored. When it swung round from the north or the west, they hoisted the sails. From Mallaig they moved to Tobermory and from there on to Oban, establishing a soothing pattern which suited them, free of tension and stress; days which started early; days in which silence and conversation were equal partners; days which ended in the deepest slumber either of them had ever known.

When they were sailing, Lucy was content to defer to Seymour. It was Seymour who watched the winds and the currents. It was Seymour who trimmed the sails and plotted their course. But in every other respect, they had become a team, assessing their daily plans and their shopping lists together; agreeing where to anchor for lunch or whether home-made omelette was preferable to a battered sausage from Wee Jocky's chip shop in Oban.

"We're like sea gypsies," said Lucy. A basking shark had just passed them off the island of Mull.

"I never knew monotony could be so exciting," said Seymour.

By the time they reached Fort William, the boat was their home. Under the black shadow of Ben Nevis, they refuelled 'Gratitude' and persuaded a hotel manager to let them share a lukewarm bath. Two days later, they entered the Caledonian Canal behind a barge loaded with malt whisky.

Three days after that, anchored alongside Urquhart Castle on Loch Ness, they allowed themselves a weekend off. On the shoreline nearby, an elderly man in a waxed green jacket scanned the water constantly for the monster.

"I wouldn't stay there long," he shouted. Lucy and Seymour had been for a morning swim and were resting quietly on the deck. "Nessie eats Englishmen for breakfast."

Twice a day, without fail, they squeezed around the radio to listen to the shipping forecast. For two weeks, they had been blessed with good visibility and calm waters, but at Inverness, as they slipped into the North Sea through Dochgarroch lock, each of them could feel change on their skin.

"The Moray Firth," said Seymour. "Now it gets serious."

The balmy shelter of the islands was gone. Creamy-topped waves rolled in constantly from the north under flint-grey skies. Every few seconds, the boat was washed with bitter spray, and the cold stabbed relentlessly at their extremities. Under full sail, however, progress was swift, and Rehab's boat seemed to come alive.

Luckily, neither of them suffered from sickness. Even when the swell deepened, 'Gratitude' held such a reassuring line through the turbulence that Lucy's forebodings were displaced by a buzz of excitement which cut through her exhaustion and fear. And whenever she looked at Seymour, fussing contentedly with his ropes, Lucy felt calmed.

"Were you always like this? Was I missing something?"

Seymour simply grinned happily. So far, he thought, so good. But only just. From Inverness to Fraserburgh harbour had taken five easy days; there'd been no alarms; and they were on schedule for the wedding. Unless conditions deteriorated, they'd be fine, and yet once or twice he'd been secretly shaken by his own inexperience, and their week on open water had left him mentally drained.

"Halfway there," he told Lucy, as they walked unsteadily into town. "Plain sailing south from now on."

"It's weird to be still," said Lucy. "I feel a bit woozy."

"Land sickness. I'm the same. A large brandy should clear it."

Tucked in safely between two pale blue trawlers, they permitted themselves another short break; two long lie-ins, fresh water and an inch by inch inspection of the boat. Privately, they were both thankful for the time to nurse their bruises, and neither complained when two days drifted into more.

"Don't we need to go?" asked Lucy on the fifth morning. The winds had eased, 'Gratitude' was restocked with tins of condensed soup, and the sun was rising over the harbour wall.

"Yes, Cap'n," laughed Seymour.

Over the next ten days, conditions remained perfect. Without ever losing sight of land, they moved swiftly down the east coast, from one anonymous granite port to the next, crossing destinations off a list which had once felt like the stuff of dreams. Peterhead. Stonehaven.

Arbroath, Anstruther. North Berwick. Eyemouth. Seamlessly, unknowingly, they had become sailors.

Whenever Seymour fretted over tide times down in the cabin, Lucy took the wheel and followed their compass bearing. Nothing troubled them; they never argued; and they had each grown to love the fraternity of the sea; from the trawlermen with gifts of fresh fish to the lighthouse-keepers waving from their bleached turrets.

For Lucy, especially, it was an epiphany. Much more than Seymour, she was struck by the mute romance of the sea. All those years, she had looked out on it and felt nothing. Now she sensed the company of countless ghosts, and as they pushed on, she thought only of the Vikings, seeing the same Northumbrian shoreline as them with its endless beaches and its rich, ink-fingered monks.

"That's Holy Island. Lindisfarne. The first monastery the Vikings ever raided."

It was Seymour's turn to be the lookout and since crossing into English waters, he'd turned into an assiduous tour guide. A mile away, on their starboard side, they could see the outline of a castle perched on a solitary, green plug of rock.

"Let me guess. In 793AD?" said Lucy, raising her voice to counter a troublesome wind which had been building all day.

"Ha. Ha. Ha."

"We read the same leaflet in the pub."

The previous night – in Berwick on Tweed – the pair had mapped out the remainder of their voyage over a beer. Another week that was all. Just a week. As a reward, they'd eaten steak before huddling under the bedclothes with the radio. Both had seen the needle on the cabin barometer creeping left.

'*Tyne, Dogger. East veering North East. 6 or 7. 8 later. Thundery showers. Moderate or good. Poor later.*'

403

"That's bad isn't it? Force 8 wind? That's very bad."

"It's not great," said Seymour.

For the next few days, however, the storm appeared stuck. They could see rotating curls of black cloud in every direction; the sea and the sky were no longer divisible; but there was still no rain, and the winds – although strong – came at the perfect angle for speed. On board 'Gratitude', Seymour and Lucy saw their chance.

On one day they covered forty-four miles, sailing eight hours without a break. On another, they clocked up thirty-six. Amble. Blyth. Newcastle. Hartlepool. They were almost there, but the relentless anxiety of the chase had fatigued them and when they crawled into Whitby harbour shortly after 4pm on June 16th, they slept in each other's arms for fifteen hours.

"You're incredible. It's like you were born to all this." Seymour had stirred first. The cabin was swirling with the smell of fresh coffee.

"We're not there yet. I still might go off it."

"Can I ask you something?" A rubber fender had become trapped between the boat hull and the harbour wall. As the tide rose, it was squealing like a trapped animal. "What are we going to do after the wedding? Do you still want to teach?"

Lucy took a cautious sip from her mug. The windows were beaded with condensation.

"Can I ask you something first? Is sailing as cold and difficult as this in the Mediterranean?"

"You're kidding me?" Seymour sat up sharply, his back resting against the bulkhead.

"The gulf of Naples, Sardinia, Corsica, Majorca......"

"....Ibiza. Yugoslavia. Turkey. No tides. Not much wind. Warm, clear blue seas."

"You could buy me a bikini. I've got the bosoms for one now." Lucy sat up, wrapping the bedclothes around her shoulders. "Yes, I do want to teach. But next year. Not now. If we can afford it, I think we should carry on. I think you need to get this out of your system. And I like it. I really do. Even more if it was sunny."

"We could live really cheap. We could afford another year. Definitely. Just about. After that, we'd both need to work."

"Back on the newspaper?"

"No." Seymour waited until their eyes were locked. "I'd like to set up a boatyard."

"Building boats?"

"Building boats. Small ones," he said, quietly. "Maybe even join the lifeboat crew, finally?"

"That would be perfect," said Lucy.

"Just like your tits," said Seymour.

All the next day, they rested up and watched the weather. After breakfast, they climbed the steep steps to the abbey; shocked by the weakness in their legs; lifted by the tumbling red maze of roofs and the miraculous calm of the harbour.

Beyond its grey walls, a high sea was running, and the air was sticky with salt. Every few seconds, white spray lashed high over the barrier, followed by the distant tremor of its impact. Nothing on the water was moving. An entire fleet of black trawlers rocked idly in the swell.

By late afternoon, there'd been a slight improvement. A wedge of sunlight flitted across the pantiles, and a knot of fishermen stumbled out of a pub to look hopefully at the sky. For the third time that day, Seymour pressed his ear to the radio, desperate to hear that the storm had evaporated.

"Well?" asked Lucy.

"It's slowly moving north. It'll be better tomorrow."

"You do know we could catch a bus to the wedding from here?"

"We're almost there," said Seymour. "We'll be fine. I promise."

They were eight miles south of Whitby when it hit them. In a heartbeat, the wind twisted, first from the east, then wildly from every direction. Suddenly, every rope was alive, snapping and snaking, and as the sea erupted, 'Gratitude' screwed sideways, deep into the trough between two enormous, black waves.

"Sails. Sails." Seymour reached down and turned on the engine.

But Lucy was already ahead of him. The two sails were slithering down, and Seymour was back in control. It had taken them less than twenty seconds. With a surge of the throttle, he pointed 'Gratitude' south again, comforted by the proximity of the shoreline and the receding black puffs of exhaust.

It was their good fortune to have caught only the storm's weakening tail. The worst of it had passed through the previous night and by early afternoon, its remnants were gone. After seven relentless hours, they were edging past chalk-white cliffs, under the gaze of a familiar lighthouse. For the first time in a week, the air felt warm and with spreading blue skies came the nervous yank of excitement.

"I can't believe what we've done," said Lucy. A few miles off the starboard bow, they could see the twin piers of the finishing line.

"My dead boat is under here somewhere," said Seymour, peering curiously over the side.

"You can build another one." Lucy squeezed his arm. "I won't be such a bitch this time."

"We should arrive back under our own steam. Let's cut the motor."

With a practised hand, Lucy raised both the sails and cleated them off securely. A fully laden pleasure-cruiser had slipped out of the harbour into the bay and Seymour knew exactly what it was. He could hear wartime music serenading its customers. He could see the wheelhouse where a smoke-stained Rehab had crept after the long-ago fire that had changed all their lives.

There was an ear-thumping blast of its horn. A rotund figure in a blue gansey was yelling into a megaphone.

"This is the skipper of The Burlingtonian speaking, known only to his friends as Harry Spanners. Mr and Mrs Pilbeam are requested to stand while we applaud and then follow me into port where there will be a modest reception."

"How did they know?" asked Seymour, rising to his feet.

A boatload of passengers was throwing their hats in the air. Most of the hats appeared to be falling back into the sea.

"I rang Eunice last night," said Lucy, sheepishly.

"Welcome home. See you back in the harbour," screamed Spanners, as the boats crossed.

"I can't hear you," blurted Seymour.

"We should have a quick wash," said Lucy. "I think we might smell."

Fifteen minutes later, their voyage was over. After a private, tearful embrace, the couple stepped gingerly into the arms of their welcome party. Over a hundred people had turned out to cheer; two rockets fizzed skywards; and as Seymour guided Lucy up the barnacled steps, his old boss lurched forward clutching a microphone and a huge bouquet of roses.

"Mr. Latheron?" said Seymour.

"Teshting. Teshting. Hello. One Two. One Two. Everyone hear me OK?"

A few doubtful thumbs were raised in Soapy's direction.

"In a world starved of heroes, this town is thrilled, nay delighted, to have its very own Christopher Columbus back in its bosom. Eh? Eh? And so say bally well all of us. Hoorah. Up school. Chocks away. And now we've got a job for him to do."

A gap had opened up in the crowd leading back to the old stone flagged market square overlooking the fishing boats. Beyond it, Seymour could see window lights flashing in the novelty shops which lined the parade. People everywhere were eating – huge mounds of chips shining with gravy; pink clouds of candy floss; paper cups piled with pickled grey shellfish – and when he breathed, he took in the glorious smell of a British seaside summer.

"You can't beat it, love," said Seymour, filling his lungs. "Vinegar. Fish. Sea air. Fried Onions. Donuts. It's all in there somewhere."

But Lucy wasn't listening. They'd been propelled up onto the square where every side was lined with onlookers. In front of them was a statue covered by an old canvas sail. Among the crowd, she'd spotted Frank and Eunice, holding hands, alongside Harry, now miraculously transformed in a tight-fitting suit.

"This town knows all about sacrifice…"

There was a respectful hush. Soapy was speaking without a microphone, but his voice sounded strong. And, for once, quite sensible.

"….Fishing folk all know the price they sometimes have to pay…."

Over in the amusements a machine was spewing out pennies like a tommy gun.

"….and this magnificent memorial, paid for by our readers, is for every single bally one that didn't come back. So, if you could now please remove the sail."

Seymour pulled a cord and watched the drapes fall. It was perfect. Everybody in the audience who'd known the Captain felt the same. From his shoulder-length hair and bobble hat down to the battered wellington boots, it was Rehab. Captain Rehab. Jansen Fallowdown cast in bronze, standing eight-foot-tall with his eyes firmly fixed on the precise spot where he'd lifted his last lobster pot.

"Jane and Celeste. They'll have to come and see this."

A mangled aside to Lucy was all Seymour could manage. Seeing Rehab's face had melted him, and he was sobbing uncontrollably. Through his tears, he could make out the pub where he'd once stood with the Captain, watching his dinghy fall apart on a sad, summer weekend.

"Ten quid? You were done," Rehab had chuckled. And then the mast had fallen down, and everything else had started....Goodrun, Phoenix and Gratitude.

"They will come," said Lucy. "And they'll love it."

The spectators were quickly ebbing away. Only a handful of locals were still circling the statue.

"I still can't believe he had a kid," said Frank.

"It's just so wonderful to see you, Lucy," said Eunice, drawing breath for a volley of questions. "Where do we start? I thought you hated boats. I can't believe it. What did you use for a toilet? Or a decent wash? I've got so much to tell you. Can you make it on Monday? To the wedding? Only a small affair. It's at 11, followed by drinks at The White Horse. What are you doing tomorrow?"

"Calm down. Of course we'll be there. It's what we nearly killed ourselves for."

"I still can't believe he had a kid," said Frank. But, by then, everyone had gone.

There were just two nights left before the wedding. After a month of on-board privations, they took a large room in the town's biggest hotel, with an ocean-facing balcony and a bath with hot water which wasn't the colour of peat.

It felt strange sleeping in cotton sheets; odder still to be served breakfast at a table which wasn't in perpetual motion. Each of them had woken refreshed – Seymour had even hacked away a month of whiskers – but they spoke little over their poached eggs, preferring the sea view to eye contact; each of them waiting for the other to speak.

It was Seymour who caved in first. "Were you serious about carrying on; to the sunshine?"

"Completely."

"Then I think we should set off as soon as we can; check the boat over; wash everything; restock, refuel, recharge and get underway."

"That's fine. Relax. I'll be ready. Will it still be warm when we get there?"

The morning sun was flooding the breakfast room with heat. Just a few yards away, the tide was retreating from the seawall where entire families were already setting up camp with their windshields and their picnic baskets.

"If we catch the trade winds it'll be September. So yes, it'll be warm. It'll be lovely."

"And we'll come back in Spring?"

"Yes, we'll come back in Spring," said Seymour. "And we'll make everything work."

"I love you," said Lucy.

"I never stopped loving you," said Seymour.

They spent the rest of the day apart. Lucy had an outfit to prepare; Seymour needed some 'stuff' from the chandlery; and (as they readily admitted) they were 'long overdue a little break from each other'.

Leaving the hotel, Seymour strode out to the lifeboat station where a tall young man in yellow waders was sluicing sand away from the pavement. Through the open doors, he could see the Roll of Honour. A new coxswain's name had been carefully added in gold paint. Stan Clough's tenure was over.

"What happened to Stan?"

"No-one knows. It's like he vanished." The volunteer switched off his hosepipe. "You're Seymour Pilbeam? Wow."

"I am. Need any volunteers?"

"Always. Always."

"I'll see you next year, then."

Next, he walked to their old house, passing the junk shop (now a nail salon) and the gasworks (still a gasworks) before stopping outside the familiar bay windows. It was shocking to see what the winter had done. Toadstools grew in rotten window frames and fly-tippers had heaped the yard with bags of broken tiles.

In the workshop where he'd built Phoenix, Seymour perched on a pile of offcuts and waited for a few happy memories, but none came. He thought of Lucy sleeping in a darkened room. He thought of Isaac burning his boat. He thought of the long nights watching Rehab through a blizzard of sawdust. And he thought of the most important thing his three boats had taught him.

Being happy in himself had always been easy. Being happy together took graft.

"I thought I'd find you here." Lucy was silhouetted in the door. "It makes me feel ill. I hate it. Please let's leave."

Like Seymour, she'd found herself on a dismal pilgrimage. Where The Titanic Hotel had once towered, only rubble remained behind a billboard promising '52 bijou retirement flats'. And since December, the sea had continued its merciless destruction of the Clough family plot. Every fragment of the building had been swept away leaving only a gaping brown cavity.

Even her old shoe shop was no more. A giant 'SOLD' sign had been plastered across its frontage. Apart from a few abandoned boxes, the shelves inside were bare. Along the broad promenade – thronged with holidaymakers – nobody else seemed to care. And nor, to be honest, did Lucy.

Later that night, comparing notes in the bar, they would each say the same thing. The sea, the sand and the cliffs were still majestic. But the town felt smaller; the distances shorter, and the fabric more broken than they'd remembered. They'd noticed something else, too.

Since Christmas, a new name had appeared over Stan Clough's arcades. And the name, in sickly neon letters, was 'Frank's'.

"I added it up once," said Frank the next day. "I reckon I took over 400,000 photographs when I was still wearing the orange blazer. £1 a piece. Think about it. Maybe I'm not so dense after all."

They were gathered in the back garden of The White Horse; forty or so carefully-picked guests who'd just witnessed Eunice and Frank's wedding; the first of her five to have opted for the town's register office, a handsome, if modest, Georgian building sandwiched between a fishing tackle shop and a VD clinic. Not that the happy couple had shown any matching restraint in their outfits.

412

Despite a proven lack of Scots ancestry, Frank's suit had been cut from the tartan of an obscure Highlands clan. Alongside him somewhere beneath a wide-brimmed yellow hat, Eunice had opted for a bespoke floral-patterned silk trouser suit. "I lost my virginity before he was even born," she confessed to Lucy later. "White was never really an option."

"They look like they're auditioning for the circus," muttered Harry, during the breezy procession down to the pub. A trail of confetti swirled behind them and the bride's hat had been blown under a parked milk truck from where Frank was instructed to retrieve it.

"Don't spoil your bloody suit," she'd barked.

"No, dear," said Frank, checking the knees of his trousers.

No-one had ever seen The White Horse so clean. Every horse brass had been polished. The old round wooden tables gleamed. Streamers and balloons hung from every beam. Ale-soaked beermats had been replaced with dry ones. Even the fire grate was swept and blacked for the occasion.

"This way. This way. You won't have been in my garden before. It's a proper treat."

Nor had anyone (especially Seymour) ever seen Nellie looking quite so magnificent. Squeezed into a plum-coloured dress, she looked younger – and somehow, more exotic – than anyone could recall.

"You won't hear these words from me very often, but help yourself to drinks from the bar," she announced. "Buffet food will be circulating shortly. Please, please, relax and enjoy yourselves. Oh, and big thanks to Eunice for loaning her magnificent stereogram."

A little soft jazz was playing in the background. Guests were stripping their jackets and ties, and the warm hum of conversation rose off a dozen separate clusters of friends.

"400,000. That's a lot of crap snaps," sniffed Harry, returning from the bar with three pints of bitter and a bowl of nuts.

"Portraits, not snaps," spluttered Frank, who had found a cigar from somewhere and was contentedly sucking the wrong end.

"Your name is over Clough's amusements," said Seymour. "You must have been stashing cash away for years."

"Have a potted beef sandwich, darling? Your favourite." Eunice darted in, and then out again, with a tray of bulging bread rolls.

"I know. I still can't believe it. Pretty soon after Stan disappeared, they suddenly popped up on the market for a daft price and it seemed mad not to buy."

"They didn't do him much good," grumbled Harry, rubbing his bad leg. "Nor you either probably."

"Bollocks," said Frank, through a mouthful of meat paste.

"You're number five, mate. It's only a matter of time."

"Another sandwich, cherub." Eunice was back again. "And let me get you all a refill."

"Double bollocks. They were natural causes. All of them."

"Are you feeling alright, mate?" said Harry. "You're looking a bit peaky."

"Anyway, we're moving to Spain next week."

"Woooooooooooh," wailed Harry, wafting his hand in front of Frank's face with the five fingers spread wide. "Only if you live that long."

"Leave it, you pissing git."

"It's weird to think of you being rich," said Seymour.

"I know. It's great," said Frank, sounding uncharacteristically serious.

"But Eunice doesn't love me for my money."

"What does she love you for then?" asked Harry, forming his two index fingers into the shape of a cross.

There was a long pause. Frank had located the correct end of his cigar and was frisking himself for a box of matches.

"That's easy," he snorted, "You all saw the photograph."

At the opposite end of the garden, Lucy had smiled when Harry held up his mock cross. Everyone at the reception was thinking the same. At least seven of the guests had attended each of the bride's previous public declarations of eternal love; not to mention the four funerals which had followed soon thereafter.

"Till death us do part?" said Eunice, slipping back alongside Lucy. "This one feels right. This one's a stayer."

"You're certainly feeding him up, anyway."

"Potted beef. They're his favourites." The smoke from Frank's cigar was drifting their way. "Are you alright, poppit? Are you happy? I can't believe you were in a boat."

"Yes. Yes. And neither can I," laughed Lucy. "We'll be off again in a few days."

"People are saying that Stan Clough threw himself off the cliffs."

"Not a chance." Lucy took a long slug from her glass. "He loved himself too much."

"He had a place in Cornwall too, I heard. Right on the sea."

"That's where he'll be then. With a garage full of pennies, probably. But do I care? No, I do not."

"Actually, I'm – we're – going away soon too. A little place in Spain. We'll probably be the first British people living there." Eunice looked over at Frank's empty plate. "Mind you, he's been a bit peaky recently. Not his normal self at all."

Lucy took a sly glance at Seymour. The voyage from Scotland had done him good. Against the white cotton of his shirt, his arms looked tanned and strong and she felt a serious half-drunken need to see him naked.

"I saw that the shop was sold," she said, turning away from the thought. "Are you keeping the house?"

"Sold. Like everything else. Apart from the records."

"Never coming back?"

"Over my dead body," said Eunice. "And nor should you."

There was a gentle groan from the direction of the bridegroom. Frank was holding his stomach and easing himself down onto a chair.

"I feel shit," he muttered. "Those sarnies tasted off."

"Everyone else is fine," said Seymour, slipping into the cool of the pub. "I'll get you a glass of water."

Nellie was washing plates behind the bar. He could smell the soapy water. He could see the purple fabric shimmering down from her neck to the tight clinch of her waist.

"I think Frank needs a cold drink," he whispered. There was a strange croak in his voice.

"I reckon he does," said Nellie, reaching for a tea towel. "But what does Seymour need?"

"I....I...think I've found what I need," he stammered. The landlady had slid from behind the bar. "You won't tell her, will you?"

"There's nothing to tell, is there?" she smiled. "Your trousers were wet. You took them off. We all lived happily ever after."

"I'm sorry," said Seymour. They were standing so close he could feel the weight of her left breast on his arm.

"What's there to be sorry for, love?"

"Because you're still on your own?"

"Ha. When I'm surrounded by deluded men gawping at my tits every night of the week? Hardly."

"Because in another life....?"

"You have got to be kidding, my sweet," chortled Nellie, dropping a scarlet kiss on Seymour's forehead.

"I'm hurt," laughed Seymour. "Now you've got to tell me why."

"Because I have never been on a fucking boat in my life."

There was a voluptuous flash of powdered skin, and she was gone. Left alone in the bar, Seymour helped himself to a fresh pint, and wandered across to the empty trophy cabinet. Frank's picture was still inside it. Rehab was still clutching his abacus. Next year, maybe he could reactivate the team in the Captain's memory. Maybe even Lucy would play. Definitely. She would. The mere idea flooded him with happiness.

"You've got lipstick over your eye."

Lucy unearthed a tissue from her bag, licked a corner, and wiped the smudge from Seymour's face.

"She's an attractive woman." Lucy was grinning. "Isaac always reckoned she fancied you."

There was an awkward hiatus. Both were looking at the empty cabinet.

"Are you sure about all this?" blurted Seymour. "What about Olive and Bill? We don't have to go now. We could make a stab of things here. We could go another time. Just tell me what's best."

"I'm seeing my parents here tomorrow; Vietta and the baby the day after. It's all fine. We're not going forever. Unless we choose to disappear somewhere."

"We could go another time."

"Stop it. Look. Read my lips. We. Are. Sailing. To. The. Sun. Alright?"

There was something in the photograph Seymour had never noticed before, a lone figure in the background smirking by the door to the gents.

"He let me win, you know. The night this photograph was taken."

"I know. He told me."

"Do you miss him?" Seymour had taken both of Lucy's hands.

"It had its moments. But not many."

"I always got the feeling he pitied me…I think that's why he let me win."

"You're wrong. It wasn't pity," said Lucy. "It was jealousy."

"We'd better go and say our goodbyes," said Seymour.

There was a tinkle of breaking glass from the garden. Frank had slumped forwards in a deckchair with his head between his knees and a plate of half-eaten sandwiches between his feet.

"Listen. Truly. I think I'm being poisoned."

"Wooooooooh," said Harry, flapping his arms like a B-movie ghost. "Wooooooooh."

"We're going to go, everybody. We've a lot to do. It's been a lovely afternoon."

A few late rays of sunshine stirred the flowers on a trellis sagging with clematis.

"She wants my money. I'm being poisoned."

"It's the drink talking. He'll be fine," said Eunice. "Thanks for coming. I'll take care of Frank. You two look after yourselves."

There was a warm wind blowing down off the Wolds when Lucy and Seymour closed the pub door behind them.

After a few minutes walking, they stopped and looked left. The windows of their old house were dark. A solitary child was kicking a plastic ball against the gate.

"Still sure," said Lucy

"I'm so sure," said Seymour, reaching for his wife's hand and steering her, softly, towards the sea.

Postscript

There was to be a fourth boat in Seymour Pilbeam's life, although sadly it was not one that he (or Lucy) would ever see.

It was 5.52 am on July 14th when the fishing vessel 'Alain Fournier' picked up the first distress call. In another hour, she would have been discharging her catch on the quayside at Brest and although most of the crew were asleep, nobody complained when the First Mate knocked them from their bunks. Each of them knew a friend or a relative who'd died at sea. Nobody lasted long in these waters. Not even in summer.

In the official report that followed, the First Mate (who happened to have been born in Kent) reported that this first call was delivered calmly by a man with a Northern English accent. After giving the boat's name (which the mate heard as 'Lassitude') the caller provided an approximate location, adding that their vessel had been holed in the night beneath the waterline by a large cargo vessel.

"We are in grave and imminent danger," he had said. "Please come quickly."

The second call was received at 6.18am, just as the 'Alain Fournier' was approaching the given location. This time it was a female speaker, clearly in distress, and clearly unfamiliar with the Mayday protocols. "If you hear this, please hurry. Anyone. Please. The boat is filling with water and we're attempting to board our life raft."

Approximately fourteen minutes later, the trawler had arrived under full steam at the stated bearing which they proceeded to scour for any trace of life or wreckage. None was found.

After an hour, they were joined by a vessel of the French coastguard whose skipper informed them that they were now at liberty to proceed home with their catch. Despite extensive enquiries, no cargo vessel ever came forward to report a collision. And despite a widespread search involving several helicopters, not one fragment of the missing boat was ever found.

It was only some months later – after an English couple was reported missing by their son – that the French authorities realised a mistake may have clouded their investigations. As a result of these later disclosures, the official verdict of the marine enquiry concluded that *"given the lack of evidence to the contrary, the 'overwhelming, but not conclusive, likelihood must be that 'Lassitude' and 'Gratitude' were one and the same."*

For the official record, the magistrate noted that Mr.Isaac Pilbeam, resident of Kyle of Lochalsh in Scotland, was privately funding an ongoing search along a track between the boat's last known bearing, and its intended destination in the Bay of Naples. At the time of writing, his efforts have failed to shed any light on the mystery.

Several weeks later (in ignorance of the above proceedings) a retired maths professor was walking his dog on a beach several miles north of Pointe Sainte Mathieu when he spotted a small wooden box floating in a tidal rock pool. Inside, he found a ribbon-bound batch of illegible letters (which he discarded) together with a badly damaged English concertina which he handed in at the local gendarmerie.

Following a severe outbreak of summer flu, the police station was manned at that time by volunteer reserves and the discovery was never linked to the missing boat.

To this day, the instrument remains unclaimed.

Author's note

Having spent my first twenty years in the Yorkshire fishing town of Bridlington, I owe my greatest thanks to the people who inhabited my life there such a very long time ago; most especially my parents who moved there shortly before I was born.

Today, it is a place much changed but the coastline and the beaches never disappoint; and nor does the streak of bloody-minded resilience which has kept the town going even as its visitors headed off to warmer alternatives.

During the writing of this book, I have been back many times looking for ghosts, but finding none (that I recognised, at least). Times are hard for Britain's seaside resorts, but there are still some wonderful chinks of light. In Bridlington, the Sailing Coble Preservation Society, is battling hard to save the survivors of a once vast fleet. On the quayside, it runs a small, but fascinating museum. And some of its older members – like the indomitable Joe Gelsthorpe – were (and sometimes still are) working shipbuilders whose skills are being passed quietly on. To Joe, and many others in the group, my sincere thanks. Keep up the good work.

It was in their shop that I picked up a long-deleted book 'The Coble' by John Salmon. That text, together with Uffa Fox's 'Joys of Life', provided many useful insights into the art of shipbuilding and the psychology of the sea.

Finally, I would like to thank Practical Boat Owner for leading me to the story of John and Diana Rogers, whose restoration of 'Essex Melody' quietly inspired the final part of this story ; my good friends

David and Jenny Hunter for local knowledge from just a few miles up the coast at Filey; my former agent Mark Stanton; my dear friend Chris Baxter, who lived on the West Coast of Scotland in the 1970's and recalled a time when the 'Weefrees' even tried to stop the trains running a service on Sundays; Martin and Philippa Clunes for many things; Katy at Quacks for tidying my words; Lesley Seeger for permitting me to use her artwork around the cover; and last of all, my wife for her tireless patience and loyalty. I promise you, Kay, this is the last.

For many years, I have sailed dinghies and, in the tide-free warmth of the Mediterranean, much bigger boats in friendlier waters than those which circle Britain. No doubt, there will be many experienced hands who find fault with the details and descriptions contained within this book. But please be gentle. This is a novel not a sailing manual and – although it is mostly born of direct personal experience – I make only modest claims as a sailor, and absolutely none as a shipbuilder.

No more than Seymour did. And look what happened to him.

Bill Jones

September 2020